April

Lying Lainey

Underground Omega Syndicate

Elizabeth Knight

The best cons are the ones you never see coming

Creative Wonder Publishing

Lying Lainey – Copyright © 2023 by Creative Wonder Publishing LLC

All rights reserved.

This is a work of fiction. Names, characters, places, and incidents are either the product of the author's imagination or are used fictitiously, and any resemblance to actual persons living or dead, business establishments, events, or locales is entirely coincidental. No part of this book may be used to reproduce, scan, or be distributed in any printed or electronic form in any manner whatsoever without written permission of the author, except in the case of brief quotations for articles or reviews.

Please do not participate in or encourage piracy of copyrighted materials.

Knight, Elizabeth

Lying Lainey

Editing: Swish Editing

Cover artist: Jodielock Designs

Formatting: Creative Wonder Publishing

ISBN: 979-8-88958-004-1 (ebook) / 979-8-88958-040-9 (paperback)

Here is to the women who own their space in this world. Who don't need a man but still keep one around because they want to. Grab a drink and your favorite 'me time' toy and settle in for a good time.

Authors Note

Dear Readers,

Lying Lainey is a book that contains subjects that could be triggering to some people. If you feel like this could be a problem for you, please protect yourself. No work of fiction is worth your mental health.

The full list of content warnings is available on my website.
Link found here: Click or Scan

Contents

1. Lainey — 1
2. Lainey — 13
3. Lainey — 26
4. Lainey — 38
5. Halstead — 46
6. Lainey — 58
7. Lainey — 70
8. Lainey — 81
9. Quintin — 92
10. Lainey — 105
11. Lainey — 116
12. Lainey — 126
13. Kerian — 138
14. Kerian — 150
15. Lainey — 157
16. Quintin — 169
17. Lainey — 182

18.	Lainey	193
19.	Lainey	204
20.	Halstead	214
21.	Lainey	224
22.	Lainey	235
23.	Lainey	247
24.	Lainey	258
25.	Lainey	270
26.	Lainey	281
27.	Kerian	291
28.	Lainey	305
29.	Lainey	315
30.	Epilogue	324
About Author		337
Also By		338

One

Lainey

There are two types of people in the world. Those who let their circumstances dictate who and what they become and those who say fuck it and choose to make the life they want by any means necessary. I'm the latter.

Born to an addict, an Alpha no less, my mother lost me the moment I took my first breath. I was handed over to the foster system before she could even name me. Really, I should be thanking her for being such a fuck-up and exposing me to the reality of the world.

It's been thirty-two years since that event occurred, and damn, if she could see me now. Here I was walking down the steps of the most exclusive high-end hotel in Marlios, wearing a gown that cost more than the average person's yearly salary. That's not even adding in the accessories that went along with it to complete the whole look.

It hasn't all been ball gowns and roses, but the life I've lived thus far has taught me many valuable lessons and skills. However, I will admit my mother did teach me the most important lesson in life—*never count on anyone to look after you, they don't give a shit.* If I hadn't been forced to own that truth and do what was necessary to build the life I deserved, who knows what dead-end town or job I'd be stuck with. At least now I had a life I could control, and provided me everything I could ever want. To me, that was the true measure of success.

"Good evening, Ms. Emmalina. Mr. Gilani wanted me to inform you that he'll be meeting you at the gala," the driver greeted as he opened the limousine door for me.

"Thank you, Walter," I said, slipping into the limo, trying to mask my irritation at his words.

I spotted my favorite brand of champagne on ice, ready for me to pour a glass which surprised me. Then I noticed a note tucked into a large bouquet of purple flowers—*Emmalina's favorite color*—the man had been paying attention. Plucking the note out of the bouquet, I flipped it open.

My petal,

I'm sorry I couldn't be there to pick you up tonight as I promised. This new drug launch needed a bit more of my attention. I hope these flowers make you smile as you have made me smile these past weeks. Can't wait to see you in that dress.

~Z

I smiled at the letter but not for the reason he'd thought I would. This simple note and gesture made all my fears vanish about *my snookums* getting bored of me. I'd been playing a risky game of hard to get, drawing out the anticipation of what was going to happen tonight. Zarin Gilani ran one of the biggest pharmaceutical companies, Blissmeds, and they were about to launch an off-brand version of a competitor's drug that would crush the competition. The thing about it was that Zarin stole intellectual property from an intern who used to work for him. That intern felt undervalued, so he offered the competition his idea, and they ran with it. That drug became a game changer in the medical field, making Pharmigo the number one pharmaceutical company. Blissmeds started to lose stock and loyalty until they announced the creation of this off-brand version.

Furious, the CEO of Pharmigo hired me to get nice and comfy cozy with Zarin so I could plant some information. Specifically, this information would flag doctored findings of the data they collected during the drug trial. It was a report that the authorities were required to read in their final review happening on Monday. Once that was uncovered, the drug would be rejected, Blissmeds investigated, and Zarin Gilani would lose millions. Pharmigo would remain on top, I would get a hefty amount of money deposited into my account, and we'd all be happy.

Well... not Zarin.

As a con artist specializing in manipulation, counterfeiting, stealing, planting evidence, and occasionally, blackmailing, I keep busy. With each new contract, it's important I make it clear my customers are paying for the end result—nothing more. They don't get to dictate anything other than who the target is, what the end result needs to be, and the deadline. If they want the best female con artist in all of Breona, they'll do as I say, or I'll cut my losses. They need to understand I'm in high demand, and if I don't like a job, I don't need to take it. There are always more jobs waiting for me at the snap of my fingers.

Over the past five years, there's only been a few times a client has refused my rules. Typically, it's because they want me to promise certain things on top of the end goal. Such as ruining a marriage, making sure they are blacklisted in an industry, or ensuring they are left destitute and will never recover. This is where I need to explain none of this is personal to me—it's strictly business. All I care about is what I might get out of the transaction on top of the cold hard cash in my pocket. Some understand, while others can't see past their anger and find someone else.

The limousine pulled up to the museum where the gala was being held. An attendant came to the limousine and opened the door for me, extending a hand. I took his offered assistance, making sure I led with my left leg to show off the dramatic slit my dress had. The man gave an audible gulp at the sight, making me grin. It was always smart to test your effect on a stranger to make sure you nailed your desired response. Tonight, I wanted Zarin to think of nothing else other than taking me back to his home and stripping me out of this dress. I'd teased him for almost two weeks, ensuring he would follow through tonight so I could finish the job.

I gave the man a sweet smile before I tucked my clutch under my arm and adjusted my fur stole. It was spring, but the nights in Marlios were still a bit chilly, being the northernmost city of Breona. Marlios was the third largest city in the province and the epicenter of all the medical companies. This made it a rich city as well as a favorite of mine to work in.

My stilettos click-clacked on the museum's marble steps, alerting the door attendants that someone was approaching. They each gave me beaming smiles as I passed through the double doors and into the museum entry. This was normally the space you bought your ticket before proceeding into the museum's main room. I paused before a woman in a simple black dress with a tablet and an earpiece telling me she was an event coordinator. The gala had started earlier, but I'd suggested we go slightly later to avoid the press and overwhelming crowds.

"Good evening. May I see your ticket, please?" the woman requested.

"Unfortunately, my date has them, and he's meeting me here. The name is Zarin Gilani," I explained. "I'm more than happy to wait—"

"There's no need for that," she said, cutting me off. "Mr. Gilani reached out to us and said you'd be arriving before him. I'll just need to see your ID to confirm you're the person he said would be joining him."

"That's wonderful. My name is Emmaline Cresswell," I shared, pulling out my ID. There on a carefully crafted counterfeit was my smiling face, fake name, address, and the mark of being a Beta.

In our hierarchical society, a person can be born as into three designations—Alpha, Beta, or Omega. The moment your designation presents itself during puberty, your life and future are categorized. Alphas are the best of the best, the cream of the crop, so to speak. They have all the advantages in appearance, education, and society, which is why the majority of them make up the top one percent of the wealthy. This gala would be predominantly Alphas in attendance, with maybe a few Betas if they were lucky, and the rest would be Omegas, the preferred female partner to an Alpha since they're the only ones who can give birth to another Alpha or Omega.

She glanced over it quickly, handing it back to me. "A Beta, I'm impressed. You should teach a class or something on how the rest of us can become a whore for a rich Alpha like Mr. Gilani."

I couldn't blame her for being a bitch, since Betas got the shit end of most deals. However, that didn't mean I had to take it either. Just because I could pull off something she couldn't didn't give her the right to act like a cunt.

"That's the thing..." I started, pausing to give her a look from head to toe. "You either have it, or you don't. No one can teach class."

The woman's jaw fell open at my brash words, but I didn't give a shit. Betas might be the middle-lower class of our world, but many have made a name for themselves. If she wanted to have a better life, then *she* needed to be the one to fucking do something about it. Yeah, Betas were less desirable for Alphas since they could only produce Beta children, but I knew plenty of packs with Beta lovers as well as an Omega.

"Well, you have a good rest of your evening," I said, offering her a dazzling smile as I snapped my clutch closed. She muttered a few choice words under her breath, but it simply proved my point. She didn't have enough of a backbone to stand up for herself, and there was nothing I could do about that for her.

Next, I stopped at the coat check but decided to keep my clutch with me. I had things far too valuable in there to risk letting anyone else hold onto it. With all that out of the way, it was time to join the gala's guests.

The museum's main room had been transformed from a mundane space full of education into a glowing golden grotto filled with music and sparkled with the gowns and jewels the women were wearing. This gala was a fundraiser for the new hospital wing they wanted to build, specifically to treat children with terminal diseases—a place meant to accommodate the patients as well as their families.

Taking an offered glass of champagne, I wandered the outside edge of the event, looking at all the photos of the children they planned to help along with their stories. Of course, they made sure to pick the images that made them look the most pitiful or on the brink of death. How else would they squeeze every last penny from these calloused Alpha high rollers?

My guess was that some of these kids weren't even sick or in the hospital. It's amazing what the right makeup and lighting can do in a photo shoot. My thoughts on the matter—*disgusting*. I'm sure it seems contradictory for me to be upset by this when I am a con artist. However, I've had firsthand experience knowing what it's like to be exploited as a child.

At the tender age of ten, I was adopted by a man who turned out to be a fucking con artist. He would adopt various kids and teach them how to be his helper. Depending on the job or scam, he needed a specific look or age. Trent is the man who taught me everything I know and use, even to this day. He used to tell me I had a gift, and if I stopped being such a bleeding heart, I might go places when I was older. The joke was on him since he's the one rotting in prison for the rest of his life, and I'm the one who put him there.

"Emmalina, my petal, I hope I didn't keep you waiting too long," Zarin said from behind me.

His sharp scent of pepper and earthy sage made my nose itch, but I'd learned long ago to ignore the scents of others. We might be hardwired to acknowledge them, using it as a barometer of compatibility, but that didn't matter when I was working. Flicking the switch, I fell into my Emmalina character twisting around to face the man of my dreams.

There he was in a sharp dark gray silk tux that matched his olive skin tone well. Zarin was shorter than me by only an inch or two, but the heels made it more distinct. His black hair was combed straight back, showing off the start of his receding hairline. Warm brown eyes stared at me with such affection, I knew if I weren't the hardened woman I was now, I'd feel bad for what I was about to do. Sadly for him, the five zeros that came after the three on my contract for this job meant more.

"You're finally here," I gushed, grabbing his forearm and beaming at him. "Thank you for the flowers. They were so pretty, and how did you remember my favorite champagne? You're too good to me."

"My petal, I keep telling you, it's like the gods themselves formed you just for me," Zarin cooed, leaning in and dropping a chaste kiss on my lips.

He was an affectionate man, but when it came to public settings, he was beyond conservative. I thought he wasn't into me at all, yet the moment we found ourselves in a private area, I saw the Alpha side of Zarin come out. That's when I knew he enjoyed the hunt and made the call not to sleep with him but make him work for it.

"I feel the same way." I sighed, looping my arm around his. "Thank you for inviting me to this event. I can't believe a woman like me gets to be on your arm."

"Emmalina, how many times do I have to tell you not to listen to what your parents have to say?" Zarin scolded. "Just because you're a Beta doesn't mean you have less value in the world. Your late mother was a Beta, and your father loved her enough to bond with her even though the rest of the pack disapproved. They seek to tear you down because they are jealous of what your father got to experience."

Who would have known that an Alpha such as him would be a champion for equal rights for Betas? It was one of the things I'd learned about him and used to set the trap and reel him in.

"I know you're right. It's just I'm scared to tell them about us. What if they cut me off, and I'm left with nothing?" I murmured, adding a slight sniff to up the emotion.

Zarin stopped and tucked a finger under my chin. "Emmalina, I am a man with no pack, no children, and no extended family to look after. If they cut you off and toss you away, it would be my honor to care for you for the rest of my life. When this new drug goes on the market, it will secure my company's future, and no matter what happens, I'll be able to take care of you."

Oh, you poor, poor, romantic fool. In a mere two days, your future will be so bleak you won't want to get out of bed.

"Truly, I don't know how I ever got so lucky. Who knew spilling a glass of wine in your lap would bring me so much joy," I said, letting my eyes brim with tears before stepping back and pretending to wipe them away. "There is no time for silly tears when we have a wonderful night ahead of us."

Offering me his arm again, he smiled. "I couldn't have said it better myself. Let me introduce you to a few friends of mine who are in town just for the gala. They run a large technology company in Corzina."

Even as my expression stayed light and cheerful, my blood ran cold at the mention of that city. Corzina was the largest city in all of Breona and where Trent made his headquarters. A feeling of fear I hadn't felt in a long fucking time churned in my stomach. *What if I knew these men from there?* The chances of anyone recognizing me tonight with a wig and contacts on were slim to none, not to mention it's been twelve years since I'd left Corzina. Once I knew they didn't need me for Trent's trial and they could crush him like the cockroach he was, I ran and never looked back.

"Zarin, you finally made it," a man said, pulling my date into a hug.

Then he paused when he saw me, letting his faded blue eyes trail down my body. His skin was tanned, but almost overly so, like he worked at it with artificial assistance. It made his light blond hair stand out as well as the wrinkles around his eyes and mouth. They appeared deeper and harsher, giving him a hard look. He might be the same age as Zarin or older, it was hard to tell, but I was thankful I didn't recognize him.

"Who is this?" the man asked.

Zarin reached for my hand, and I gave it to him with a quick, shy smile. "This is Emmalina Cresswell... her family owns Elegant Clear, the gin distillery."

The man's pale blond eyebrows shot up. "Is that so? What brings you out here?"

"My family feels that I need more education in learning the business, so I was sent out here for two weeks to learn from the Wentworths," I explained.

"I see. They are a giant in the business, that's for sure," he commented, then offered a hand. "Forgive my rudeness. I'm Reuben Watts, owner of Cyclone Software."

The shock of his name and getting a waft of raw onions off him must have shown on my face as he chuckled. "I guess that means you've heard of us?"

Pressing a hand to my chest, I let out a laugh. "Heard of you... of course, I've heard of you. Truthfully, I think anyone who hasn't must live under a rock. To think there's a possibility for someone *not* to use your search engine at least once a day would be ludicrous."

Reuben laughed at that, a deep belly laugh that had people turning to see what could be so funny. "I suppose you might be right about that. We weren't always a household name, though. My pack and I worked long hours with blood, sweat, and tears to make it happen. Take this time you have with the Wentworths and make it count, young lady. Who knows what you'll end up doing with your family's company one day."

"I will absolutely take that advice to heart," I said, leaning a little more into Zarin, letting him know I was comfortable being here with his friends.

We stayed and chatted for a little longer before being called into a second room where tables were set up. We each had assigned seats that separated us from Reuben and the others in his pack. Now Zarin and I sat at a table with no one we knew or were interested in getting to know, allowing me to set things in motion.

As the night progressed and plate after plate of food was situated before us only to be removed and another to take its place, I picked at a few things here and there while alternating between water and my champagne so I didn't get tipsy. We watched videos, listened to stories, and then the medical director came out to talk. Thankfully, I had my own game to play, or I would have been bored out of my mind.

I started out with simple touches brushing the back of his hand, rubbing his knee, or leaning in close to whisper something, letting my chest brush his arm. These were all coy, subtle movements that had the man sliding his hand further and further up the slit in my dress. When he finally brushed his fingers over my pussy, he was greeted with the knowledge I wasn't wearing anything under the dress.

"Naughty, petal," Zarin whispered, his voice rough with desire. "If you're trying to show me that you're finally ready to let me have you, you've succeeded."

Letting my legs fall open a little more, I leaned my chest into his arm as I answered, "Does that mean we can leave soon?"

"The second the presentations are done," Zarin confirmed. "I'm not going to let my precious petal suffer."

It took far longer than I thought for this night to be over, and with the amount of liquids I'd been drinking, I had to excuse myself to use the restroom. As I weaved my way through the tables, I darted out of the way of a drunken man and knocked into another. The scent of fine whiskey, the musk of bergamot, and a rich tang of cigar tobacco enveloped me as his hands settled on my hips.

"Careful there," a deep voice rumbled, shooting right to my pussy.

Mumbling my apology, I didn't pause to look at who I'd run into, instead fleeing to the ladies' room. I spotted a room for nursing mothers and hurried inside, locking the door behind me as I sank onto the chair provided. My head fell into my hands as my heart beat wildly at what just happened. That man, whoever he might have been, was a scent match. It was a phenomenon that occurred when an Alpha and Omega were a perfect match for each other. Their scent would be so intoxicating to the Omega that it would draw them to that Alpha and vice versa.

So why would this be a problem when I'm a Beta? Well, I'm not.

I, Lainey Caddel, am an Omega.

I'm an Omega who has been hiding her designation as well as her identity from the world through suppressants and scent-altering drugs. No Omega could be what I am or do what I do, not without an Alpha by her side. We Omegas were expected to be dutiful women to our Alphas, allowing them to dote on us as we took care of their needs. I say fuck that—we can hold our own just fine. Who needs a man of any designation to dictate what we do with our lives?

People say it's a magical moment when you meet an Alpha you're scent matched to. Well, I'd just met one, and I felt anything but magical. I prayed my scent-altering drugs were strong enough to keep me hidden from him. This job was almost over, then I'd get the hell out of dodge and away from that intoxicating scent along with the man who went with it.

Two

Lainey

True to his word, the moment the final person spoke and the dance music started, Zarin yanked me out of my seat, and we were off. I tried not to grin like an idiot at how my plan was working out, forgetting all about the mysterious Alpha I'd run into. Then I reminded myself I should be smiling. *Emmalina was finally going to get fucked by her dream man.*

There was a brief stop to get my fur stole from the coat check before racing out to the limousine. Walter already had the door open waiting for us when we reached the vehicle. I slid in with Zarin right behind me, tackling me to the long bench seat, making me giggle.

"My darling, you're going to smother me," I admonished.

Zarin ignored me as he kissed along my neck down to my collarbone. "I want to smother you in my love. I've waited so patiently for you, my petal, and now I need my reward."

Internally groaning at his words, I placed a hand on his chest. "You'll get your reward, I promise, but I want our first time together to be beautiful and romantic and not in the back of a limo."

He cupped my face and kissed me, his tongue forcing its way into my mouth. I pretended to moan with pleasure at his god-like skills of kissing as he slobbered all over my face. When he broke the kiss to look down at me, I had to fight the grimace as a string of spit connected the two of us.

"You're right, my perfect petal. You deserve all the romance I can give you. As an Alpha, I sometimes get a little carried away, but I've gotten ahold of myself," Zarin explained, stroking my cheek, and then we sat up.

Reaching for the button of his tux jacket, I popped it open. "I didn't mean we had to stop completely but more to savor the experience. This is a moment I want to remember forever with you." As I talked, I loosened his bow tie and then started on his shirt buttons. "I know something that will help take the edge off."

Sliding to the floor of the limousine, I put myself between his legs.

"No, petal, there's no need for that," Zarin argued. "I'll be able to manage until I can bury myself deep inside you."

"What if I want to? You do so much to take care of me and let me know how much I mean to you, so let me do this," I urged, undoing his belt and opening his pants to free his cock.

It was hard and already leaking pre-cum, making my job all that much easier. His dick was average in every way, but it meant I would have zero trouble getting this done before we arrived at the house. Getting situated, I grasped it at the base with two fingers so I didn't take up any of the length but could hold it steady. Locking eyes with Zarin, I licked him from his balls to the tip, making him hiss and toss back his head. Instantly, he went to grip my hair, but I removed his hand.

"No helping," I instructed. "This is all about me taking care of you."

He nodded frantically, and I resumed my work. Not all jobs or targets required me to be this intimate, but sometimes it was the only way I was going to get any. My life was all about moving from place to place, job to job, and changing my name, identity, and personality to fit what needed to be done. One place I didn't have to worry about how I acted was during sex. Some people, like Zarin, weren't going to get sex from me, but I enjoyed giving blow jobs and hand jobs, so he was in luck. If I had the right person and could get them to take a risk, I loved to be an exhibitionist.

If I thought I could have talked Zarin into finger-fucking me right there at that table, I would have let him. However, that was the real me, the thrill seeker, looking to see just how far we could go before getting caught. Unfortunately, that wasn't who the timid Emmalina was, and that's who needed to be in control of this moment.

I took all of him in my mouth, humming as I licked and sucked, giving all the enthusiasm I could so this man believed it all. The sounds of my efforts filled the limousine as Zarin moaned, clutching at the seat beneath him to keep from interfering. "Fuck, that feels so good, petal. You just wait... I'm going to eat you raw, then fuck that pussy of yours, filling you with my cum as I knot your ass to me."

Disregarding all the things that were wrong about that whole visual picture, I moaned, lifting my head from his cock. "Yes, darling, keep talking dirty to me. I want to know everything you have planned for us tonight."

"Yeah? You like it when I tell you you're a naughty girl? Well, get that naughty mouth back on my cock so I can fuck your mouth," Zarin ordered, his Alpha side coming out swinging.

Knowing I needed to do as he said, I swallowed him and let my jaw go soft, allowing him to fuck my face the way he wanted. With a grip on my wig, he used it to control how deep I was taking him. When he shoved my face down so my nose was pressed to his skin, I'd never been more thankful for a man with a manageable dick. Don't get me wrong, I can deep throat like a motherfucking champ, but it was on my terms, not theirs. It was easy to tell how erratic he was thrusting that this would all be over soon enough, so I didn't fight him or argue. I just took it.

Thankfully, he let me back off as I felt the knot at the back of his cock starting to swell. Gripping it with both hands, I squeezed tightly as he came, giving him that feeling of being knotted in an Omega. This was the second reason Alphas preferred Omegas over Betas because Omegas were built to take an Alpha's knot. They could accommodate the base swelling two to three times the size of the rest of the dick as it essentially locked them together. The purpose of this was to ensure that the Alpha's cum wouldn't leak out and raise the chances of the Omega becoming pregnant. The thing was, Omegas only get pregnant during a heat or mating cycle that happens twice a year.

When an Omega goes into heat, they become mindless sex addicts driven by instinct and the need to be bred. The first heat an Omega goes through is the worst, and it was a moment I never wanted to think about. It was buried in the past, along with the rest of my pain to be forgotten.

Thanks to the suppressants, I controlled when it happened and with whom it happened. I only allowed myself to have one heat a year. I learned the hard way if I skipped them both, there was a chance the suppressants would stop working, and I'd be fucked—literally. To an Alpha, an Omega in heat is like drugs to a junkie. So if I spontaneously went into heat, there was no controlling how things would go down. Not to mention if it happened around an Alpha who wasn't disciplined enough to keep control of his response, it could be awful for the Omega.

This is why as soon as this job was over, I'd ensured I had some time off to deal with my heat before starting the next job. Reminding myself of that fact explained why I was so fucking turned on right now. Zarin wasn't my type, nor did his cock do much for me, but goddamn if I didn't lick it clean after he came down my throat.

He grabbed my chin, drew me up, and then pulled me onto his lap so I was straddling him as he kissed me. His hands groped at my breasts over the dress, trying to keep from ripping it off me. Kissing this way was better than lying down. It seemed to keep things more contained, or I'd managed to take the edge off.

"I want you so bad," Zarin whispered against my lips. "If your pussy feels as good as your mouth, I'm never going to let you leave my bed. I'll fuck you till your pussy is imprinted by my cock, and no one else will ever be able to satisfy you the way I do. This way, you'll never leave me."

It was sad to me that he felt this was what women wanted from him. Really, he was a catch to someone who actually wanted the life he could provide for them. So many out there wanted to be the princess like that Beta who checked my ID. If he made the same offer to her as he did to me, I bet you anything she'd leap at the chance, thinking she'd won the lottery. Me, well, all I see is a man who wants to trap me by taking all my freedoms away. Never would I want to be in a relationship where I didn't make my own money. If I wanted to buy something or go somewhere, I did not want to be forced to check with a man first.

I do admit that because of my profession, I know all the dirty details of the world and see the worst of humanity on a daily basis. Fuck, I was a card-carrying member of the worst of humanity. However, it just showed time and time again the first lesson I learned—don't ever count on someone to care about you. Taking care of yourself was the only way to ensure your future, and even then, life, as a whole, was a risk.

A knock on the limousine window had me gasping and pulling away from Zarin.

"Shh... my petal," he soothed. "It's just Walter. We arrived at the house."

Sliding off his lap to sit next to him, I took a second to grab my clutch and pulled out a small mirror. I cleaned myself up a little and gave Zarin an apologetic look. "I'm sorry, I never act this impulsive, but you make it so hard for me to control myself. I know he's your driver and probably fully aware of what was happening back here, but I can't go out there looking like a hussy."

"You are right about him knowing, which is why he knocked. Take your time. I want you to feel comfortable in my home, starting at the driveway," Zarin assured me.

Double-checking my wig and contacts, making sure nothing was out of place, I cleaned up my smeared lipstick before announcing I was ready. Zarin exited first and reached in to help me out, not allowing Walter to get a good look at me. This man might have some shady business practices, but fuck if he wasn't the world's sweetest and most thoughtful man.

His home screamed single man with lots of money. It was modern, with many glass walls, streamline wood, and metal accents, along with tons of green ferns, succulents, and other plants that needed no maintenance. A warm light emitted from it, making it surprisingly welcoming for something so stark. Seeing it in person versus the blueprints that I'd been working off of gave me more appreciation for the person who designed it. The interior was something out of a Zen garden magazine—lots of warm wood colors with little areas of stone with bonsai trees or other similar plants.

"Fancy a drink?" Zarin asked as I paused to take in the place.

Pretending to shake myself back to reality, I smiled and nodded. "Love one, anything but champagne. I think I've reached my limit on that beverage this evening."

We walked up a flight of stairs into an open living room with a wet bar in the corner. I took a moment to wander the room as I visualized the space compared to the blueprints. Up here should be the living room, office, bedroom, bath, and a spare room I've heard him refer to as his meditation room.

"Your home is absolutely fantastic, just like you described it to me," I shared, running my fingers over some weird-ass-looking sculptures made out of marble.

"I'm glad you like it," he said, handing me over a rocks glass with a clear fizzy beverage. "Gin and tonic. I even used your family's gin. You'll have to tell me how I did," he teased with a wink.

One of the reasons I picked gin and the Elegant brand to represent was simply because it was my favorite. If I was going to put my fake name and reputation behind something, it had to be something good. Not to mention I knew I'd probably have people doing what Zarin just did, assuming I liked my family's product.

Taking a sip, I was surprised at how good it was. "Is this a special tonic?"

Zarin grinned. "Yes, it's an herbal tonic that I find compliments the gin perfectly, wouldn't you agree?"

"It's wonderful. I'm going to need you to tell me who makes it," I commented, taking another greedy gulp.

The man stepped closer, settling his hand on the curve of my hip as he leaned in. "That would be me. It's my private recipe I concocted some years ago in college. What else would a medical nerd like myself do for fun in the labs while watching mold grow all night."

"I'm deeply impressed," I admitted truthfully. "This really is something special."

"Maybe your family might be interested in working with me to get it out of the lab and into the market?" Zarin questioned. "Something tells me adding to their bottom line all thanks to you will soften them up to the idea of you staying here."

Reaching out, I cupped his cheek and brushed our noses together. "You are amazing, you know that... always looking out for me." I placed a tender kiss on his lips before letting my hand fall away. "Will you let me make a drink for you?"

"I would be honored," he answered, grinning at me. "It's not every day that a powerhouse in the liquor industry shows up at my house making that kind of offer."

Laughing, I playfully shoved him away and walked up to the wet bar, setting my clutch on the bartop and flicking open the latch. "Anything you don't like?"

"Not the biggest fan of rum, but in the right mix, I can drink it. My favorite would be tequila if that helps?" he shared.

It did, and it didn't. The drug I wanted to use had a strong bitter taste and was amber in color. Then I spotted the reposado tequila in a rich amber hue, making it perfect for what I needed. Zarin had a refined pallet with his tequila, allowing me the perfect vehicle to seal his fate. At least it would go down easily. The number of times I've pretended to be a bartender to get close to someone made this exercise all that much easier. His bar was stocked with all the essentials, giving me many options, but I decided to keep it classy by making an old fashioned.

Watching for my chance, Zarin turned to start the gas fireplace, and I slipped the small vial of amber liquid out of my clutch and squeezed it into the glass. Giving it one final stir, I called it good enough, taking a careful sniff, but all I could smell was the orange I'd rimmed the glass with. With my drink in hand, I offered him the one I had made, which he accepted eagerly.

"How did you know I loved old fashioneds?" he inquired before taking a sip and groaning. "Oh, that's it! I don't care what your family says, I'm not giving you back."

"So all it takes is a little muddling, and you're ready to commit? If I'd known that, I would have pulled out that skill sooner," I teased.

"Come sit with me. I know I got all hot and heavy on you in the limo, but as you said, tonight is a night of romance," Zarin explained, taking my hand and guiding me to the couch.

While this worked in my favor, I needed him to drink a few more sips for the drug to take effect. Over the years, I've used this technique, and one important thing I learned was when we got to this part of the evening, guaranteeing they would drink the whole glass wasn't going to happen. So I countered this by making it three times as strong, so even if they only got a quarter of the drink down, it would work. In the rare case they did drink it all, the drug wouldn't harm them—they would just wake up a day or two later.

"Romance, you say... that is something the world is sadly lacking," I commented, curling up next to him and resting my head on his chest.

"I couldn't agree more, my petal," he murmured, kissing the top of my head. "Tell me, how is it that a stunning woman like yourself hasn't found a pack before now?"

"Same question to you. I hardly think it makes sense how you don't have a pack and an Omega sharing this house with you," I countered, not interested in coming up with some sappy story.

"Hmm... well, there was a pack once." Zarin hummed. "They were my fraternity brothers... thick as thieves, the five of us. However, that all changed when I started making it big in medical research. I was the only one career-focused, and after a time, they resented me for my accomplishments. They were my family, and I wanted to build a life alongside them as packs should. Yet it seems they didn't feel the same, always telling me I was throwing my wealth and success around in their faces. In the end, we all went our separate ways. It's been almost twenty years, and if I ran into one of them now, I'm not sure what the reaction would be." That tale had him tossing back a good portion of his drink, wiping his mouth with the back of his hand.

Twisting, I pressed a hand to his chest as I looked into his eyes. "You're better off without them. If they couldn't support your success, then they don't deserve to be a part of it. I've learned that others will be drawn to you for many reasons, but I don't want them to be because of my money, family, or wealth. We deserve to be loved and valued for who we are as people regardless of the trappings that accompany it."

His fingers brushed along my cheek as he smiled. "You are just too perfect, my petal. I don't think anyone has ever explained that to me in a way that makes so much sense. Each time I think there isn't anything you can do to make me fall for you even more, you prove me wrong."

"Just goes to show you never truly know everything about a person. If you did, what would the fun be in that?" I reasoned, then kissed him deeply but backed off quickly, knowing I could knock myself out with the residual drug left on his tongue.

Pushing off the couch, I stood, setting my drink on the coffee table. The dress he'd picked out for me had a strapless corset-style top with off-the-shoulder straps. I tugged down the zipper as I held up the front until I got it loose enough. When I released my hold, the dress slithered down my body to pool at my feet, leaving me completely naked except for the jewelry I wore.

"Have I surprised you again?" I asked, making sure my voice was breathy and full of sultry desire.

Zarin just sat there staring at me for a moment before he was on his feet, wrapping an arm around my waist and latching his mouth to one of my nipples. I gasped, clutched his shoulders, tossed back my head, and moaned. "Zarin."

"Yes, my petal, tell me what you want. Anything, and it's yours," he assured me.

Grasping his face, I smirked. "Do you remember what you said to me in the limo about me being a naughty girl?"

"Of course, the naughtiest of girls." He all but growled.

"Will you punish me..." I started, dropping my eyes and biting my lip like I was ashamed of my request, "... then fuck me, bent over your desk like in a forbidden-romance novel?"

Zarin let out a shaky breath as he grabbed my ass with both hands. "Is that what you really want?"

"Yes," I whimpered, clutching his shirt desperately as I put my lips to his ear. "Headmaster, I've been so *very* bad. I think I need to be punished."

"Naughty, naughty girl, there's nothing to be done. You knew the consequences when you chose to misbehave," Zarin said, playing along as he lifted me, so I wrapped my legs around his waist. "Let's go to my office, young lady. This conversation needs to happen in private."

"I'm at your mercy, Headmaster. Do what you want with me." I purred, letting my fingers comb through the hair on the nape of his neck.

Zarin wasted no time marching over to the office door, punching in the code, and pressing his hand to the sensor before the lock snicked open.

"I didn't realize your office was so secure," I said, sounding concerned. "It's okay if you don't want to do this in here. I don't want to get you in trouble for having me in here."

"You, my petal, are not who I'm worried about being in here," he answered, kissing along my neck as he kicked the door shut. "I host many parties here for various business reasons, and there is a lot of valuable information here, so it's better to be safe."

"Wise, handsome, and romantic... I've hit the jackpot," I gushed, kissing all over his face.

Abruptly, I was placed on his desk as he frowned at me. "Don't think you can talk your way out of your punishment, you naughty girl."

I coyly bit my bottom lip and leaned forward. "There must be something I can do to make you forgive me..."

"What are you willing to offer?" he challenged, really getting into this role-playing.

I walked my fingers up his shirt. "Anything, Headmaster. Please, my parents can't find out about this. I'll accept my punishment as long as you don't tell them."

He snatched up my hand and pressed it to his crotch. "Think you can take care of this?"

"If that's what it takes to keep you from telling my parents, I'll do it," I answered with the slightest pretend sniff, making sure he realized it was fake.

"I'm not sure I believe you," Zarin grumbled, placing his hands on my knees and pressing them outward. "You know what I think? I think you need a test to see just how serious you are about this. Now show me your naughty little pussy so I can decide what to do with you."

Sitting in his office chair, he rolled forward, positioning himself in the perfect spot to spend some quality time between my legs. From how he'd been talking in the limousine, I got the feeling this man really loved eating at the downstairs restaurant. How long I'd let this go on until the drug took effect in a few minutes depended on how good he was at it.

The answer to that question was fucking amazing.

Within the first few strokes of his tongue, I knew I was in for a treat. He teased the skin around my pussy, making me buck and wriggle, trying to get him where I wanted his mouth. When he finally descended upon my clit, I let out a cry that wasn't faked in the slightest. Gripping the edge of the desk, I dug my nails into the wood as I held on for dear life. The kisses might be sloppy, but when it came to licking the envelope, it was the best way to make sure that shit was secure. His tongue thrust inside me, causing my back to arch as I felt the freight train of an orgasm heading my way. Only the train never made it to the station as the conductor crashed to the floor.

Three

Lainey

There I was, lying on the desk in the dark with my legs spread wide. It was not my proudest moment, that's for sure. For a moment, I considered finishing myself off before getting to work so I had a clear head.

Knowing I was lying to myself, I channeled my inner Smurfette, accepting I'd been fucked by some blue balls. Shoving myself off the desk, I stood on slightly shaky legs but managed to reach the office door. I knew that once the door was unlocked, it would stay that way until he locked it again, but to be safe, I made sure I stuck a book in the way to keep it from closing. Snagging my drink as I walked to the bar where my clutch was, I chugged the thing, needing the fortitude to deal with my unexpected bluevaries.

I needed to make a detour to Zarin's room for some clothes, not wanting to put my dress back on. Plus, when I slipped out of the house, a black hoodie and sweatpants were easier to sneak around in. In preparation for tonight, I'd made sure everything at the hotel would be taken care of, and my go bag was within walking distance to here. The hardest part of these jobs wasn't pulling it off but the exit after. The person I'd been for the past two weeks needed to vanish into thin air and never be traced back to me.

Dressed, I headed back to the office and dragged the snoring man out of the way. Removing two USB jump drives from my clutch, I plugged in the first one—a code breaker that would get me access to the computer and files. While I might be a lot of things, a computer wiz, I was not. This is the reason to make friends on the dark side of the web that had as many morals as I did. My contact was brilliant. There hadn't been a request he couldn't fulfill, and he undercharged himself to the point where even I felt like I was cheating him.

Resting an elbow on the desk, I drummed my fingers on the wooden surface as I waited. Two minutes later, there was a chime of bells, and the computer screen opened to the desktop. Once I was in, it took me far longer than I would have liked to find what I was looking for, but Zarin had put in some effort to hide the access point to the Blissmeds' database. Removing the one jump drive, I plugged in the other, typed in the activation code, hit enter, and watched as the files downloaded. A notification popped up asking if I wanted to delete the original version and replace it with these.

"Why yes... yes, I certainly do," I told the computer as I clicked yes. "God, sometimes this job is too fucking easy."

This part took the longest as the program I'd been given scattered the false information throughout the entire database. This was to ensure if anything was discovered, there would be no way they'd find it all, and something would slip through. All it took was one person doing the audit to get suspicious and dig deeper to find the rest. When it was over, the whole screen glitched for a moment, and the scent of smoke had me snatching the jump drive out of the computer. A thin trail of smoke wafted from the device, telling me it was toast.

Smart, then you ensure I can't hold it to use as blackmail. Pharmigo was quickly becoming one of the companies I put on my don't-fuck-with list. With the job complete, I shoved up out of the chair and looked down at Zarin, trying to decide if the couch or bed might be better. Feeling it was best to give myself the time I needed, I dragged the man to his bedroom. I stripped him down and got him on the bed, face down on his stomach. Getting in the bed, I rolled and thrashed around so it looked like wild sex had happened. Just to make him feel good about himself, I tipped over one of the lamps on the nightstand.

Taking a moment, I wrote him a quick note about being called back home due to an emergency, but I would forever try to get back to him. Putting on lipstick, I pressed a kiss to the sheet of paper and left it on the pillow. With that matter put to a close, I headed to the living room.

Bundling up the dress, I shoved my clutch in the pocket of the hoodie and pulled up the hood. I double-checked to make sure I wasn't leaving anything incriminating behind before jogging downstairs. Knowing he never set the security system, I slipped out the back door where it butted up to protected forest land. I just had to make it through a corner of the forest to end up in the neighboring subdivision where my go-bag was located. I quickly looked in either direction and booked it through the backyard.

I was home free with another successful job completed.

Once I entered the forest, I slowed to a walk, pulling my burner phone out of my clutch. Using the encrypted messaging app, I sent a confirmation to the client, adding the tidbit about the jump drive so they knew I'd used it. Hearing a twig snap behind me, I paused, thinking it was Walter coming after me, but there was no one. Scowling, I scanned the forest once more before continuing.

Just as I was about to leave the forest, I was yanked back with a leather-gloved hand covering my mouth as I screamed. Thrashing in my attacker's grip, I cursed myself for choosing to steal flip-flops for shoes as I slammed my heel into the top of their foot. Pretty sure that hurt me more than them. It did jack shit and caused them to tighten their grip, followed by the burn of a needle puncturing my neck.

Fuck, fuck, fuck.

This can't be happening.

There's no way I screwed up badly enough to warrant this reaction. *Shit, was Pharmigo trying to get rid of all the evidence? Motherfuckers.* If I came out of this alive, I'm going to hunt down whoever was behind attacking me, and they were going to pay. Whatever it took, I was going to make it fucking hurt.

Never had my head throbbed this bad after a night of drinking. I was always so careful. Hangovers made you careless, easily irritated, and that's when people slipped up. One drink too many and the con you'd been planning would be gone in an instant. So why the fuck did my head feel like someone used it to hammer nails into concrete?

Rolling over, I groaned at the stiffness of my body, making me wonder if I'd been in an accident. I took a deep breath and waited for the sharp pain across my chest where the seat belt had been, but there was nothing. *Okay, not a car accident—thank God.* I took a moment to take stock of my body and didn't notice anything out of the ordinary. So I gathered my courage as I rubbed my eyes to see where the hell I ended up last night. Cracking open one eye, just in case I needed to shut it again, a bedroom came into view.

My eyes snapped open as I shoved myself up, taking in the strange room. The room itself hadn't bothered me all that much. What had me panicking was the picture of me and three other kids at a park smiling at the camera. I was around thirteen in that picture with rosy cheeks, bright hazel eyes that still believed my world could get better, and rich golden-brown hair.

The other children had been orphans like me who he'd allegedly adopted with his various identities. We'd been told to play and have a good time at this park in a super fancy neighborhood. Of course, it had been for one of his cons, and the second he got the pictures he needed, we were shoved back in the car and brought back to reality. That day had been wonderful, and it was one of the few happy moments of my childhood.

What was scaring the shit out of me as I looked at the photograph was how the fuck they connected it to me. Since the moment I walked away at the age of eighteen, I've never once used my legal name on or for anything. Typically, I went by Angelina when I wasn't on a job, which was nothing close to Lainey. How someone managed to figure out who I was had my stomach revolting. Looking around wildly, I spotted the bathroom door half open and stumbled my way over, falling to my knees as I threw up. There wasn't much in my stomach telling me that I'd been passed out longer than I thought.

Once my stomach accepted the fact I had nothing left to give, I used the sink's counter as leverage to get back on my feet. Not daring to look in the mirror, I kept my eyes on my shaking hands as I turned on the water. Rinsing out my mouth, I grimaced at the acidic taste from vomiting. I really fucking hated throwing up. My biggest fear when getting sick was that it would be a stomach bug. Being sick made you weak already, but being forced to stay near a bathroom was a level of vulnerability I didn't want to commit to.

My skin still feeling clammy, I splashed water on my face, scrubbing it vigorously, trying to pull my shit together. Giving in, I faced myself in the mirror, not flinching from the mess that looked back at me.

"Get it together, woman," I scolded myself. "This is no time to have a panic attack over a fucking photo. You need to figure out where the hell you are, then you might get some clues. Remember, your next job isn't for another two weeks, so there's time to fix this."

Those same hazel eyes looked back at me with makeup I'd slept in smeared all over my face. There was no wanderlust found in them any longer. Instead, they reflected the reality of the life I've lived fending for myself. The baby fat was gone from my cheeks, allowing the elegant slope of my bone structure to show through. Natural full lips were made just a touch more pillowy with some filler, giving the barest pout to them. I took great pride in how well I looked after my skin, investing in the greatest asset I had in a con—myself.

It was the same for maintaining a good weight, not too skinny taking away my curves, but not too much. I worked out every other day and watched my diet, owning up to the fact I had a terrible addiction to sweets. Moose Tracks ice cream was my drug of choice. I could slam a pint like it was nothing if I wasn't careful. That was a piece of Lainey I couldn't seem to shake, no matter how hard I tried. Guess some things are so ingrained it doesn't matter how deep you try to bury them, they still pop up.

Seeing my hair, I actually flinched as I absorbed the fact someone ripped the fucking wig off my head. The wig cap was barely holding on, and my natural hair was sticking out all over the place like I had no idea what I was doing. That wig had been glued down tight, knowing it needed to last the two weeks I was going to be Emmalina. Whoever brought me here wanted to prove they knew I was hiding who I was. Then I realized they'd removed my contacts as well. Whatever drug they used, they weren't fucking around if I stayed passed out through all that.

While I would kill for a shower, I couldn't be that exposed until I knew what the hell was happening. Walking back into the bedroom, I scanned the space looking for anything that would give me a clue as to why I was here. Instead, all I found was that this room is exactly what I would have designed for myself. The walls were white, but with the artwork on them, you didn't really notice. Everything had a modern feel with vintage touches that were so my style—the advantages of the current era with the elegance of the past blended together.

Taking in the bed again, I couldn't help but be surprised at how nest-like it was. Tons of fluffy pillows in creams, light pinks, and robin's-egg blue sat on top of a pure white comforter that had an ivy pattern stitched into it with white thread. There were even soft gauzy curtains to pull from the head of the bed to give it that cozy feel as you snuggled in, a must-have for most Omegas. Seeing these rather specific features of the room told me that not only did they know *who* I was but also *what* I was.

With each second that passed, I got thrown from one emotion to another as I tried to process what the hell was happening. Clearly, I wasn't going to learn much from this charming yet frustrating bedroom, so it was time to explore the rest of this place. Half expecting the door to be locked, I paused when the handle turned easily. Stepping out into the tiny hall that took me to the living room, I couldn't help but gasp at how beautiful it was.

A crystal chandelier hung from the ceiling casting little prism rainbows over the cream-tufted furniture below. More pillows filled the loveseat in pinks, gray, and white, making me want to run and jump into the pile. A glass coffee table sat in the middle with a fresh floral arrangement of roselilies, a rather unique flower and my favorite. Right below them was a tented card with Lainey scrawled across it in elegant handwriting. Picking it up, I found a simple black smartphone underneath. Reading the card, it had one sentence and a four-digit code to unlock the phone.

USE THIS CODE TO READ MESSAGE.

I flipped the card over, but no more information was found. Picking up the phone, I tapped the screen, which prompted the request for the four numbers I'd been given. Entering them, I set the phone down, backing up as far as I could before hitting the enter button. It's not like it would do much if the damn thing was going to blow up, but it made me feel better. Closing my eyes, I hit enter and hunched over, waiting for something to happen. Peeking at the phone after a minute to make sure I really hit the right button, I was sucker punched with a picture of Trent in an orange prison jumpsuit looking at whoever was taking the image.

My legs gave out, and I crumbled to the floor as the feelings I'd hidden away for twelve years came rushing back. Overwhelmed, a single tear rolled down my cheek as I fought to regain control. He was locked away where he couldn't hurt me or the others again. I'd made fucking sure of it. Quickly, I brushed away the tear, refusing to acknowledge it had happened. That bastard didn't deserve any more tears than the ones he robbed of me as an innocent. I was far from the Lainey who sought that man's approval and believed he might have a shred of affection for me. The woman I was now could make men crawl on their hands and knees if I chose to. I had nothing to fear from a picture.

Reaching out with a shaky hand, I fisted it, took a deep breath, and tried again without a hint of fear. Grasping the phone, I steeled myself to see his picture, but now that I was over the initial shock, he didn't look like the personal demon I always pictured in my nightmares. He'd gotten fat which was hard to believe since he'd been such a stickler about his appearance, knowing as I did how important it was. Although I suppose since he wasn't ever getting out, he had no one to impress. His jaw was covered in salt and pepper stubble while his hair had gone all gray, and it wasn't a good look for him. Everything about him now looked like he was defeated until you got to his eyes.

Those amber orbs were full of the intelligence I knew that conniving bastard had. It wouldn't surprise me one fucking bit if he were using this appearance to throw people off. He probably ruled that prison without anyone the wiser. Having recovered from the shock, I remembered the note said to read the message, so I swiped his photograph away to see what the hell was going on.

> *Hello, Lainey Caddel, and welcome to the Underground Omega Syndicate.*
>
> *You have been chosen for a very important project based on your particular set of unique skills and/or connections. We've taken the liberty of relocating you to your apartment in Corzina. This location will serve as the starting point for your new role within our organization.*
>
> *There are three rules you must abide by:*

1. *Keep this phone with you at all times. It is your sole source of funding and anything else you may require to be successful in your mission.*

2. *Follow any and all orders given within the time frame provided. If an issue arises, reach out to the number provided immediately.*

3. *Never discuss the Syndicate or your affiliation with the Syndicate.*

Follow these instructions, and you will be considered to earn your freedom.

Should you choose to ignore or deviate from these guidelines, the penalties will be swift and severe. Any attempt to expose our organization will immediately activate Termination Protocol, which includes but is not limited to: the release of damaging evidence relating to your role in putting this man in jail, as well as sending your identity to all the targets you've conned. Immediate termination of funding and available resources will also occur. In some cases, loss of life might be called for to protect the Syndicate.

For now, please make use of the home and items provided. They are for you to use in completing this mission. We're glad to have your skills at our disposal, helping to further our cause—putting Omegas in positions of power globally. Together, we will strive for equality and a better, safer, and more prosperous tomorrow for all designations.

Further instructions will follow shortly. Remember, we are always watching...

U.O.S.

"What. The. Actual. Fuck?" I said in disbelief, staring at the phone.

Thankfully, I was already sitting down, or I'd have ended up on my ass over the shock of reading this psycho-babble bullshit. Now the picture in the bedroom made sense—they wanted to prove, without a doubt, they knew who I was. This syndicate has dug up all the dirt on me and, for fun, left a surprise for me to wake up to. I'll hand it to them, they had my attention, and I wasn't one to scare easily. Trent might have a choke hold on me from my childhood, but adult Lainey didn't give two shits how big or bad you were. If you find the right piece of information, you can bring anyone down. A point this syndicate was trying to make as I sat here.

The phone vibrated in my hand, making me yelp in surprise. I have no idea how they were uploading things to this phone because it wasn't an email, text, or any other messaging system. It's like they added it to the phone's operating system, and by typing in the code and reading the message, I activated the protocol. Document after document flashed on the screen, followed by pictures of men, women, city buildings, and a home. Once the phone stopped freaking out, there was a pause then another full-screen message appeared.

> YOU ARE THE NEWEST EXECUTIVE ASSISTANT TO HALSTEAD NORLUND, THE CEO AND OWNER/FOUNDER OF ENIGMA TECHNOLOGIES. MONDAY IS YOUR FIRST DAY ON THE JOB. THEY EXPECT YOU TO BE AT THE LOCATION PROVIDED BY 8:00 A.M. SHARP. COMPLETE ONBOARDING, OBTAIN YOUR EMPLOYEE BADGE, AND FAMILIARIZE YOURSELF WITH THE FACILITY.

> FURTHER INSTRUCTIONS WILL BE PROVIDED WHEN THESE STEPS ARE COMPLETED.

Four

Lainey

Picking myself up from the floor, I swiped the message out of the way and was prompted to complete the biometrics setup. I scanned both pointer fingers and thumbs to ensure I could open whichever way necessary. The information they'd provided had been organized into neat little digital folders I needed to unlock each time I entered. These folks were serious about their security, but I suppose it's also a way to track if I'm doing what they wanted.

Back out of the information, I pulled up the contacts, and there were two names listed—Home and Pharmacy. Why the hell anyone would have a pharmacy listed in their phone, I have no fucking clue but whatever. I guessed that home would be the number to call if I had any trouble, but I was curious about the pharmacy. Pulling up the contact information, I found a note in the memo section—*For Mom's emergency prescription.* Apparently, this wacky syndicate was providing healthcare while I was on the job. How kind.

There wasn't much else on the phone, at surface level, that is, for which I was grateful. I'm not sure I could take much more between being drugged, kidnapped, blackmailed, and forced to be back in a city I never wanted to come to again. Padding over to the window, I looked out at Corzina, expecting to recognize where I was. In a way, I did—this was the ritzy northern part of the city I never had a reason to spend time in. This apartment was several floors up, fourth if I were to guess, in an older building with a view of the Lovisa Arboretum.

Corzina was a beautiful city, the oldest and largest in Breona near the ocean. This apartment was facing the wrong way to see the ocean. However, it was a breathtaking sight if you're fortunate enough to live on a high-enough floor to see past the trees and buildings. Lots of history has happened in this place—it was what I loved most about it. That and the government worked hard to keep that front and center while still advancing the city into modern infrastructure. They held a delicate balance in their hands, and I was pleased to see at first glance not much had changed since I left.

Setting the phone on the kitchen counter, I decided to take them at their word and make myself at home. If this was where they were putting me up for this *mission,* then I was damn well going to use it. Yanking off the hoodie I'd taken from Zarin, I wrinkled my nose at the smell of it.

Just how long had I been passed out?

This had me glancing at the clock in the bedroom as I made my way to the bathroom. It was early evening, meaning I'd been passed out for well over twelve hours. Chucking the clothes into a hamper that was placed in the bathroom, I opened the shower door to see if there were any supplies inside. Sure enough, my favorite brands of everything I used in my daily life were sitting there waiting for me to use. An oversized fluffy towel also hung on a hook inside, making it so I didn't need to search for a thing.

It took me a minute to figure out the faucet, but it was well worth it as the dual showerheads kept me nice and toasty warm as I washed. I scrubbed my body from head to toe, getting a good exfoliation before shaving from my big toe to my pits. If tomorrow was my first day at a new job, then first impressions were of the utmost importance. After all the shocks I'd experienced in the past hour, falling into my routine with my normal products was comforting. I kept running that first message through my head, trying to ascertain if this syndicate was legit. It's not like I could get on the internet and ask Cyclone if there was such a thing as the Underground Omega Syndicate.

Furthermore, I have no idea how they could find out about me and who I really was if they weren't some criminal organization or law enforcement. The latter didn't make any sense. Why would the government go so far as to pull a stunt like this? If they knew this much about me already, then they'd have more than enough to arrest me. No, this syndicate had to be treated as a real threat. I couldn't risk Trent ever finding out what I'd done. Even from prison, that man could destroy my life with his connections. While I'd gotten really fucking good at my job, there was a reason Trent hadn't gone down before I handed him over on a silver platter.

Twisting my hair up in a towel, I pulled on the silk kimono-style robe I'd found on the back of the door. It was a beautiful soft gold color that set off my bronzed skin, tanned from the job I'd finished up before Zarin. The mysterious syndicate implied that I would have everything I needed, so I investigated the dresser and closet to see if they were right. I pulled open the door to the moderately large walk-in closet full of clothes for all occasions from casual jeans to a ball gown tucked away in a dress bag. Behind the door was a rack of shoes in basic colors and styles that would meet almost every need.

Satisfied with what I'd found so far, I moved to the dresser and pulled open the top drawer. Jewelry and other accessories were revealed, organized expertly to show me what all I had to use. How they'd managed to pin down my style was just creepy. I loved combining the old with the new, pulling inspiration from the famous femme fatales of the silver screen along with a dash of vintage glamour. Even the lingerie provided had that classic silk-and-lace vibe going for it that would thrill any man who might happen to get a glimpse.

In no way was I a slut who slept with all my targets, but to be good at this job, you had to use *all* your tools. Men were simple—they were all drawn to the same things, and I just happened to use it against them. After slipping on some underwear and a silk nighty, I returned to the bathroom and blew out my hair. I wouldn't bother doing much with it before the morning, so up in a messy bun it went.

Wrapping back up in the robe, I headed to the kitchen, desperate for some food. The space was simple with no official dining area, instead using the kitchen counter as the table. It seems whoever designed this apartment wanted to have more space in the living room, but the open concept made it feel so airy I couldn't help but agree with the choice. I tugged open the refrigerator door and found it stocked full of food. Snooping around the cabinets, it was just as it was in the bedroom. Everything I could ever fathom needing was here at my fingertips. If I weren't so worried about what they were blackmailing me to do, I'd consider staying on just to live in this adorable place.

Too bad this was all as fake as the rest of my life. They'd made me my perfect home. Moving on from that thought, I returned to the refrigerator and grabbed what I needed to make a simple dinner for myself. I loved to cook, and I missed being able to do it as much these days with my busy schedule. It started out as a necessity. If I wanted to eat, I needed to do it my fucking self. The group home was run by a decent couple, Charles and Imogen, but neither knew how to cook. There are only so many nights you can eat mac and cheese, hot dogs, and frozen pizza before you're begging for something else.

Being young and lacking the skills to know how to cook, I sat and watched cooking shows with Imogen's mother, Penelopy. We kids all called her Poppy, and many of us considered her our surrogate grandmother. She'd once been a skilled chef and was always muttering about how Imogen was such a disappointment and couldn't even boil water. When we watched the shows, I would pepper her with questions, but she never minded, always happy to talk about her first love—good food. I'd just started to help in the kitchen when Trent showed up to take me away.

Thank God for Poppy and all that she'd taught me because Trent didn't have time to worry about feeding me or the other kids who cycled through his home. Some of the kids knew how to cook and would help me, but the majority of the time, it was left to me. Once I was on my own, I discovered the true joy of cooking. Experimenting with flavors, new ingredients, and the best part was I didn't have to lie about a fucking thing. The food told the story—you were good or you weren't—no way around it.

I whipped up a simple salad, chopping the ingredients and tossing it with a balsamic dressing I made. This was a go-to meal since there really wasn't much 'cooking' involved in the process and could be made with whatever was in the refrigerator at the time. Even now when I never had to look twice at my bank account to make sure I can afford to pay for this or that, some habits are hard to break, such as making sure to only buy what I need for food and never letting something go to waste. If anything, I'd rather make food and give it to the doorman, the homeless on the street, or even the neighbor next door I've never met before. That way, I know someone is making use of the food.

On my way to the living room, I snatched up the phone, planning to look over the information I'd been given. Plopping into the midst of the pillow pile, I noticed a television was mounted on the wall, but it had a picture frame around it, making it part of the décor. I searched for the remote and discovered it was in the side table drawer. Flipping on the television, I turned my attention to the phone and grinned as I found what I was looking for. Seconds later, my phone was displayed on the much bigger screen allowing me to read everything easier.

My new job was with Enigma Technologies, a company specializing in cyber security. I was to be the executive assistant to Alpha Halstead Norlund, the man who created the company and put it on the map with a military defense contract. From there, it grew to the giant in the market it was today—the number one company to turn to when you wanted to know the latest and greatest in cyber security. Scrolling through his information, he seemed like the typical shrewd businessman who knew what he wanted out of life and took it. Then his picture popped up, and I sat up so quickly and almost dumped what was left of my salad on the floor.

"Holy silver fox," I blurted.

Halstead sat casually in a leather armchair with a glass of what I would guess to be whiskey in one hand and a cigar raised to his lips in the other. His hair was that dark steel gray with lighter strands highlighting it. His beard matched for the most part, maybe a half shade lighter with more white mixed in. The attention to detail this man took with his appearance was noticeable. Not even an eyebrow hair was out of place, yet it didn't seem *too* perfect. He had 'classic gentleman' written all over him. This was only made more apparent with the three-piece suit, leather strap watch, cufflinks, and thick ring on his middle finger with a monogram on it.

"How the fuck am I going to get any work done being around him?" I muttered to myself, flopping back into the pillows. "Maybe I can test the waters and see if he's a man who's willing to take risks outside the boardroom."

Then I realized how stupid that sounded. There is no way a man like that didn't have a pack and some pillow princess of an Omega at home—*lucky bitch*. Letting out a frustrated sigh, I stabbed another forkful of salad and shoved it in my mouth. I continued reading and was intrigued to find out Halstead wasn't a man to keep an assistant for long. Due to the secretive nature of the man and the amount of NDAs and contracts he put on each canned employee, no one was willing to talk about why they were fired.

This had me flipping back a few pages to see if they had any personal information on him, but it seemed I was on my own with that. I suppose for someone whose whole purpose was to keep the world safe from hacking or the spread of personal information, it would serve to reason he'd do the same for himself. While this would have worried others, I saw this as a challenge and couldn't be more excited. Even without the other part of this job I have yet to learn about, just being the one to quit on this guy would be reward enough. What the hell could he be looking for in an assistant? He's had both men and women, so it wasn't a case of leaning toward one gender over the other.

Tapping my fork on my bottom lip, I stared at his picture, almost mesmerized by his vibrant blue eyes. Halstead might show physically that he's been alive for fifty-five years, putting a solid twenty-three years between us, yet everything in that look he was directing at someone sitting across from him told me he was mentally sharp as a diamond. He'd taken all that pressure as a younger man, honing it into the rare jewel he was now.

The question was would that put us on equal footing during this?

It seems like there's only one way to find out, and the first step was to show up for work in the morning. This was going to be fun.

The rest of the night I read over everything important to do with the company itself, such as the competition, friends, enemies, and the ins and outs which prepared me for anything. I've never pulled off a job in any type of security world before. To me, it seemed like tempting fate, something I never liked to do, *ever*. If the Syndicate had the reach it appeared they did, then I had to trust they'd make sure my cover wouldn't be blown with a carelessly thrown-together identity.

When I started to go cross-eyed from reading so much information, I decided to call it a night. Taking a moment to clean up the kitchen from dinner, I washed up, leaving them to dry in the sink and deal with it in the morning. Even though I'd been drugged and was passed out for most of the day, I felt like I hadn't slept in days.

Laying the robe on the padded bench at the end of the bed, I crawled up into the fluffy cloud of a mattress. Then I tossed back the blankets and slipped under them, only to snuggle in, tucking the blankets under my chin. Inhaling deeply, I counted to four then let it out again, repeating the same action three times, grounding my body and mind before I risked closing my eyes. My biggest fear at the moment wasn't what tomorrow would bring or the dangers lurking in the shadows from the Syndicate. No, I had a much simpler problem to worry about...

Making it through the night.

Seeing Trent on top of being back in Corzina for the first time in twelve years would absolutely trigger my nightmares. I wonder if the Syndicate knew about those too? Guess they will after tonight—fingers crossed the walls are soundproof.

Five

Halstead

Each time I walked up the steps of this company and saw the name I'd thought of all those years ago as a college student printed on the building made it worth the bullshit I now dealt with on a daily basis. Reaching the top step, I didn't even have to worry about pulling out my keycard to get it—someone was already holding it open.

"Good morning, Mr. Norlund," the security guard greeted me.

"Morning, Thomas," I answered with a nod.

Reaching into the breast pocket of my vest, I pulled out my mint strips and popped one in my mouth. I had a meeting first thing with the new Department of Defense contact to go over the latest project and why I refused to do it. There weren't many times I would turn down a job they requested, but I couldn't support this one, nor did I want my name or the name of my company associated with the damn thing. My phone buzzed in my pocket, and I groaned as I took it out and then my glasses from my inner suit pocket. Getting old made things fucking complicated with extra steps to read a goddamn text. I muttered my greeting to the security guard near the elevators as he held back the door for the private elevator upper management used.

Quintin: *The new hire is starting today, and I don't want to hear a word about it, H. You need someone to pick up the pieces you* *leave behind all day. I have enough work of my own to do, and putting out fires you caused is no longer one of them. The contract she is signing says we will keep her for a minimum of two weeks as a trial period.*

Cheeky asshole, thinking he could box me into keeping them around with that, did he? If the man didn't like how I dealt with things, then he didn't need to butt in. He wasn't my assistant anymore, hadn't been for quite some time, but it would seem old habits die hard. In fact, he'd just celebrated being the CFO for the thirteenth year last week. There was a party and everything for him.

Quintin: *I can see you read my message. I expect a response.*

I snorted at that. Quintin and I have worked side by side for eighteen years, longer than anyone else in this whole damn company. It was one of the only reasons he felt so free to speak to me like I was his child rather than his boss. Well, I suppose I'm not his boss either since he now owns equity in the company, a gift he more than earned on his tenth anniversary with the company.

Me: *K*

I couldn't help but smirk, knowing that was about to get his perfectly pressed slacks in a twist. He wanted an answer and damn well knew I wasn't happy about him going behind my back to hire this person I hadn't even met yet. It seems she was a referral from another company in Marlios but recently moved out here and was looking for a job. Why the hell she moved without having a job lined up makes me question her ability to do this job. I wasn't looking for a secretary to book my lunch meetings, get me coffee, or pucker up to kiss my ass every morning—that's what Sam was for. Well, minus the ass-kissing, the last thing I needed was a damn lawsuit for sexual harassment.

Stepping out of the elevator onto the building's top floor—a space I shared with four other people, soon to be five, if my pushy business partner had anything to do about it—I started walking. Quintin's office was on the opposite end from mine since we both acknowledged a little distance between our offices helped us to work more efficiently. That man really didn't know how to give up a role he once held, and not allowing him to be aware of all the comings and goings of my day was better for everyone. In the middle was Kerian's office, our chief coder who ensured we never sent out a project that hadn't been thoroughly vetted. Sam had a space in my lobby area for his desk outside my office door. He greeted guests and made sure they were comfortable as they waited but also ensured no one just wandered in without me knowing.

As a person who rather enjoys his privacy, I can't stand it when people violate the sanctity of my office. I suppose it's one of the reasons I created a security company to provide that same sense of safety to anyone who wanted it. Out of all the secretaries, Sam has lasted the longest—almost six months, come to think of it. A surefire way to be out of a job was to allow someone to enter my office when I wasn't there or given express permission to do so. Which is why walking up on the scene of the twenty-five-year-old man plastered against the double doors to my office, fending off another man, warmed my heart.

"Sir, I understand you have a meeting with Mr. Norlund, which I've stated is in a half hour," Sam explained as best he could with the man's hand around his throat. "It doesn't matter what you threaten me with, I still can't allow you to enter his office. He doesn't let anyone in there without being present, and he hasn't arrived for the day."

"Do you know who I am, you little shit?" the man seethed.

"Yes, Mr. Hays, I'm incredibly aware of who you are," Sam answered, then he spotted me, and his whole body went slack with relief.

I strode forward, not bothering to look for the security guard who was supposed to be watching this floor. Dropping my briefcase, I grabbed the man by the back of the neck and yanked, tossing him onto the couch where he should have been sitting.

"What the fuck do you think you're doing?" I bellowed.

For the most part, I was a mild-mannered man, or I'd like to think so. However, if you messed with my people, that was tossed aside, and the protective papa bear came out. It was not a pretty sight for those who got the full brunt of my anger, creating the fires Quintin complained about putting out.

"You dare come to my office and attack my employee for doing his job? To turn your question back on you... do you know who *I* am?" I demanded.

The man gawked at me. I knew what he saw—the contradiction of me owning my age and the ease at which I just treated him like a ragdoll must be making his brain explode.

"Mr. Norlund..." he started, but I held up a hand to stop him.

"If I don't hear you begging for your life or that poor man's forgiveness, then for your safety..." I paused and leaned forward so we were eye to eye, "... Do. Not. Speak."

Leaving him to decide what he would choose, I left him in a terrified puddle on the couch to check on Sam. The Beta's eyes were wide, his breath coming in quick, shallow puffs as he rubbed at his neck. Gently, I caught his wrist and pulled it away from his skin so I could see. At the moment, the skin was only red—no signs of bruising yet—but I wasn't going to take a chance. I guided the man to his desk and urged him to sit, which he did without protest.

"Are you unharmed?" I asked.

Sam nodded his head slowly. "I'm fine, sir—"

"I know you're not all right, so don't even try that bullshit on me," I warned, giving him a stern look. "My question wasn't, are you fine. It was... are you hurt somewhere I can't see?"

He swallowed, licked his lips, and dropped his gaze. "When he shoved me against the door, the handle slammed into my back. It makes breathing rather uncomfortable."

Grabbing the phone, I hit the extension to the security office. It rang twice, then someone answered. "Fernando speaking."

"It's me," I stated.

"Mr. Norlund, is Doc Brown needed?" Fernando asked, using the security phrase to ask if I was in danger.

"No, but I will need Angela. It seems she hasn't shown up at work yet," I informed our head of security, who started yelling at people setting things in motion. "Fernando, I also need you to call for Dr. Bardas. I need him to look over Sam for me."

"I have people on their way to you, and I'll send a car for Dr. Bardas. Then I'm going to hunt down whoever was supposed to be on your floor and find out why the fuck they weren't there. Is there anything else you need, sir?" he asked, his irritation clear in his voice.

Whoever that person was, I felt bad for them. Fernando took his job dead seriously, and hearing that Sam was hurt would set him on a rampage. Neither of them knew I noticed, but the two men had been seeing each other and was how Sam got the interview. I didn't give a shit about the fact they were together as long as it didn't keep them from doing their job. In fact, I felt like it kept me safer to have his lover sitting outside my door.

"No, that's all," I shared, then paused, considering my next words. "Tell Dr. Bardas there are no major injuries, more of a precaution to ensure there's nothing we need to keep an eye on."

Fernando didn't say anything right away but let out a sigh of relief. "Thank you, sir."

With nothing more to be said, I hung up and gently patted Sam on the shoulder before returning my attention to our guest. In a move I respected but also felt was moronic, Mr. Hays met my gaze, jutting out his chin at me. "While I do acknowledge my actions were uncalled for, your man there provoked it."

"Did he now?" I commented, sliding my hands into my pants pockets and leaning against the front of Sam's desk. "If you could explain, that would help and be appreciated."

"When I arrived for our meeting, the front desk called up to let this young man know, and he had the audacity to make me wait at the front desk until he came down to get me. The security guard at the elevator then patted me down before joining us to arrive here. When I tried to enter your office, this *Beta* threw himself in my way, causing me to accidentally slam him against the door. It certainly wasn't on purpose like he's making it sound," he blathered on, showing his entitlement loud and clear.

Before I could respond to that pile of garbage that came out of his mouth, three men in black suits arrived. They stood side by side, hands clasped in front, waiting for my orders. While we specialize in cyber security, I believe in knowing all aspects of the security realm, which is why we have our internal personnel we trained to handle our needs.

Pushing off the desk, I walked over to my briefcase, picked it up, grasped the long vertical handle, and pulled open one of the doors. "I think the best way to settle this is for me to see the whole thing for myself. Why don't you join me, Mr. Hays, just in case I have any questions." Turning my attention to the guards, I also handed out their instructions. "One of you with me, please, and the other two will stand stationed outside this door. No one enters, and no one leaves until I say."

They nodded, and one broke off to follow the troublemaker into my office. "Sam, the moment Dr. Bardas arrives, let me know."

"Of course, sir," Sam assured me.

"Don't let him out of your sight. One of you will follow him to make up for the fuck-up that happened this morning," I ordered, pinning Sam with a look not to argue with me. He sighed and accepted his fate, flinching as he sat back in his chair.

Seeing that made me grit my teeth as I walked to my desk. Mr. Hays sat in one of the two chairs in front of it. I took joy in slamming my briefcase down on the chestnut-colored surface, making the man jump. With a grunt, I settled into the large leather office chair and stared at the man for a moment.

"If what I see on this video contradicts what you told me out there, I'm throwing your ass out of my building," I warned.

"What?" Mr. Hays squawked, his eyes going wide.

Grabbing a remote, I flicked on the projector that was hidden in the ceiling and connected to my computer. "You think I should be scared since you work for the DOD... well, I'm not. I'm sure you're used to getting a certain type of treatment, getting what you want just because you ask for it. That shit isn't gonna fly here. I don't care if you're the Prime Minister himself, no one treats my people the way you just did."

"Mr. Norlund, I really think we've gotten off on the wrong foot here," Mr. Hays said, nervously fidgeting with his clothes. "This is all just one large misunderstanding."

"Is that what you think it is?" I asked, peering at him over my reading glasses as I pulled up the video file I was looking for. "I suppose we'll see if I'm overreacting or not in just a moment."

With a few clicks and the hit of an enter button, I witnessed firsthand this shitbag assaulting my secretary outside my office. Sam escorted Hays to the seating area, and I watched him ask the man if he wanted anything to drink, which he turned down. Hays ignored the instruction to sit on the couch and went for my office door. Sam cut the man off, trying to explain quickly and calmly that he couldn't go in there. This would be the moment Hays lost his proverbial shit and slammed my secretary into the door.

No wonder Sam was hurting. That wasn't just a simple shove—the bastard used his whole body weight against a man who was half his size. Having seen enough to know this asshole had lied about everything, I stopped the video and turned off the projector. If I looked at it any longer, I was going to strangle the man.

"I think it's safe to say this will be the last time you will ever be setting foot in my office or this building, Mr. Hays." Flicking my gaze to the security, I waved my fingers carelessly at the man sitting before me. "Please ensure Mr. Hays finds his way to the exit without attacking anyone else."

Hays shot out of the chair as the guard approached. "You can't do this."

"Why the fuck not?" I demanded. "This is my company, my building, and you *assaulted* my secretary. If I'm not able to do anything about that, then what's the fucking point of being the boss of this place?"

Of course, the man was all bluster, and when I called him on his shit, he didn't have anything more to say. The guard grabbed his arm and escorted him out of my sight. Glancing at my watch, I realized it was only eight fifteen, and this was how my day was starting. Scrubbing my hands over my face, I got up and went to the office door, yanking it open almost crashing into Quintin.

"What in the holy hell are you doing just standing there in front of my door, Quin?" I snapped.

Quintin raised a perfectly sculpted brow at me as he adjusted his glasses. "I believe it's customary to knock before entering into someone else's space, is it not? To do this action, one must come to a halt, plant their feet, lift their—"

"Oh, for fuck's sake, Quin, I know how knocking works," I grumbled, cutting him off before he rattled off the seventeen muscles used in the motion of knocking. "I assume you needed something?"

"Two things," he corrected.

I rolled my eyes. "How would I have known that, Quin? You know what, never mind. How can I be of help to you?"

"Are you all right? I was alerted there was a situation up here, and Fernando is on a rampage," Quintin explained.

Seeing the worry in his dark green eyes behind his tortoiseshell glasses made my irritation slip away. I grasped his arm and squeezed it. "I'm perfectly fine. Sam is the one who got the short end of the stick in that encounter. Although I have a feeling when I tell you I just had the man removed from the building and banned, you're going to be the one to watch out for."

Quintin let out a heavy sigh and cocked his head. "You already told me you weren't taking the contract, and I agreed. Also, why would you think I'd be upset with you tossing out a man who attacked one of your employees? There was no other option, and our people need to know they are safe here. Just think of the PR nightmare if the security company doesn't provide any *security* to their staff."

That was Quintin in a nutshell. He saw the world as checks and balances that needed to be maintained at all costs. It was one of the reasons he was the best person to run the finances in this company—nothing slipped past him. However, the downfall to that was he lacked empathy. He tended to see people as assets rather than living, breathing humans, which made for some challenging moments with the employees.

They couldn't see past the crisp, starched suit, perfect hair, rigid posture, and resting unimpressed face he always had going on. He was a tough boss to be sure and expected excellence in all things at all times. What they didn't realize is he imposed that rule on himself as well. If they removed the glasses and the suit he wore like armor, they'd see the man *I* knew, who's stood by my side for almost twenty years, a man who feared failure and carried scars on his body as a result of past failures. Trauma created when you're young is the hardest to overcome, and his mother literally beat into him the consequences of failing.

"You're absolutely right," I agreed with a soft smile. "I shouldn't have assumed you'd be upset at me for the fact that I'm going to call that man's boss and get him fired. Our employees take priority, and they should know and trust that no matter who the asshole is, we don't fear doing the right thing."

"I'm sorry, did you just say you're going to get that man fired?" Quintin asked, backtracking and growling. "You can't mean that you're going to call the Secretary of Defense about this, are you? He's already pissed at us, so why are you trying to make it worse? This is exactly what I'm talking about, H. You can't keep doing things like this if you want our company to expand."

"Quin," I cut in, taking him by the shoulders. "Breathe in through the nose, out through the mouth, and count to five."

You'd think after all the time we'd spent together, he wouldn't be surprised when I pulled shit like this. The trouble was, even though he was a ball buster in our business, he panicked when it came to outside authority, especially higher-up authority like the Secretary of Defense.

I wanted to kick myself for having told him in such a casual manner when I knew I needed to take the time to explain myself better. If he understood the why behind the choice—the repercussions we may or may not encounter and allowed him the chance to ask questions—we wouldn't end up where we are now on the verge of a panic attack.

"Do you want to sit down and talk this through?" I asked, pained that in my effort to protect Sam, I ended up doing this to Quintin.

Closing his eyes, he breathed like I instructed, holding onto my forearms and grounding himself. You'd think with all my life experience, I'd be better at shit like this, but thankfully, I knew how to own my shit and fix it if I fucked up.

"I'll be fine... there was just a lot all at once. Fernando said he didn't know much, and then I saw Mr. Hays being escorted away, so I was thinking the worst. Now that I've seen with my own eyes you both are fine, I'll be able to pull myself together," Quintin shared as he dropped his hands and gave me a soft smile. "There is too much to be done today. I can't afford to let my personal issues interfere."

"You know I don't give a shit how busy we are. If you need to take the day off, then do it. None of this is worth it at the cost of your health," I argued. This wasn't the first time we'd had this particular conversation, and it wouldn't be the last. I was sure of it.

"Excuse me," a woman's voice called to us. "I'm so sorry to interrupt, but Mr. Price instructed me to bring Ms. Collins up once we got her security badge."

Peering past Quintin, I spotted Sarah from our Human Resources looking a little nervous, wringing her hands. That was my fault—the last time she brought up an assistant who had been hired for me, I didn't handle it well. I glanced at Quintin to make sure he was okay, but he'd already wiped away any sign of emotion and was adjusting his clothes—a habit and coping mechanism he had developed to give him time to collect himself.

Taking the lead, I stepped around Quintin, giving him the time he needed, and attempted a reassuring smile at Sarah. "Thank you for doing that, Sarah."

Her cheeks flushed at my attention, dropping her eyes. "It's not a problem at all, Mr. Norlund."

When I looked around, I didn't see anyone other than the people who already worked for me. Just as I was about to ask Sarah, the most ethereal beauty stepped out of the small office next to mine. Her hair gleamed in the office lighting that did no one any favors, and her skin had a healthy glow complimented by the olive green skirt suit she wore.

Normally, I wasn't one to notice fashion, but as a man who loved vintage, this was a surprising sight. It was a high-waisted skirt that fit snugly against her curves, coming to midcalf. There was a simple black shirt under the cropped long-sleeved jacket that was equally conservative yet revealed the fact she had curves in all the right places. Finally returning my gaze to her face, I met her intelligent hazel eyes studying me almost as closely as I was her.

"I'm sorry, they said it was going to be a moment, so I thought I'd look at the space I'd be using," she apologized as she tucked her hair behind her ear.

Goddamn, this woman is going to be trouble. I can feel it. The question is will it be the good kind of trouble or the bad? Only one way to find out.

I walked up to her and held out my hand. "Nice to meet you. I'm Halstead Norlund, the man you'll be assisting."

Six

Lainey

I was so fucked.

There standing before me was Halstead Norlund, the fucking Alpha I'd bumped into at the gala. Like an idiot, I stood there staring at him as his scent wafted around me like a hug. I didn't know if you could get drunk off the smell of whiskey, but I sure as shit felt like it. His smoky cigar and musky bergamot only added to his confident, commanding presence.

Shaking myself out of the scent-induced stupor, I took his hand, giving it a solid grip as we shook hands. "It's lovely to meet you, sir. I'm Elaine Collins, and I hope we can work well together."

When I awoke to an unfamiliar ringtone this morning, I answered it without thinking, still mostly asleep. A creepy electronically-altered voice informed me there was a packet at the door for me that I'd need for orientation. When I retrieved the manila packet from the doormat, I dumped it out on the kitchen counter. This was the moment I learned my fake identity and was provided all the legal documentation I'd need for the onboarding process.

Picking up the driver's license, I cursed as I saw the first name was Elaine. Since my mother never named me, someone else in the system did and landed on Elaine. I'd never been a fan of it, so I always went by Lainey. The fuckers made me use my original name before Trent officially changed it to Lainey when he adopted me. Thankfully, Elaine was connected to nothing other than an orphan girl who was handed to the state and then adopted at age ten. Still, I knew this syndicate was flaunting the fact they knew every detail about me. Now here I was, blackmailed into this job, shaking the hand of an Alpha I was scent matched to. *This was just perfect.*

"Allow me to also introduce you to one of my business partners, Quintin Price, our CFO," Halstead said, drawing me forward toward the man.

I'd seen his picture in the collection of important people, but I hadn't paid much attention to details since I assumed my job had to do with Halstead. I extended my hand to the handsome man who could be on the cover of *Alphas Quarterly* fashion magazine. His style was impeccable with classic designers that would never go out of fashion. As he grasped my hand, I closed my eyes as the most soothing aroma of earthy matcha, the spice of ginger, and the brightness of lemon blended to make the perfect mixture of scents.

Fuck me sideways. How can he be another scent match?

Realizing I still had my eyes closed, I looked at the man from under my lashes demurely with a soft smile. "I hear I have you to thank for this chance to work here. My thanks for taking a risk on me." Letting go of his hand, I allowed my fingers brush along his in an almost caress, hoping to draw his attention away from my odd reaction.

"Yes, well..." Quintin muttered, seeming flustered as he tugged at his cuffs before meeting my gaze again. "Let's hope you'll be able to do the job, and that will be thanks enough. Halstead isn't going to be an easy sell, but you have two weeks to make it work."

His tone was crisp, and his words were direct and to the point. I didn't see any animosity in his body language for me to assume what he said was meant to be rude. It was as if he was so tense and rigid that it came out in his words as well. *I wonder how many people working here think he's a prick?*

"Thanks for the warning. I'll keep it in mind," I assured him. "Who better to take advice from than the man who used to be in my position?"

The fact I knew that seemed to surprise him. "You certainly did your homework."

My lips twitched, trying to hold back a grin. "Isn't that what you're supposed to do when you start a new job? It's important to make sure your values align with the company, so what better way to do that than studying who you plan to apply for."

"So tell me, what did you learn in your study of my company?" Halstead inquired as he took a seat on the couch, looking up at me expectantly.

Quick on my toes, I flashed him a smile as I clasped my hands behind my back and rocked on my feet. "Oh, am I being tested already?"

Quintin let out a sigh and took a seat in one of the armchairs. "So it begins."

Halstead gave him a disapproving grunt before answering me, "If that's what you want to consider it to be, sure. I, however, view it as market research. It's important for me to know what perception the public has of my company. The power behind the people who choose to give their loyalty and hard-earned money to my business is a monster you must always watch."

I cocked my head going over everything I read last night and also what I heard people saying the half hour I'd been here. "The biggest thing I noticed is that your company has been able to hold steady or grow over the years, even during economic trouble. To me, that says you have consistent results and offer a product people genuinely need, regardless of how much money they have to spend. Your ratings from employees who have left the job all say good things and rate you well in all categories offered. I've also seen a few news articles on the fact you don't cave in to larger companies or government organizations if you don't believe in something, you won't do it. What I find even more interesting about that is how the public views those choices."

Taking a moment to pause and read the two men before me, I needed to ensure I was giving them what they were looking for, but what I wasn't expecting was the third person who walked up.

"And what are their views?" he asked, coming to stand behind the couch, arms crossed.

Tongue-tied for a moment, I took in the stunning man before me. Amber eyes watched me with an intelligence that set me on edge, almost as if he could see through my act. His skin was a rich umber, with flawless perfection that anyone would envy. A simple goatee graced his face, adding to his artistic flair. Neatly maintained dreadlocks that had a silvery-blue color weaving into them were an interesting contrast to the natural warmth of his overall appearance. Unlike the other two men who wore formal suits, this man chose a more business-casual approach. They were all designer articles that gave off a professional perception but slightly more approachable.

"Enigma gained more brand loyalty from them because they turned down the work, no matter how large the price tag would have been. Doing this caused a few companies to take another look at the idea or product and came to agree with your choice," I answered, not dropping my gaze from this newcomer.

With the flip of a switch, the man who had me almost sweating, fearing he already knew I was a fraud, was now blessing me with a smile I couldn't help but return. It changed everything about his features, showing a more youthful, playful side to him.

"You must be the new assistant Quin snuck in under the radar. I'm Kerian Lewis, head programmer here at Enigma," he said, introducing himself. "I have to say I only caught part of what you were sharing, but that is some damn good research on your part. Not many people would think to look at those types of things once they decide if the hourly wage is enough."

This man had me almost blushing with his compliment, which wasn't a thing I did without purpose. "Thank you," I murmured.

"Oh, now look what you've done," Halstead grumbled. "How you manage to take a strong self-assured woman like that and turn her into a simpering fool, I'll never know."

That had me snapping back to attention, anger flaring as I instantly locked gazes with the older man. "Excuse me? What did you just call me?" Halstead opened his mouth to speak, but I held up a hand. "No, wait. I'm pretty sure it was *simpering fool*. Forgive me, I had to wash the male ego off the phrase to tolerate saying it aloud. Please, I'd love to know how me thanking Mr. Lewis for the compliment is turning me into a fool? Where I come from, it's known as good manners."

Halstead cocked a brow at me, almost as if to ask if he could speak, and I dropped my gaze in acknowledgment, realizing with horror what I'd just done. *What the fuck was I thinking? In what world was it smart for me to speak to a mark like that? Goddammit, I haven't even started the job, and I'm fucking it up.*

"It would appear that I spoke too soon," Halstead admitted. "While I don't advise pulling that kind of stunt often, I did deserve it."

My jaw nearly hit the floor, hearing him admit that, making me audibly gasp as I met his gaze once more.

"Since you seem to be a straight shooter like me, I'll lay it out for you. I need an assistant who can *assist*," he stated, crossing one leg over the other and resting his hands in his lap. "To me, that means thinking on your own and anticipating what will be of value to a meeting I might not have thought of. If you see a problem with something, speak up, and we'll have a conversation about it. Obviously, I don't expect you to know the ins and outs of this business, but if you're as clever as I think you are, you'll catch on quickly. Your job is *not* to baby me, fetch coffee, or worry about managing my daily schedule. That is what I have Sam for... he is my secretary and support to balance real life with work. Now hearing my expectations, do you think this is a job you can or want to do?"

Not like I had a fucking choice in the matter. If I wanted to continue living my life without constantly looking over my shoulder, I would do whatever it took to keep this job. The fear of Trent or my other marks learning about me was a looming threat breathing down my neck, that's for damn sure.

"I can absolutely do this job," I answered, far more confidently than I actually felt. "As you said, I catch on quickly. Give me a day or two to get the lay of the land and see what you personally handle day to day, and you'll be wondering how you did this without me."

Halstead chuckled but clapped his hands together before standing. "Challenge accepted. If by the end of the two weeks that doesn't happen, then we call it quits, and I find a better place for you to work."

"I have no doubt it will be right by your side," I quipped.

Kerian let out a bark of laughter and slapped Halstead on the back. "Oh, I like her. Not many would have the courage to sass you, H. I'm off to work. There's a glitch in the program I'm working on for Cyclone. Now it makes sense why they begged me to help them on this... it's a bitch of a problem."

That made my ears perk up. "Cyclone, as in Cyclone Software company?" I questioned.

My question seemed to garner all their attention, making me realize I'd done something I shouldn't have.

"What do you know of Cyclone Software?" Quintin demanded, his tone frosty.

It was clear there was no love loss between the two businesses, and it made me wonder what the hell could have happened. "Nothing really. I knew the name since they are your company's biggest rival in certain markets. Of course, they're not a security firm, dealing more with the everyday user with their search engine, but everyone knows that."

Quintin stared at me for an uncomfortable moment with a look so piercing I felt bare to him. "Just so you're aware, since you haven't begun your onboarding yet, but Cyclone tried to steal from us. Kerian started with that company, mentored by Reuben Watts himself before he wised up to the shady dealings of Cyclone. According to our company guidelines, you are not to have any in-person interaction with *anyone* from that business. If it has been discovered you have, you will be fired and slapped with so many NDAs, court gag orders, and lawsuits it will make your head spin."

Holy fuck, talk about a Jekyll-and-Hyde situation here. One minute, the man is uncomfortable with our interactions, almost bashful, and now he's threatening me with the corporate hammer. I can picture Halstead being an angry grizzly bear as Sarah had painted it, but Quintin was like a viper you didn't see coming until it was too late. No wonder they made the man in charge of money—no one was going to steal from him.

"Understood. I apologize for touching on a matter that has such awful memories," I offered, unsure what the right response should be.

It was made real fucking clear to me that Halstead can never know I was at that gala or that I'd had a rather lengthy conversation with the owner of Cyclone. Getting in that much legal trouble would do about the same damn thing to me that the Syndicate was threatening me with. Lawsuits were public knowledge, not to mention they'd want to do a television interview, or paparazzi would be hiding in the bushes trying to take my picture.

"Elaine, it's fine," Kerian interjected. "You didn't know any better, and I'm the one who brought it up. Hearing me talk about working with them and being our biggest competition must seem rather odd. I would have questioned it too."

"Kerian, it's rude to call a person by their first name if you haven't been given permission," Quintin scolded. "Furthermore, there was no need to come to her rescue. I wasn't being mean nor was I going to get her in trouble. My intention was to simply inform her of the severity of such conversation."

"Plus, he's a little on edge from a situation this morning," Halstead added, looking back at Kerian. "I had to ban the DOD's new rep, who insisted we have a meeting about the project I'd already turned down. The bastard attacked Sam, so I had to call for backup, and Fernando is... well... being Fernando in this situation."

"Jesus, that's one way to start your morning," Kerian muttered. "Good thing I decided to take Tater-Tot on my ride this morning which made me late getting in."

"I wondered why he wasn't here with you today. Poor guy is probably a puddle of wrinkles on the floor right now," Halstead commented with a chuckle.

It took everything in me not to ask any questions. I desperately needed to try to understand these men and their dynamic. Without social media or a personal internet presence, it made things challenging. Two of the three men were scent matches for me, and at best guess, I would say they are best friends. Although that sounded weird to say about two grown-ass men over forty. However, it was the best I could come up with to explain their interactions thus far.

While I could tell they cared for each other more than employee and boss, I didn't think it was of an intimate nature. Kerian fit in the mix somewhere as well, but he was so different in personality and energy I couldn't quite fit that puzzle piece in the picture I was building. It was almost like I was missing a corner piece that made it all fit together correctly.

"Forgive us, Elaine, we have a terrible habit of getting lost in our conversation when the three of us are together," Kerian explained and got a disapproving grunt from Quintin, making the younger man of the group sigh. "Do you mind if I call you by your first name, or would you prefer to keep things more formal?"

"Not at all. Elaine is fine. I rather enjoy the fact you three are so close and comfortable with each other," I commented.

There was a slight pause before Quintin stood. "I asked Sarah to bring you up to make introductions, but today you'll be going through our company onboarding. It's going to be a lot of watching dry HR-mandated videos and answering questions. Once that is done, we have some legal forms for you to sign before I can give you access to Mr. Norlund's calendar. Sam can help you find whatever you need as far as materials. You'll have to understand that while on the trial basis, even with the non-disclosure agreements, there will be some proprietary to the company you won't be able to know."

"Sounds reasonable," I answered. "Where would you like me to do these courses?"

Quintin started to answer, but Halstead cut him off. "In your new office, of course. Even if you're not shadowing me today, I think getting a feel for how the office runs will be useful to you."

"Is that computer even set up to access the network right now?" Kerian asked as he headed over to the office.

"Don't you have a code to work on?" Quintin muttered as he followed after him.

I stood there for a moment then glanced at Halstead. "They aren't related in some way, are they?"

"Why on earth would you ask a question like that?" Halstead countered, grunting as he stood.

"I can't put my finger on why I think that, but the way they treat each other seems slightly more familial than coworkers," I shared.

"Aah, well, that's simple. The three of us are family to each other," Halstead stated. "Quintin and I have known each other for almost twenty years, and Kerian joined our company roughly seven years ago. None of us have family around, so I guess you could say we adopted each other. We all own equal shares in this company and have an equal say in how things go."

Leaning in as if he were going to whisper something to me, I couldn't help but inhale his scent deeply, almost missing what he said.

"If you want a tip on how to keep this job, know that their opinion matters a great deal to me," Halstead murmured.

Before I could say anything, Kerian popped his head out of the office. "Hey, I'm gonna need you to set up a password."

"O-of course," I stammered, feeling as if I'd been caught in an intimate moment with Halstead. "I'll be in my office if you need anything from me," I said, to which I got a grunt, and we both entered our offices.

Kerian held out the black leather rolling office chair for me, and I took a seat. The moment he leaned across the desk to type something into the computer, I was smacked in the face with crisp juniper berry that reminded me of my favorite gin, with the added woody depth of sandalwood and the grounding notes of sage rounding out his scent with the earthy aroma.

Three for three, I really shouldn't have been surprised. With how close these men were, why wouldn't the universe decide they should be a pack and share an Omega? As soon as I got back to the apartment, I was going to reach out to the Syndicate and tell them I needed my scent-altering meds and a suppressant. Whatever job this was, it better not take me more than a week—two at the max. I'd pushed this heat off for far longer than I should have to finish the last job. This week was supposed to be spent holed up in a hotel with some random-ass Alpha helping me through my heat.

If the suppressant didn't work and my heat was triggered, there was no stopping it. Within minutes, I would be in full-blown mindless sex mode, willing to let whoever had a knot fuck my brains out. That was not something I ever wanted to experience again because all I was left with was regret at who I found in my bed and the fear I might be pregnant.

"Elaine..."

"Hmm?" I answered, opening my eyes that I'd closed at some point and found my face far too close to Kerian's neck.

Jerking myself back, I covered my mouth with a hand, horrified at what I'd done. "Oh God, I'm so sorry. I have no idea what came over me... that was so incredibly rude."

Kerian shifted so his hip was resting on the edge of the desk. "What is your designation?"

"B-beta," I answered, pausing a second to clear my throat. "This is going to sound ridiculous to you, but your scent reminds me of my favorite gin. However, that is no excuse for invading your personal space, especially just before taking these courses."

He smirked at me. "Actually, if you think about it, it's better you didn't do it after because then there's no way for you to claim you didn't know."

"Are you teasing me?" I demanded, scowling at him.

Kerian raised a hand to his chest, a scowl on his face. "I would never be offended to have a stunning woman think I smell good enough to lean in closer. That is a lofty compliment if you ask me."

Quintin, who I'd almost forgotten was in the room with us, cleared his throat loudly. That had Kerian and me sitting up straight like we'd been scolded. "If you're both quite finished."

"Yes, quite," I mumbled, brushing my fingers through my hair, settling myself. "I'm sorry... one of you asked me a question, and I quite clearly wasn't focused. If you'd kindly repeat the question?"

"We need you to enter a password, must have—" Quintin started to say, but I was already typing in my choice.

The meter that indicated how secure the password was, turned green, and an approving chime sounded. With the password set and accepted, the desktop was revealed, displaying various icons for programs I'd be using.

Kerian let out an impressed whistle. "Damn, first try. That's impressive."

"I, too, am a lover of good security, another reason why I chose this business," I shared. "Passwords are the first line of defense and shouldn't be overlooked. Now, what's next?"

Seven

Lainey

For a day filled with endless paperwork and mind-numbing forms to fill out and sign, I was exhausted when I left Enigma.

"We'll see you here tomorrow at seven-thirty," Sam told me. "Once you get the swing of things, you can decide when you want to arrive, just so long as it's before Mr. Norlund. I have too much to do before he steps foot in the building, and I feel like the extra half hour is vital."

"Seven-thirty it is," I agreed. "Do you drink coffee? I can pick some up tomorrow on my way in if you'd like?"

Sam gave me a wide smile. "That is so sweet of you. I appreciate it, but my partner is trying to get me to give up caffeine, saying it makes me too hyper. However, if you happen to stop by a place for yourself and they make a Golden Milk latte, I would be thrilled."

"Golden Milk?" I asked.

"Oh, it's turmeric, ginger, and cinnamon with a dash of black pepper," Sam explained. "It's an acquired taste, but I think it's all about what milk you use. Coconut has been my favorite so far."

"Huh… who would have guessed," I mused aloud. "Well, I'm new to my neighborhood, but if the coffee shop I try tomorrow has it, I'll be sure to bring one."

"Where did you land? Are you close to the city? I commute about forty-five minutes to get into the city, but it's worth it to get this experience," Sam gushed.

Sam was younger than me, probably around twenty-five or twenty-six. This was his first corporate job, and he took it incredibly seriously. I planned to make us best buds since he would be a valuable asset to get information from, and he had access to pretty much everything I couldn't while on probation. If it took finding or even making a fucking Golden Milk latte, then that was an easy sell.

"I was fortunate enough to find a little place up in Bayside East, thanks to a connection I had," I shared, tucking my purse under my arm. "Is there anything else I should know or prepare for tomorrow?" I asked, feeling the need to steer him away from this topic.

Clicking on the calendar, he glanced over the notes for the day before answering, "He has an important meeting with New Wave Financial and, later in the day, a meeting with Solarbyte. It might be smart to at least glance over what they do and the services they offer. Mr. Norlund won't be expecting you to be perfect your first few days here, but I've learned it's always better to know what you're walking into. Sometimes the companies will do something or, through negligence, have allowed something to happen that endangered the public's safety in one way or another. I know when this happens because I can hear him through the doors and even down the hall in the conference room."

"I see, and who is normally the one to deal with the clients after he's offended them?" I inquired.

"Mr. Price, and he's getting tired of it," Sam answered.

Nodding, I tapped a finger against my chin as I processed that information. "Thanks, Sam, you're a lifesaver, and I'm glad you're okay after what happened this morning."

During the midst of training, I heard the doctor come by to look over Sam. On my lunch break, the whole building was talking about it, so I got the full picture of what went down this morning. If Halstead only knew how big of a hero he was to his staff after kicking that man's ass out of the building. They'd already respected him for how he ran the company in general, but now he'd proven his people meant more to him than a defense contract.

"Just goes to show you how serious it is not to enter his office without him giving you permission," Sam pointed out, giving me a look like I should take note.

"Let's hope people will hear about this and decide for themselves it's a bad idea," I added, then gave him a small wave. "I'm off... have a good night."

"Night," he called after me.

Stepping onto the elevator, I hit the lobby button and sagged against the back wall as I watched the numbers tick by. Knowing this was the private elevator that accessed the top floor, I was surprised when I got to the tenth floor, and it stopped and opened. Kerian, head down studying something on the tablet in his hand, absently hit the button for the top floor.

"Um... Mr. Lewis, this elevator is going down," I said softly.

His head snapped up as if utterly surprised to find me in the small space with him. Little did he know the torture it was for me to be trapped in here with his goddamn scent drawing me to him.

"Oh shit," he blurted as if the words I'd said just registered in his brain. Clicking off his tablet, he hugged it to his chest like I was going to take it from him as he smiled at me. "Well, looks like I'll just take the ride with you before heading up. How was training?"

"I never knew corporate regulations could be so thrilling," I shared, my voice as deadpan as my face. "Then there's the moment I realized I might be signing away my firstborn, any inheritance I might have, and my left kidney should it be needed."

This had Kerian doubling over in laughter. "Oh God, if that isn't the truth. I'm a man who looks at lines of code all day, every day, and I couldn't make heads or tails of what they had me sign. When I got my share of the company, it was three pages... *three*." He held up his fingers to emphasize his point. "How can I own one-third of a company with less paperwork than being hired?"

My eyes grew wide. "You own one-third?"

His smile faltered. "Ah... yeah. Halstead and Quintin have the other two-thirds of the business. Look, I wasn't really supposed to disclose my share. It's not something H likes us to talk about."

"Sorry, that was a bit of a dramatic reaction. I just figured Mr. Norlund would prefer to keep the majority share. Then again, he doesn't seem to be like most corporate bigwigs I've interacted with before. It's a rare breed who can throw out someone from the DOD," I offered, trying to mitigate the awkwardness.

"Rare breed is the right term for H, that's for sure." Kerian chuckled.

The doors opened to the elevator lobby and the security guard who held the door open. "This is me," I said, stepping out.

"You planning on coming back tomorrow?" Kerian questioned.

I grinned at him and rolled my wrist. "I better. If I get carpal tunnel from all that paperwork, I'm gonna need the insurance to cover it."

"Something tells me you're gonna fit right in. See you in the morning," he said before hitting the button for the top floor once more.

The pleased smile at those words lingered on my face as I walked through the lobby to the front doors. Interestingly enough, today had been a first in a certain area. Instead of acting like someone else to fit the needs of the job, somehow being myself had done the trick. Almost nothing of what I did or how I acted was fake.

When I made it down to the street, I'd planned on flagging down a cab, but an all-black sedan pulled up at the curb. The passenger window rolled down, and the driver wearing sunglasses and a mask, leaned over to peer up at me. "Get in."

"I'm gonna go with no," I replied instantly.

He grabbed his phone and flashed a picture of Trent at me. "Get. In."

Well, fuck, the Syndicate. Just what I needed.

Pulling open the back door, I slipped in as if he were a taxi. Wasting no time, the man pulled away from the curb and was off to who the hell knows where. The man didn't say anything further, and I didn't ask any questions. The Syndicate had proven enough to me that I didn't want to know any more. Tell me what my job was and let me get to it. This whole dropping tidbits of information was getting old real fast.

Ten minutes later in true evil-mastermind fashion, we pulled up to a warehouse on the docks. The building looked like it shouldn't still be standing with how dilapidated it looked. When the driver still didn't say anything and just hit the button to unlock the doors, I got out. My purse buzzed from the phone, and I pulled out.

Enter the warehouse, go up the stairs then hit enter on the laptop in the office.

"Super," I grumbled, shoving the phone back in my purse. "Like I haven't watched enough horror movies to know this is how I die. Guess what, girl? You're not the main character in the story of your life. Nope, you get to be the leading lady's best friend or rival. It'll be fun, go on, enter the creepy building that must be the entrance to hell."

Turning the knob, I pulled, but the door didn't budge. Trying again, I put some weight into the pull, and it popped open, sending me stumbling back a few steps. I brushed my hand off on my skirt, checking to see if my oh-so-pleasant driver had witnessed my floundering. Thankfully, the asshole was looking at something on his phone. Shoulders back, head held high, I entered the warehouse, assuming there was surveillance set up and I wasn't going to look any more like an idiot than I already had.

My heels echoed in the empty space as the sunlight filtered in through various holes and cracks in the building. It gave me enough light to notice the metal staircase to walk up, which I grimaced at seeing it was the type with all the holes in it that my heels could easily slip through. Gripping the railing, I tried to walk on the balls of my feet so my foot didn't get stuck. Once at the top, I realized the decking was also made from this same material.

"Did they really think I was going to be wearing sneakers to work today?" I muttered as I carefully made my way to the office.

Hearing the metal groan, I sped up the pace, practically leaping into the office. Inside there was a folding table and chair with a laptop open on the table. These items had clearly been placed here recently since they were the only things not covered in an inch of dust. Gingerly, I sat, not trusting that the floor under my feet was going to hold, but I was sure the Syndicate didn't want me dead just yet. Looking at the phone once more to ensure I remembered the instructions, I hit the enter key.

The screen went fuzzy as if it were a vintage television set before a person sat at a table, folded their hands, and leaned forward. The way it had been filmed, I couldn't tell who the person was other than their shape made me believe it was a man. When they started speaking, it came out as the same robotic-altered voice I'd heard this morning.

"Now that you've proven yourself capable of infiltrating Enigma Technologies, you will be provided with the mission details," they announced, as if they weren't really sure if I would be able to pull it off. *"Your target is Kerian Lewis, more specifically, the code he's working on for Cyclone Software. Reuben Watts is aware of the UOS and is trying to create a code that will scour the dark web for information about us. This cannot be allowed to happen."*

I don't know about that. It doesn't seem like it would be all bad to have a kidnapping, blackmailing, and criminal organization removed from the world.

"The UOS has been working behind the scenes to prevent and alter events that would affect Omegas negatively. Our world would not be as fair as it is today without the UOS intervening. It would be catastrophic if this code is completed, and we are forced to cease all activities to keep the world a safe place for Omegas to exist. We feel that as an Omega yourself, whether you choose to ignore what you are or not, would be the right person to get this job done."

"That's rather presumptive of them," I mumbled. "Truthfully, I feel like living as a Beta is far easier, and if I could remove the need for having heats, I would. Not like I want any kids as it is."

"Cyclone has hired Mr. Lewis to fix a problem with the code telling him it's for advanced data protection from dark web hackers. It is imperative that Mr. Lewis remains unaware of the true nature of the code's purpose. Your job is in two parts... one, to destroy the code as it currently is and replace it with the code we give you. Secondly, to remove all traces of the original code on all devices Mr. Lewis could have worked on it and ensure that Mr. Lewis will never be able to recreate the code again.

"This last part is up to your discretion on how you wish to make that happen. As I've stressed already, this code must never exist. If the loss of life is the only way to guarantee this outcome, the UOS will protect you

from any and all backlash. Should you need any materials or money for bribery or goods, use the number provided for you. An additional number has been added to your phone for the driver who brought you here today. He will take you wherever you need to go outside of work. Do not use taxis or public transportation when completing work for the UOS."

Hell yeah, for free car service in the city. Not having to wait around for a taxi or using the grimmy underground train wouldn't be a hardship for me. That's one rule I'm happy to follow.

"Remember, Ms. Lainey Caddel, the UOS is always watching. My advice... complete your mission, further the goal of supporting Omegas, and you will reap the benefits. The UOS is not an organization you want to double-cross." With those ominous parting words, the laptop screen fuzzed out again and went dark.

Sitting back in the chair, I stared at the computer for a moment, trying to figure out what the hell I'd been forced into. Not only did they want me to destroy every single trace of the code but potentially the man who helped to write it, just so they didn't get discovered. What that said to me is I needed to do a hell of a lot more investigating into Cyclone Software if they had the Syndicate that ruffled.

Done being in the creepy death warehouse that could collapse at any moment, I headed back out into the waning sunlight. The sky was turning a brilliant color of sherbert pink with swirls of orange. It reminded me why I loved living in Corzina with the mild weather and clear skies. Too bad the place held so many haunting memories—I'm not sure I could truly ever enjoy life here. Giving the sky one last glance, I got back into the car, finding another manila envelope on the seat next to me.

I opened it and peeked inside but found it was full of more paperwork. Not feeling the urge to sort through it all now, I placed it on my lap and let my head fall back against the headrest. "So if you're going to be my driver, I feel like I should have something to call you by," I commented once we were back on the road.

There was no immediate response, so I thought I was being ignored.

"Gilles."

"Seriously, Gilles?" I said with a snort. "Why don't you just wave a red flag telling the world it's a fake name."

"Then you pick. It doesn't matter what the fuck you call me. I'm just doing what needs to be done to keep my family safe," the man snapped.

That got my attention. "Wait, you don't work for them voluntarily?"

"Fuck no," he spat. "I don't think anyone works for them willingly. They just blackmail people all willy-nilly so no one can trace anything back to anyone of importance."

"I suppose that makes sense," I agreed. "Well, seeing as we're in the same boat, do you think you could stop being such a prick?"

"No," he stated.

"Great, at least we're on the same page then, Wadsworth," I quipped.

"Wadsworth? How is that any better than Gilles?" he muttered.

Grinning, I shrugged. "It's not, but this name will make me smile every time I say it, so that's a win-win for me."

His response was an irritated grunt and for him to turn on soft classical music, indicating he was done talking. That was fine with me. I was exhausted, and all I wanted was a bowl of pasta and to watch some trashy reality television show while I ate. There was still a lot of work for me to do, but I needed an hour of mindlessness before diving back into the job. Maybe somewhere in this envelope, it would tell me what my deadline was to pull this off. I was running short on time, and the faster I could be done with this whole fucking mess would be great.

That reminded me to send them a message, asking for a suppressant booster and more scent-altering drugs. I was impressed to see it showed as normal when I typed it, but when I sent it, the words changed into a string of weird symbols. Okay, this syndicate knew their shit, that's for damn sure. My question was, how would I be able to read it when they responded? I didn't have to wait long. Two minutes after I sent my request, an answer popped up. When I clicked on it, a decoding app appeared and translated it for me in seconds.

> *REQUEST ACKNOWLEDGED AND ACCEPTED. SUPPLIES WILL BE GIVEN TO YOUR DRIVER, WHO WILL DELIVER THEM TO YOU TOMORROW.*

I couldn't tell if it was creepy that I didn't need to tell them what drug I used, the dosage, or that it was so readily available to them that they could get it to me that fast. When I ordered it from my supplier, they had at least a week, sometimes two weeks' lag time for the scent-altering shot I used. The suppressant was more common since many Omegas used it for various reasons, but still, the following morning was impressive.

Wadsworth dropped me off at the steps of my building, and he was off before I even managed to close the door. "He's going to be delightful to spend time with."

Finally back in my temporary apartment, I headed right for the closet, kicked off my shoes, stripped out of my clothes, and pulled on sweats. My final act of being done with my so-called work day, I threw my hair up in a messy bun as I headed to the kitchen. As I further investigated the kitchen, I found all the fixings to make homemade alfredo sauce. Doing a little happy dance, I turned on the television and landed on a show about a group of rich Omegas and the dumpster fire they made out of their lives—the perfect background noise as I cooked so the unfamiliar space didn't feel quite so empty.

Cooking was one of those things that no matter what mood I was in when I started, I was smiling and relaxed by the end. Then again, who wouldn't be smiling with a giant bowl of fresh fettuccine alfredo and a thick toasted chunk of garlic bread? Just as I was about to settle in on the couch, a knock came at the door. Frowning, I set the bowl on the counter and grabbed my phone. I'd noticed there was a front door camera attached this morning and an app already installed on the phone.

There, standing in front of my door with his suit jacket missing, sleeves rolled up, and hands in his pockets, was Halstead.

Eight

Lainey

The gasp that came out of my mouth upon seeing him standing there could probably be heard through the door, it was so loud. Looking around the room, I spotted the two manila envelopes with everything the Syndicate gave me sitting on the side table next to the couch. I darted forward, grabbed them, and ran to my bedroom, lifting the mattress and shoving them under it. Not the most secure place in the world, but it had to do for now.

What the hell could he possibly be doing here? Should I answer or just let him think I'm not home? Wait, fuck, the television. He's probably hearing it through the door. Shit, shit, shit.

Looking down at myself, I groaned, knowing I looked like a frat boy, but he's the one who showed up out of nowhere. Letting out a frustrated sigh, I headed to the front door and peeked out the security peephole.

Yup, still there.

Shaking myself out of this funk, I took a slow, deep breath and opened the door. "Mr. Norlund? What are you doing here?" I asked, pleased that I sounded more surprised than irritated.

"I'm sorry to drop by unannounced like this, especially on your first day, but could I have a minute of your time?" he asked.

Stepping to the side, I pulled the door wider to allow him through. "I just made dinner. There's more than enough if you'd like some?" I offered, shutting the door and grabbing the remote to turn off the television.

"No. Thank you for the offer, though. I don't want to take up your personal time... that's going to become a rare occurrence as it is," Halstead commented as he looked around the room.

"Oh?" I questioned, hopping up on one of the barstools.

When his gaze met mine, it was as if he was *seeing* me for the first time. His eyes trailed over me as if he couldn't get enough of the sight of me in casual clothes. Then he must have realized it and snapped his eyes back to mine with a slight head shake.

"Yes," he blurted, then cleared his throat, scrubbing a hand over his neatly trimmed beard. "Sorry, I don't usually do something like this, but I thought it was best to have this conversation off-site."

With those words, the man had my full attention, causing me to sit up straighter.

"I took the liberty of reaching out to your previous employer and the man who referred you to Quintin. What I needed to know was something a resume couldn't tell me but would be vitally important to working for me," Halstead explained.

"Color me intrigued," I commented. "So does you standing in my living room mean I passed the test and got your approval?"

"Let's not get ahead of ourselves," he warned, lifting a hand as if to slow me down. "For now, I'll tell you what you need to know, and if things go well, I'll expand on that knowledge."

"I can work with that," I agreed, resting my arm on the counter to lean on. "Do you mind if I ask what you were looking for and their answers?"

Halstead started to pace the width of the living room, making it clear to me he wasn't a man who liked to sit still for long. "You already know that Cyclone had hired Kerian as a contractor to help with a project. The thing of it is, I don't trust Reuben, the owner of Cyclone. He's up to something. Well, he's always up to something, but this time he's involved one of my people in his scheme. As for what I asked those two..."

Pausing, he faced me and stepped forward so we were only a foot apart. Until that moment, I'd been doing good controlling myself around his scent, keeping him at a distance. Now with him so close, it took all my willpower not to lean in and meet his advance with my own.

"I needed to know your skills at discretion as well as observation, gathering intel, and rooting out the truth of the matter. Anyone can see you're bright and quick on your feet, but I needed to know just how far that goes," he informed me.

A smile bloomed on my lips at the prospect of what he wanted me to do. "My guess is they told you I was all of those things and more." Giving into the urge, I sat up, putting Halstead a mere few inches away, and I could taste his scent on my tongue. "Tell me, Mr. Norlund, are you perhaps looking to get some information on a rival company? One which is as locked down in the security department as you are?"

"Not on the company, but Reuben and what the fuck this code really is. You see, I'm a coder myself. In fact, that's how Reuben and I met the first time. We attended the same college, and he was a snake even then," Halstead said with a growl. "I've looked over what Kerian is working on, and it's only a piece of the puzzle. Yet no matter how I look at it, what they've been telling us it's being used for doesn't make sense."

"There it is, the true purpose of this visit," I whispered. "You want me to find answers so you can make sure Kerian isn't standing in quicksand?"

"Yes, that's exactly what I want to know," Halstead murmured, his head dipping closer as his fingers brushed a rogue strand of hair off my forehead. "I will do anything to keep those who are important to me safe, no matter what needs to be done to make it happen. It would be in your best interest to keep that in mind because it's the only warning you're going to get."

"Noted," I said, my voice breathy as *need* grew like a hot coal in the pit of my stomach.

My nose brushed alongside his, and I almost let out a needy whine at the contact, which would have betrayed me as an Omega instantly. Where Alphas purr to soothe and reassure their Omegas, we could demand attention with a single sound. Such is the dynamic of our world thriving on the codependency of designations. Yet I couldn't deny how incredible it felt to touch him. This was one of the dangers of a scent match. It slowly consumed an Omega until they were all we wanted in life, unable to be without them and taking away our independence like every other drug in existence.

"Why?" Halstead asked as he tugged at my bun, pulling the hair tie free so my hair tumbled around my shoulders. "Why do I need to taste you so desperately? It's all I can fucking think about."

"No one's stopping you," I goaded. "Taste me."

His hand slid into my hair and fisted it at the base of my skull, pulling so my head tipped back before he slammed his lips to mine. There was no stopping the moan that erupted from me as his tongue brushed against my lower lip, asking me to open for him, which I did instantly. He tasted just like he smelled—that rich whiskey taste with an edge of smokiness and the tang of bergamot. I tried to keep myself restrained, but he had other thoughts as he released my hair only to grab my hips. Kicking the stool out of the way, he set me on the counter, wedging his muscular body between my legs as he deepened the kiss.

It had been ages since I'd experienced something as mind-blowing as this kiss. My brain seemed to be short-circuiting as I fisted his shirt in my hand, wrapping my legs around his waist, trying to keep him close. Then as quickly as it started, he was ripping himself away from me, backing up until he bumped into the couch. His blue eyes were wild, but it wasn't with the same emotion I felt if the look of horror on his face was an indicator.

"I'm sorry," he said, his chest heaving. "That... that never should have happened. Forgive me, Ms. Collins... that was unacceptable for many reasons."

Confused, I slid off the counter and approached him, but his hand shot out.

"No," he barked, and I flinched.

All Alphas could create a certain edge to their words that Betas and Omegas submitted to. It was much harsher to an Omega, almost like a slap to the face and was only ever used when truly needed. Thankfully, his internal battle kept him from noticing my response as he charged to the door.

"Halstead, wait," I called, not wanting to risk him leaving so upset and telling me not to show up to work tomorrow.

Spinning on his heel, the gentle man I'd just been talking to was gone, and the dominant Alpha was in its place. "Don't. This was a mistake, a truly horrible mistake I never should have let happen. Things between you and me will be the picture of professionalism while you still have a job at Enigma. You will refer to me as Mr.

Norlund or sir, and I will only ever call you Ms. Collins. Are we understood?"

"Yes, sir," I answered. It was the only thing I could say at this point.

"You will not speak of this *ever*," Halstead demanded. "I am not unattached as many would believe. For their protection, we keep things private, and now I'll need to discuss this with them. The last thing I need is rumors flying around the office until I've addressed matters."

My hands covered my mouth as I backed away from him. One thing that was off-limits for me was fooling around with men who had any type of significant other. The only time that changed was when it happened as part of a job that was business and not personal. However, Lainey Caddel would never be the other woman to someone. I deserved so much better than that.

"Get out," I rasped, turning my back on him, trying to keep my anger in check.

"I'm sorry. I shouldn't have lashed out at you like that. You didn't know there was anyone, making it doubly my fault because I did. If this changes our ability to work together and you don't show up to work tomorrow, I'll understand. Should that be your choice, I'll do everything in my power to get you another job. However, if there's a chance you might be willing to let me prove I'm not this kind of despicable boss or man, I would be eternally grateful. Either choice you make, I will respect your decision."

When I didn't answer or turn around, the sound of the door opening and closing told me he left. My hands started to shake, and it had nothing to do with my anger or the way my heart ached hearing he had someone already. Sweat broke out over my whole body as I crumpled to the floor, my legs unable to hold me up.

"No," I whispered. "This can't be happening. I refuse to let myself go into heat."

Hot tears burned down my cheeks as I crawled my way to the bathroom like a pathetic fool. Turning the knobs of the tub on, I got the temperature I wanted and slumped against the cool porcelain surface.

Tomorrow. I just had to make it until tomorrow. Wadsworth would have the drugs, and I would be in the clear.

Stripping out of my sweats, I left on my underwear as I rolled myself into the freezing tub of water. The shock to my system was just what I needed to clear my head and look at this problem with a somewhat clear mind. My skin was so hot I was honestly surprised the water didn't steam and bubble off it. Taking the time to wash my face, I sat in the tub until my teeth started to chatter and my skin felt normal, if a little chilled. Feeling more in control, I got out and drained the tub, knowing I needed to have a little chat with myself.

Standing at the sink, I stared deep into my eyes. As I did, I mentally went through every reason why I'd chosen to live my life as a Beta. At the top of the list was the simple fact that I could do anything with my life. There was nothing holding me back from entering any establishment I wanted to, going completely unnoticed. No Alphas were stalking me, trying to check if I had any bond marks on my body to see if I was available or not. I was allowed to purchase things like a car or home without being asked if I had my Alpha's approval. People didn't hound me about when I was going to have kids or why I didn't already.

Life as a Beta was simpler. End of story.

There was nothing about being an Omega that I couldn't have as a Beta, but the same couldn't be said for the opposite. Besides, the only person you can ever rely on is yourself. Did I let my emotions and biology get the better of me tonight? Yes. Was I going to allow that to stop me from finishing this job and getting the Syndicate off my back? Absolutely the fuck not.

"Listen up," I told myself sternly. "You're going to dry off, eat your fucking pasta, watch a damn show, and look at the information you were given today. These men are your targets... nothing more, you hear me? They are not scent matches. Betas don't have those, so you better get it the fuck together and do the goddamn job."

With one more searching look, I shoved away from the mirror that was revealing far too much and got dressed. I purposely left the soaking-wet underwear on to keep my damn pussy on ice, as it had done quite enough already. The bitch was in time-out.

Two months.

The code was to be completed and delivered to Cyclone Software in two months. I'd done long cons before, but not when it was around three Alphas who happened to also be scent matches so close to a heat. There was no way I'd be able to get around this unless I took some time off from work, but they'd need to know why. Everyone knows you don't pull shit like that when you've just started a job. It makes you look bad, and I don't have any of the resources that I line up for dealing with my *needs* during a heat.

I was so distracted by this information I didn't notice Wadsworth handing something to me until he let out a shrill whistle.

"What the fuck," I snapped, glaring at his stupid mask and sunglass-covered face.

"Take the fucking thing. They said it was important," he grumbled and gave the rectangular case a toss, forcing me to lean forward to catch it.

I unzipped the protective case and found the normal single injection for altering my scent, but instead of something similar for the suppressant, I found a vial and four needles. A note was tucked under it all so I slipped it out.

Use 10cc of the medication, injecting it in the area between your pubic bone and belly button. If any issues should arise, please reach out to the medical staff we have programmed into your phone.

"You have to be shitting me," I muttered as I picked up the glass vial with no label or marking on it whatsoever. "They really expect me to just inject myself with this stuff, no questions asked? Yeah, well, I choose life. Thank you very much."

Putting the vial back, I removed the injection pen and tugged down the left side of my slacks so I could inject it into my hip. It was the easiest one to know if it was working or if I managed to get the injection deep enough because that motherfucker burned. While this medication was also not on the up and up, I knew who made it and what was in it for me to research the ingredients. The lab also had people who'd been using it and shared with them any and all side effects they might have had. That was a far cry from an anonymous note with instructions on it.

Zipping the case back up, I dropped it into the leather tote I was using for a purse today. It was going to be a long day, and I planned to be prepared with snacks, an alternative pair of shoes, and a spare dress because I was wearing white. I would love to have a study done of the number of times someone spills on average, then compare it to the days you wear a crisp white shirt. My money was on the white-shirt day being worse than usual since you're far more worried about your actions that it backfires.

Wadsworth pulled up at Enigma, not uttering a single word since tossing me the medication. When I went to open the door, it remained locked, and there was no button for me to press to unlock it. "Is there a reason you're not letting me out?"

"You have to take the other medication," he answered. "I was told you couldn't leave this vehicle unless you took both."

I was so shocked I merely stared at him with a look of incredulity. "What are you supposed to do if I don't?"

"You will not exit this car without having taken it," he repeated.

"Meaning you'll climb back here and do it yourself if I don't," I translated.

He just removed his sunglasses and looked at me with an expression that told me I would find zero sympathy from him. "Wow... what the fuck do they have on you that you would go so far to make sure their orders are followed?"

"Let's hope you never find out," he responded. "Now take the medication and use this moment as an indication you need to fear the UOS a little more than you do. They are not an organization to fuck with."

Left with an impossible situation where I was on the losing side of all options was not a fun place to be. Either I took the medication, and it did who the fuck knows what to me, or I refused, and Wadsworth did it for them. Let's say I managed to get away, make a run for it, then the whole world would know who I was, including Trent. No matter how I looked at it, I had no choice.

Grabbing the case out of my purse, I uncapped a syringe, lifted the vial, and poked through the rubber seal. Drawing out the proper dose, I freed the needle and made sure there were no bubbles before injecting it right where they instructed. The needle was so thin I didn't feel the injection, but if I thought the burn from the scent drug was bad, this was worse. It was almost as if I'd just shot liquid fire under my skin. Leaning my head back, I closed my eyes and waited for the pain to settle.

"Fuck, fuck, *fuck it all to hell*," I yelled, throwing the needle across the car so it smacked into the opposite window. "You happy now, fuckwad?"

The click of the doors unlocking was my only response which I was fine with. I'm not sure I would have held back from punching him in the face. However, I did chuck the rest of the medication at him just before slamming the door closed. "Bastard."

"Ah... Ms. Collins, are you all right?"

Spinning around, I found Quintin standing at the base of the steps.

Nine

Quintin

The morning hadn't started off the way I'd hoped, and it seemed I wasn't the only one suffering from this fate. I'd noticed the car stopped as if to drop someone off, but when I saw Ms. Collins burst out of it, slamming the door closed, I couldn't help but pause.

"Ms. Collins, are you all right?" I asked, surprising myself that I would interject myself into this situation.

That was more H's department, dealing with employee relations. My job within the company was to ensure we ran at peak performance, with the best people in place for optimization, while remaining within our budget. None of this required me to become overly invested in the personal lives of our employees. While that might make me callous and pragmatic, it's one of the reasons we've done so well over the years. A sob story might work on Halstead, lord love the man, but it would roll off me like water on a duck's back.

"Yes, totally fine," she answered, brushing her hair out of her face. "Just had the delightful experience of an ever-so-cheerful taxi driver."

I stared at her for a moment, the picture of elegance and daringness in an all-white pants suit. You could tell she was a woman who liked expensive clothes and had refined taste. Yet something about how she went about it didn't make it feel like she was flaunting or showing off. This woman was different enticingly so, and I couldn't seem to put my finger on what it was exactly. Nor could I discern if it was good or bad, but I was intrigued enough to take note.

"Yes, that is the downfall of taxis... you're at the mercy of whoever your driver might be. This is why I prefer to drive myself to work. There's no guessing in that," I answered as we started up the steps together.

"Oh, is there parking here?" she questioned. "After this morning, I might think about getting a car."

What had that driver done to upset her so? Furthermore, why do I even care?

"There is a parking garage under the building, but there is a fee to use it. Most of our employees rent a parking spot and pay for it monthly. This way, we can keep track of how many people are using it and if we have space to accommodate more. I believe in the last report I read there were a few open spaces left, but you'll want to check with HR to make sure," I explained.

"Thank you, Mr. Price, I'll look into it." She smiled as one of the security guards opened the door for us. "Next, I'll have to see if the cost of my peace of mind is worth having a car. The way Mr. Norlund and Sam talk, I don't think I'll have the time to be driving to many places other than here."

That would be true, especially if she found a way to get H to keep her on staff, then she'd be incredibly busy keeping up with his schedule. When I became CFO, I felt like I was given a massive pay raise for less work in comparison. Of course, I was far busier now that I was running things and Enigma had quadrupled in business from that time.

"If you need the name of a car service, I can provide you with a list of a few I know have been used before and are reliable," I offered.

For Christ's sake, what am I doing?

In a seamless move, Elaine turned to look at me and somehow managed to toss her hair out of the way as she slung her purse over her shoulder. "So it's not just Mr. Norlund who looks after his employees above and beyond the norm."

I didn't know how to respond to that because it wasn't true. Normally, I would have taken her at her word that she was fine and been on my way, but for some reason I can't seem to explain, I wanted to be around her.

"It is far more uncommon for me," I admitted, unwilling to let her believe something false about me. "Halstead is the one the employees like. As for myself, well, I'm sure you'll hear for yourself around the common areas. Unlike Halstead, I'm not driven by my emotions and prefer to rely on hard evidence. People perform up to my expectations and are rewarded for their effort, or they are replaced by someone who can achieve what I'm looking for."

"Pragmatic... I like it," she stated with a nod as she entered the private elevator.

Her answer caught me so off guard I paused for a moment before entering. Nothing about this woman was making any sense at all. Each time I expected the same response I got from everyone else in my life, she put a different twist on it.

"Yes, precisely," I mumbled as I entered and hit the button for the top floor.

We fell into a comfortable silence, and I surreptitiously leaned a little closer, taking a deep breath. Her paperwork declared her a Beta, not that it would have mattered what designation she was. However, if she didn't believe that and was really an Omega, it might explain my peculiar behavior toward her. When I got a good read on her scent, I scrunched my nose at the chemical smell coming off her.

Was it her makeup? Perfume? I'd never smelled a scent like that unless at a hospital. Wait, was she sick? A growl of irritation at myself slipped out, and just as the elevator doors opened, I rushed out to head for my office. I'm sure my abrupt exit after making such a sound caused her to think I was being quite rude. It wouldn't be the first time someone thought that, nor the last, so I stopped caring somewhere along the way.

Once in my office, I hung my coat in the hidden closet behind my desk and set my briefcase in its spot under the desk. Taking a moment, I took a deep breath counting to ten, forcing my hands to relax as I exhaled until there was no more air in my lungs. Repeating this, I felt more grounded, cooling off the chaotic emotions building up in my head.

Unnecessary feelings make you sloppy, Quintin. I hear my mother so clearly in my mind, almost as if she's speaking right into my ear.

I snapped my eyes open and marched over to my beverage bar. Flipping on the kettle, I got the water boiling as I collected the items I needed to make my favorite matcha tea. Over the years, I'd been in therapy to overcome the severe mental damage my mother had done to me growing up. I found this ritual to be soothing. One of my therapists had suggested I find some routine or coping mechanism to put my focus on instead of the intrusive memories of my mother's teaching.

Green tea not only had many health benefits, I found not having a high caffeine intake was helpful as well. My brain needed less stimulation, not more. The anxiety I lived with regularly was plenty to deal with, thank you very much. The kettle beeped, letting me know the water was ready just as I completed sifting the tea through a strainer. I poured a small amount of water into the mixing cup before grabbing the whisk.

In the beginning, I used to tell myself the steps of making the tea were teaching my brain that I was confident and competent to instruct this activity. Now I could do this with my eyes closed, knowing exactly how many rotations I needed to make before the blend was perfect enough to add the rest of the water. So my goal at this moment was to tell myself ten things I was good at or I was proud of myself for. This might not seem hard for most people, but five years ago, I was only able to come up with one thing. The fact I now have ten things to say is nothing short of a miracle, and that is the first of ten things I'm proud of.

"I, Quintin Price, am a skilled gardener, and I'm proud of the many plants I care for in the conservatory at home," I verbalized aloud. "Another thing I'm good at is managing the finances of Enigma Technologies, a company I'm proud to work for, and I've supported for almost twenty years. I'm proud to be business partners with Halstead and Kerian, and they see value in my guidance and knowledge."

"You forgot to add how much we love you," Halstead's deep voice said from behind me, the only warning I got before his arms wrapped around my waist. Instantly, I leaned into him as his lips brushed the back of my neck, chasing away the last of the shadows of my past.

"Quin, what's got you so unsettled?" H asked, resting his chin on my shoulder. "You seemed fine when you left the house this morning, or did I read that wrong? Is it because I asked for space last night?"

Setting down the whisk, I turned to face my partner and lover for the past fifteen years. "No, H, it's nothing to do with you or asking for a night to yourself, I promise. You and I have worked to find a healthy balance where you can ask me for things like that, and I'm secure in us. In fact, Kerian and I took that opportunity to get a drink at the jazz bar you hate."

"Then, my brilliant, capable Quin, why are you saying your affirmations ten minutes after showing up to work?" he pressed, resting his forehead against mine. "Do we need to have Alexis stop by and have a check-in with you?"

"We already have an appointment for next week, and I've got to grow stronger in managing these moments without her on speed dial," I pointed out.

"Who the fuck said you needed to grow stronger alone?" H challenged. "Quin, I love you so fucking much. I wish to God I could just reach into your head and pluck out every lie that cunt ever said to you. There is no weakness in having support when you need it. All you need to do is tell me what will help, and I'll make it happen."

I looked into his deep blue eyes, seeing the love, devotion, and desire to free me from this struggle. We both knew he couldn't and, through many group sessions, owned up to the truth that it's not his battle to fight for me. There were days when he struggled with that more than others, but he just didn't understand I wouldn't still be alive without him. He and Kerian have saved my life each day I wake up with them in our home, telling me they loved me.

"If I tell you what happened, I need you to promise something," I warned.

Halstead kissed me soundly. "Anything."

"You can't get upset and fire anyone because I don't know how to regulate emotions well," I ordered.

His brows furrowed as he clasped my face between his hands. "Someone *here* upset you?"

"No, quite the opposite, they accepted me," I explained the best I could, not feeling like that was the right way to put it. "When I got here, I ran into Elaine..." Halstead stiffened at her name, making me pause, and then it was my turn to frown. "Did something happen between you two? I thought things had gone well so far."

"We'll talk about that later, but right now, we're focusing on you," he countered. My frown deepened, but he just kissed the crease between my eyes and chuckled. "No, Quin, I'm not going to let you turn this around on me and my issues. You're going to be dealt with first. Now you were saying something about running into Ms. Collins."

It didn't escape my notice that he referred to her so formally, but once Halstead decided something, there was no changing his mind. If I wanted to know what happened, I had to talk first. Pushy bastard.

"We happened to arrive at the same time, and I noticed she was rather upset getting out of the car that dropped her off. I paused to make sure she was okay physically before asking if everything was all right. H, I was genuinely concerned about her and then chatted the whole way to the elevator. Hell, I offered to get her in touch with a few car services so she didn't have to deal with rude drivers ever again," I blurted as all the overwhelming feelings started to rush back in. "Why? Why would I care so much when I've known the woman for merely a few hours? I thought possibly she might be an Omega hiding her scent, but when I tried to get a sense of her, she smelled like chemicals or a hospital. Is she sick? Do we need to find out what's going on?"

"Okay, okay," Halstead soothed, pulling me into a hug and stroking my back. "We're going to process this one thing at a time. I can see why you needed your tea... that was an avalanche of things to field all at once. Let's start with the car situation since that's what upset you first. Tell me more about why that made you pause in the first place?"

Having him ask me to explain it made me realize I didn't know what triggered me to notice the car parked there in the first place or how I knew the second the woman got out it was Elaine.

"Her hair," I murmured. "I spotted a woman in that car brushing her hair out of her face, and it reminded me of Elaine. When she stepped out, I caught a glimpse of how upset she was about something, and it was as if I had no choice but to ensure she was going to be fine."

"I mean this with all the love in my heart, but clearly, you're not used to your Alpha instincts kicking in, are you?" he questioned.

A harsh laugh burst out of me. "Not in the slightest. How can an Alpha who doesn't know how to protect himself do that for someone else? I was never meant to be—"

"You finish that sentence, and I'll let Tater-Tot use your greenhouse as his personal bathroom. Because *that* was about to be a giant pile of shit coming out of your mouth," Halstead threatened.

I about swallowed my tongue with how fast I ate my words, imagining the horror of Kerian's English Bulldog running rampant in my sanctuary. Halstead had the nerve to chuckle at my reaction knowing full well that his threat would be more than enough to do the trick.

"Since we have that settled, I'm more curious about why you'd feel so strongly about her," he mused aloud as he ran his nose along mine before kissing me.

A sharp gasp had me jerking away from Halstead to see Elaine standing in the doorway to my office. The idiot had forgotten to close it when he came in. For being the one who pushes so hard for us to keep our personal life private, it was ironic he was the one who didn't take precautions. It had taken me some time to accept that his not wanting the world to know about the three of us being a pack didn't reflect how he felt about Kerian or myself. He viewed it as keeping us safe from those who would want to use that information against us. Personally, I thought he was being dramatic until a friend of ours had a pack member kidnapped and held for ransom. They owned a Fortune 500 company as well, proving to Halstead he'd made the right choice.

"I'm so sorry, the door was open…" she muttered, dropping her gaze and backing out.

Was it truly that shocking for her to see us together? Once again, her reaction wasn't at all what I expected. Relationships with the same gender were common and almost assumed if you were a pack. Some packs did develop with just friendship in place. However, ninety percent of the time there was at least one, if not more, couples in the group. Our pack was unusual for being so small with only the three of us, but with my issues, Halstead's overprotectiveness, and Kerian's indifference in adding anyone else, we didn't go the common route of adding an Omega into our family.

"Ms. Collins, did you need something?" Halstead asked gruffly, not letting me pull out of his hold.

She took a moment to clear her throat and met my gaze. "The way you left the elevator had me wondering if I'd done something to upset you and wanted to apologize. I realize I'm an extrovert and don't always notice if someone isn't interested in conversing or wishes to ride the elevator by themselves. In the future, I'll make sure to be more aware."

Not even waiting for my response, she turned and left, not acknowledging Halstead. Looking from the door where she'd been back to H, I scowled. "Now you're going to tell me what the hell is going on between you. She seems just as upset with you as you are with her."

Halstead sighed and released me, backing up a step to slide his hands in his pockets. "I stopped by her home last night."

"Excuse me?" I snapped. "Why in the world would you go to her place?"

He met my gaze with a grim set to his mouth. "I went there with the purpose of talking to her about looking into the project Reuben has Kerian working on. As for why I did that outside of work was because

I didn't want to upset you or risk that someone might overhear me asking her to do it. Reuben is a touchy subject with you, as you clearly displayed when she simply mentioned Cyclone, so I felt it was best to have the conversation off-site."

"You make it sound like I'm the only one who has issues with the man, but here you are going behind our back asking someone we barely know to look into the company. After what they did to Kerian, I don't know how he can even consider doing this for them," I fumed.

"They played on his love of coding, gave him a taste of the project to get him interested, and he couldn't say no," Halstead answered. "Reuben mentored him, put him through college expecting to have this perfectly trained programmer prodigy who flipped and turned on him the moment Kerian realized how shady they are. I *need* to know this code won't bring him down or harm him."

"I understand that, but why go to Elaine to do it?" I challenged. "How do you even know we can trust her?"

"Because I reached out to her previous employer and Mitch who told you about her in the first place. They used her to do the same thing for their companies, but she wanted out of corporate espionage so she moved here. Now I'm asking her to do the one thing she was trying to leave," Halstead explained. "Not only that, I... I kissed her."

Stunned at his confession, my jaw fell open. I didn't even know how to process what he was saying.

"Wh..." I couldn't even finish the question with how blindsided I was.

"There is no excuse for my actions, and I won't even begin to give you one other than to say I royally fucked up. There we were talking in her apartment, she'd just made dinner... fucking fettuccine alfredo, which made her home smell so comforting," he shared, hanging his head. "If I could explain to you what happened and how we ended up in that situation, I would. Her scent wasn't at all how you described being astringent. No, everything about her, from the messy bun and baggy sweats to the spicy sweet fragrance I caught a whiff of, drew me to her like nothing I'd experienced before. The second I realized what I'd done, I backed away and explained to her that I was in a relationship. That would be the moment she looked at me like I was scum, and that fucking hurt way more than it should have."

"Did you tell her who you were in a relationship with?" I questioned, folding my arms, trying to deal with the hurt and disappointment I felt in Halstead. Then my mind spiraled, wondering if she was being so kind to me because she knew my partner had kissed her making her feel bad for me.

"No, I told her that I was going to have a conversation with you and Kerian but didn't name names. My goal at that point was to make damn sure she wouldn't say anything to anyone before I got the chance to tell you the whole story," he answered.

"I see," I commented. "So when she walked in just now seeing us together, it wasn't the fact she couldn't bear to look at us because we were men, but because she realized who you were in a relationship with."

"Everything about this has been handled wrong. I own and accept that," Halstead said, finally looking me in the face again. "How do I fix this?"

"Are you looking to add to our relationship?" I inquired.

We'd never really talked about a situation like this. Kerian happened so naturally as we worked together just like things with Halstead and I had. It was normal and natural in our society to have polyamorous relationships which is why we lived in family units or packs as many referred to them. With our schedule and workload, I'd never considered that any of us would find someone they might develop feelings for. While my initial reaction was to be shocked and hurt, I knew that was coming from a place of selfishness and insecurity. Kerian had fit so seamlessly into our lives that it was almost as if he'd always been there. Who's to say there wasn't another person out there who could do the same thing?

Truthfully, when I look back on how things developed, Kerian and I bonded over our love of jazz music. He'd managed to talk me into joining him at an outdoor concert at the arboretum, drawing me in with my love of nature. Then by the end of the night, we were dancing under the stars and have been ever since. Once this started to become more serious, he went to Halstead, and the two of them had an open conversation about the situation. They started working out together to build a friendship outside of work. Soon working out turned into spending time doing the various physical activities that I did not find enjoyable, meeting a need I couldn't for either of them.

All of this started off with Kerian pursuing only me, but in the end, we all became friends and fell in love. Such is the nature of being open to loving more than one person. Before any of us realized it, Kerian had practically moved into our home. Shortly after that, we made it official, creating our family.

"I honestly don't know," Halstead answered. "Even if I was, the way things unfolded wasn't fair to my existing relationships or her. I lashed out, ashamed of my actions, and I don't think that went over well."

"Sounds to me like you need to have this conversation alone with Kerian to allow him the chance to process how he feels before we talk about it as a family," I pointed out. "It might also be wise to smooth things over with Elaine if you want a chance. That was an incredibly frosty interaction."

"Yeah," he said more as a groan. "I gave her the option to quit, and I'd find her someplace else to work if she didn't want to be around me.

However, if she decided to come back, I'd show her I'm not the ass I was last night. Looks like I'm not doing such a great job there either."

"Sit, I'll make us both a cup of tea, and we'll start this day over," I offered, gesturing for him to take a seat in my seating area.

"What about you?" Halstead asked.

I dumped out the now cold tea I'd been making and washed the mixing cup. "What about me?"

"Do you have any interest in adding to our relationship? If you're feeling protective enough over Elaine for you to get so worked up about it, that leads me to believe you might have an interest," Halstead reasoned.

My hands stilled as his words hit me like a ton of bricks. *Was I interested in Elaine?*

"I will need time to consider that question," I answered. "Speak to Kerian, and I mean today, H, and then we can all see how we feel."

"Done and done," he agreed. "Now hand me this magic tea so I can see if it will help me pull my foot out of my mouth."

"Oh, if that's what you want it to do, then I'm going to need a much bigger cup," I muttered, making Halstead laugh, a sound I loved to hear from both my partners. This had me curious about what it sounded like when Elaine laughed. *Maybe I was interested after all.*

Ten

Lainey

After the morning I'd had, I was happy things started to smooth out by lunchtime. Halstead made sure I took a lunch break and even handed me the company credit card.

"There is a fantastic deli just around the corner with amazing food. If you're willing to pick up an order there for the meeting with New Wave, then I'll happily buy you lunch," he explained. "The order should be a dozen vegan pastries. Tabitha, the woman we're meeting with today, loves them, and I always try to make sure we have them for her since she is a major client with us."

"That's not a problem," I answered. "It will be nice to try a place so close by and stretch my legs."

"Good afternoon, Elaine," Kerian greeted as he entered Halstead's office. "Are you joining us for lunch?"

"No, I'm actually on my way out to pick up an order at the deli," I shared.

He gave Halstead a disapproving look. "What happened to… she's my assistant and not wanting her to run your errands?"

"Hey, as a thank you for doing that, I'm also buying her lunch there," he pointed out. "Sam had to deal with another situation for tonight's meeting with Solarbyte. It would appear they'd like to do the meeting over dinner so it doesn't draw attention from the press. Seems that their servers being hacked has been leaked. Now they don't want to make a statement until they can say the best in the business has been hired to fix the problem."

"Smart on their part if you think about it," I commented.

Both men looked at me questioningly.

"How so?" Kerian inquired, cocking his head.

"Really? It's not obvious to you?" I demanded, hands on my hips. "Solarbyte is one of the biggest companies that run multiplayer computer games online. They are used and played all over the world by millions. If one hacker can get into their systems to steal credit card information, then what's to stop someone else from figuring it out? Just think if another person using the same weakness in the system hacked in and started holding user profiles up for ransom. Something along the lines of pay, or I'll delete everything you've spent years building with a click of a button."

"Huh..." Kerian grunted as he rubbed his chin. "A hundred percent something like that would work on people. I mean, I'd be willing to pay whatever it takes to make sure I don't lose progress or rare items."

"Exactly, so if Solarbyte came out saying, yes, we know there's a problem, but we're still working on a solution, it would be a disaster. One, because it tells hackers it's still vulnerable, and second, it sends their users into a panicked frenzy. Stocks would fall, subscriptions would be canceled, rogue bootleg servers would appear, and all hell would break loose," I shared, painting the picture for them. "So if I were you, I'd pick a restaurant you love and leave them the bill to pay. This isn't a meeting for you to win them over, it's them begging you to take them on as a client."

Halstead grabbed the phone, hit a button, and waited a moment. "Sam, call The Forest House and tell them I need a reservation for six people..." he paused, listening to whatever Sam was saying, nodding along, "... yes, that works fine. Oh, and make sure you speak to Jean-Marc, and tell him it's for a business meeting, not pleasure. No, I think the only person who will need a change of clothes is Ms. Collins."

That had my brows shooting up. "I will?"

Halstead covered the bottom of the phone as he held my gaze. "You, madam, just earned your seat at the table with that analysis. I'm going to have someone else pick up the pastries, and a driver will be waiting at the front to take you home and grab a dress for dinner. Sam should be emailing you the rules for The Forest House so there won't be any issues."

My mouth fell open. "Wait, are we talking about *The* Forest House? The restaurant in the founder's mansion?"

"Yes, now go. I need you back in time for the meeting with New Wave," Halstead instructed, waving his hand in a shooing motion.

Spinning on my heel, I raced for the office door past a chuckling Kerian, who I had to struggle with the urge to stick my tongue out at. He could tease me all he wanted, but this was a once-in-a-lifetime chance, and I wasn't going to risk being unable to go. Snatching up my purse, I hurried to the elevator, and once the doors were closed, I gave in and did a little happy dance.

It might seem silly to be so excited over this, but since I was a little girl, I'd been dreaming of a day I could eat at that restaurant. The mansion sat on a hill you could see from most of the downtown area. Anders Forest, the founder of Corzina, built his home there so he could always keep watch over the city he built. When he passed, it became a museum, and then about twenty or so years ago, the current living family decided to turn half of it into a restaurant. I'd seen pictures of it, and it was every woman's fantasy with a stunning art deco atmosphere that just spoke to me.

Walking through the lobby, I calmly opened the door and spotted the car waiting for me. Thankfully, it wasn't Wadsworth back to ruin the happy moment I was having. Slipping into the backseat, I gave the driver my address, and we were off. My phone vibrated with a notification that I'd gotten an email. It was from Sam listing out the rules for the dress code of The Forest House. Nothing about it surprised me since I knew their goal was to recreate the feel of the house back in its prime. Women had to wear formal dresses that went past their knees, dress straps needed to be two inches wide, and no prints, solid colors only. The men had it easy, stating it had to be a three-piece suit or tux in black, navy, or gray.

"Miss, I'll wait right here for you to get what you need. I've also been instructed to take you anywhere else you might need to go as long as I get you back in an hour," the driver explained as we pulled up to my building.

"Thank you, I shouldn't be too long," I said, offering him a smile before stepping out of the car.

Back in my apartment, I headed for the closet and pulled out the five formal dresses that were in there. I glanced at the cocktail dresses, but they would be too short for this dinner. It seems floor length was going to be the winner tonight. Instantly, I had to put two off to the side since they had patterns on them. My gaze settled on a stunning gold silk dress that was high in the front but backless with beautiful draping. Slipping out of my suit, I pulled the dress on and inspected it in the massive full-length mirror.

I'm not sure what it is, but there's something about a killer dress that can make a woman feel like she's capable of taking over the world. This was one of those dresses. My grin reflected back at me, radiating my excitement. It was an expression I hadn't seen in a while and was nice to experience. I matched a pair of heels and jewelry to the outfit, impressing me with the skills of the person who'd done the shopping. They'd really thought of everything I could need, down to the simple black clutch.

Packing everything safely into a garment bag, I reached for pants to get dressed when I felt a twinge of pain in my gut. Frowning, I looked down, brushing my skin with my hand, making sure I didn't have anything noticeable going on. Then I spotted the mark where I'd injected myself with the strange medicine was red and tender. Probing around the injection mark, I found the muscle was tender as well. Worry started to trickle through my veins as I searched for where I'd placed my phone. Snagging it off the kitchen counter, I hit the number for the 'pharmacist' and listened to it ring twice.

"UOS Pharmacy, is this an emergency?" the woman on the other end asked in a monotone voice.

"Um… I'm not really sure," I answered.

"Are you bleeding out or in danger of dying?" she questioned with the same lack of emotion.

"No?" I said, feeling like it was more of a question than anything. "Look, I was forced to take a drug this morning with no label or ingredients listed. The only thing it told me was dosage and injection placement."

I could hear typing going on as I spoke then it paused. "Have you been taking suppressants or scent-altering medication for a long time?"

"Yeah, like since I was nineteen," I told her.

"When did you administer that drug?"

Rubbing my forehead, I started to pace, my anxiety rising with each question. "This morning around seven-thirty. Listen, the injection site is red and tender. Doesn't that mean I'm having a bad reaction to this? Should I be going to the hospital?"

"Absolutely not. If you are in need of emergency care, then we will be the ones to provide that for you," she scolded me.

"Great, what do I need to do for that to happen?" I asked.

The woman let out an irritated sigh. "First of all, you need to warrant emergency care, and this matter doesn't qualify. Ma'am, this is a normal side effect of the drug and will go away on its own. With how long you've been taking suppressants and alerting drugs, stripping those from your body will have some unpleasant moments."

"Excuse me?" I snapped. "Did you just say stripping? Are you saying that what I just took this morning will remove whatever traces I have of either drug previously from my body?"

"Yes, ma'am, that's exactly what I'm saying." The woman drawled like she was bored with my questions. "We are the Underground *Omega* Syndicate, and they don't like it when Omegas deny what they are. So when they come across Omegas such as yourself, they fix the problem. You were picked for your skills and your designation as an Omega. I suggest you make peace with the fact you're going through a detox."

"How long will this take? What is about to happen to me?" I demanded, panic roaring in my ears.

"There's no way to know as each person is different. Since I've determined you are not in any life-threatening danger, I'm going to hang up now. Thank you for calling UOS Pharmacy. Call us back if you find yourself in need of our assistance." With that, the line went dead.

"Fuck," I screamed, hurling the phone at the wall. By some twisted fate, it didn't break as it crashed to the floor.

Running my hands through my hair, my body started to shake as I wracked my brain trying to come up with my next steps. *This can't be happening to me. How the fuck am I going to pull this off when I suddenly turn into an Omega right before their eyes?*

"I need the real drugs," I told myself. "You got this, Lainey. The driver will take us to a local pharmacy that has a clinic, and you'll get them to administer a suppressant there. There's no way this mystery drug can break down a fresh dose of suppressant."

Taking deep breaths, I tried to calm myself, but it was almost as if I'd been given a shot of pure adrenaline with how fast my heart was beating. Dropping onto the edge of the bed, I let my head fall into my hands and focused on calming down. I hadn't had a panic attack in a long fucking time, but it wasn't something you forgot the feeling of. It took longer than I wanted it to, but I managed to pull my shit together. There was no time for this if I wanted to get to the pharmacy before the meeting with New Wave in forty minutes.

I focused on nothing but getting dressed, grabbing the few things I would need to do something with my hair, and slinging the dress bag over my arm. Glancing at the phone still on the floor, I debated leaving it there and telling the syndicate to fuck off. Then I reminded myself that getting outed to these people that I was an Omega wasn't the same as the whole world knowing my name and face. My jaw clenched, I stomped over to the damn thing, scooped it up, and jammed it in my pocket.

Eye on the prize, Lainey. Finish this job and be done with the Syndicate and Corzina once and for all.

The moment the driver spotted me, he hopped out and took the dress from me, laying it out in the trunk. "Did we need to make a stop anywhere?"

"The nearest pharmacy, please. I seem to be out of hair spray," I answered.

"Certainly, there is one just around the corner," he said as he opened the back door for me.

In mere minutes, I was heading to the pharmacy counter praying they had a fast-acting suppressant on hand.

"Hello, how can we help you?" the woman behind the counter asked.

Taking note of her name, I smiled. "Hi, Annabeth, I was hoping you might have some fast-acting Intervestron in stock. I was supposed to get my dose yesterday, but the pharmacy I normally used was out. There is a super important meeting I need to be at tonight, and it's a group of high-powered Alphas."

She seemed hesitant but typed the name of the medication in her system. "We do have it in stock..." she paused, glancing sidelong at me, "... however, we do need a doctor's note to ensure we're giving you the correct dosage."

I'd been expecting this, and thankfully, this wasn't the first time I'd had to pull this trick and kept a fake prescription on a cloud server so I could access it.

"I don't have it physically, but I do have a copy of it from the pharmacy that couldn't fill it. Will that work?" I questioned.

Annabeth chewed her lower lip, debating. "I'll get the pharmacist and have him make that call."

Thank fuck it's a man. If it had been another woman, I'd have managed, but knowing all I had to do was convince a man to help me was so much easier. Annabeth returned with a gentleman in the typical white lab coat with his badge hanging off his pocket, but something seemed off about it.

"This is the pharmacist," Annabeth said, gesturing to the man as she glanced at his name. "Dr. Roberts."

Her hesitation had me thinking this wasn't the normal pharmacist. He took one look at me with a disgusting grin that I'm sure he thought would be charming. "How can I help?"

"I need to get a dose of Intervestron," I explained. "Annabeth was asking for the prescription, but I only have the record from the pharmacy that ran out of it. Will you honor it?" Seeing how this man was already eye fucking me, I didn't bother laying on the dramatics or batting my lashes. It was obvious this idiot was already in the bag.

"Of course, of course," he assured me. "Let me see the prescription, and I'll get it pulled together."

Handing over my phone, he looked over it and handed it back. "Give me a few minutes, and I'll call you back to administer it."

Both Annabeth and I looked at him, confused by that statement.

"Aah... I'm more than comfortable doing it myself," I explained.

Dr. Roberts nodded with that creepy smile and walked away without saying a word. I looked at Annabeth, who was frowning, staring after the man. "I'm really sorry about him. Our normal pharmacist is on maternity leave, and he's been the replacement while she's gone. The man is odd but does decent work."

"As long as I get the medication, that's all I care about. I need to grab something really quick, then I'll come back to settle the bill," I commented as I headed off to find a can of hairspray.

It was at this moment I realized the only money I had was either the company card from Halstead or the card from the Syndicate. Something told me that the Syndicate wouldn't be happy with what I was trying to do and might see it as retaliation or something equally unpleasant. My only choice was to pretend I used the Enigma card by accident and have them take it out of my paycheck.

I'd been a little worried as Annabeth swiped the card for the medication since some company cards have certain categories blocked so people couldn't do what I had. Fingers crossed behind my back as I waited, holding my breath. I all but sagged in relief at the confirmation trill and receipt being printed.

"Perfect timing," Dr. Roberts announced as he walked back up. "I've got it all situated, so if you come around to the clinic door, I'll let you back."

Everything in me screamed not to do this, but I was desperate, and no good choices happened when you were desperate. He led me to a small barren exam room where the shot was ready and waiting to be used. Thankfully, he put on gloves without me having to ask and sat on the short-wheeled stool.

"If you'll undress from the waist down and bend over the exam table, I'll get this taken care of," Dr. Roberts instructed.

"You want me to do what now?" I demanded.

"Undress and bend over," he reiterated. "The shot has to go in your buttocks. Surely, this isn't the first time you've had this medication?"

"Like I said before, I typically do it myself," I shot back. "If you give me the room, I'll have it done in two seconds."

"While you might have been able to do that before, a new law was passed, and now only medical personnel can administer the medication," he explained, giving me this look like I was a petulant child.

Stepping up to him, I snatched his name badge off his jacket and looked at it more closely. "This is shit work."

"Give me that back, or I'll have you arrested for assault," he yelled, shooting to his feet.

With the tip of my nail, I picked at the corner of the badge feeling the added layer of adhesive and got under it enough to peel back the whole layer. "Would you look at that... it seems the real Dr. Tarance Roberts is not only sixty years old but also a black man," I shared, flashing him the photo. "Neither of which you are unless you're going to try and tell me he stole your badge first? If he did, then I need to find out who his contact is because damn, this looks fucking perfect, almost as if it's the real deal."

"Who the fuck are you?" Dr. Roberts liar-liar-pants-on-fire blustered.

Tucking the badge in his pocket over his heart, I patted it roughly. "I'm the person who knows your dirty little secret. So I suggest you walk out of this exam room, let me give myself the shot, and forget we ever saw each other."

He blinked at me, almost dumbfounded. "That's it? You're just going to let me go?"

"Is there a reason I shouldn't? Did you fuck with the medication or switch it out for something else to drug me?" I questioned, crossing my arms and pinning him with my gaze.

Shaking his head vigorously, he backed up. "N-no," he stuttered. "It's just the suppressant like you were prescribed."

"Excellent, now get the fuck out of this room before I change my mind," I ordered.

That might have been the fastest he'd ever moved in his life, but dear Robby bolted out of the exam room. "Fucking perv, making women undress and bend over," I muttered as I grabbed the syringe, yanked off the cap with my teeth, and injected it into my bicep, the other alternative place you can administer the drug.

Dropping the used item into the appropriate container, I collected my purse and hurried out of the store. Glancing at my watch, I cursed under my breath. I had ten minutes to get back, and it was going to be close.

Eleven

Lainey

By some miracle, I made it back only five minutes late when I thought for sure it would be ten. The meeting with New Wave Financial went smoothly. Tabitha gushed over her love for the vegan pastries for far longer than was needed, but it set the right tone for the meeting. I could see why Halstead made sure they were here for her because the conversation they had after was tough and honest.

"Halstead, surely you don't mean that," Tabitha said with a disapproving tone. "We agreed last time that when we added on the new branches, the price wasn't going to change."

"When I agreed to that, you were only taking over three banks," he countered. "Tabitha, can you tell me you don't see a difference between three and thirty? Your company expanded to a whole-ass other province. New Wave took over the entire operation instead of testing the market with the failing locations like you told me was the plan. If I keep the cost the same with that massive of a shift, my other clients will be beating down my door like an angry mob."

Tabitha leaned back in her chair, studying Halstead. She was an Alpha in her late forties who was fastidious about her appearance being neat and tidy. Her hair was in a slicked-back ponytail, not a hair out of place. Even her eyebrows were immaculate. The only thing she didn't have perfect was her fingernails. Clearly, she was a nail-biter and clipped them as short as possible. However, that didn't stop her from picking at them, causing irritated red skin around her cuticles. This woman was a high-powered, no-nonsense sort who wanted results and to feel like she got the best deal.

She was in charge of New Wave's security from boots on the ground, staffing every branch, to cyber security, which is why she was here today. I knew the fastest way for her to agree to the price increase and be happy with it was to offer something she would see adds value but doesn't take from our profits.

"Halstead, we've been working together for *years*. You know I like you, and you're the best at what you do. However, my bosses are under the impression the cost is going to stay the same. We now have thirty locations to train, switching them over to our systems and procedures. If you can't work with us on this, then I'll have to go back to them with a number that's a quarter of what we paid to buy out this company. Three locations were in the red and needed a complete overhaul, but the rest weren't far behind," Tabitha explained. "Maybe it's better to pick another option that's cheaper for these new additions since we're not sure how many will last."

Oh, she's good. I had the utmost respect for a woman who thought she had a chance to make Halstead feel guilty about charging her more when she's the one who changed the rules.

"Look, I want to help you, Tabby," Halstead started, sighing heavily. "Truly, though, from three to thirty isn't a small amount. If you'd come to me and said five, maybe I'd be up for doing that. Thirty is just too big a number for me to get there."

"Trust me, I get it. They put us both in a shit spot with this," Tabitha admitted, shaking her head as she started to pick at the skin around her thumbnail. "The board was actually divided on this deal, but they got one person to flip their vote, and the deal was done. I was told to see if you would play ball, but I had a feeling it was too big of an ask."

"Once you get those locations up and running making a profit, then we can have this talk again, maybe end up with a better situation," Halstead offered.

What? That's it? Neither of them were going to try?

"Um... excuse me," I interjected, rising from the seat I'd been told to sit in against the wall. They both turned to look at me with questioning expressions. "Hi, I'm Elaine Collins, Mr. Norlund's executive assistant."

"Oh?" Tabitha commented with a smile. "So he hasn't chased you away yet?"

"Too early to tell... it's only day two," I shared, returning her smile. "Although I have to admit I'm not that easy to get rid of. If you don't mind me asking, when it comes to your security, what is the most expensive part of that for your company?"

"Oh, that's easy... labor," Tabitha answered. "We pride ourselves on ensuring we do everything in our power to keep our clients' money safe. It's the main reason we use Enigma. Their record is the best out there."

Thrusting my pen at her, I smiled. "That, right there, what you said just now... it's not only something you pride yourself in, it's your damn slogan. '*New Wave Financial, the bank with a new way of looking at your future.*' So tell me how your customers would feel if they find out these new branches you're trying to get off the ground that already aren't doing well don't meet the same standards of security as the others? Would you want to put your hard-earned money somewhere less secure?"

Tabitha leaned forward, resting her arms on the table. "You make a valid point. If they are already struggling, and we don't hold them to the same standards, there's no way for them to improve. However, that still doesn't change the fact I have a budget that hasn't been adjusted for anything more than covering the payroll increase."

As I sat at the conference table, I looked at Halstead. "Can I float this idea without committing us to anything?"

"Since I'm interested to know what you're going to say, go ahead. Before you do, though..." he started then looked over at Tabitha, "... everything about to be said by Ms. Collins is hypothetical. Nothing is in writing or backed by me or my business partners."

Tabitha laughed. "Goodness, Halstead, make me out to be a tyrant or something, why don't ya? I get it... we're spitballing, nothing more. Hell, if you want to call it training for her, then by all means, do so, but let the woman share already."

He grunted and motioned for me to go ahead.

"Now, Mr. Norlund already mentioned that thirty is just a bridge too far, but five he could see keeping at the same rate. Hypothetically, if he only charged your company for the additional twenty-five, accounting for the increase that would cut into our bottom line, it would bring the cost down. In addition, Enigma will train your cyber and in-person security here while you are switching things out and setting up the new system. Legally, while training, you can drop their pay to minimum wage. It cuts the cost but keeps it legal. Once they've been fully trained and they're sent back to work, pair them with a seasoned employee at another location.

"This way, they can see how a fully functional branch should work. Then you can take those displaced employees and have them work in the new branches. This will get things optimized and running ten times faster. With the blend of old and new, you can advertise the training they're getting which boosts our visibility, plus it will show your customers that nothing is changing for them. No matter where they go with New Wave, they can expect the exact same treatment and security you've always had," I explained.

When neither of them said anything, I feared I might have overstepped.

"Darling, if this grumpy old ass doesn't keep you, I'll find a job for you with me. That is brilliant," Tabitha praised. "The bosses won't like the increase, but if they hear training at minimum wage and only being charged for twenty-five branches instead of thirty, it makes us both look good. Also, the suggestion to pair a newly-acquired employee with a seasoned New Wave employee is just goddamn genius."

Halstead leaned back in his seat, staring at me as he stroked his beard. I started to squirm under his scrutiny, unsure if it meant something good or bad. No matter how hard I tried, I don't think I've ever had a harder time reading someone before now. Nothing gave away what he was thinking. Finally, freeing me from his intense azure gaze, he shifted it to Tabitha.

"Forget what I said before... that was a real offer," Halstead announced. "The only thing I'm going to add is that the training by my company will be a one-week intensive course. We do the same thing for the DOD when they have a new batch of recruits who need to be caught up quickly. Once that week is over, pair them with the seasoned employee to make sure the training sticks."

Tabitha reached a hand across the table. "Put it in writing, and I'll get it done."

"I have no doubt," he answered with a smirk. "We both know who really runs that place when it comes down to it."

"Only when it comes to operations. Anything else, and it falls on deaf ears," she grumbled as she stood. "Ms. Collins, it was a pleasure, and don't forget about what I said. As long as I have a job with New

Wave, the offer stands." Pulling a card from her purse, she passed it over to me.

It never made it into my hand as Halstead snatched it first, crumpling the thing in his hand. "I like you, Tabitha, but don't go poaching my people while I'm sitting the fuck here."

"Oh good, you do realize she's something special," Tabitha quipped. "A brilliant mind like that shouldn't be put in the corner to take notes, Halstead. Next time we meet, she's going to be sitting at this damn table. It will either be by your side or mine, but she'll damn well be here."

The two shook hands, and Halstead walked Tabitha out of the conference room, leaving me there, too stunned to move. *What the hell just happened?* One minute I was worried they'd hate the idea only for it to become the deal they could both agree upon. Dropping my head into my hands, I massaged my temples, trying to figure out what threw me the most—the fact I was actually *good* at this, or I was enjoying it.

Being a con artist taught me to analyze people, find out what they were all about, and then manipulate weaknesses to get what I wanted out of the deal. Here I was doing the same thing, but instead of using it against them, it helped me to negotiate terms that might be agreeable to both parties. This was like doing a job on the fly, using the limited time I interacted with them, coupled with the basic research I'd done beforehand. Interestingly enough, I didn't research Tabitha herself, just the company, since I didn't expect to interject myself into the situation.

"That was certainly unexpected," Halstead commented.

Not bothering to lift my head, I just grunted. Things all day with Halstead had been hot and cold, leaving me with no clue how to navigate our situation. Honestly, I hadn't allowed myself to dwell on it all that much. My mission was to get Kerian to stop writing the code, destroy said code, and find a way to make sure the code was never going to be recreated. Playing nice with Halstead was important to keep this job, but I felt I'd more than demonstrated I could be useful to him today. There wasn't much else I was willing to do beyond that since he was in a relationship with Quinton, and my guess would be Kerian too.

"Can we talk for a moment?" Halstead asked.

Raising my head, I found he was standing on the other side of the table from me. "Did you have a particular subject in mind?" I sassed, knowing full well he wanted to address last night.

"I deserve some of that attitude, but I will remind you that I'm still your boss," Halstead cautioned.

I planted my hands on the table and stood, trying to keep my face clear of the irritation I was feeling right now. "Then unless this is a work-related conversation, I think it's best we leave all other topics alone. As you pointed out, you *are* my boss, and we wouldn't want anyone here to get the wrong idea about us. I have a feeling it could really upset others if the wrong impression of us were to spread." Grabbing my notebook and the few files Halstead asked me to bring in, I started to head out of the conference room.

"Quintin and Kerian are both my lovers as well as business partners," he announced.

"Yes, I gathered that," I tossed over my shoulder. "I'll make sure to keep it to myself. Don't worry."

This was the last thing that I wanted to deal with at the moment. After the encounter with that creep of a pharmacist, I'd had my fill of men thinking I was some easy target. These men might be my scent matches, but if they never found out, it would be simple enough to leave them behind when this was all over. Just another reason I needed to get this job done a hell of a lot sooner than two fucking months. *How hard could it be to destroy a code?* I'd done work like that many times before. The trickiest part would be getting to his devices at home. My guess is he put it on a central cloud location to work on it in real-time, no matter the device. However, I wasn't going to chance that, not with everything on the line.

Entering my office, I set the paperwork down and sat at my desk. There was some prep work I wanted to do on Solarbyte to see just how bad their situation was. One thing Enigma didn't need was bad press. If Solarbyte knew about this issue and ignored it or if there was some other dirt such as this happening in retaliation for something, I wanted to know.

"Elaine, we can't go to dinner tonight without having this conversation," Halstead stated as he walked into my office and closed the door.

Clearly, he wasn't going to drop this, so I crossed my arms and waited. There was no fucking way I was talking first—I'd done nothing wrong. He's the one who showed up at my door after hours and needed to chat.

"I feel like I should tell you both of them know what happened between us. Quintin asked that I tell you what happened this morning had nothing to do with that matter. It's not my place to go into detail, but let's just say that Quintin faces a fair share of demons. Simply meaning that not every situation is handled as people expect from him," Halstead explained.

Hell, if I didn't understand that on a soul level. You roll with the punches until one comes at you out of left field and knocks you on your ass.

"First, I would like to once more apologize for putting you in that position because of my poor choices," he offered. "It was wrong of me to even think it was a good idea to visit your home after hours alone. That put you in a situation you never should've been in. Secondly, it's not your fault for what happened with the kiss... you didn't know I was in a relationship with my partners. That was all on me, and I've made it clear to Kerian and Quintin of this fact. Neither holds any ill will toward you, nor do they see you being at fault."

While I can't say my anger or irritation over this matter lessened, I did appreciate that he took full responsibility. It was refreshing to see a man who could own up to a mistake. He didn't try to sugarcoat it or tell me I tempted him into doing it because if I'd known he wasn't single, it never would have happened.

"I appreciate your apology and accept it," I said, knowing he wouldn't let this go until I gave him the resolution he clearly needed.

In the long run, none of this mattered. I was going to be gone and out of their lives when this was over, letting them return to their normal routine. Allowing my emotions to tell me I should feel slighted and lied to, I had no room to talk. If they found everything I'd been lying to them about, they'd have every right to be furious.

"I'm not sure I deserve to be let off that easily with how I handled this whole mess, but I'm grateful for your forgiveness. My reasoning for pushing this conversation is that Kerian and Quintin will be at dinner tonight, and I wanted you all to be on the same page. It wouldn't be fair for them to know all the details and leave you in the dark," he explained. "You've impressed me today, Elaine. The suggestions and insight into matters are exactly what I'm looking for in an executive assistant. My hope is that we can build trust between us and see if we're the right fit for each other."

Relief flooded through me as I realized he was genuinely pleased with how things had gone with Tabitha. Standing, I walked over to him, reaching out a hand. "Why don't we start things over? Hi, I'm

Elaine Collins, feel free to call me Elaine. I look forward to working with you and this company."

He smirked as he took my hand. "It's a pleasure, Elaine. I'm Halstead Norlund, one of the owners of Enigma. My two partners and packmates, Quintin and Kerian, also own this business with me. Welcome to the team, and I hope this works out for the best."

"Me too," I answered with a genuine smile. "Now, if you'll excuse me, I'm going to do a deeper dive into Solarbyte. You know, to make sure nothing bites us in the ass taking them on as a client."

Halstead chuckled. "Be my guest, but we've had them looked into before accepting the meeting."

"Not by me," I countered. "As you've been made aware by my previous employers, I have certain skills for finding things they don't want to be found."

"Then I shall leave you to it," he said, reaching for the door handle. "Please be ready to leave by four-thirty. Our meeting is at five."

"I'll be ready and waiting," I assured him. "This is a once-in-a-lifetime experience not only to be at the restaurant but to prove my worth to you."

He gave me a lingering look, his gaze softening as I earned a genuine smile from him. "I'm looking forward to it."

Taking a deep breath, I walked back to my desk and sat. "Let's get down to business."

Twelve

Lainey

Halstead had thought of everything for his employees down to a locker room on the lower level next to the company gym. Taking a peek at the gym, it wasn't anything extravagant, but it covered everything someone would need if they wanted to use it during their lunch break or even after work. The locker room was well maintained and had most things you could need from lockers, changing rooms, showers, and even a steam sauna I would need to try out another day.

Taking one last look in the full-length mirror, I pinned back an unruly strand of hair into the chignon hairstyle I'd thrown together. The dress demanded a classic look, and that's what I was giving it—a soft, smoky eye made the green in my hazel eyes pop, bold red lipstick, and subtle blush. Since the dress was a champagne-color gold, I went with rose gold for the earrings that dangled but not adding anything else accessory-wise. This was dinner after all, not a gala like a few nights ago. In fact, I felt like this might be a tad too much, but none of the other dresses would have worked.

It didn't matter now. There was no time to make any changes. It wouldn't be the first time I'd drawn attention for going a bit overboard or the last. Of course, those had been a character I was playing, but so was this if I were being honest. Yes, Elaine might be the closest to who I think of myself to be, but I hadn't been Lainey Caddel since I was eighteen. If someone asked me what *I* truly liked, not what I thought I should or needed to like, I don't know if I could answer that.

With a glance at my watch, I hurried to collect my things to head back upstairs. When I stepped out of the elevator, Kerian was coming out of his office wearing a sharp, light gray three-piece suit that had a slight sheen to it. We spotted each other at the same time and froze in the middle of the hallway.

"You look stunning," he said at the same time I spoke. "That suit looks amazing on you."

He laughed and did a little twirl. "This old thing? I have to be honest... when it comes to suits, they are not my area of expertise. You'll have to thank Quintin for this ensemble."

"What am I being thanked for?" Quintin asked, preoccupied with fixing a cufflink to his shirt with his tux jacket slung over the other arm.

Stepping forward, I stilled his hand. "Here, let me. It's kind of an awkward angle, isn't it?"

Quintin froze under my touch, and I was worried that I'd done something to upset him. Yet when I met his gaze, I only saw surprise and appreciation as he took me in.

"Thank you..." he said absently, holding out his wrist.

The cufflinks were of a tree, not the typical Tree of Life symbol, but something else. "Do these mean something or just a show of appreciation for nature?" I asked as I got the branch that had been stuck in the buttonhole free.

"They're oak trees that represent strength, stability, and endurance. All things I feel I'm rather lacking in, so Kerian got me these to remind me that isn't true," Quintin answered, far more honestly than I ever expected.

Giving his wrist a gentle squeeze before releasing him and stepping back, I smiled. "I know we've only just met, but it's rather obvious to me that he's right. No one can handle the work you do without those qualities. Not to mention, from what I hear, Enigma wouldn't be what it is today without your skills."

"That is very kind, Elaine, and I'm glad you believe that. Sometimes it's hard to trust what someone says when they love you and want to see you happy. You have no need to cater to my emotional well-being, so I find it easier to hear and accept if that makes any sense," Quintin shared as he pulled on his jacket.

"I understand that logic completely," I admitted.

"Then please accept the truth of my words when I say you look ravishing in that dress. Not to say you don't always have impeccable style, but this look you've pulled off is just beautiful," Quintin whispered, holding my gaze with his deep green eyes, revealing the sincerity behind his words.

A reaction I never expected occurred as my cheeks burned with a blush, and I dropped my eyes. Combining his sweet words with his bright green tea and ginger scent had me all kinds of flustered, to the point I thought I would have to fan myself.

"Thank you," I murmured, pressing the back of my hand to my cheek to cool off the reaction.

"Oh good, you're all her—" Halstead started to say but stopped when his attention landed on me. "I think we need to cancel this meeting," he decided abruptly.

Frowning, I turned to face him. "Why on earth would we do that? I know I forwarded the information I found on them, but every company has a few skeletons in its closet. None of them were bad enough to warrant not speaking with them," I reasoned.

"I don't think that has anything to do with why he wants to cancel," Kerian commented.

"Oh," Quintin blurted. "I didn't see the back of this dress yet, but now I understand."

Glancing over my shoulder at him, I cocked a brow. "Care to enlighten me because I have no idea what the back of my dress has anything to do with this matter?"

"It has everything to do with this matter," Halstead practically growled. "The owners of Solarbyte are young men in their late twenties. They will have no idea how to act around a woman of your caliber, not to mention I don't want them gawking and drooling over my assistant."

"Um..." I started, then paused, "... thank you, I think?"

"That was absolutely a compliment. Halstead is just tongue-tied because he's not used to having such a gorgeous woman around. Technology, more so cyber security, tends to be predominantly male, and I think he's worried these men—"

"Boys... they are not men... they are still boys," Quintin interjected, cutting off Kerian.

Kerian rolled his eyes but shifted his terminology all the same. "These *boys* won't show you the proper respect distracted by the fact you look, pardon my candor, sexy as shit."

"Oh..." I said, my mouth popping open in surprise. "So we're still doing this, though, right?"

Kerian and Quintin looked to Halstead for the answer.

There weren't many times I noticed the age difference between us beyond his looks. He did a remarkable job keeping up and was in phenomenal physical shape, something that the dark gray suit he was wearing displayed well with his arms crossed like that. The man stared at me as we waited for his answer, truly weighing all options, which I thought was ridiculous.

"You'll sit between us. I don't want you within touching distance of those two, understood?" Halstead ordered.

I couldn't help but smile. "That's fine with me. I won't argue with you on that."

"Oh, thank fuck." Kerian sighed. "I was not looking to go to jail tonight for beating some punk's ass."

"Good God, it's like you three don't think I'm capable of dealing with pervy men on my own," I pointed out. "I'll have you know I manage just fine, so there's no need for the white-knight act."

"Oh, I wouldn't be a fucking white knight, Elaine," Halstead warned. "No, they would have been introduced to their worst nightmare."

"Damn right I would be," I stated and headed for the elevator. "Seeing as it's fifteen minutes until our reservation, I think it's best we get going."

The sound of grumbling behind me told me they were following, making me smirk. It was flattering to have these men acting like this on my behalf. Unlike others who wanted to keep me as their shiny new toy all to themselves, these three were worried I wouldn't be treated right. I'll hand it to them, they know how to make a person feel valued, even if they've only just started working for them.

Unsure how we planned to get there, I left them to hit the button for either the lobby or the underground parking. Then again, Quintin had walked up the main steps this morning, so these three might have private parking. Kerian hit the 'L' and came to stand next to me, leaning casually, but I kept catching him glancing at me out of the corner of his eye. I couldn't tell if he wanted to say something to me or was simply being a typical male and scoping out my curves.

"I heard Tabitha was impressed with you," he finally commented.

Halstead grunted. "You mean because she tried to poach Elaine right in front of me?"

"That, and I know you got a call back from her bosses agreeing to the terms you set up," Kerian clarified.

My head snapped to look at Halstead grinning at me. "That's true... I just got off the phone with them. Congratulations, Elaine, you helped negotiate your first deal. Let's see if you're able to swing two for two."

"How on earth did she get them to agree that fast?" I questioned.

"Let's just say that I'm not the only one who likes to keep certain aspects of my life to myself," he answered cryptically.

Wracking my brain, I tried to figure out what the hell he was talking about until it dawned on me. "It's her pack that owns New Wave, isn't it?"

Halstead gave me a wink as an answer just as the doors opened, revealing the lobby guard.

"Evening, sirs, ma'am," he greeted, holding back the door. "Will we be expecting you back tonight?"

"No, we'll be back tomorrow," Quintin answered bruskly as he exited.

Halstead clapped the man on the shoulder. "Have a good night, Eddy. Keep the place safe tonight for us."

"Absolutely, Mr. Norlund. Enjoy your evening," Eddy assured, giving a nod.

Kerian offered me his arm, which I took, grabbing the bottom of my dress as we exited. It wasn't that it was too long, but I didn't want to risk it getting stepped on or caught as we passed through the busy lobby. A car was waiting for us—a modified SUV with seats facing each other like a limousine but not stretched. Quintin got in first, then offered a hand to help me in, making my heart flutter in a way that worried me.

Why the hell was I acting like a silly teenager being treated like a lady for the first time?

Taking my seat, I tried to get a fucking grip on my emotions. That went out the window when he chose to sit next to me. I had to fight the urge to rest my head on his shoulder so I could breathe in his scent with every breath, savoring the taste. I was momentarily distracted as Kerian slid in last, and the second the door was closed, he grabbed Halstead's chin and kissed him soundly.

"I know you wear suits all the time, but damn, there is something about the way this one fits that is just fucking sexy," Kerian shared, pressing another quick kiss before getting comfortable, resting his hand high on Halstead's thigh.

Kerian's warm amber eyes met mine, telling me I'd been blatantly staring at the two of them. "Don't you agree, Elaine?" he asked, not breaking the hold he had on me.

My mouth had gone dry, but I recovered quickly. "It's the cut of the suit. The others I've seen him wear are a looser style, and this one is far more tailored, showing off his well-earned physique."

This had a wide grin appearing on his face, lighting up his features and making him even more handsome than he already was. "Then I think I'm just going to have to get rid of all his other suits and replace them all with these."

"No," Quintin snapped. "If you did that, then we'd run into the same problem we're having with Elaine wearing this dress. He's chosen to keep our relationship quiet, which comes with benefits and challenges. Having others believe they even have a chance with him is bad enough, but alerting them to the fact he has the body of a Greek statue will only make it harder on us."

I choked on my spit at the directness of Quintin's words, but damn, if that wasn't the truth. "Speaking as someone who unfortunately experienced this situation, I have to agree with Quintin," I commented after I stopped coughing.

"Elaine, please don't think that was directed at you. It's not the first time someone has made the wrong assumption, but it just happened to be the one time Halstead let it get out of control. Normally, he would have cleared the air and made you sign an NDA regarding that matter," Quintin explained.

Kerian groaned. "Quinny, you're totally not making this situation any better. We promised to do our best not to bring up the matter unless she did."

"I made no such promise. H requested I do that, but I never agreed," Quintin stated. "Personally, I think it's best we get it out in the open. Then we can clarify that we hold nothing against Elaine for what happened, which would provide closure for her." He shifted his attention to look at me. "Don't you agree?"

"I agree that I would like there to be closure and for us all to pretend the situation never happened," I answered. "I'm here to do a job, he is my boss, as are all of you, for that matter. If we are to do dinners and such like this, then we all need to be on the same page, but once this discussion is over, I'd like the matter to die with it."

"There's no reason why I don't see that being possible, right, guys?" Halstead asked, but his tone didn't give them room to argue.

Kerian leaned forward, loosely intertwining his fingers as he rested his elbows on his knees. "I have one question, then I'll drop the matter altogether."

"That's fair. Quintin, do you have any questions before we put the matter to rest?" I inquired.

"No," he answered succinctly.

Satisfied, I motioned for Kerian to go ahead and ask, bracing myself for what I assumed would be a brutal question.

"At the core, I supposed it's two questions, but they go together in my mind," he clarified. "Did you want him to kiss you? Would you want him to do it again if there was a possibility to make that happen?"

My mouth fell open at his question. Out of all the things I thought he'd ask or say, that wasn't even close to what I considered. However, since he did ask, I had to take a moment to consider my answer. My gut reaction was fuck no, I didn't want anything to do with that man other than fulfilling my mission. Things were already risky enough being their scent-pair and not saying anything about it. Now I was being asked flat out if I would want to experience that mind-blowing kiss again. *Fuck*.

"To answer the first question, yes, I one hundred percent wanted him to kiss me. In fact, I goaded him into it when he seemed to hesitate. Of course, now that I understand the reason behind it, I simply thought it was the boss-employee aspect," I shared, then dropped my gaze from his. Needing to do something with all these chaotic emotions that didn't draw attention, I stroked the glass surface of my watch with my thumb.

A hand came to rest over mine, stilling the motion causing me to look up at Quintin. "No matter what your answer is, I promise you we will not treat you any differently. While this particular situation didn't start on the best foot, it's not uncommon for people in our society to fall for someone outside their current partners. What matters most in these situations is communication, which I think Kerian is trying to do. In his roundabout way, I believe his intention is to ascertain if you have any interest in developing something beyond a work relationship."

That had me frowning. "Why would you be okay with that?"

"Because this is how Kerian joined us," Quintin explained. "He knew I was with Halstead but took a chance to see if I was interested in him. We went on a few casual and innocent dates, and the moment we decided that something deeper might come of our time together, we both went to Halstead to share our intention. From there, as a group, we found the best way to manage work and relationships. Halstead might be too selfless and would never ask Kerian or me to share him with another person. Yet both of us love Halstead too much for him to give up on something or someone who could make him happy. Possibly all of us, as was the case with our third."

Returning my attention to Kerian, I searched his face looking for anything that would clue me in on some scheme or trick they were trying to pull, but all I saw was an open and honest expression. "Is Quintin right?" He just nodded.

My gaze flicked to Halstead. "I feel that question should come from you unless your partners are making incorrect assumptions. However, I feel like that would be odd since the three of you have clearly had conversations on this matter today."

"I was going to bring this up later, after dinner, in a more pleasant atmosphere," Halstead offered with a sigh. "That being said, it would seem my partners had other ideas on how this should happen."

"Well, if you don't ask her out, then how the hell am I supposed to? Wouldn't it be more awkward?" Kerian questioned, getting a glare from Halstead that had the man throwing up his hands. "All right, all right, I'll leave you to it."

Sitting back, he tucked his hands behind his head like he needed to forcibly keep himself from interacting. Halstead watched him for a second, almost as if he didn't trust his lover would let him do this himself. When he was satisfied, he fixed his gaze on me, a firm hold on my attention as he spoke.

"Elaine, I would greatly enjoy the chance to get to know you in a setting outside of work... or your home," he added. "You have captured my attention in a way that not many people can, and I would jump at the opportunity to see where all the possibilities might take us."

I had to bite my lip to keep from laughing, but a snort slipped out, betraying me. That was all Kerian needed before he burst into laughter, and even Quintin chuckled.

"You know what, fuck you both. I told you I wasn't good at this shit," Halstead grumbled, shoving Kerian. "Look, Elaine, that kiss has been living rent-free in my mind since it happened. Not only are you drop-dead gorgeous, but that brilliant mind has to be the sexiest thing about you. My hope is that if we could have a chance to drop the roles we have to keep while at work, it would be nice to see if there is anything deeper than initial infatuation."

That offer had been honest, blunt, and far truer to the person who I was coming to know as Halstead. "I'm assuming, since you're asking in front of them, that both are fine with this? It's a little late to ask, but I really don't want any trouble."

"Elaine, did you miss the part where I said I wanted to ask you out?" Kerian stated, crossing a leg over the other. "There will be zero trouble from me."

"The same goes for me," Quintin answered.

I paused at that. "Which part?"

"All of it. While I wouldn't have asked you as quickly as Kerian seems to be planning to, I feel when we both are a little more settled with this change, I would have made my interest known," he expounded. "I've never had a protective response toward someone, and yet I did with you this morning. Clearly, there is something drawing me to you, and I'd like to explore what that might be."

"Ah-hem..." Halstead cut in, clearing his throat loudly. "What does it take for a man to get an answer around here? I'd like to know if I've got a shot before we head into the restaurant."

That had me looking at my surroundings and realized The Forest House was looming out the window to my right. Fingers gripped my chin and turned my head to meet Halstead's gaze once more.

"I'm not a man who's used to being ignored," he commented as he released me, but the move set my body on fire. The command in his voice was clear and added to the physical redirection. "I'll accept any answer, even if it's 'I need some time to think about it,' but I will insist you give my request acknowledgment."

A shiver of delight trilled up my spine, loving the dominance. "Yes," I answered, my voice slightly breathier than I would have liked. "Yes, I will go out with you, Halstead."

The smile that appeared on his face transformed the man. He'd always been handsome in a regal way any silver fox of a man should have, but this added a warmth to him I hadn't seen before. "Then let's get this meeting over with so we can have a drink in peace after. I took note of how excited you were to come here, so I wanted to make sure you got to see the place as one should."

My heart actually skipped a beat as my breath hitched at the intensity of Halstead's gaze, like a man on the hunt. I was so screwed, but I didn't give a fuck. Who said I couldn't enjoy myself while working this job?

Thirteen

Kerian

The Forest House was a favorite of ours. The owners knew how to be discreet, and it gave us a place where we could have dates or just a lavish dinner out as a family. Here, we didn't have to worry about who saw what or if they would use it against us. No one could come here if they didn't have a substantial net worth with their own weaknesses at risk. Shared danger kept things amiable, and if you broke that unwritten rule, then you'd never step foot in this place again, no matter how much you made.

I smiled as Halstead helped Elaine out of the limousine and tucked her arm through his. The look on his face was one I hadn't seen in a long time—it was full of excitement. Not that I would say our life was boring, but I'd be the first to admit we're all workaholics who didn't take much time out of our day to do anything new. We had hobbies, but we'd also had those for years, making them far from exciting. Elaine was an intriguing and gorgeous new puzzle for us all to figure out, and it was clear we all had a unique interest in her.

Halstead mentioned Quintin's protectiveness over her, and that was huge. H was clearly intrigued with her drive and passion for whatever she put her mind to. He'd shown me the research she pulled up on Solarbyte that no one had been able to find in all the deep dives we've done on this business. Then there was the meeting with Tabitha, creating a solution none of us would have thought of based on the information she'd gathered sitting in that meeting.

As for me, she posed a unique challenge. Everything about her was so carefully put together, from her appearance to how she responded to situations. I'd spotted one or two moments that were genuine authentic reactions to something. One of them being my scent. The second she realized what she'd been doing, the panic that flashed through her eyes had my attention. Each time I dug into who she was and where she came from, I found the bare minimum. She'd never had social media, and there were no records of her graduating high school, only college. However, when I looked into that, I had a hard time finding anything about what classes she took, her grades, and things like that. It was almost as if it was a damn good false identity.

Was she hiding from someone? Maybe she's in witness protection?

"Keri?" Quin questioned as I stood there at the foot of the steps like an idiot, staring at the other two.

I smiled, grasping his hand and lacing our fingers together. "Sorry, just lost in thought. Shall we head in?"

The skin between his brows started to crease, so I leaned in, cupped his cheek, and kissed him. Not the basic, we've-been-together-for-over-five-years peck. I wanted to steal his breath away like he did to me every damn day since I met him. This stiff, prickly man who always said the wrong thing had a heart of gold that loved endlessly. He had no idea how much he's helped me become the man I am today, knowing I needed to be better for him. It was crazy to think how a kid abandoned at five to my mom's pimp turned criminal hacker could end up here with this amazing life.

"What was that for?" Quin asked, his eyes a little glassy with pleasure.

"Because," I offered. "You know how that damn bow tie makes me want to strip you naked and have you call me Master Lewis as you bounce on my cock."

Right on cue, the blush flamed to life on Quintin's cheeks. "Kerian, we are in public. You can't talk like that," he scolded in a harsh whisper. "Let's go before you think of something else outlandish to say."

"Hey, honesty is the best policy, right?" I teased, wrapping my arm around his waist and urging him toward the entrance. "We better hurry. Who knows what might happen if we leave those two alone for too long."

"Did we make the right choice?" he asked, as I smiled at the entrance attendant in thanks for holding the door.

Passing the coat check, we headed into the main foyer of the mansion, which served as the split between the restaurant and the museum. Head to the left for the history, whereas going right would place you in a magical place where the food was made from heaven.

"What do you mean? Encouraging Halstead to pursue Elaine or the fact that we also find ourselves interested?" I inquired, curious as to his answer.

Quin let out a heavy sigh. "Both, I suppose. Keri, I'm not the man who does impulsive things like ask a woman to date me when I already have two partners I'm happily in love with. My heart is more than willing to explore this new interest, but my brain is not quite on board, even though I realize this is completely normal for everyone to experience."

Pulling Quintin to a halt, I turned him to face me. "Don't answer me right away when I ask you this. Let's say out there is a person we scent-pair with, the three of us together. Would there be the same hesitation? I suppose what I'm trying to say is if you're hesitant in general or if it's because your mother told you that you'd never be good enough for anyone."

"That is a question I'll have to think on," he said after a moment.

"Mr. Lewis, Mr. Price, so good to see you," Jean-Marc greeted with a slight bow. "I just took Mr. Norlund back to the private room I've set you up in tonight."

"Good evening, Jean-Marc. It's a pleasure as always to be here," I said, reaching out to shake the man's hand. It had been my mission to break down the barriers this man put up with everyone he interacted with. He was of the mind that a maître d didn't build personal connections with the guests—he was there to be of service—and that was that.

He gave me a disapproving look but accepted the handshake, albeit a quick half-hearted one. "Please, follow me."

The Forest House lived up to its name, keeping the interior design of the restaurant a deep emerald green with gold embellishments. Even the chairs were emerald velvet with a gold frame. Tabletops were green, white, and gold marble, setting off the white and gold dishes they used. Soft hanging twinkle lights set the ambiance with illuminating wall sconces showing off the art deco designs on the walls. Decadent—that one word said it all about this place—but it had a charm to it that made you want to linger.

The main restaurant was what had once been the ballroom, with a stunning floral mural painted on the ceiling. Rooms branched off the ballroom that at one time had been small parlors for women and men to relax separately. There were six of these, and Jean-Marc always seemed to find a way to keep us in the same room each time. It was Quintin's favorite because of all the plants and greenery that decorated the room along with a small water feature. Interestingly enough, though, tonight he brought us to a different room. This one was a soft cream color with gold and green accents, but the crowning feature in this room was the massive floor-to-ceiling windows that showed the backyard, which also happened to look out over the city.

Corzina was a beautiful city, especially at night when the sun had gone down and you could see how large it was. Elaine stood at the window, her hand over her breasts like she was trying to keep her heart in her chest as she took in the sight. I let my eyes take in the bare skin of her back and the curve of her muscles as she moved to tuck a strand of hair behind her ear. With the dress she was wearing and the innate elegance she had, I almost believed she should be the woman living here.

Everything in me wanted to slip the straps of that dress off her shoulders and watch the silk pool at her feet. *What would she be wearing underneath? Just underwear?* Possibly nothing at all with how smooth the fabric flowed over her ass. Then I'd press her up against the window, letting the cool glass contrast the heat of her body as I finger-fucked her until she came screaming my name.

"Took you two long enough... get stopped by someone?" Halstead questioned.

"No, hot make-out session in the coat closet," I answered, making Elaine turn to stare at the two of us, heat smoldering in her gaze. *So she likes the idea of us together. That's helpful.*

"I'm kidding, guys. We just thought the two of you might have a few moments together before we had to flip to business mode," I said, taking a seat so I could look out the window. We'll make the other two joining us put their backs to the view. "Come sit here, Elaine. This way, you can make sure you have a good view."

To my delight, Quintin sat on the other side of her, making it so Halstead had to sit next to one of us. That shouldn't have made me smile, but it most certainly did. The man was a giant in the industry and used to getting things his way, so I like to remind him on occasion that that wasn't reality. He settled next to Quin, running his hand affectionately along our partner's thigh before pressing a kiss to his cheek. Those two were like that adorable elderly couple who still were madly in love after eighty years.

"Here you are, gentlemen. Your server will be with you shortly," Jean-Marc said as he ushered in our potential clients.

Solarbyte was owned by two brothers, Angel and Xavier LaCruze, both under the age of thirty, if I'm not mistaken. They both looked equally uncomfortable in their suits, clearly not something they were accustom to wearing. Halstead picked this place because it put us all on the same footing. These men could easily afford this meal and lifestyle, but they acted like they were still living in their mother's basement where they started their company. If they wanted to play with the big dogs, then they needed to act like they belonged here.

"Hello," Angel greeted, walking over to Halstead and shaking his hand. "Thank you for taking the time to meet with us this way. I know changing plans at the last minute wasn't the most professional thing to do, but our PR consultant suggested it would be the best plan."

We knew their public relations expert, Zimina, was a shark who could sniff out the blood in the water better than anyone else. However, she was also a raging bitch and didn't give two shits about treating her clients like humans, ordering them around and demanding things be done her way. Zimina would get you results, that's for damn sure, but you had to be willing to deal with the witch.

"I'm sure she did," Halstead commented. Zimina and H should never be left alone in a room together. If that happened, the fight that would go down would cause buildings to collapse and the earth to split. Just think of any of the Godzilla movies, and that would give you a clue as to what would happen. "Allow me to introduce my business partners, Quintin Price and Kerian Lewis. I felt it was best to have them here to hear you out as well since they would be involved in this whole process too."

"And who might this vision of a woman be?" Xavier asked, coming around the table to stand near Elaine.

"Ms. Elaine Collins, Mr. Norlund's executive assistant," Elaine answered, taking the hand he offered.

My hackles went up as Xavier kissed the back of her hand, letting his lips linger longer than they should have. "It's a delight to have such a beautiful woman joining us. These meetings can get so boring, so it will be refreshing to have a female perspective."

"Goodness, that puts a lot of pressure on me now, doesn't it?" she responded, pulling her hand from his. "Although it worries me that your company is in such a crisis, and yet you find meetings like this boring? Does the future of your company mean so little to you?"

I nearly choked on the water I was sipping, trying to distract myself from the urge to toss this man out of the room. Elaine had, in the most polite way possible, called his ass out, and I don't think he even realized it yet.

"No, my company means everything to me, which is why we are here. We need the best of the best if we are going to keep this from happening," Xavier countered.

"Then I suggest you kiss his hand instead of mine," Elaine quipped, a tight, polite smile on her lips. "He's the one who will make the final choice on the matter."

I knew better than to look at Halstead. If I did, there would be no chance of hiding the delight I felt at her smackdown of this man. She'd been right to tell us to back the fuck off and let her prove herself to us because I don't know of a more elegant way to watch someone being told to fuck off than I was right now.

Xavier's charm dimmed slightly as he stepped back from her and realized his normal routine wasn't working. Unable to help myself, I reached out a hand to the man. "Kerian Lewis, head programmer as well as part owner."

Taking the lifeline, he grasped my hand firmly and shook it, but I held onto it, pulling it close to kiss the back of it. Xavier's expression went from shock to disgust, telling me all I needed to know about how he felt about men.

"My apologies. I thought that's how you were greeting everyone," I said, releasing his grip. "I thought it was a rather daring greeting since it's a rather intimate gesture. However, I knew your family migrated here from Echana and assumed it was customary there."

Take the hint, asshole, and don't touch her again.

Xavier cleared his throat and moved back to the other side of the table to sit next to Halstead, leaving Angel to take the one closer to me. "Our parents did migrate here, but Angel and I are first generation raised in Breona Province."

"So you are living the dream, creating a company out of your mother's basement, and now you are here treating us to a meal at The Forest House. That is quite remarkable. I bet your mother is so proud," Elaine gushed, leaning her elbows on the table to rest her chin on her clasped hands. "Did you ever think you'd make it this far?"

Angel glanced at Xavier when she mentioned that they'd been the ones to suggest this place, but his brother was no help, still salty about my kiss. "It's something we dreamed of but never thought would happen. Video games have been around for quite some time, so trying to change the process is a risk. Whenever you have to retrain your users, it's a gamble. As for our mother, she is beyond proud, but no matter how hard we try, she won't move out of that original house. Says it's full of good luck, and it's risky to throw it away."

We all smiled at that and, in some ways, understood. Each of us had a good luck charm of sorts that we kept from where we started.

"While it's no house, I kept the tie I wore when I got the loan I needed to start Enigma, and it was the same one I wore when I got that first defense contract," Halstead shared. "Some things you just don't risk getting rid of."

Our conversation was brought to a halt as the server entered the room. We gave her our drink orders and were informed of the menu. The Forest House didn't allow you to order, they had a set meal for the night, and unless it was allergy related, they did absolutely no substitutions. This stayed true to the exclusivity of the restaurant, making it an experience each time you came, never getting the same thing twice.

"So we all know why we are here," Quintin announced once the server left. "Now my biggest question is *why* should we take you on as a client? You had ample opportunity to prevent this incident from occurring but, in my eyes, you seemed to put the security of your company at the bottom of your list. Now you've seen the impact of not having reliable security, you come running to us."

Damn cutthroat Quin was sexy as fuck, more so because I loved to see him take charge and stand up for us along with himself. He fought every day to better himself, proving to that dark voice in his mind that made Quintin believe he was worthless. In the past three years, he's made amazing strides and never would have been bold enough to lay down the law like this. Alexis, his therapist, found that viewing certain things as protecting us and our future together allowed him to assert himself better.

"You have every right to question us on that, and our only defense would be to say it was sheer stupidity," Angel answered. "That being said, I would like to point out that we learn incredibly quickly from our mistakes, and our efforts to correct this problem aren't simply focused on this one issue but all security issues we might face. In a way, you might say we are also looking for mentors in bringing on your company."

"So you're looking to add on consulting as well as security," Elaine interjected, knowing full well they were looking for us to help them out of the goodness of our hearts. "Just so you know, Mr. Norlund is sought after by hundreds of people looking to pick his brain about things, but there are only so many openings in his schedule to make that happen. You're looking at an easy five figures just for the ability to reach out to Mr. Norlund alone, but if you're thinking of having the same opportunity for all three men here, that would be more in the six-figure world."

Xavier nearly spat out his water at her candor. "That doesn't come with bringing them on for security? All companies offer a support team."

"Oh, we most certainly do," Halstead pointed out. "That would be provided through our IT support team, not from me directly. Enigma has more than one hundred thousand clients worldwide, so there's no possible way any of the three of us could keep up with that. Not to mention the hours we'd have to keep."

"I see..." Angel murmured. "Then to you, we'd be just another client."

Now it was my turn to step in. "It seems there is an expectation here that we're not understanding. Was there somewhere along the way that you were told we'd be able to offer you specialized services you aren't paying for?"

"Zimina—"

I raised a hand, cutting him off. "I'm going to stop you right there. Zimina and our company have a complicated relationship, but I will tell you right now that whatever she said it's a lie. There is no agreement between our company and her to offer extras to her clients. That's something she's been saying and doing for years, and we've even taken her to court over it. I really can't believe the bitch is still trying to pull that scam."

Zimina working with Solarbyte was one of the things that Elaine had uncovered in her search of the company. It wasn't hard to find information on our lawsuit with Zimina, so I wasn't shocked that Elaine already knew about it. Halstead hadn't had time to look into the matter further to ensure this sort of thing wasn't happening, but it was clear she hadn't changed her ways.

"She didn't promise it," Xavier stated. "All she did was mention that you guys like to mentor younger, up-and-coming people in the tech world, so we assumed you'd want to help."

"Son," Halstead started, giving the man a hard look. "In what reality are you considered new or up and coming? You two own one of the biggest video game companies in the world. Do not insult us by believing you thought it was based on age alone. Clearly, you are smarter than that."

Angel held up both hands as if to stand between the verbal battle playing out between them. "Clearly, we've gotten off on the wrong foot somehow, and I'd like us all to take a step back."

Halstead sat back in his chair, crossing his arms and looking like a grumpy bear who'd gotten his chew toy taken away. "Why don't you just tell us what you're looking to get out of hiring us, and I'll tell you if one, we are interested or two, if we want to take you on. Right now, you're looking like a lot more work than I think is worth it. Out of respect for what you've done in the industry at such a young age, I agreed to take this dinner meeting, which is taking away from other things I'd rather be doing."

As if the universe knew we needed it, the server returned with our drinks and a light salad to start off the meal.

"If you don't mind, I think it's probably safe to put in another round of drinks right away," I suggested, making Elaine smack my leg playfully as she took a dainty sip out of her gin and tonic.

Damn, is there anything not perfect about this woman?

Fourteen

Kerian

The rest of the meal was rather boring as we listened to the brothers tell us their woes about the past week's events. I noted all the things they'd done wrong and where I'd need to improve things along the way. That is, if they ended up hiring us and if we took on the job, a matter still up for debate. No matter how droll our company was, the food was just outstanding.

The pan-seared scallops with champagne sauce melted in your mouth with how perfectly they were cooked. Then came the duck confit with roasted vegetables that I devoured every single bite of. It was over too quickly, but Elaine took pity on me and gave me her leftover roasted vegetables she didn't want to eat. It seems our girl wasn't a fan of peppers or mushrooms, so I guess that means more for me.

"So what do you think?" Xavier asked as our dinner dishes were being collected. "Have we done enough to deserve your help?"

The room fell silent at the flippant words that had just come from that man's mouth. Angel looked at his brother horrified and tried to quickly fix the damage he'd just done. "I realize that sounded rather antagonistic, but I think what—"

"No," Xavier snapped, slicing his hand through the air. "From the moment we stepped foot in this room, they've done nothing but belittle us by treating us like children. We've worked our asses off to get here, building the company from the ground up. I get that Mr. Norlund is one of the most respected people in this tech world, however that doesn't mean you can treat us like idiots."

Welp, it looks like we'll be getting a free dinner out of this, and that's about it.

There was no way Halstead would let something like that slide.

What these boys didn't realize was that it wasn't the money in the bank that made them our equal. Each of us had given our blood, sweat, and tears to get to where we are now. Solarbyte had only been around for five years, and Enigma was going to be turning thirty this year. It had taken ten years of endless labor for Halstead to obtain that first defense contract that put him on the map. That man earned the right to be respected by all who came after him, including myself. He might not program anymore, but that's what built this empire. Fuck, I still went to him when something didn't make sense to get another perspective, and he could pick up on things as if he'd never been away from the keyboard.

"Instead of puffing out your chest and beating your fist on it like some alpha gorilla demanding respect, maybe you should think about why you don't have it in the first place," Halstead commented as he traced a finger aimlessly around the rim of his whiskey glass. "As everyone knows, respect isn't just given, it's earned. So why don't I respect you? That's the question you should be getting all ruffled about because if I don't respect you, chances are no one around you does either. Your own brother doesn't respect you, so how can I?"

"Angel respects me," Xavier snapped. "That's beside the point, I asked you if we made the cut or not."

"No," Halstead answered simply. "You most certainly did not make the cut. In fact, I have one piece of advice to share with Angel before I ask that you both leave before the dessert comes. Fire your brother."

"What?" Xavier demanded, shooting to his feet and knocking over the chair. "Who the fuck do you think you are to say something like that?"

"A man who once had to fire a person who was very dear to me at that time in my life. You might say we were once brothers," Halstead shared. "He wasn't good for my company, wanted to cut corners, take too many risks, and in the end, I had to cut him out of the company. I bought out his shares and paid him handsomely for them so he wasn't left without anything while he decided what to do with his life. However, not having him was the game-changer I needed before I got that defense contract. That was all the confirmation I needed. So, Angel, if you ever decide to fire your brother from the company that he already does so little for, we'll talk about how Enigma can help your business."

Angel looked at Halsted with a pained expression. It was clear he already knew that one of his biggest issues was his brother. However, it wasn't that easy to cut a person, especially a family member, out of the business.

"Thank you for your time," Angel murmured and pulled out a checkbook from his pocket, filled it out, and handed it to Halstead. "Your consulting fee as well as enough to cover dinner... my way of apologizing for taking up your time this evening."

"Don't fucking do that," Xavier grumbled. "The old man didn't give you any advice worth listening to."

My heart hurt for the kid—his brother would sink him if he weren't careful. I'd heard, like the others, that he was the one to say that security wasn't a priority over the ability to get more games and updates out. Now they had a PR nightmare, and their one hope in fixing it just asked them to leave.

"Shut your damn mouth, Xa. You've done more than enough tonight," Angel barked, which interestingly enough, had Elaine jumping in surprise.

When it was clear Xavier wasn't going to play nice, I stood, planting my hands on the table. "You've been asked to leave. I suggest you do so while it's been requested nicely. If you want to play with the big dogs, then I suggest you realize when you've lost a fight."

Angel grabbed his brother's jacket and hauled him out of the room just as the server was entering through the other half of the double doors. The woman gasped and spun, nearly dumping the tray full of dessert. Since I was already standing, I caught the tray and held it steady until the server regained her balance.

"Thank you." She sighed, clutching a hand to her chest. "Spilling this would have been a nightmare."

Glancing at the food, I understood why. It had been dessert fondue with bowls of steaming hot caramel and chocolate that had little burners underneath to keep them warm. Once I was sure the woman had the tray, I took my seat again, excited for the treat. I wasn't a major sweets person, but this type of thing I could get behind since I could control how sweet it was. As the waitress set out the items for us to dip, I kept trying to find out where the cinnamon scent was coming from.

No, it wasn't just cinnamon. It was almost like a chai with the clove and cinnamon spiciness but the warmth of vanilla. The scent had me all fucked up because I couldn't place where it was emanating from, and I *needed* to know. My mouth was watering, but at the same time, my cock was getting harder by the second. Finally, I closed my eyes and let my nose lead me to the source. When I felt the warmth of skin under my lips as I let myself drown in this spicy heaven I found myself in, I snapped open my eyes.

Here I was up in Elaine's personal space with my face buried in her neck and the rumble of a purr in my chest. Two things registered in my brain at that moment. Elaine was an Omega who I was scent-paired with, and she was in motherfucking heat.

"Elaine," I managed to rasp out as I fought against the urge to ravage her body that was screaming for an Alpha. "It would appear you might have left a few things out about yourself on your application."

"Kerian," Halstead snapped. "What the hell do you think you're doing? I realize we agreed to test out a personal relationship with Elaine, but don't you think..." Halstead paused as Elaine let out a gasp in reaction to me taking her breast in my hand and finding her nipple.

In doing that, the subtle perfume she'd been releasing exploded, filling the air with her spicy-sweet scent. My lips placed teasing, featherlight kisses down her neck, and I used my other hand to slide off the fabric covering her shoulder, revealing the perfect skin underneath for me to keep kissing.

"Holy fuck," Halstead blurted.

"More like thank fuck," Quintin interjected. "This changes everything."

Forcing myself to pull back, I looked at my other lovers watching me with our Omega. Their pupils were blown, nostrils flared, and chests heaved as they tried to draw in her scent deeper.

"Tricky, tricky, Omega," I purred, grasping her chin and turning her to face me. There was a mix of fear and unfocused need brought on by the heat. "Did you know you were ours?" I questioned.

"Yes," she whispered. "The second I met you all, I knew we were scent-paired."

"Then why lie to us? Do you find us so unappealing that you needed to hide who and what you are to us?" I pressed, needing to know where we stood before anything went further.

If she didn't want us, then I was certainly not going to force myself on a woman, heat or no heat. There were plenty of other ways to deal with that issue. None of this made sense—why work with us? Why entertain the idea of dating us if she knew we were already hers? Yes, there were those who were scent-pairs who decided to go their separate ways, as it wasn't a biology without flaws. However, ninety percent of the time, those who were scent-paired were perfect for each other in most ways.

"I'm hiding from someone," she admitted. "I've been running a long time, and it's safer to be a Beta."

"*Who?*" Halstead demanded, but I glanced past her and shook my head slightly.

Now was not the time to deal with that. A cry tore out of her as a wave of need hit her, pulsing through the air, calling to the three of us, demanding we satisfied our Omega's needs.

"Elaine—"

"Lainey, please call me Lainey," she corrected. "I fucking hate the name Elaine."

Why the hell had she chosen it then? No, that's not what I needed to worry about right now. After we settled things with her heat, we would circle back to all these other matters.

"Lainey, you're in heat," I pointed out, unsure if she realized it or not. "Do you want us to help you through this?"

She started to shake her head and wobble around like she was drunk. I grasped her face in both hands so I could keep her focused on me. "No, we can't do that. Then you'll be sad when I leave. No getting attached."

"Lainey," I snapped, using my bark to pull her out of the heat haze.

I'd heard many things about heats, and I'd even seen the beginnings of a few over the years. However, I'd never seen one hit so intensely that it literally made her act like she was drunk. The bark seemed to do the trick and snapped her back to her more normal self.

"Lainey, we need to get you out of here. What I need to know is if we are taking you back to your home, where you'll deal with your heat, or if we are taking you back home with us. If you come back to our home, we're going to fuck you through this heat, understood? I want it to be crystal clear what you're agreeing to."

Her stunning hazel gaze seemed so lost at what to do, but I wasn't going to make the choice for her. She needed to say in her own words how this was going to go down. None of us could live with the knowledge that we'd taken advantage of our Omega.

"Take me home with you. I won't be able to handle this heat on my own," Lainey answered. "I skipped a heat this year already, so this is gonna be intense."

"Thanks for the warning, but I have a feeling the three of us will find a way to manage," I murmured before I slid my hand to the back of her neck and slammed my lips to hers.

She tasted like fucking heaven.

Fifteen

Lainey

My brain seemed to short-circuit as Kerian kissed me. It's almost like my body exploded with need as my scent-pair pulled me onto his lap so I was straddling him. His touch on my burning skin felt like the sweetest relief, cooling the fire building within me. Unable to fight my attraction and need for him, I simply stopped fighting, allowing myself to fall into the depths of my heat. When this ended, I'm sure I'll be cursing myself, but right now there was nothing in this world I wanted more than to be naked with his cock inside me.

"More," I rasped as our kiss broke. "I need more."

"Oh, you'll get more, my needy girl, but first, I think it's best we get you out of this restaurant," Kerian reasoned.

For the first time in my adult life, I let out an Omega whine to voice my displeasure at his choice.

His hand shifted to grasp the front of my throat and gripped it tightly enough, even in the haze of my heat, he had my attention. "That's not playing fair, you little vixen. Keep pulling that kind of stunt, and you'll get more than you bargained for. It's taking everything we have not to rip your fucking dress off, rub you down in this chocolate sauce, and eat you out for dessert."

That had my slick gushing out of me at the mere thought of them doing that. *Fuck, I needed to get fucked like right now.* "Yes, please. Can we do that?"

Kerian's eyes went wide, and his gaze shifted to one of them behind me. "Did you hear that, Halstead, we have a performer on our hands. That seems like something more up your alley."

"It most certainly does. Shall we put it to the test?" Halstead asked, and I could hear the clink of dishes being moved.

While I realized I should take note of what Halstead was doing, all I could focus on was the man before me. I tugged and loosened his tie, yanking it over his head and tossed it aside. Now I could start unbuttoning his crisp white shirt revealing his skin for me to touch and savor. When I got enough of it exposed, I started to kiss down his neck as I rocked my hips against the cock I could feel resting along his thigh. Kerian was packing some major equipment, and I couldn't wait to get my hands, mouth, and pussy around it.

"One of you better take her now, or I'm going to see how hard it is to rip fucking silk off a woman." Kerian groaned as I flicked my tongue over his nipple. "Fuck, that feels so fucking good, my naughty little vixen."

Large hands grabbed my waist and pulled me off Kerian which had me mewling in need, reaching for him.

"Shh, doll, I've got you," Halstead murmured, the roughness of his beard making me shiver as he kissed my neck.

He placed me on my butt only long enough to turn me around to face him before he picked me up again. Instantly, I wrapped my legs around him as I curled my fingers along the back of his neck. His deep blue eyes seemed to drink me in with a look that was far less tortured than they had been since he kissed me.

"Do you realize the emotional shitstorm you caused in my family because you didn't admit what you are to us? Here I thought I almost cheated on my partners with a strange woman I'd barely known but desperately wanted to be close to," Halstead informed me, a slight frown on his features.

That bothered me much more than it should have, but I didn't want him to be upset with me. "I'm sorry," I whispered. "Finding three men I was scent-paired to was the last thing I expected to find when I arrived at this job, and I didn't know how to handle it."

"Now, that I understand, but you should have spoken up after what happened. Plus, I distinctly remember you getting mad at me in return," he countered.

"I will never be the *other* woman in a man's life. All you told me was that you had someone, but you didn't come clean with me either. It made me feel horrible for making a pass at you in the first place. Committed men are off limits," I explained.

"Yes, but scent-pairs will never be the other woman, they will be the only woman," Halstead stated. "Packs only have one Omega, and when you have a scent-pair, that's it. The search is over, and you've met the perfect match."

"What if you already had an Omega, and I came along and ruined everything?" I pressed.

"That's not something you need to worry about because we don't, and we never will now that we have you," Halstead assured me before capturing my lips in another life-altering kiss that exceeded the one we had in my kitchen.

It was most likely because I was in heat, and any physical touch sent me through the roof, but I was here for it. Bring on the overstimulated endorphins and dopamine dump that made up the bubble I was existing in right now. My nails scraped along his scalp as I shifted the angle to kiss him deeper, making him groan. I hadn't noticed we were moving until my back touched the surface of what I assumed to be the table. Halstead let his hands slide up my legs, pushing the fabric out of the way until it was bunched around my waist.

He drew back, looking down at me with an Alpha hunger so strong it made me grin. Right now, I was the trapped little bunny with the big burly bear looming over me, teeth bared, ready to eat me. My response to that was to let my legs fall open as he took a step back, and I released my hold on him.

"Fuck me, she wasn't wearing underwear this whole time," Kerian muttered in an almost pained voice.

"Look at her," Quintin said, his voice having a tinge of awe to it. "She's dripping wet, and her scent is making me want to bury my face between her legs and lap it all up."

Seeing and feeling the three of them standing there watching me as I bared myself to them kicked my outrageous libido into supersonic. "Someone needs to touch or fuck me. I'm about to lose my mind with need."

Halstead shrugged out of his jacket and handed it to Quintin, then rolled up his sleeves to reveal his forearms. God, it was like watching porn happen right before my very eyes. My breath quickened as I groped around for something to hold on to, or I was going to roll right off this table and tackle someone.

Kerian noticed my struggle and came around behind me, taking each hand, drawing them above my head, and pinned them to the table. "Be a good little vixen and stay right where you've been put."

Now that Halstead tucked the length of his tie into his shirt to ensure it stayed out of the way, he pulled up a chair and sat before me. He traced my leg starting at my ankles, removing my heels, then let them stroke over my skin as he moved upward. When he got past my knees, he started to massage the flesh of my inner thigh, slowing his progress toward the holy land. I panted, watching his every move, small sounds of need and pleasure slipping through my lips.

This was pure torture.

"Quintin, can you hand me a small cup of the chocolate fondue and a spoon?" Halstead requested.

A moment later, Quintin was handing them over to him, but instead of going back to stand behind Halstead to watch, he came to stand at my side. Reaching out, he brushed a few strands of hair off my face that had been irritatingly close to my eye.

"You are simply ravishing, Lainey," he remarked as his fingers traced along my jaw and his thumb brushed over my lips. "To think I would be gifted such an honor as to be your scent-pair alongside my packmates."

I let my tongue flick out to lick the tip of his thumb, making him hiss with pleasure. "Kiss me, Quintin."

"You want me to kiss you?" he asked, seeming genuinely surprised.

"Desperately," I answered, arching my body toward him since I couldn't draw him to me with my hands.

He seemed to hesitate for a moment, then let his fingers slide into my hair, cupping my head as he leaned over. His kiss was tentative, almost as if he was afraid to hurt me, so I nipped at his lower lip, making him jerk back from me. I watched as his intelligent green eyes searched my face.

"You're not going to hurt me, I promise," I assured him. "Kiss me just like you would your other lovers. I'm no different because I'm an Omega."

"No, you're different because you're a woman," he whispered just loud enough for me to hear. "I've never..."

I could feel myself melt at the sweetness of this man. "No matter the gender, if you kiss with your feelings, you will never be wrong. Same with sex. The mechanics are exactly the same, but I have a few more choices for where you want to thrust your cock into."

Kerian snorted behind me. "I cannot believe you just said that."

Shrugging, I smirked. "Well, it's true."

Before anything else could be said on the matter, something hot was being drizzled on my pussy, making me gasp. With Quintin still hovering over me, I couldn't see past him to find out what the hell Halstead was doing down there. Then the sensation of his tongue stroking over my skin cleared all questions from my mind as I moaned. The beautiful bastard really had covered me in chocolate and was eating me like dessert. Arching, I squirmed my hips trying to get his mouth right where I wanted it, but the Alpha knew what he was doing and avoided putting any chocolate on my most needy part.

Quintin took this as the perfect opportunity to ease my suffering as he kissed me again. This time there was no hesitation, and he owned me as he thrust in his tongue, twining it with mine and making me whimper. I was utterly at these men's mercy with Kerian holding my hands hostage while Quintin feasted on my mouth and Halstead reapplied his chocolate dessert to my body.

Just when I thought my body was going to explode with the pent-up need my heat was driving, Kerian took pity on me. "H, I think you need to give her something. At this point, she's going to be perfuming so strongly they'll be able to smell it in the next room. Then we're going to end up with a restaurant of horny Alphas looking for the Omega in heat."

Halstead didn't say a word one way or the other. He simply dragged his knuckles through my slick, letting his fingers run on either side of my clit, making me scream into Quintin's mouth. When he got to my entrance, he straightened his fingers and slipped them inside. There was no resistance as my body welcomed the intrusion with open arms begging for more. With a skill I've never experienced before, he used his fingers to stroke in a rhythmic fashion as if tapping out the beat of a song. Yet somehow, he managed to have his fingers hit my G-spot every time.

Tap-tap-tap-tap—*stroke*.

It was inconsistent in its pattern, not allowing me to get used to it or numb from the assault on my senses. Quintin slowly pulled back from our kiss, his eyes slightly hazy with the enjoyment of what we'd just been doing.

He looked up and motioned for Kerian to let go. "I want to see her breasts."

"Yeah, not gonna argue with that suggestion," Kerian agreed as he released me from his hold.

Quintin smoothed his hands down my neck and over my shoulders, taking the dress with him. Once my arms were free, Kerian caught them again, assuming the same position as before. "Sorry, vixen, but I just don't trust you to be a good girl right now."

Frowning down at my chest, he took in the silicon bra I'd used to hold the girls together while wearing a backless dress.

"What do I do with this?" Quintin asked.

"Peel it the fuck off so I can feel your hands on me," I directed. "It's just sticky, so rip it off like a Band-Aid."

He didn't seem convinced but grabbed the edge of one of them and did just that. With one quick snap of the wrist, my breasts were free, and he was holding a pair of chicken cutlets. He regarded them with disdain as he placed them on the table before returning his attention to me. Evidently, Halstead was feeling like his work was going unnoticed and latched his lips around my clit and sucked—hard.

With a scream, I arched off the table, but Kerian quickly smothered the sound with his lips as he kissed me. Halstead kept up his finger-fucking and clit-sucking action as Quintin explored my chest. Kerian seemed quite content to swallow down all the elicit sounds coming out of my mouth, shifting his hold to just below my elbows. He'd maneuvered me more to the side, putting his body closer to mine, and with my hands now free, I tugged down the zipper and slipped a hand into his pants.

Kerian growled as I grasped the base of his cock. "Vixen, what did I tell you about being a good girl?"

It took me two tries to form words, but I managed to answer, "That I couldn't be one."

"H, make it quick," Kerian ordered. "Our Omega doesn't mind a public setting, and I'm on the verge of telling Jean-Marc it was worth it as we get banned for life from here."

This caused Halstead to chuckle, which then vibrated his mouth, sending shockwaves through my body from my clit. He took the suggestion to heart, though, as he thrust harder, hooking those two fingers so they hit just right. Then when I thought I might be able to contain my soul in my body, Quintin wrapped his lips around one of my nipples sucking, licking, and nibbling as if unsure what was the best choice, so he did them all.

My first orgasm of the night came barreling down the line like a freight train and slammed into me. If Kerian hadn't put his hand over my mouth to smother my cries, there's no doubt in my mind that the whole damn restaurant would have heard me. Halstead turned me into a shaking, shivering mess as he continued to lap at my pussy, leisurely flexing his fingers to set off one aftershock after another. This seemed to appease my pussy, which was clamping down in search of a knot to squeeze.

The whole purpose of a heat was to attract Alphas to breed with the Omega when they were at their most fertile. There were measures you could take if you didn't want to have kids just yet or ever because the only way to cool a heat was medically or with cum. Our Omega bodies didn't believe we'd done our job unless we were on the receiving end of more cum than I'd ever like to admit to. However, since I wasn't planning on having a heat anytime soon, I didn't have the medication for the guys or myself. Looks like we were going to play a game of *how lucky do I feel*?

"Okay, that seemed to do the trick," Quintin announced. "Kerian, text the driver, and let him know we need to leave right away. Halstead, I don't care how you take care of the bill, but that needs to happen outside this room. I'm going to wrap her up in my suit coat. It should help ease Lainey and keep the whole restaurant from scenting her."

Kerian grabbed Quintin by the lapels and kissed him long and deep. "I fucking love when you get all bossy, Quin."

At the sight of them, my body decided it rather enjoyed it as well, causing the fire of my heat to flare back to life.

"No, no, no, vixen," Kerian chided as he helped me get the top half of my dress back on sans bra. "You can't get all excited right now. You need to keep things cool, calm, and collected."

"Then stop doing things that I find so exciting," I quipped. "You three are hot all on your own, but when you manhandle each other like that, it's sexy as sin."

Kerian dropped his head to my shoulder. "Fuck, woman, you're really trying to test all the control I have, aren't you?"

"I feel like we've already established I'm not the good-girl type, especially when my body is demanding a fuck," I pointed out.

"Enough," Quintin cut in. "Kerian, did you do as I asked?"

"The driver will be waiting for us the second we step through the doors," Kerian assured. "Let's get her wrapped up in your jacket."

I was going to argue that I didn't need it, but the second it settled around my shoulders, I shut my mouth and enjoyed being wrapped in Quintin's scent. The bright ginger and comforting green tea had me taking long, slow breaths, savoring the aroma. He scooped me up in his arms and tucked my head against his neck protectively.

"All I want you to do is close your eyes and count my heartbeats until we get to the car. We need you to keep your heat under control until we get you out of the building," Quintin instructed. "I don't think you realize how strong your scent is right now. I realize that I don't know much about Omegas, and that will change, but this seems out of the norm, even to me. If we weren't Alphas who had complete control over their biology, I don't think we'd be leaving this restaurant until your heat was over."

While I don't think this was his intention, a spike of fear shot through me, quelling my heat and banking its flames. I knew exactly what he was talking about. I'd seen it before, even experienced it myself during my first heat as well as when I learned not to forgo both heats. Those memories drove me to make sure I was safe when my heats happened, which was why I was willing to let these men take care of me. The fear of being left alone in my apartment, where anyone could break in and assault me, wasn't the experience I wanted.

Kerian held open the door, my shoes and clutch already in his other hand, making me want to kiss him for being so thoughtful. I did as Quintin asked and closed my eyes, focusing my attention on the sound of his heartbeat. The strong, steady rhythm was comforting, and I could feel my heart slowing from the panic I'd felt moments ago. It took more attention than I assumed to keep count of his heartbeats. Each time I lost track, I started over again, but I knew the purpose of it was to give me something to keep my mind busy, not worrying about the people in the restaurant we were passing.

I knew the moment we were outside as the cool air teased my hot skin, making me sigh with relief.

"You got her?" Kerian asked.

"Yes, I'll be fine if I take the first seat," Quintin responded.

Another pair of hands helped to keep us balanced as we made it into the limousine without Quintin surrendering his hold of me. When I felt like he was seated, I lifted my head, watching Kerian climb in and move to sit opposite. Halstead wasn't with us, but I remembered he was in charge of taking care of the bill, so it might be a moment for him to get that settled. My body pulsed with need, almost as if it was a physical thing inside me demanding to be acknowledged. It caused my muscles to tighten and my breath to catch at the force of it. A whine emitted from my mouth as the wave rolled over me, taking its sweet time to pass.

"I need one of you, please," I begged, sweat breaking out on my skin, something that had never happened before.

In a fleeting moment of clarity and realization, it dawned on me that I'd been forced to take that medication. Clearly, going to the pharmacy for the suppressant had been pointless unless it was the reason I'd been able to make it this late in the day because of it. God only knows, but right now, all I cared about was my pussy getting the attention she desperately was screaming for.

Quintin shifted me so my back was to him and urged my legs to fall on either side of his legs. There was a slit in this dress, but it only came up to my knee as this was a classier dress than others I've worn. In an action that had me swearing, impressed, and, if possible, even more turned on, Quintin grabbed the fabric and ripped it from the end of the slit up to my hip. That done, he swept the fabric aside like a curtain revealing my weeping pussy to Kerian.

"You need to help me do this," Quintin told Kerian. "I can't fail her, not now of all times."

Kerian's expression was one of love and understanding. "You won't fail her, just like you've never failed me or H, but I will help you forever and always."

Sixteen

Quintin

I had to prove myself.

Lainey needed me, and I was sorely lacking in skills and knowledge when it came to Omegas as well as women. Of course, I knew the basics that everyone was taught in school and biology classes, but I'd never been interested in women. The trauma I'd suffered at the hands of a woman who was supposed to love me unconditionally left me with a bitter taste in my mouth. It wasn't that I'd written off all women or didn't find some women I was comfortable being around. The core of the matter was I never thought I had a chance past basic friendship.

The guys would yell at me for thinking this, but who would want an emotional basket case like me?

Now here I was in a limousine with a woman in my lap. Not just any woman, an Omega who I was scent matched with. The need to bury my face in the back of her neck and lick her skin, knowing Lainey would taste as amazing as she smelled, was hard to resist. Right now, it wasn't about me but about her. As I held her, I could feel that last wave of her heat growing stronger, having still been denied a knot. We needed to maintain it until we got home, and it was safe for us to give her that. When a knot expands, locking the Omega to the Alpha, it could last anywhere from fifteen minutes to forty-five, depending on the situation.

Meaning if any of us knotted her here or in the restaurant, we'd literally be stuck for a minimum of fifteen minutes. That was a risk none of us were willing to make with something so precious to us. Not every Alpha had a scent-paired Omega, and with so many people spread out all over the world, it wasn't always a guarantee you'd be able to find them. Thus, it was why our culture as a whole viewed them almost as soulmates, a person who completed their pack in a way no one else could. How true all that was, I didn't know, but I was coming to realize there was a special connection with Lainey.

I wouldn't say I was instantly madly in love with her, but my instinct was to protect, nurture, and give affection to Lainey. Everything in me wanted to provide for her. While that might sound like an absolute cop-out to many, I would tell them I didn't believe it either until this very moment. It's like how people try to describe the instantaneous love you have for a child the moment it's born. You had no reason to feel those emotions, but our biology knew it had to do something to protect this small life that couldn't protect itself. Therefore, it triggers a bond between parent and child to ensure that the child can grow to become an adult furthering the species.

However, even knowing this was a biological response toward Lainey, and we had a lot of work ahead of us if she chose to be part of our family, I was going to enjoy the feeling for as long as it lasted. The sound of her breath catching as I slipped my fingers between her legs, lightly stroking her pussy, made me purr for her. My chest rumbled with the deep sound as I used my other hand to grasp the front of her throat, my forearm nestled between her breasts.

"Did you know you're the first person I've ever purred for?" I murmured in her ear as I held her tightly against me. "Alphas only purr for their lovers, children, and their Omegas. I have two lovers who mean everything to me, but it seems that this sound was meant for you and you alone."

Tilting her head slightly, I kissed and nipped along her neck as I slowly toyed with the outer parts of her pussy, teasing the entrance that was practically vibrating for me to enter. The erotic sounds of her whimpers and cries made my cock so hard I feared I might come without even touching it.

Spotting movement out of the corner of my eye, I saw Kerian across from us, his cock out and his hand fisted around it, stroking it lazily. "Look at Kerian. Do you see what you're doing to him? How your scent is so intoxicating, it makes us hard the second we smell it. I'm fairly certain with just your sounds alone, you could make one of us come. I know I'm on the verge. Then there's this seductive body you have, plush with soft skin and enough of you to grab hold of as we fuck you into the mattress when we get home."

The more I talked, the faster her breathing became, and the thundering speed at which her heart rate was going felt as if she was running a marathon. I could feel the frantic pace under my grasp, and it had me gripping ever so slightly tighter and forcing her head back so I could capture her lips as I slipped one finger inside her. To my shock and amazement, she came instantly, the walls of her pussy clamping down on my finger as if it feared I would leave. Instead, I languidly stroked my finger in and out of her, drawing out the orgasm and moving on to the next one I hoped to achieve fairly quickly.

I broke our kiss as the car door opened to reveal Halstead, who had to pause a moment as her perfume slammed into him. "Holy fucking shit, I think I just dry orgasmed right here." He grunted. "Why is it so strong? There's no way it should be like this, even if she skipped one. This is next-level potent."

"They made me take a drug," Lainey muttered as she sagged in my arms. "I didn't want to, but I had no choice."

My brows snapped together. "Who?"

Pulling out my fingers, I shifted her so she was now sitting sideways. Halstead kneeled on the floor of the limousine as it pulled away from the restaurant, placing a hand on her bare knee. "Lainey, what kind of drug?"

She shook her head vigorously. "No, I can't tell you. I shouldn't have even said that... it will get me killed."

The stormy expression that crossed Halstead's face reflected my own emotions. "Doll, there is no fucking way I would ever let someone harm you. I know nothing has been set or agreed upon, but no matter what you choose to do at the end of your heat, you are still our scent-paired Omega. No one better fucking harm a hair on your head, or I swear to God I will take all the power I have in this world and the next to crush them."

I couldn't have agreed more with that sentiment. None of us were foolish enough to believe that just because we had this interaction and understood we were scent-paired, it changed things between her and us. We were all grown adults with lives, homes, and careers. It wasn't like we could just throw everything out the window and start a new life. If we weren't willing to do that for her, how could we expect her to do that exact same thing for us? Everything was about communication and negotiation, which would take time.

"Not them... you won't be able to touch them," she answered. "We can't talk about this. They are always listening, watching, and know your weaknesses. Please forget I said anything. After this heat, everything will be back to normal."

She was right about one thing, now wasn't the time to talk about it. However, that didn't mean we'd forget or drop the matter. If someone threatened her to this extent, forcing her to change even her name to keep safe, then we would get to the bottom of it.

The rest of the drive home was quiet as Lainey dozed in my arms. Something I felt like I should treasure since I knew I wouldn't be able to do that unless I felt some kind of trust in that person. We lived outside the city in a more rural area which consisted of older homes that had once been farmland. It gave us bigger plots of land which meant distance between houses that Halstead favored. The grumpy bear liked his privacy and felt that two hundred and eighteen acres might do the trick. Not to mention a gated entrance to our driveway which was two miles long. He didn't want anyone to see what went on in our daily lives, leaving us free to do as we pleased.

Kerian and I moved into his home instead of finding a new place. This wasn't because it was more than large enough for us and three other people, but neither of us had a home of our own. We'd both been renting, and Halstead hadn't done much with the place, having only owned it for a few years, so together we made it our own. Halstead and I had similar classic tastes whereas Kerian would have preferred things more modern, yet we managed to come to a compromise with shared spaces but allowed each other to have our own rooms and offices we did with as we pleased.

Our limousine pulled up to the front of our brick and limestone home or estate, as Halstead referred to it. This time, I handed Lainey off to H since getting out of the limousine proved to be more of a feat than getting in.

Ruth, our housekeeper and cook, greeted us at the front door. "Welcome home, gentlemen. Kerian alerted me to what was going on, and while the nest room isn't perfect, it will work for now. I plan to stop in tomorrow and make a whole bunch of things you can come down to grab that won't need to be cooked, just heated if you like. Do we know if your Omega has any food allergies?"

That had us all pausing for a moment.

"I see. Well, I'll steer clear of some of the major problem foods until we have an answer to that. Sezer and I will keep to the coach house unless you need something from us. Don't hesitate to ask. I'm going to be driving my men crazy not having the normal work to do while we give you this time," Ruth said with a chuckle.

Ruth was a Beta who'd been working for Halstead since he bought the place. Somehow, she ended up in a relationship with the two Beta brothers, Sezer and Adem, we hired to tend the grounds. They lived on the property in the two-story coach house set a little further back on the property, which made it convenient for all of us.

"Can I just say how happy I am for the three of you," Ruth gushed, clutching her hands together. "I know the three of you love each other as much as I love my husbands, but I can't wait to see how this brings your family closer."

"Ruth," Adem called from the kitchen. "Enough, woman. You've said your piece, and now it's time to let them be. You're acting like their mother popping by during their honeymoon."

That had Kerian snorting and trying to cover it up by coughing into his hand. Ruth gave him a glare telling me it hadn't worked, but she gave us all one more assessing look and turned on her heel.

Adem caught her hand when she was close enough, tugged her to his side, and kissed her temple. "Always gotta put your nose in everyone's business, don't you?" He then turned to look at us. "We'll make sure the place is still standing when you emerge, so don't worry about a thing. So..." he hesitated as if wondering if he should say the next part but gave in, "... enjoy yourselves." Kerian gave a salute and headed upstairs.

Our rooms, offices, and a private living room were on the second floor, where we spent most of our time. The third floor is the library where Halstead kept his rare books and my vinyl record collection.

"Hey, you guys go ahead. I need to make sure Tater-Tot is settled for the night," Kerian informed us as he paused at the landing. "The last thing we need is a howling bulldog interrupting things."

"If you didn't spoil him so much, he wouldn't be so codependent," I pointed out.

Kerian just shrugged. "Too late for that, the pup's already three. Not sure I'm gonna be changing much now."

Tater-Tot had an automatic feeder and waterer, along with multiple doggie doors for him to go out whenever he needed to. Ruth was also one of his favorite people and would be happy for her to spoil him while Kerian was busy, but I realized it wasn't about that. The two of them were partners in crime, and we didn't know how long Lainey's heat was going to last, not giving him much time to spend with the dog.

A whine of need snapped my attention to Lainey as Halstead carried her up the steps. "Pretty sure that's our signal that the lull is over," he called over his shoulder. "Make it quick, Kerian. You're the youngest of us all, and something tells me we're gonna need your stamina."

"Hey," I grumbled while jogging after him. "Did you forget that I'm ten years younger than you?"

"Nope, but I don't need to bribe you away from a canine," Halstead pointed out. "That man will get distracted and leave things to the two of us, which I'm sure we can handle for a while. However, with how intense this has been so far, I'm thinking we're gonna need all hands on deck."

"Could you two please stop talking about me like I'm some crazed sex monster," Lainey muttered as she wrapped her arms around Halstead's neck, rubbing her face against his skin. "Why the fuck do you smell so good? It's like I can't get enough of it, no matter how close I get. I just want to bathe in it."

"How you managed to control yourself around us until now is rather impressive," Halstead commented. "It's taking everything I've got not to just ravage you against the wall."

"I'd be okay with that," she commented in a soft, sultry voice. "I'm not shy when it comes to sex."

"That is becoming rather evident," I interjected as I turned the handle and shoved open the door to the nest.

Whoever H bought this house from must have had a specialty designer put this space together because the layout was amazing. The bed sat in a half-moon alcove that you could pull gauzy drapes together and make more private. Vaulted ceilings in a sloping peak formation gave the room a spacious feel. I walked over to the double doors and pulled them open, revealing a patio that looked out over the backyard. The soft evening breeze made the curtains dance at its touch.

Other than the window seat couch and the bed, there wasn't much in this room. We never really planned on needing to use it at this point in our lives. Ruth always kept up hope and made sure to clean it once a month. Thankfully, she did so the quick refreshes she did of the space could be done in the time we gave her heads-up from the restaurant. She even managed to get a small couch and simple coffee table up here. A cooler full of water bottles and sports drinks, a container of ibuprofen, and various bowls full of snacks were on the coffee table.

That woman was awfully presumptive for selecting things she felt we'd need, but I couldn't blame her. While none of us were spring chickens, we weren't geriatric either. However, something about turning forty sure made your body ache in ways it hadn't before.

Thankfully, we were incredibly active and worked out, knowing we couldn't afford to let our bodies slow us down.

"God, yes, keep doing that," Lainey moaned, making my cock pulse at the sound.

Looking over at the bed, Halstead had stripped Lainey out of her dress, and he was shirtless. The sight of her sprawled across the bed, hair loose in the soft moonlight with my lover's face back between her legs had me groaning. I made quick work of removing my clothes, folding them, and placing them neatly on the couch. Padding over to the bed, I found the alcove fit the massive bed and left more than enough room for us to move on either side.

Lainey's hands gripped the sheets as she thrashed her head from side to side at whatever Halstead was doing to her. Her mouth was open in a silent scream of pleasure as her back arched. I almost hated to intrude on the moment, but I couldn't hold back anymore and climbed up beside her. Taking her hand, I freed the sheet and gave her my cock to hold onto. She opened her glassy eyes to look at me with her heat back in full force.

"Come closer," she instructed, giving my cock a slight tug. "I want to taste you."

"Hold on," Halstead cut in, flipped Lainey onto her stomach, grabbed her hips, and pulled her ass up. "That's better," he announced and gave her right cheek a slap.

The cry that burst from her wasn't one of pain, stilling my urge to scold him for his actions. Halstead was a demanding lover, a big strong man who knew exactly what he wanted and had zero problems taking it. Of course, he always wanted pleasure and enjoyment for his partner, but we didn't know Lainey or what her boundaries were. Then again, I was always the one out of the three of us to proceed with caution.

I tucked a finger under Lainey's chin and urged her to look up at me. "You need to speak up if we go too far or you don't like something. This family is all about communication, and we expect that a person will voice their needs so we can make adjustments."

"I'll tell you if I don't like something, I promise," she answered. "Thank you, though, for always checking in with me, Quintin. Not many have in my life."

"That changes now," I warned her. "Because as long as you are in our care, I will always make sure you feel safe and comfortable with us."

Sitting up, she wrapped her arms around my neck and kissed me. Her fingers scraped along the nape of my neck, making me shiver. The bed shifted, and Lainey broke our kiss to let out a cry of ecstasy as Halstead thrust into her.

"I couldn't hold back anymore seeing the two of you like that," Halstead shared as he seated himself balls deep in her, then grabbed the back of my neck, dragging me into a kiss.

The feel of Lainey's body rubbing along mine as Halstead thrust into her was erotic on so many levels. Then the feel of her soft hand covered in slick grasped my cock and started to stroke it against her stomach. Not wanting to risk her moving away, I twined my arms around her, pressing tightly as I thrust into her hand, matching Halstead's rhythm. He saw what I was doing and used his body to sandwich her between us, lips, hands, and bodies all intertwined with each other.

"Why is this so amazing?" Lainey whispered before a moan erupted out of her as I slid a hand down to her ass and pressed against her asshole.

I didn't answer her right away, even though I knew the answer. Kerian had been blown away by this realization too, after the three of us had sex together for the first time. Personally, I wanted to know if Halstead would be the one to tell her or not. He could be an emotional man, but sometimes when it came to sex, he lost that aspect, distracted by the goal of getting everything out of the moment and his partner as he could. It was that damn competitive nature to one-up himself in performance or ability. Tonight it would be bad because, like myself, he felt he had something to prove to Lainey.

"It feels amazing, my sweet, tempting doll, because you're ours, and we are yours. Four bodies and four souls meant to fit together in harmony to create something perfect," Halstead answered, thrusting in deeper each word he wanted to make his point on.

This had her crying out, clawing at my skin as she clung to me, desperate for something to ground her as he pounded into her. The onslaught of sensation and emotion I'm sure she was feeling, if my reaction to what was happening was any clue, rendered her speechless. That is until she came screaming so loud I thought my eardrums were going to burst. Halstead slowed, but he didn't stop, which told me he hadn't come. Otherwise, he'd be knotted up in that needy pussy.

He shifted back, pulling himself free, and guided her as she crumpled to the bed panting, her body covered in a sheen of sweat. "Why didn't you knot her?" I asked, glancing at his glistening cock that was impossibly hard and twitched under my stare.

"Because I want you to be the first to knot our Omega as I come in your perfect ass while Kerian is fucking her mouth," he shared. "Speaking of the man, he better get here quickly so we can start this heat off right. We've fucked it up so far, but I really want all four of us to be together this first knotting."

Lainey chuckled, rolling onto her back, brushing her dark brown hair out of her face. "You're making it sound like this is a huge deal,

Halstead. I'm thirty-two years old, I've had more than a few heats in my life, and I know what it's like to be knotted."

Halstead and I both snarled at the casual way she mentioned sleeping with other men. While rationally, I knew none of us had any leg to stand on when it came to sleeping with others, I still wouldn't talk about it with my new lovers.

"You might have experienced being knotted before, but none of us have ever been with an Omega. Both Kerian and Quintin are skilled and talented lovers, but neither of them could ever handle my knot. They weren't built for it, and that's perfectly fine... that's what knot clamps help with if the need arises," Halstead informed her, making me blush to hear him talking so casually about it.

"H," I chided. "She doesn't want to know about that."

"Why?" he challenged. "If she's going to be with us, she should know these things. There's nothing to be ashamed of. Males aren't made to take a knot up the ass, plain and simple. While I'm sure there are some who find a way to manage it, I don't need that kind of effort from either of you. I get more than enough satisfaction from how we've been doing things, and I fucking love how we fuck."

Lainey took her foot and poked at Halstead's thigh. "You make it sound like you're never on the receiving end of the deal."

He caught her foot, but instead of being irritated with her for doing that, he started to massage her foot. "That's exactly right, doll. Let's just say I'm more of a giver than a receiver. I've never been one to enjoy that part of sex. I'd much rather focus all my attention on my partner."

She moaned as he reached a certain part of her foot, making me feel a little jealous for how good it looked like it felt. There was nothing better than the feel of his strong, rough hands on my body, with or without sex. I simply loved the fact that he was so free with his physical touch here at the house since we had to keep such a distance at the office.

"Sounds like someone is enjoying their heat," Kerian commented as he entered the room wearing only low-slung sweatpants.

"Oh, I feel like I'm going to be enjoying it a lot more now that you're here," she quipped, making me smile.

I glanced at her, seeing the delight and attraction on her face as he yanked down his sweats before joining us. She had a natural knack for adjusting her responses and mannerisms to interact with all three of us in a different way that matched the energy we gave her. It truly seemed she was a woman made to fit into our lives perfectly.

Now we just needed to make sure she stayed.

Seventeen

Lainey

The orgasm that Halstead gave me took the edge off this wave of my heat, but I could feel the next one gearing up to slap me in the face like the others had. I needed to be knotted, and it needed to happen now. This pussy of mine wasn't going to take pity orgasms any longer. Either she got to catch herself a knot, or this pussy was going to be hissing something fierce.

My hope was now that Kerian was here, Halstead would make good on his detailed vision of what would come next. I wanted to get my mouth on a cock and suck it dry as I got pounded. What would be even better is to have one of them in my ass as well as my pussy and mouth. Three men, three holes, seems like a no-brainer to me. There was still time for us to manage that before the heat was done. For now, we'll start with Halstead's idea and see where we go from there.

I curled a finger at Kerian, making him grin as he crawled across the bed toward me. "Did you know that gin is one of my favorite liquors in the whole world?" I asked, gazing up at him from where I was lying on my back.

"I did not," he commented as his hand stroked over my stomach, moving toward my breasts. "However, it doesn't surprise me that a woman with such fine taste in things would pick such a liquor."

"Oh, look at you, smooth talker." I giggled. "The reason I mentioned that is because, to me, you smell like the best gin has to offer. Now I want to see if you taste just as good," I shared as I grasped his cock and signaled for him to come closer.

Kerian groaned. "Fuck, woman, that mouth of yours is something else."

"All the more reason for you to put it to good use," I pointed out as he positioned himself so I could easily get my mouth around him. Before I started my investigation, I looked over Quintin. "How do you want me, on my back, stomach, knees? You pick whatever you'll be most comfortable with."

"I want you just how you are now," Quintin answered. "What I need is to be able to see your face and know you're enjoying what I'm doing."

That had me sitting up. "While I appreciate that sentiment, I get the feeling you're saying it like you don't think I will be enjoying myself."

"Sex is an incredibly personal thing, and everyone likes something different. Seeing as we hardly know each other on a personal level, there's a high chance I'm not going to be good at this," he reasoned.

Wrapping my arms around his neck, I drew him to me and kissed him slowly. I kept this up until he began to relax in my hold and pressed against me as his hands slid up my back. Leaning back, I coaxed him to follow until he was nestled between my legs with his upper body resting on mine. My fingers moved up his neck until they slid into his hair, and I could hold him there as I maneuvered my hips to catch the tip of his cock at my entrance. Once I got him in the door, he did the rest on his own, *slowly* pushing himself into me as if he were trying to torture me. I knew he wasn't, but it sure felt that way as my pussy screamed for someone to stuff her good and hard. Quintin wouldn't be the one to do that, but the odds were, out of Kerian and Halstead, I'd have a pretty good chance.

Finally, his hips met mine, telling me we'd managed to get all of him in me. I pulled back from the kiss and cupped his face. "Quintin, will you please fuck me until I come all over your knot as you fill me with your cum?"

His expression was shocked at my candor, but I felt like he needed to understand I wanted him *badly* right now. This wasn't a pity fuck or because I'd lost my mind to my heat. I wanted to be fucked by Quintin Price in the worst way, and it was going to happen *now*.

"How can I resist such a request?" Quintin responded as he drew back his hips then snapped them forward, making me gasp.

Could it be I've misjudged Quintin this entire time?

The other guys seemed to be willing to give Quintin a moment to get his rhythm before adding themselves into the mix. Kerian caught my chin and turned my head to where his thick cock awaited me. I opened for him and moaned as he filled my mouth, shifting slightly so he was now directly behind me and could use my whole-ass throat to fuck. He was big, and, at first, it made my jaw ache to hold it open that wide, but my heat realized what was going on and joined the party.

I felt like my skin would scald anyone who touched it, but none of the guys seemed to have any trouble. Quintin found a pace giving me long deep strokes, building my climax as he toyed with my clit. Kerian matched Quintin while he played with my nipples, finding all the ways to make me moan. Halstead watched us for a bit standing next to the bed, stroking his cock as if he was trying to take a mental picture of what was happening. It was so fucking sexy to be watched, and the look of enjoyment and appreciation on Halstead's face made it that much better.

Then he vanished, and I wanted to ask what happened, but my mouth was full of cock at the moment. I shouldn't have worried as he was back in a moment with a bottle of what looked like lube in his hand as he climbed onto the bed. It didn't take long for me to figure out he was working on getting Quintin ready as the man slammed into me and dropped his whole upper body on mine. Kerian had to pull out quickly before he choked me.

"Oh God, yes." Quintin groaned. "I love the way your mouth feels on my ass."

There was a chuckle from Halstead, and now that I could move, I spotted his face buried in Quintin's ass.

"Oh fuck, *fuck*." Quintin panted. "Yes, get that tongue in there, lick out the cum Kerian left behind last night."

I'm not sure there is a moment where I could have been more shocked at the words that were coming out of Quintin's mouth right now. This man had some major dirty-talk skill hiding, and I felt a little cheated over the whole thing.

Quintin's eyes rolled back in his head as Halstead pulled back and slipped a finger in the man. "I love those fucking thick fingers working my asshole, making sure I can take your cock when you ram it into me."

"Okay, where the hell is this coming from?" I blurted, unable to keep my thoughts to myself.

Kerian is the one who answered as he cupped my face to look up at him. "That, little vixen, is a side of Quintin only H can seem to draw out. Now the man clearly loves dirty talk, but with me, it's more on the receiving end. With Halstead, he loves to dish it out and make sure his top knows what a *good* job he's doing."

Before I could say anything else on the matter, Quintin started to thrust into me as he clung to my body in fast, hard strokes. It took me a second to realize it was the pace that Halstead was setting as he fingered Quintin. Not that I was complaining because, holy shit, it felt amazing, and the orgasm that had backed off at the interruption was now building once more.

"This feels so good, Quintin." I gasped, curious how he would react. "Yes, pound my pussy... take what you want from it."

Quintin's face was buried in my neck, and I could feel his hot breath on my skin as he moaned, grunted, and cried out at what Halstead was doing. "I never knew a woman could feel so good. The toys I've tried are nothing compared to the real thing. It's so warm, slick, and the way you clamp down on me when I hit the right spot is mind-blowing."

He'd used toys? That was an interesting tidbit I shouldn't be surprised by, but I suppose I was since he hadn't seemed all that keen on bringing a woman into the relationship.

"Okay, I think you're ready," Halstead announced, slapping Quintin on the ass. "Now come on, sit up tall like a good boy so I can hug you as I fuck you both."

Oh. My. God. These men were going to *kill* me with all this dirty talk. I thought I was more into the exhibitionism side of things and didn't get all that into the dirty talk. Clearly, I'd been missing out on what dirty talk was supposed to be.

"Doll, you better get that pretty mouth of yours around Kerian's cock. It's not fair for him to be left out of this," Halstead warned.

"That's right, my pretty little vixen, I'm going to use that hole until I'm coming down your throat, and you get to taste me for days after this," Kerian whispered as he stroked the side of my face and neck. "Open wide and let me worry about the rest."

I nodded and did as he asked, swallowing down the urge to choke as he hit the back of my throat. Taking a second to adjust and keep that from happening, he placed a pillow under my head. *Fuck, sexy and considerate. I'm never going to want to leave when this is over.*

That single thought sent a stab of fear into my gut. I couldn't think that way. This wasn't permanent, they didn't know who I really was, and if they did, I doubt they'd want to keep me as their Omega, scent-paired or not. My whole purpose in being here was to cheat them out of a code and contract I'm sure they valued, even if it was with someone they despised. Nothing about what was going on between us was real—heats clouded your judgment just like a drug or alcohol. Nothing said or done during a heat should ever be trusted.

Enjoy the moment, Lainey, because that's all it is—a moment.

Quintin cried out, bucking his hips into me as Halstead held the man in a bear hug, face resting on his shoulder as he thrust. It was hard to watch them from the angle I was at, so instead, I closed my eyes so I could feel and listen. Kerian's hands were holding me so lovingly as he fucked my mouth, making me gasp for air when he pulled back to give me a break. While I couldn't feel Halstead directly, I noticed a difference in how Quintin moved. There was a slow build as I'm sure Halstead needed Quintin to warm up and relax into being fucked. It was important since men didn't have the same natural lubrication abilities we women possess.

Once things got rolling, though, I lost track of everything else but what was happening right now. Sounds of pleasure filled the air, skin slapping, moans, the gwak-gwak of Kerian fucking my mouth, and the telltale sound of a good make-out. This enticed me to open my eyes and find Kerian and Quintin tongue fucking each other's mouths right above me.

It was hot a fuck.

That sight was all I needed before I exploded from an orgasm that had been building for way too long. Now as it wracked my body, I screamed while all my muscles went rigid, meaning the walls of my pussy slammed down around Quintin. It was hard enough he pulled away from Kerian and groaned as he dropped his head to ride the wave with me as Halstead didn't slow a beat. The screaming must have been enough vibration to set Kerian off because he pulled out enough not to get his knot stuck in my mouth and came.

"Holy fuck, I'm coming," he shouted as hot ropes of cum filled my mouth which I swallowed without reservation.

My mind wasn't firing on all cylinders right now as Quintin still rutted into me as I was coming, so before the first could even fade, I was hit with another making me arch off the bed. Thankfully, Kerian had removed himself from my mouth, or I'd have been worried about biting him. Then I felt the swell of Quintin's knot as he shouted his climax, but he started to back away, making me panic. I shouldn't have been too worried, though. Halstead was right there to slam him back into place as the knot locked us together.

There was no better feeling in the world than a knot pushing you to the limit of what you could handle, only to have it send shockwaves of euphoric pleasure through your body. Then you add the feel of his cum filling me, and for the first time since my heat came on, it truly cooled.

I reached for Quintin, needing him to hold me right now. "Please, I need to feel you," I whined.

It took a second for my words to penetrate the euphoria of climaxing the way an Alpha should in an Omega. While I know there were tools and toys that simulated getting their knot squeezed like an Omega did, it wouldn't be the same as the real deal. He leaned over and wrapped his arms around me, but instead of rolling on his side or resting on top of me right then and there, he pulled me up so I was sitting in his lap. This forced the knot deeper and made my whole body shudder as I came again and clung to Quintin.

"I think my soul has left my body." I panted. "Never have I been knotted so deep... holy shit."

Quintin brushed the hair off my shoulder so he could kiss along it and up my neck to my ear. "Does that mean I did it right?"

A shaky laugh burst out of me as I practically draped myself over him. "Oh, my sweet innocent Quinny, you just fucked my soul right out of my body. I'd say you aced that test."

Another pair of arms wrapped around us as a body pressed to my back. "I can't wait to see how I get an A-plus on my test," Kerian murmured.

Halstead, not willing to be left out of the hug, enveloped all three of us as he kissed my temple. "Just you wait, doll. I held back earlier. Let's see if you have what it takes for me to give you an outstanding grade."

"Challenge accepted," I countered, then yawned. "But I think I'm going to take a nap first. For some reason, I'm so incredibly tired I can barely keep my eyes open."

"Oh, thank God." Quintin sighed as he rested his head on my shoulder. "I know I complained before about you thinking I didn't have what it takes to keep up, but after that, I could use a break too."

With the help of the other two, Quintin and I managed to find a comfortable way to lie all curled up. Kerian and Halstead switched, and my silver bear wrapped around me, resting a hand on Quintin's thigh as I drifted off to sleep, letting out a deep sigh of contentment.

The way Kerian's cock filled me as I slowly lowered myself until I could sit down was a little overwhelming. If this is what it felt like to just have his cock in my pussy, what would his knot do to me?

I'd been able to nap for about an hour before I was needy and whimpering. Quintin slid out from between Kerian and me, letting the younger man try his luck to see if he could make me come as hard as Quintin had. His hands settled on my hips as I sat there, letting myself adjust, panting like a bitch in heat. Oh wait, that's exactly what I was.

"You doing all right there, vixen?" Kerian asked, with a cocky smirk on his lips.

I grabbed his nipple and gave it a quick pinch, making him yelp and thrust up into me. Suddenly, this joke had turned into me riding the bucking bronco of a cock, trying to stay on as he squirmed under me.

"Oh fuck!" I gasped, planting my hands on his chest. "I regret that choice."

"Why would that be, you naughty vixen? It couldn't possibly be that my cock is too much for you to handle, is it?" Kerian teased then reached up and tweaked my nipple in return. Only instead of freaking out at the gesture, I moaned and arched into the feeling. "Would you look at that? Is this how you make the kitty purr?"

Shoving his hand away as he tried to go for the other nipple, I glared at him. "What am I? A fox or a kitten, pick an animal and stick with it, or I'm going to get a complex. I won't know if I'm supposed to be sly and crafty or needy and mewling for attention."

"Lainey, I think you're selling yourself short here. Why can't you be a crafty vixen who demands attention just as a kitten would?" Kerian countered. "Personally, I think I'd shoot for the best-of-both-worlds scenario."

I leaned down so our noses almost touched and flicked out my tongue to lick the tip of his nose. "You have no idea how crafty I can be," I whispered as my nails scraped down his chest. "I know just what to do to make people see things my way so they give me what I want without ever having to demand it. Most of the time, they have no idea I'm even doing it, and that's what makes it fun and challenging. When they notice, they tend to get upset."

Kerian's fingers dug into the flesh of my hips as he held me down while his hips rolled at the feel of my nails. He groaned in pleasure, tossed his head back, and gave me a perfect chance to nip at his neck until I found the right spot and bit. As an Omega, when I bite an Alpha, it doesn't matter how hard I bite, nothing will happen other than bruised and bleeding skin, maybe an infection.

However, if an Alpha, especially one scent-paired to the Omega they planned to bite, did so, it would create a *bond* of sorts. No one can really explain why or what causes it, but it can only happen when an Alpha administers the bite. When the bond is created, they have a metaphysical ability to 'feel' their partner's emotions. Some researchers say it's to ensure that the Omega is happy and healthy, so the chances of becoming pregnant are higher when we go into heat. In this day and age, it makes no sense, but at one point, there clearly was a need to ensure the population was growing steadily. It seems to me like the only thing Omegas were built for was sex and baby-making.

My train of thought was abruptly halted when Kerian flipped us over, pulled out, and rolled me on my stomach. He held me down with a hand on the back of my neck and rammed his cock into my pussy. I let out a scream, the action being a mix between pain and pleasure. In no way was I hurt, but the action certainly meant Kerian now had my full attention.

"That wasn't just naughty, it was foolish, Lainey," Kerian snapped. He timed his thrusts to match his words, making me cry out. "Do you know how hard it is for us not to fucking mark you? Bonds are forever, and if we make that mistake, it doesn't matter what you want in the end, you'd be *ours*. Is that what you want, Lainey, for us to claim you and never let you go? To wrap you up in our arms every night so tightly you'll never be able to escape?"

My heart and body screamed *yes* to all those questions, yet my brain which still seemed to have an ounce of common sense, gave a resounding *no*. It would never work—they would mark me in the heat of the moment, and then when they found out the truth, they'd be stuck with a liar and a thief forever. This is why it was better for me to be on my own. No one would be able to accept that I con people out of their money, marriages, and companies. I was a criminal, and these men ran a fucking security company, for Christ's sake.

Kerian gripped a fist full of hair near my scalp and pulled back, making me arch toward him. "I asked you a question, Lainey. Look, even H and Quin want to hear your answer. Tell us there's no need to manipulate us to get answers or a reason for you to be crafty in getting us to the point you want to make. All you have to do is tell us, what does Lainey want?"

If only he knew how hard that fucking question was. I didn't know. I had not one fucking clue what *Lainey* would want. She hadn't had a choice in things for so long, I honestly haven't a fucking clue what I really want or like out of the personalities I'd built and been over the past twelve years. Even before I became a true con artist, Trent told me who I was and the part I needed to play. *Have I ever known what Lainey wants?*

"Keri, she's crying. Stop," Halstead barked.

I was crying? That can't be right. I don't cry anymore. Well, not for real, anyway. Why would I be crying now?

Eighteen

Lainey

Instantly, Kerian's hand was gone from my hair, and he slid out of me as gently as possible before Halstead scooped me up. The silver bear curled me up in a ball and cradled me against his chest like I really was a little kitten. His chest rumbled with his deep purr as I reached out and fisted some of his chest hair, making him grunt, but he didn't stop me.

"Shh," Halstead soothed as he nuzzled the top of my head with his cheek. "It's okay... things got a little out of hand, is all. You both pushed each other farther than you should've, but it's gonna be fine."

A sniffling hiccup caught me off guard, proving to myself I was indeed crying. "I don't cry," I mumbled. "Why the hell am I crying?"

"You're asking the wrong man. I never know why women are crying around me when it happens," Halstead admitted. "If I were to take a guess, though, it's probably due to the fact you're in heat and hormones are running rampant."

That made sense. I suppose no one I've ever been with before would venture on a topic that would be remotely close to making me cry. First, there would have to be talking past the fuck yes, just like that, harder, and get-the-fuck-off-me-you're-heavy moments.

A glass of water appeared, and I found it was Quintin who offered it to me. "Hydration is important."

Bless this man for having no idea what to do with a crying woman but still wanting to take care of her. I took the glass because he'd been sweet and brave enough to do something, even if it might not be right. After our few discussions of him struggling with me being a female partner, I was slowly figuring out it had more to do with the fact he didn't want to fuck up things. He didn't care that I was a woman and not a man. What he did care about was doing things right and meeting expectations.

"Thank you," I whispered, taking a sip of the water, then pausing in surprise. "You put something in it?"

"Oh, ah... yes, lemon and cucumber are in the water pitcher," Quintin explained. "I find that drinking plain water isn't that appealing, so I like to infuse my water. If you don't like that flavor, I have others." He moved as if he would get them all right this moment if I reached out.

"Quin, it's fine... this tastes delicious. I wasn't expecting the flavor, but it is a nice surprise," I assured him. "It's smart to make your water more interesting so you drink it. I might have to steal the idea."

"Go right ahead. I got the idea from someone else as well," Quintin murmured, his cheeks blushing slightly.

Since the water tasted so good, I ended up drinking the whole glass before I handed it back to him. Feeling much better and more myself, I tried to extract myself from Halstead's grasp, but he had other thoughts on that. Instead of letting me go, he maneuvered me so I sat on his lap while his legs were crossed with arms loosely wrapped around my waist.

"Nope, you're staying right here until you and Kerian talk about what just happened. Things don't need to be perfect, but I would appreciate you at least telling him what pushed things too far and then hearing Kerian out on his side of things," Halstead instructed. "As the saying goes, there are two sides to every story, and I've found in my fifty-plus years of life, it's important to hear them both out."

While I understood where Halstead was coming from, the last thing I wanted to do right now was have a heart-to-heart moment during the middle of my heat. Granted, the emotions had dampened the need to be fucking someone right now because what woman feels sexy when they're upset? However, when I looked over at Kerian, my stomach dropped. The man looked so upset as he sat on the edge of the bed with his back to me, head hung low with his dreadlocks hiding his expression. I didn't need to see his face to know he was upset, though. It radiated off him.

It was clear that while I might not want to deal with this issue right now, I wasn't the only person in the situation. Letting out a sigh, I had to agree with Halstead—this needed to be addressed. "Kerian," I ventured. "What just happened is not anything you did. I'm fine, really. I didn't even know I was crying until Halstead said something."

Kerian turned to look at me, his eyes full of shame and uncertainty. "I got too carried away. The way I manhandled you like that..." his voice drifted off as he shook his head, "... it was wrong."

I struggled against Halstead, trying to get to Kerian, but he held me firmly in place. "Doll, when he gets this upset, he doesn't want to be touched. Doing so will not help matters, and is why I'm holding you here. As an Omega, you want that physical connection with him because that's what soothes you, but not everyone is like that," he whispered in my ear low enough only I heard him.

That had me instantly stop my efforts to get free. Halstead was right. Everyone processed things in their own way, and as his partner, Halstead knew exactly what Kerian needed right now. Top of the list was clearly not being touched.

"I like rough sex," I blurted. "Honestly, I like rough sex more than any other kind of sex. Scratch that, I like public sex. More so the threat of being caught doing something naughty, like getting fingered at the table in a restaurant or a bathroom hookup. Things like that. Seriously, you guys have unlocked a new kink in the way you approach dirty talk. Never understood it until I heard what was coming out of Quintin's mouth. Then there you were pounding me like I hoped you would when I bit you, but clearly, I misjudged how that would affect you."

Pausing, I chewed on my lower lip, trying to decide how much to explain or say about what actually made me cry. "Look, I didn't have a good childhood. My mom was a druggy. I got put in the system at birth and given the horrible name of Elaine. At the age of ten, I was adopted by a man, but he didn't want a kid, not in the traditional sense."

That had them all growling with dark looks on their faces. I knew what they were thinking, but I couldn't tell them it wasn't like that because it was. Just not with me until my first heat came about.

"He was, well is, a con artist," I explained, hoping that would be enough without going into details that would give me away if they researched it. "What he wanted was a 'daughter,' and I use that term loosely to help him with cons. I think what might have triggered the emotional response is you asking me what I wanted. Growing up, I had to become whatever character he dictated to meet his needs. All that to say there are genuinely things I don't know if I like because I like them or because I was told to like them. Do I prefer ketchup over mustard because that's what I prefer, or was it because I was instructed to be that way? It's a total mind fuck, let me tell you, and I've been avoiding asking those very questions my whole life."

As I spoke, Kerian finally decided to face me, holding a pillow over his crotch, trying to be respectful of our conversation, making my heart melt just a little. "Where is this man now?" he asked.

I suppose there's no harm in telling them the truth. It's not like they were going to know his name or how long he's been locked up. "He's in jail. Finally got caught and sentenced to life for all his crimes they discovered during the investigation."

"That's the best answer I suppose we could have hoped for, all things considered," Halstead grumbled. "Dead would have been my preferred response, but jail for life I can accept."

"Yeah, while things were bad, it wasn't bad enough for the death penalty," I added with a sigh. "So, now we've established that it's my fucked-up past and nothing you did to me physically or mentally which caused the waterworks."

"Do you really not know what you like?" Quintin inquired.

Okay, it seems we aren't going to be moving on from this subject as I hoped.

My body seemed to be in agreement with my plan to move on as my need started to flare up, causing my skin to feel hot and my pussy to throb, making me dig my nails into Halstead's thighs.

"I got you, doll, just give me a second," Halstead assured me as he picked me up only to settle me back down, impaling me on his cock.

Moaning, my head fell back to rest against his muscled chest while my pussy was thrilled to be full once more. He used two fingers and rolled my nipple between one as he swirled another around my clit. My breath quickened as pleasure assaulted me from all areas of my body. Kerian crawled forward until he laid on his stomach and urged Halstead to open his legs so he could get an unobstructed view of Halstead thrusting into my pussy. I was about to make a sassy comment, but it died on my lips as Kerian removed Halstead's hand, only to replace it with his mouth.

"Oh my God," I screamed at the feeling of him sucking and lapping at my pussy.

Never had I experienced something like this, but I also didn't normally sleep with more than one person at a time. It was hard enough to find someone who wouldn't get attached during my heat, let alone more than one person. That's not to say I haven't had a threesome or an orgy in my life, but none seemed to have the creativity these three men did. Was this the benefit of going for someone older? Who the fuck cared? All I knew, I was going to have some amazing sex over the next few days.

Kerian seemed to be making his apologies through his efforts toward my clit because that little gal was feeling all kinds of affection for the man. With a sharp suck, I was flying high as I climaxed, body bowing, but Halstead's solid arms made sure I didn't go far. He purred as he kissed along my neck and shoulder, making everything vibrate, including his cock. This sent another wave of ecstasy through my body right on the heels of the previous orgasm.

"Fuck yes, don't either of you fucking stop," I managed to get out as my eyes rolled back in my head when Halstead's knot started to swell.

He thrust up into me as he used his leverage to push me down, making sure his cock was as deep as he could possibly get it. With a shout, he came, locking me into place as he grunted and kept trying to thrust into me, making my body implode.

"That's right, doll, come all over my fucking cock." Halstead growled into my ear. "I'm gonna put my cum so deep inside you, it will be leaking out of you for days no matter how hard you try to clean up. That way, every time you feel it, you'll be reminded who your Alpha is."

His words alone had me coming again as Kerian took me at my word and didn't stop his assault on my clit with that wicked tongue of his. I could feel how fast Halstead's heart was thundering in his chest as he flopped back onto the bed, taking me with him. My body was like putty as I lay sprawled on his chest, everything exposed to the other two men in bed with us who stared at me hungrily.

Quintin came behind Kerian and shoved the man forward so his ass was up in the air. Then he spread his partner's ass and began to feast on him, making Kerian moan. "Yesss. That's right, Quin, put that mouth to good use, get me all nice and loose for you to fuck. Show Lainey just how good of a top you can be as a bottom."

Taking some effort, Halstead grabbed some pillows and propped us up so I could watch them easier. "You mentioned how you liked the thrill of almost getting caught... well, our dear sweet Kerian enjoys watching and being watched. The cocky boy likes to put on a show for me some nights, don't you?"

Kerian arched his back as he reached between his legs and started to stroke his cock. "I fucking love it when you watch... it's the best feeling in the world. There's no need for porn if you have a partner who's more than willing to provide something for you to watch. Plus, there's the added bonus you might get to participate. No video can do that for you, can it?"

Yup, it was official. These men needed to teach a class on dirty talk. It came so effortlessly to them, and it didn't sound cheesy, at least to me. I suppose if you're not a fan of any kind of vulgar or raunchy conversation, then it might be a bit much, but hell, sign me the fuck up.

"What about you, Lainey? Do you enjoy watching, or are you more interested in participating?" Quintin asked. "Or is it more torturous to you that you're sitting there, knotted to the hilt with Halstead's cock and unable to play with us?"

"Both, I want to watch you, but I also want the option to play," I answered, my voice breathy with how turned on I was.

Halstead took note and slid his hand between my legs to lazily stroke my clit. It was fucking sensitive after all the attention Kerian gave it, so I was thankful he wasn't aggressively trying to get me off. Instead, it was almost as if he was trying to edge me, keep me wanting more even as I was sitting there knotted up.

Quintin grabbed the bottle of lube and covered his cock and Kerian's ass in the thick liquid, shoving two fingers in the man without a second thought. "Should we tell her why I can do this so easily?" Quintin asked as he draped himself over Kerian's back. "Something tells me she'll find it hot as hell."

Kerian's hands fisted in the sheets as Quintin shoved his cock balls deep in one go. Then his already-lubed hand grasped Kerian's cock and stroked it in time with his thrusts. It was glaringly obvious that Quintin had taken it easy on me the way he pounded into Kerian, the slapping of skin so loud it betrayed how hard he was thrusting.

"Come on, Keri, tell our Omega how you like to make sure you're good and ready for either of us to fuck you whenever you want," Quintin pressed, wrapping an arm around his neck and pulling him to sit up, displaying Kerian's cock to us.

The pure ecstasy written all over Kerian's face as he met my gaze made me a little jealous that I didn't get the same treatment from Quintin.

"I'm a horny slut who likes to keep a butt plug in my ass," Kerian admitted between thrusts. "I removed it before coming up here so you wouldn't know."

"So it wasn't just Tater-Tot you were taking care of," Halstead rumbled behind me. He'd removed his hand from my pussy to lazily stroke whatever skin he could, setting me on fire with need. "That would be why I don't remember you asking my permission if you could take out that plug I put in this morning."

Quintin pulled out of Kerian and slapped him hard on the ass. "You naughty boy, I didn't know you'd been instructed to leave it in. You don't deserve my cock if you broke the rules."

"No," Kerian cried out. "Please, don't leave me like this. I'm so close."

"Don't beg me. I'm not the one who broke the rules," Quintin pointed out.

That had Kerian crawling over to Halstead, but he didn't stop when he reached us. Instead, he draped himself over me so his weeping cock rubbed against my stomach as he cupped Halstead's face.

"Please, papa bear, will you let me come? I know I broke the rules, but I feel like with Lainey here, it changed the situation. It won't happen again... please let Quintin fuck me until I come," Kerian begged as he humped against me, trying to get friction wherever he could.

Halstead grabbed a fist full of Kerian's locks and slammed their mouths together in the most Alpha make-out I'd ever seen. They each fought for control without even realizing it in the way they nipped at each other. After a few moments, Halstead pulled him back, both panting as they gazed heatedly at each other.

"You can come..." he answered but held up a finger to stop Kerian from speaking, "... but I want you to stay right there so your cock rubs on Lainey's clit. When you get her off, then you can come."

Kerian nodded eagerly as he shifted himself so he was positioned right where I needed for this to work. Thank God he was lubed up because with the knot blocking my slick, it would have been fucking painful. Quintin came up behind his lover, applying more lube to his cock, and surprised me when he slipped his hand between us, making sure I was taken care of as well.

"Can't risk rubbing you raw this early in the heat," he commented before lowering himself to kiss me.

No longer was he afraid or timid in his actions. I'm not sure what changed—if it was taking charge with Kerian or because he'd knotted me, but I was a big fan of this commanding side of Quintin. With a final nip, he pulled back and gave Kerian's ass a warning slap before he dove back in. He didn't go quite as hard as before. This time he picked a rhythm that would benefit me as well as Kerian.

"How does it feel to know I'm fucking him to get you off?" he asked, staring into my soul.

To hold myself steady, I coiled around Kerian, hugging him to me tightly as he kissed Halstead. "It's hot as hell," I admitted. "Never would I have thought of something like this while I'm knotted to someone else."

"This is the fun of having a pack... all of us have different ideas to try out," Halstead interjected, purring in my ear as he wrapped his hand around my throat, tipping my head back so I was looking at him. "Just think of all the things we can come up with now that we have you to add to the mix. We've tried just about every combination of things there is to try with a partner who only has two options for us to explore. You doll, have three, the perfect number if you ask me."

I shivered in his grasp, his words ratcheting up my level of horniness, making Kerian's movements even more intense. A moan worked its way out of me as lips closed around one of my nipples, a hot tongue flicking at the overly sensitive peak.

"Does that turn you on, Lainey... the thought of us using you for our pleasure?" Halstead pressed. "Tell me, when this is over, if I brought you into my office and pinned you up against the wall of windows, would you let me fuck you? Would you risk knowing someone could be watching from another building?"

The vision of his words floated through my imagination and had me coming almost instantly as Kerian bit down on my nipple. With the combination of dirty talk and all the sensations going on, I let myself fall off the cliff into one of the most intense climaxes ever. My body shook as it clamped even tighter around the knot in me. Apparently, it had calmed enough that it shifted deeper into me than I thought possible, the tip of Halstead's cock hitting the back of my cervix, making me scream.

Halstead roared as he pulled me up and off his cock. "Fuck, fuck, fuck, woman. Are you trying to break my damn cock by squeezing it that hard?"

"No," I whined. "Put it back in, please. It was perfect, but now I feel so empty."

Another pair of hands grabbed me, slid me down Halstead's body, and filled me with a cock that stretched me to my limit. "Don't worry, my sweet vixen," Kerian whispered in my ear. "I've got a knot for you. It's ripe, ready, and waiting to pop so it can fill you with my cum. Now take a deep breath because I'm going to make you see God."

With a growl and one more fierce thrust from Quintin, Kerian came. The feel of his knot swelling had me writhing and babbling gibberish before I could feel the flood of cum filling me. Why this sensation was so much more fulfilling than anything else I'd ever felt, I didn't know, but at this moment, I didn't think I'd be mad if I ended up pregnant from this heat. They did their damndest to make it happen and had me begging for more.

When Kerian's knot stopped swelling, I truly understood what the word stuffed meant because that's what I was. Stuffed with his cock along with his cum to the point I came again so hard I blacked out. In that split second before I slipped into the darkness, I didn't see God, but I saw the face of a man who deserved the title, that's for damn sure.

Nineteen

Lainey

For the next two days, I was fucked within an inch of my life and in every which way possible. We might have also managed to christen all the furniture in the room when we got bored of just fucking on the massive bed. In the moments when I wasn't sleeping, fucking, sucking, or knotted, they managed to get water and food in me.

This heat had been unlike any other in my life. It was almost as if I'd been given an accelerant that kept my heat from dying down as the days went on. Instead, it got more and more intense, unable to pause for any sort of meaningful conversation. The more I was pumped full of cum, my head cleared enough for them to check in on me and get coherent answers. My brain just felt like it was in a fog, completely lost in this heat haze.

Finally, on the third—or was it the fourth day—my heat broke.

"Hey there, beautiful," Quintin murmured as he brushed hair off my face. "It's nice to finally see you with some clear, focused eyes. You really had us worried there for a bit. Halstead was about to call the doctor to come check you out."

My mouth felt as dry as the desert and had a gross film over my tongue that I didn't want to think about. "Water, please," I croaked out.

"I got it," Kerian called from somewhere in the room. A moment later, I saw the man himself looking as tired as I felt. "Can you sit up?"

It wasn't until I started to move that I realized how sore I was. My body felt like I'd been worked over with a meat tenderizer.

"H, help her," Quintin ordered.

"Easy now, Quin, I was going to," Halstead's deep voice chided from behind me. "I wanted to give her a moment and see if she could manage on her own. This isn't her first heat, and I've heard not every woman likes to be touched after things have settled down. What we just went through was a shit-ton of physical contact."

I turned to look at him with a raised brow. "Is that what we're calling it now, a shit-ton of physical contact?"

"Best I got on the fly," he answered with a shrug. "Would you like a hand?"

"Yes," I admitted as my arms started to shake.

Kneeling behind me, he sat me up, but instead of putting me propped up against the pillows, he settled me between his outstretched legs. It was then my brain realized he was wearing sweatpants—they all were.

"Is it over?" I asked, even though it sounded more like pleading.

"From what we can tell, it subsided around three this morning," Quintin answered. "Your scent changed to a more normal level, and the fever broke as well."

"I had a fever?" I questioned.

"A really bad one for at least a day, but it didn't slow you down one bit," Kerian shared as he handed me the water. "It's one of the reasons H was so worried about you. We managed to take your temp while you slept, and it was a hundred and three."

A moan tumbled out of me at the taste of the cool, refreshing liquid. Never in my life had water tasted so good to me. While I'd heard what

Kerian said, my body's demand for me to finish off the water was more important. Once the glass was empty, I could relax against Halstead and let Kerian take it from me.

"How are you feeling now?" he asked, searching my face. "Do you want more water?"

"I would love more water, but I think I'm gonna need to work on that slowly. Right now, all I want to do is guzzle it down," I explained. "As for how I'm feeling, let's just say I'm really glad the meat is dead when we tenderize it because, damn, this sucks."

Quintin slid off the bed then paused, catching my eye. "I'll be right back. I just want to see if we have a glass with a straw for you to drink from. That should help you to slow down the water intake enough so you don't overdo it. Is there anything else I can get you... painkillers, a snack?"

The mere thought of taking any medication right now had my pulse racing with panic. "No, I think I'll be okay. If you guys have a bathtub I can use to put some Epsom salts in, that will be all the medicine I need." Quintin nodded and left the room, closing the door softly behind him.

Kerian draped a ridiculously soft blanket over me as he came to sit cross-legged before us. "Lainey, something tells me that wasn't a normal heat for you. Is there something going on that we should know about? Are you okay... in general, I mean?"

It was kind of cute to see Kerian stumble over his words being the normally confident and boisterous man out of the three. I reached out, and he took my hand instantly, letting his thumb stroke my skin.

"I'm fine, I promise," I assured him, even though I wasn't exactly sure that was true.

Whatever the Syndicate had given me had to have been the cause of this. It had me questioning what else it might be affecting as well.

When I got the chance to be alone, I needed to reach out to the doctor again and ask more questions.

"Since I've been hiding being an Omega, I only allow myself one heat a year. Unfortunately, the second heat fell right when I needed to start working at Enigma, and I couldn't risk asking for the time off. I'd hoped to get at least a few weeks in before I got 'sick,' " I shared, using finger quotes to make my point. "My guess is since we are scent-paired, being around the three of you forced the heat, even though I'd made sure to re-up my suppressant dosage."

Kerian nodded, scooching forward so he could keep my hand in his. "That actually makes a lot of sense now that you put it that way. It was just you were here with us engaging, then a switch flipped, and you were gone. None of us knew what to do other than help you through the best we could. The craziest part was if you weren't knotted or asleep, it was like you were in real physical pain."

"I'll be honest, there are parts of all this that I truly don't remember. It could have been from the fever putting me in a daze, I'm not sure, but what I do know is that I'm completely fine now," I offered, squeezing his hand in reassurance.

He gave me a soft smile and leaned in to give me a peck on the lips. "Thank God for that because I'm not sure how papa bear here would have handled it if you didn't get better. I thought that man was going to have a heart attack trying to keep up with your voracity."

"Ha," Halstead grunted. "Says the man who passed the fuck out the moment she did during that first DP."

"Whoa, let's not point fingers," I cut in. "I'm not sure anyone, no matter their age, could have kept up in that frenzy. Let's just say job well done by all, we made it through, and it's over. You've all worked hard, so let's make today a day off... hmm?"

Halstead tucked a knuckle under my chin, tipping my head back so he could kiss me deeply. It wasn't frenzied like the others we've shared before. This one was intimate, full of emotion, and had me melting in his arms. Things were getting dangerous, and I didn't mean with the Syndicate. Right now, these three men were threatening my very existence and what I had planned for my life. Too easily was I losing sight of the reason I was even there with them in the first place. Their sweet words, gentle kisses, and tender touches were like a siren's call to me, begging me to throw the whole mission out the window and stay with them.

However, I knew that couldn't happen. I would never be what they wanted once they learned the truth. Everything they thought they knew about me was a lie or half-truth, and nothing was real. Who could accept someone who lied so easily? How would you ever know if they were telling the truth? No, this was a blissful moment I would treasure forever in my heart, but I couldn't stay.

Halstead started to purr as he pulled back from our kiss, gazing down at me with such affection in those deep blue eyes I almost wanted to cry. "You said something about a bath. Why don't we start there so you can get cleaned up? I hope you don't mind, but we sent our driver over to your place and grabbed some clothes and other personal effects. Figured you'd probably feel better using your own toothbrush and such."

"That sounds perfect," I admitted with a sigh.

"Here, let me show you the en suite bathroom here," Kerian offered, tugging me off the bed. "If you don't like this tub, there are about four others for you to choose from, but I think this one will do the trick. Suppose it helps that this was the nest the previous homeowners had put together for their Omega."

My legs were a little shaky, but I managed once Kerian slipped his arm around my waist and held me close to his side. Before I could think better of it, I wrapped my arms around his middle and nuzzled his chest. I took a deep breath of his scent, letting that fresh citrus and juniper berry scent waft over me.

"God, I love how you smell," I murmured, then froze as I realized how silly that sounded.

He didn't say a word, just hugged me back, burrowing his nose into my hair. "Under the musk of sex, I think I can still make out your scent."

I snorted then pinched his side, making him yelp and pull back. "What the hell, you little vixen."

"That's for saying I stink," I quipped before attempting to stride toward the door I assumed to be the bathroom.

After five steps, my legs betrayed me, and I stumbled, almost crashing to the floor, but Kerian scooped me up. "I did not say the smell of sex on you was bad," he pointed out. "All I said is it took effort to get past it to get to the real deal which I happen to enjoy immensely."

"Whatever, Mr. Smooth Talker," I grumbled.

He just chuckled and kissed my head as he shoved open the door. "We already put your things away here, so hypothetically, everything you need should be available." Kerian set me on a chair that was placed before a lighted vanity.

The bathroom was stunning, which is a little odd to say about a bathroom, but it was the best word I had to describe the place. White and cream marble made up the floor and counters with little slivers of gold accent. Everything else was a crisp white color. However, the detailed woodwork is what elevated the space—crown molding along the ceiling, elegant carved designs on the front of the cabinet doors, and the gorgeous large corner windows that were the backdrop of where the tub sat. A tub that could easily fit three people with water jets as an added bonus.

"Holy shit." The words just popped out of my mouth as I took in the room.

Kerian, who was already getting the tub started, just laughed. "I figured you wouldn't have a problem using this tub. You even get a view of the backyard and Quin's solarium."

"What about my solarium?" Quintin asked as he entered the bathroom with a bag of Epsom salts as well as a large tumbler with a lid and straw. He offered me the glass, which I took greedily. "This one is mint, ginger, and lemon flavored. They say it's supposed to help with stress and promote relaxation."

"Well, who can't use some of that in their lives?" I asked, taking a sip. "Oh fuck, that's incredible. That's it, I'm never drinking normal water ever again, not when it can taste this good."

Quintin's face lit up with such a radiant smile I was stunned by it for a moment. "I'm so glad you like them. I can't ever seem to get the others on board."

"What?" I gasped. "How can you not like this?"

Kerian rolled his eyes and snatched my tumbler from my hand to take a sip. He hesitated a second before looking at Quintin with narrowed eyes. "Why does this oddly taste close to your own scent? Just switch out the mint for some of that green tea you love so much, and that would be a dead ringer."

"If I did that, then it would no longer be water but green tea. However, I might have been experimenting with an infusion you couldn't resist," Quintin commented as his lips twitched, trying to keep a smile off his face. "Why do you think I asked what my scent smelled like to you?"

"I don't know. I suppose everyone is curious to know what others smell," Kerian muttered as he snagged the bag of Epsom salts from his partner. "Don't even try to make one for Halstead. I don't think there is any vegetation that can make up that scent."

"Yes, I'll have to agree with you on that. However..." he paused, letting his gaze slide over to me, "... I believe a clove and cinnamon infusion might be something worth trying. Maybe add some apple or possibly orange to it as well?"

"Okay, now that does sound pretty fucking delicious," Kerian agreed. "Guess you'll just have to make it so we can test it against the real thing."

It was at this moment my brain finally put all the pieces together. "You mean me?" I asked like an idiot, pointing to myself.

Quintin's smile was back as he chuckled. "Yes, beautiful, I mean you."

"Cinnamon and clove, huh?" I mused to myself aloud.

Moments later, Quintin scooped me up and carried me over to the tub, where he carefully lowered me into the steaming water. "Yes, you are enticingly spicy in the best way possible, which is why I didn't grab the eucalyptus Epsom because it would cover your natural perfume that we all enjoy far too much."

Why that had me blushing as he kissed me slowly and sweetly, I have no idea, but it seemed to be a superpower this man had. No one had ever been able to do that to me, and he's managed without any effort to make it happen a handful of times.

"Now, soak as long as you like," Quintin instructed as he pushed the button for the jets. "Once you're done, get dressed and come downstairs so we can have some breakfast together."

"Okay," I whispered, feeling slightly overwhelmed by their pampering.

With a parting kiss from them, they left me to relax with my infused water in the most glorious bathtub I've ever experienced. I'd been in many a bathtub, but this one seemed so special. Maybe it had something to do with the leftover emotions tied to this whole room, having been a nest for another Omega who was clearly cherished by her pack. It made me curious as to who they were and why they ended up moving. Maybe Halstead knew who they were, and I could look them up to see what I could find on them.

Having spent much of my life investigating people since I needed to delve into their lives and learn all that I could for jobs, on occasion, I would find a connection or mention to another person I didn't need to know anything about, yet they fascinated me so I'd do some research. Sometimes I used what I learned to build the characters that I played, pulling bits and pieces from other people's stories.

Why base anything off the life you know when you could create a whole new identity out of the magic of someone else's? Did she have enough partners to fill the bedrooms, or were some of them for their children? What kind of life had this Omega led? Is she the reason they have a solarium? These were the things I could use in building the next persona because the best lie was always founded in truth.

Thinking about moving on and the job I was supposed to start a week from now made my heart ache. *Just how attached had I become to these men? Why did they make me question my choice to live life on my own terms? Surely, it wasn't just that we were scent-paired. That was simply a tool to pair Alphas and Omegas who had the best chance of producing children.*

Shaking my head, I splashed my face with the bath water, trying to end this downward mental spiral. All I needed to do was use this opportunity at their home to get rid of the code. Removing it from the office computers would be the easy part since there was a central data bank. Here at home, who knew how he stored things or where? Was he the type to put things on a backup hard drive or maybe a USB flash drive? I had to be sure I'd gotten every single copy or the Syndicate would be all over my ass.

Once I was done with destroying the code at Enigma, would they send me over to Cyclone to destroy it there? No, wait, they wanted me to ensure that Kerian wouldn't ever work on the code again, even if it meant I had to kill him. Yeah, well, that wasn't going to fucking happen. There had to be some other way I could convince him to leave the code alone, and I would find it.

Thinking of the Syndicate took away some of the joy of my bath, so I submerged myself under the water for a few seconds and cleared my mind. Today I was going to enjoy the illusion of being their Omega. All I wanted was to have that experience with them before it all shattered when they found out what I was doing. Popping back up out of the water, I took a deep breath, purged myself of all the worry, stuffed it into a drawer, and locked it away.

There would be time to face the music, but now wasn't it.

Twenty

Halstead

Sam droned on and on about the changes to my schedule, making me regret calling to check in on things. I'd called him late that first night and told him there was a personal emergency and that we would be out next week. There was no telling how long Lainey's heat was going to last. Now that it was over, it meant we got three more days with her, not having to worry about going back to work, which was priceless.

"Sam," I cut in. "I really was just calling to make sure the building didn't catch on fire, and you were still in one piece."

"Oh…" Sam commented. "So you're really not coming back to work until next week?"

"That's correct. We've managed to deal with the pressing issue, but we decided it would be nice to enjoy the break. Come to think of it, I can't remember the last time we took that much time off," I mused aloud.

"You certainly deserve it, sir. I'm just impressed you're following through, is all. Oh yes, I meant to ask you, Ms. Collins hasn't been in either, but I didn't have any contact information for her," Sam shared.

A smirk grew on my lips. "That's all right, I've been in contact with her. She'll be coming back to work next week as well. Being so new, I didn't think it would be worth her time to be there when I'm not.

Kind of hard to assist someone when they're not present, don't you think?"

"Of course, I just didn't want her to be out of the loop. One last thing..." Sam said, his voice betraying that I wasn't going to be a fan of what he was going to tell me. "Mr. Watts has been relentless in trying to get ahold of Mr. Lewis. He calls the office at least four times a day, and I keep telling him that he's out for the week. Then he demands Mr. Lewis' private number, but I'm not allowed to give that to him... right?"

"Absolutely, you're not allowed to give that out... we're a security company, for Christ's sake. You just keep doing what you're doing, and I'll deal with the bastard," I grumbled. "Anything else I should be aware of?"

"Let's see... no, no, already covered that, ah yes... the Department of Defense called... well, kind of. The woman said she was General Horn's personal assistant and would like to schedule a call between the two of you. Seems they want to smooth things over from the last interaction," Sam informed me.

"I'll bet they do," I muttered, rubbing my forehead, trying to decide if I could make that wait until next week or if I needed to deal with it sooner. "Call her back, see what his schedule looks like. Take down three options, then send them to me, and I'll decide what I want to do then."

"Certainly, I'll get you that information right away," Sam assured me then hung up.

"Good thing I didn't need to tell you anything else." I chuckled, tossing my phone on the bed.

Pulling open my dresser drawer, I grabbed a T-shirt and pulled it on. While I loved my suits, those were for business, and this was leisure time, so T-shirt and jeans it was. Looking down, I realized what shirt I was wearing and groaned. It was one Quintin had gotten me for my last birthday, reading, *I'm not old, I'm vintage*. Asshole knew I wouldn't make him return it since I was a lover of collecting vintage items. The library upstairs was full of rare old books, and the second garage was where I kept my babies. Maybe I should take Lainey out there since she seemed to appreciate vintage as well.

Dressed, I glanced at my phone, debating if I was going to take that with me or leave it, but I decided to take it. I'd asked Sam to get back to me about the general's schedule, so I should be a good boss and have an answer for him. Shoving it in my back pocket, I ambled my way downstairs into the kitchen. Quintin was sitting at the small corner breakfast table with a newspaper and tea—his morning ritual.

"The world still going to hell?" I asked, grabbing a mug for my cup o' joe.

Quintin might not ever drink coffee, but he was always kind enough to make some in the morning if Ruth hadn't gotten to it yet. Since we hadn't informed her that the heat was over, I knew Quin had made this.

Bending down the top half of the paper, Quintin looked at me with an amused expression. "Really, must we start the day with the same question every single time?"

"Aah... but our day has long since started, so this time it is different," I pointed out while sitting across from him. "See, we've already been awake, gotten our Omega settled in the bath, showered, and dressed. I mean, it's practically noon, and we're acting like it's six in the morning."

Realizing I would be intruding on his reading, he folded up the newspaper and set it aside. "This is true. The day is a rather unusual one, but I have to say I am enjoying the change of pace."

"I was thinking the same thing," I shared, taking a sip of my coffee. "It is freeing not to have to worry about what's going on back at Enigma. Thanks to you pushing me, we've made great strides to put people in place so none of the day-to-day dealings are dependent on us."

"Since you're agreeing with me now, I won't bring up how hard that was to achieve," Quintin commented as he lifted his teacup to his lips, trying to hide the smile I knew was there.

The sounds of nails scrambling over the tile floor warned us that we were soon to be assaulted by a slobbering pile of wrinkles. Moments later, Tater-Tot came tearing into the kitchen and aimed right for me, jowls flapping in the breeze. The dog had never learned how to stop on the tile floor, so he'd decided on aiming for something soft to run into that would stop his momentum. At the moment, that object was me, so I set my coffee down in preparation.

"Tater," I warned, even though I knew it wasn't going to do a damn thing. "Oomph," I grunted when the dog collided with my legs.

He bounced off and ended up rolling to the side, but he popped up on his feet in a flash. Now there stood a wiggling ball of excitement watching me carefully. Tater knew better than to jump on me—that never ended well for him—but waiting for my approval so he could greet me was almost too much.

"Oh, for fuck's sake, come here, you slobbery creature," I relented, giving in like I always did. Tater leaped forward, placing his front paws on my thigh waiting for his pets. "Now, did your dad tell you we have a guest and that you need to be on your best behavior?"

"Yes, Grandpa, I made sure I told him," Kerian sassed as he joined us in the kitchen, a smoothie in his hand.

I gave him an unamused look. "I thought we agreed not to use that term."

"What term? Oh, you mean grand—"

"Aah," I snapped, pointing a finger at him. "Don't push your luck, babe. I know how sore your ass is, but I have zero problems using that to my advantage."

Kerian walked over, cupped my face, and kissed me. "If you want me to stop calling you that, then stop acting like one all the time, papa bear."

"I can't help it that I was raised in a different generation," I said in my defense. "Look, my mother was alive during one of the worst recessions we'd ever seen, making how she raised me come with certain hang-ups. I love Tater-Tot because he makes you happy, but I still can't say I'm a pet person. It's just who I am, and you're either gonna accept that or not."

"Oh, you're not going to get rid of me or Tater that easily, so don't even try. I love you just the way you are, Halstead... old fashioned in mind, body, and spirit, but it makes you exactly who I fell in love with," Kerian stated, kissing me again. "So you're just going to have to suck it up and know that when I call you grandpa or gramps, it's a term of endearment, a show of my undying love."

That sent Quintin into a fit of coughing as he choked on his tea. "Oh my God, the bullshit is strong today." He wheezed once he could talk.

Kerian simply smiled and sat with us, reclining in his chair like he didn't have a care in the world. It truly was one of the things I loved about him—he had the amazing ability to take each moment as it was. He'd leave work at work, never letting it spill over to what happened at home. Likewise, if we had an argument here, it never affected how we interacted at work. That was a talent not many people had, including myself, but I wish like hell I did.

The sound of a phone vibrating caught my attention, making me check my back pocket, but it wasn't my phone. Kerian pulled his phone out of his basketball shorts and let out a grunt before flipping it over on the table to silence the call.

"Fucking Reuben can't seem to take a hint. If I don't answer the first fifty times you call, then why would you keep trying?" Kerian asked, but I got the sense it was rhetorical.

"What has his panties in a twist?" Quintin inquired. "I thought you had two months for that project."

"Yeah, and why is he calling Sam asking for your number when he clearly has it?" I added.

Kerian took a few gulps of his smoothie before setting it down and sitting up straighter. "I gave him my direct work line, and that's being forwarded to this phone so I can keep tabs on projects if the team needs me. When I left Cyclone, I changed my cell number to the one you two have. There's a reason I don't give it out often, and it's for moments like this. Reuben has always been this way, breathing down my neck, always wanting updates even if I don't have an update to give. At first, he said it was just to push me, help me get faster, but really it's just another way of controlling us all."

"Fucking bastard," I growled out. "I swear to God, I will find a way to knock him flat on his ass one day, but damn, is he good at covering his tracks."

"Is that why you asked Lainey to look into him because you keep coming up with nothing?" Quintin asked, not realizing I hadn't mentioned that bit yet to Kerian.

"You asked her to do what?" Kerian snapped.

Quin shot me an apologetic look but didn't even attempt to bail me out of this mess. In his mind, Kerian should have already known about me asking Lainey to look quietly into Reuben and his company. So I was on my own to clean up this mess.

"I reached out to her previous employers," I started. "I'd noticed a pattern in how they both talked about how skilled she was at gathering information as well as the fact her discretion of whatever she uncovered was above reproach. You know I don't like you working with Reuben, and I still don't understand how he talked you into doing it. My intention with all this was simply to discover if the code had an alternative use they weren't telling us about. We all know that man lies through his teeth and will say whatever it takes to get someone to do his bidding."

"And you don't think I know all that?" Kerian challenged.

The look on his face and the tone of his voice told me I might have said the wrong thing in my irritation over the matter. When it came to Kerian's past, Reuben was a subject I needed to tread lightly with. In no way did I want to make one of the people I loved most in this world feel like he was an idiot for taking this job or that I didn't trust him to make the right judgment call. Reuben fucked him over once in such a horrible way that if he hadn't turned to me for help, I'm not sure he'd ever be able to work in the technology world again.

"Keri," I said, locking my gaze on him. As much as I wanted to hold him or take his hand, I knew better. Touching when emotions were high always backfired when it came to him. "None of that was directed at you specifically. He is a crafty man who thrives on manipulation, which has nothing to do with your ability to recognize it because it's a goddamn fact. My motive was purely to protect you, the company, and whatever that code truly is. Forgive me, but I don't for a second believe it's just a deep web scrubber to help protect against identity theft in his magical search engine."

"H, why do you think I took the job?" Kerian asked with a sigh as he flipped his locks out of his face, slumping in the chair. "I don't believe that's what it is either, but the only way to find out what the code is supposed to do is to break it down, look at each line under a microscope, put it back together, and see what I can make it do. Reuben didn't give me the whole thing, just the part he was stuck on, so I have to reverse engineer this damn thing with only half the manual."

This had me frowning and my overprotective nature rearing its head. "If that's true, then why didn't you tell me?"

"No," Quintin snapped, drawing both our attention. "While there are many things that should have been done with this situation, the one thing we are *not* going to do is play the blame game. The two of you did the exact same thing in different ways to us all, so in my mind, that cancels our fault. That being said, why don't we take this moment to do what should have happened the moment this job was taken and be honest about the situation."

One thing Quintin hated as much as failure had to be when any of us fought with each other. If he saw a fight brewing as he'd just done, then down would come the iron fist of mediation and resolution. It was inevitable that we fought on occasion, but I'll admit Quintin was a master at maneuvering the stormy waters to find a way to calm things down.

"He's right," Kerian grumbled.

"Yeah, I know... he's always right," I muttered, gulping down the last of my coffee and getting up to refill it. "I suggest we either work this out now or put it on the shelf to come back to when we don't need to worry about Lainey walking in on a heated discussion."

"Why would we need to worry about that?" Quintin questioned. "It's inevitable that she'll see us having disagreements in our day-to-day lives. When you have more than one person living together, they are bound to occur."

My hand stopped with the coffee pot in the air halfway into pouring my refill. Shifting, I looked back at Quintin, brows raised. "Are you under the impression she's staying here with us?"

"Well, yes. Isn't that our end goal? I realize we haven't officially extended the offer, nor has she accepted, but I feel like that is what will be happening by the time this week is over. Why hide who we are and how our family acts from someone who we wish to be a part of it?"

The man had a solid point. Keeping Lainey with us forever, becoming a permanent part of our lives, is exactly what I wanted. However, anyone could see she was a runner, ready to bolt at the slightest sign of something that would tie them down or possibly hurt them again. From the bits and pieces we'd gathered over the past few days, her past didn't paint a rosy picture, so it was understandable, which is why we needed to move ever so carefully lest we lose her for good.

"Was I wrong to assume we all felt this way?" Quintin demanded, narrowing his gaze at me behind his horn-rimmed glasses.

"No, Quin, you're not wrong," Kerian answered first, placing a hand over our clearly agitated partner. "I think the only reason H asked was to see if the three of us were in agreement on that thinking. It might also have to do with the small detail of her clearly not looking for a pack and having kept her knowledge of us being her scent-pairs to herself. I don't think she ever would have told us if we didn't stumble upon it the way we did."

"All the more reason for us to show her why that was a mistake and staying is the better choice," Quintin argued. "I won't stand by and let her walk away without being honest about how we feel. While I understand many people see sex as a physical act having the ability to remove emotions from it, that's not what happened between us.

She was truly honest about herself for the first time when she told us about her childhood. To me, that shows trust, no matter how small, has begun to build between us. If she gave us a chance, I *know* we could be happy together."

"You caught that too, huh?" I commented, taking my seat once more with a full mug. They nodded their heads with dour expressions. "It's clear she's running from something or someone and has been for a long time. I agree we should show her what we have to offer her as a pack and Alphas who can be a support as well as a safe haven. Although, I think the question of having her move in might be better received toward the end of the week when she's more comfortable with us."

Kerian gave Quin's hand a squeeze. "I agree with H on this. Let's show her how much we want her to stay by proving she can fit into our lives effortlessly, then when the weekend comes to a close, we broach the topic."

Quintin adjusted his glasses, giving him the moment he needed before giving us an answer. "You both make convincing arguments, so I will agree to waiting, but if either of you try to talk me out of it when Sunday rolls around, I'm not going to listen."

I was stunned to hear the conviction in his tone. "She's really made an impression on you, hasn't she?"

"Are you going to sit there and tell me she hasn't done the same to you?" Quintin challenged, promptly putting me in my place.

"No, I can't say that," I admitted softly. "There is nothing more I want than to build a better life with her in it. Lainey Collins has left her mark on me even if I haven't put my mark on her yet. Something I plan to make happen sooner rather than later if I have any say in the matter."

Twenty-One

Lainey

My heart thundered in my chest at Halstead's words.

I'd just been about to enter what I assumed to be the kitchen as I followed the sound of voices once I'd come downstairs. Hearing my name, I paused to listen and instantly regretted that choice, as those words were a stab to the heart. *He wanted to build a life with me? Mark me to create a bond more sacred and meaningful than any other commitment ceremony in the world?*

Tears burned in my eyes as emotion made my chest constrict to the point I was subconsciously rubbing it with my hand. *Was I having a panic attack right now?* Everything seemed so overwhelming, and I didn't know what to do as my heart thundered in my ears. Then the next thing I knew, something crashed into my legs catching me so off guard that I toppled to the floor with a yelp.

The face of an English Bulldog appeared before me seconds before half its body was on me so it could reach my face to lick it. Giggles erupted out of me as the felt of the slobbery tongue accompanied by the snuffling and wheezing sounds coming from the dog. Reaching up, I grasped the stocky fella and tried to move him off me, but he was having none of it. Instead, he stuffed his face under my chin and scrambled to fully lay on top of me, grinning with triumph, his body all one giant wiggling mass.

"Tater-Tot," Kerian barked. "Get off her *now*."

The pup whined but slid off me and hurried over to sit at his person's feet, staring lovingly up at him.

"I'm so sorry, Lainey. He normally isn't this interested in people," Kerian explained as he grabbed me under my armpits and hoisted me to my feet. "Oh God, he got you good and after you just took a bath. Come on, let me help fix this mess since my child caused this."

"Aah… so this is the infamous Tater-Tot," I said once I got my laughter under control as Kerian pulled me into the kitchen and over to the sink.

I spotted Quintin and Halstead over at a beautiful antique-looking round wooden table that could seat about six people. I flinched when Kerian started to wipe down my neck. "That's fucking cold, asshole," I yelled reflexively.

Kerian just froze, dishcloth in hand, inches away from my skin. "Aah… right, sorry."

Flipping the water on, he turned it to hot and let it run. I spotted the coffee and headed right for it, opening the cabinet above. "Yes, I was right," I cheered, grabbing a mug from the shelf.

"I suppose I don't need to tell you to make yourself at home then?" Halstead commented, humor in his voice.

Before I could answer, Kerian dragged me back to the sink. "Come here, you slobbery woman. I promise it's warm this time."

Tilting my face up for him, I closed my eyes, and he wiped away Tater-Tot's greeting. Thankfully, I'd decided it was easier to throw my hair up instead of taking the time to blow dry it. If it had been down, I would've needed a whole nother shower.

"There, now you can go get your coffee," Kerian said, giving me a little shove. "Are you hungry? In the mood for breakfast, or are we feeling more like lunch? We're kind of on the border of the two."

I glanced at him over my shoulder. "You know they have a name for that. It's called brunch."

"Oh, I see how it is, Miss Sassy Pants," Kerian quipped. "I was going to cook for you, but now you're gonna have to fend for yourself."

The delight of being able to cook for them excited me more than it had any right to. Finally, I could do something for them that I could be proud of as a way to show my appreciation. While I didn't know much about the *real* Lainey, I did know one thing—she was a fucking awesome cook.

"Perfect, since you don't mind me poking around, I'll see what you have to work with and go from there," I said, already pulling the refrigerator door open to look for cream.

My mouth fell open as I took in the shelves stocked with anything and everything I could possibly need. I grabbed a container of blueberries and popped one in my mouth. It was the perfect balance of sweet and sour, making me hum with delight. Ideas of what I could make flitted through my brain as I took stock of what I could see. Grabbing the eggs, I set them on the counter next to the blueberries. Spotting strawberries, I took those too, along with bacon, onion, and cheese.

"Would there be any reason you might keep a frozen pie shell?" I questioned, looking up from the ingredients at the guys.

I found them standing at the other end of the long kitchen island that gave me tons of room to work. Everything in this kitchen was commercial grade, and I was thrilled to test it out. What had me doubting my choice to do this was the confused expressions on the guys' faces.

"What?" I demanded, hands on my hips. "I'm absolutely positive this is not your first time seeing a woman in your kitchen, so spit it out."

"We are supposed to be taking care of you today," Quintin pointed out.

"Yeah, I wasn't serious when I said you needed to cook for yourself. Whatever you want to eat, I'm sure we can figure it out," Kerian offered.

The excitement that I'd felt over cooking for them died a little. "Oh... so you don't want me to cook for you?"

Kerian and Quintin looked at Halstead like he should know how to respond to my question. Coming around the counter, he came to stand before me and cupped my face in his hands. "What would you like to do? Our goal in cooking for you was to make you feel pampered and cared for. However, the look on your face right now tells me we're doing the opposite of that."

A riot of emotions shot through me as I wanted to kick myself for wearing my emotions on my sleeve so clearly. While I wanted to enjoy today and pretend I was their Omega, I couldn't let my emotions get the best of me. I was a character, Elaine Collins, executive assistant to this man, who just so happened to be scent-paired to his pack. Lainey was going to be leaving after this and shouldn't get all emotional over not being able to cook for them. That was stupid. *Pull it together, woman, or your carelessness is going to get us caught and possibly killed.*

"It's fine. I do enjoy cooking, but this is your home, and I'm a guest here," I answered, giving Halstead a small smile. "I suppose I just wanted to give back a little after all you've done for me the past few days."

He searched my face with a slight frown on his brow as he studied me. "Why aren't you being honest with us, doll?"

My eyes grew wide as Halstead called me out. "Wh-what?" I stuttered.

"Lainey, moments ago you were radiating happiness as you started to gather things. Then we had to go and put our big-ass feet in our mouths and make you second-guess yourself. If you want to cook, then say so, but don't do it because you feel like you owe us. All that we want is for you to feel comfortable while you're in our home. You're welcome to use whatever we have to offer," he explained. "Now I'm going to ask you again, and I want a truthful answer, or I'm going to bend you over this counter and turn your ass red."

I gulped at the intensity in his eyes and command of his tone just on the edge of an Alpha bark. "I would really like to cook breakfast," I answered.

Halstead tilted my head up so I was at a better angle for him to drop a kiss on my lips. "All right then, I look forward to eating it."

This man had me melting in his hands the way he made me feel so cherished and heard. It wasn't like he did anything major to make me feel that way, but the intention behind it made all the difference.

"Now, the next important question... do you want our help or should we leave you to it?" he inquired.

I took a moment to think through what I wanted to make. "I can handle it on my own. You guys have been cooped up in the room with me, so go catch up on things you need to. I'll holler when it's ready in about an hour."

"Do you want to tell me what other things you might need so I can point out where they are?" Halstead offered.

That was actually a thoughtful suggestion, so I nodded and rattled off the majority of things I'd need. He showed me where the pantry was with all the dry ingredients I'd need, pulled out mixing bowls, measuring spoons and cups, and various other tools I thought I'd need.

"This is perfect. I have pretty much everything I need, and whatever I didn't think of, I've got a good guess where to find it or at least start looking," I shared.

Quintin stepped up and offered me the cell phone the Syndicate gave me. "I hope you don't mind, but I added our personal cell numbers to your contacts. If you need anything, feel free to text or call any of us. We won't be far."

"Thank you," I whispered and popped up on my toes to give him a quick kiss. "Always so thoughtful and looking after me. I'm gonna be spoiled here pretty soon."

"Good, that's exactly what I want, especially over the next few days," he responded, kissing me once more before leaving the kitchen.

Left on my own, the space suddenly felt rather large and empty in a way it hadn't before. A sneeze had me looking down, finding Tater-Tot sitting on the rug in front of the sink. His tongue lolled out of his grinning mouth as he watched me with curiosity.

"Are you going to hang out with me while I make brunch?" I asked.

He let out a soft *woof* like he'd understood what I said, his butt wiggling since he didn't really have a tail. Squatting down, I reached out my hand, and he dove for it, thrilled I wanted to give him attention. He behaved himself as he sat between licking the air when my face was too far away for him to reach. This English Bulldog had the typical white fur with red-colored splotches on him, an underbite, and floppy Dorito-shaped ears. His happy snuffles and snorts were the most adorable thing I'd ever heard from a smooshed-faced pup.

"You can stay, but you can't be underfoot, you hear me?" I told him, wagging a finger at him. He promptly licked it and gave a little yip of agreement. "Okay, go back to the rug and stay there. Be a good boy, and bacon might be in your future."

It took a little coaxing since he didn't want me to stop petting him, but once I got him onto the rug and told him to stay, he promptly laid down, kicking out his back legs.

"You good?" I inquired.

My answer was for him to settle his head on his paws and watch me with those warm brown eyes of his. Satisfied, I got to work preheating the oven, then mixing the ingredients for the French toast bake I was going to use the berries with. Then I would move to the quiche since I had to cook the bacon first. Searching for a dish big enough to put the bake into, I spotted a speaker, and upon closer inspection, there was a whole speaker system in the kitchen.

Wandering around the room, I finally found the controls tucked in a cabinet that perfectly hid the thing. If I'd had my real phone, I would have had my cooking playlist, but I didn't, so I'd have to adjust. There was an MP3 player already plugged in, making me smile at the outdated technology, but in a situation like this, I could see how it made sense. Scrolling through, I found one labeled—*Ruth gets shit done*. Curious, I looked through the songs and was rather impressed with the selection, so I clicked on Sia's song, "Unstoppable."

The music blasted through the speakers sending Tater into a tizzy, scrambling to get away as I hurried to find the volume control. Now at a far more reasonable level, I took a moment to breathe, my heart still racing from the scare. Tater poked his head around the island, looking at me reproachfully.

"Hey, I wasn't the one who left it that way," I said in my defense. "Whoever used it last must have been nearly deaf for it to be that loud."

"Actually, that would be my husband, Adem," a woman said as she entered through the sliding glass door. "He knows I'm really the only one who uses that sound system and likes to think he's funny with practical jokes like that."

"How charming of him," I commented, a little caught off guard at how casually this woman just walked into the house.

"Where are my manners? I'm Ruth, the housekeeper and cook for the guys," she explained, reaching out a hand to me.

Now I felt like an absolute asshole for having any negative thoughts toward her. "I hope you don't mind that I'm borrowing your kitchen."

"Not at all, borrow away. It's your house now too," Ruth assured me, but her off-handed comment had me biting my tongue.

Of course, she would assume I would now be living here. I was scent-paired to all three men, so it was logical. No one in their right mind would turn down the chance to live with three sexy millionaires who wanted to pamper their Omega in their private mansion.

"Don't tell me those guys were so helpless they asked you to cook and didn't even bother to help," Ruth demanded, all but growling in her indignation.

I couldn't help it and burst out laughing. "Oh my God, if you only knew what it took for them to let me do this, you'd understand why I'm laughing. No, they most certainly did not ask me to cook, and I sent them on their way so I could work in peace."

"Oh..." Ruth answered, looking a little chagrined. "Here I am barging into your personal time, throwing around wild accusations and ruining it for you."

"It's fine, really," I assured her. "If I'm being honest, it's nice to have a little estrogen around right about now. Heats are intense, and they were amazing—"

"Yup, I'm gonna stop you right there," Ruth cut in, holding out a hand, waving it frantically. "I don't need to know any of the details, thank you very much. There's no way I'd be able to look them in the eye without dying of embarrassment if I knew about their..." she paused, "... um... intimate lives?" She finished, making it sound more like a question than a statement.

"Don't worry, I won't spill any juicy secrets with you. I just was going to say they were amazingly supportive," I told her. "I hope you don't mind, but I need to keep working on this so we can eat sooner rather than later. My stomach is trying to eat itself, and I've been trying to tide it over by eating some of the shredded cheese."

"No, no, go on. I was simply popping by to make sure there was still enough food ready to go in the fridge. Now that your heat broke and you're taking care of this meal, then I'll just have to worry about dinner. I asked the guys if you had any food allergies, but they weren't really sure of the answer. Only reason I ask is so I don't make meals you can't eat or have something in the house that will kill you," she explained.

Dumping the bread chunks into the baking dish, I spread them out evenly. "Nope, no food allergies, and I'm definitely not a picky eater. Although if I had a preference, fish isn't my favorite thing in the world," I admitted and was surprised to feel like that was really true for me.

"Not a problem. Quintin is allergic to salmon, so I don't make fish in general. How do you feel about shrimp?"

"Shrimp I love... nothing better than a good shrimp scampi," I answered instantly.

Ruth grinned at me as she leaned against the counter. "Well, what do you know... that happens to be Halstead's favorite food. I mean, that man would devour anything in the Italian food category, but that is by far his top choice."

"He is a man of refined taste. After all, I shouldn't be surprised," I said in a dramatic, nasally voice that had us both grinning.

"Well, I'll get out of your hair and let you finish. If you need anything, though, my number is on the neon yellow Post-it on the fridge. My husbands and I live in the coach house, so I'm pretty much always around. See you at dinner time," Ruth called as she pulled the sliding door open, waved her goodbye, and left.

Tater lifted his head to look over his shoulder at her exit but made no effort to move. He'd practically ignored Ruth ever being in the kitchen. Was that what Kerian had meant when he said Tater-Tot didn't have much interest in people? Either way, I was going to take it as a win and assume I'd earned his approval. Why that was important, I don't know, but it was for some reason.

With everything finally mixed together, put in their respective dishes, and placed in the oven, I was left with thirty to forty-five minutes for them to cook. Grabbing my cell phone, I set the timer and turned to look at the sliding glass door that opened out onto a brick back patio. Feeling like fresh air might be nice, I pulled the door open to check the weather and smiled at the slightly cool but pleasant feel. Whoever picked out clothes for me had only grabbed the softest and comfiest things to wear, so I would be more than warm enough in my yoga pants and fleece pullover sweatshirt. Tater scrambled to get to his feet, bolted out the door heading right for the large span of grass, and got in a vigorous roll. I'd never had a pet before, but I was quickly seeing the appeal the more time I spent around Tater-Tot.

I curled up on one of the lawn chairs when my phone vibrated in my hand. Glancing down, my stomach dropped when I spotted the message was from the Syndicate. It shouldn't surprise me that they would check in with me after I fell off the radar for three days. Since I'm positive they watch my house, they would know someone came to get clothes and things for me. Part of me wanted to ignore the message and let this day be one of blissful ignorance, but my fear of them thinking I've turned my back on the job had me swiping my thumb over the screen to unlock it.

Ms. Caddel,

Due to the fact that you were given a dose of our specially formulated medication that removes all suppressant and scent-altering drugs, we assume you have gone into heat as is typical for this medication. Another side effect of this medication is increased fertility, so we strongly suggest that you be aware of this and get a pregnancy test done in the following seven to ten days.

If you find yourself with child, know that you are not permitted to terminate the pregnancy due to the chances of it being an Omega are fifty-fifty. In the event you do not wish to raise this child, we will happily take the baby into our care the moment it is born. We do not wish for the child to be put in the system as you were.

Twenty-Two

Lainey

Horror at the idea of some strange syndicate taking any child, let alone mine, was met with dread at the idea I might actually be pregnant. Kids hadn't been on my list of things I wanted to have happen in my life, but if it were to happen, I would *never* allow it to end up in the system or with some creepy-ass criminal organization. No, I would either figure out a way to protect that child myself or find a family I vetted and approved of to raise them.

What did that mean for the guys? Would I have to tell them? Should I tell them? Did they even want kids? How the fuck did I end up in this situation?

Dropping my phone, it clattered to the brick as I pulled my knees up to my chest, resting my head on them. Memories of my childhood raised in the group home flooded my mind. I remember the feelings of confusion when I went to school and people asked me about my family, parents, siblings, and other things people typically had, but I didn't. Before and after the group home, I was a kid who had no one out there in the world looking out for me or even giving a shit if I was being taken care of. One thing I was eternally grateful for was that the group home I lived in was one of the best. I'd been well looked after, fed, clothed, and sent to school until Trent came along.

That's when my life turned to shit. Nothing was normal or had a routine to it. I was forced to learn and adjust to Trent's rules. He brought me to the place the bad kids went, showed me the terrible things that people would do to them, and warned me it would be my fate if I didn't do things right. That was the first time nightmares filled my dreams, tormenting me with all the possibilities that could happen if I fucked up. It's sad to say that I was one of the lucky ones. I didn't have to suffer the fate so many others did until my first heat. That's when Trent took it upon himself to teach me what it took to be a real woman as he helped me manage my heat. He'd kept me to himself the first day, then brought in others the next since I was his to use in any way he saw fit.

What is it they say about trauma? You either spend your life running from it or running toward it. I suppose I managed to fall in the middle of that. I'd been running from the girl that event happened to, but at the same time living in a similar world, using all the lessons Trent taught me to get the job done. Now I might be faced with choosing what to do with a child in this whole mess. I'd never seen what it means to be a parent other than on television, and we all know that's *so* realistic.

Once more, my phone started vibrating, informing me that it had been thirty minutes. Clearly, I'd been trapped in this mental spiral for far longer than I'd realized. Somewhere during that time, Tater-Tot had climbed up on the lawn chair, curled up at the end of it, and kept me company. When I moved, his head popped up, and he watched me intently as if he understood I wasn't doing well. Standing, he walked up, rested his head on my knees, and gave a soft whine, so I reached out to stroke his head, reassuring him as much as he was reassuring me.

"I suppose there's not much I can do about it right now, can I? There's no way to know if I'm pregnant or not until the end of the week. Thankfully, though, they have those rapid tests so I can find out pretty quickly," I murmured as my hand moved over his velvet-soft fur. "Guess I should check on brunch. We don't want it to burn after putting in all that work."

Tater hopped down and waited for me like he knew what I'd said, making me smile. Back in the kitchen, I found Kerian peeking in the oven. He jumped as he heard the sliding door open and gave me a guilty look. "It just smelled so good... figured it had to be nearly done."

"Actually, the timer just went off, so if you think it looks cooked, then let's pull them out and double-check," I informed him.

Without a second thought, he grabbed a hot pad and set the dishes on top of the stove. Leaning against him, I held onto his arm as I peered at the food. The quiche looked perfect, and the French toast bake bubbled happily but appeared to be done. I grabbed a knife from the drawer and nudged Kerian with my hip to move out of the way. He decided it would be better to slide me in front of him, rest his hands on my hips, and watch what I was doing. I tested the middle of the quiche just to make sure it was done and grinned happily.

"I'd say we're good to call the others," I announced.

Kerian wrapped his arms around my waist and pulled me against his chest as he kissed along my neck. "I think I might like to keep you to myself for just a minute more if that's all right with you?"

For the men who can talk so dirty to also be unfairly skilled at whispering sweet nothings into a woman's ear is just wrong. It's like they can cheat at life, making us swoon and fall into their arms before they ravage us in the bed, bringing out the primal nature of a good fuck. I let out a groan as I twisted in his arms so I could look up at him.

"And if I said no?" I questioned, truly curious to know what he would say.

"Then I would accept that choice and text the others to come and eat," he answered.

Slowly, I slid my hands up his chest, then twined them around his neck, pulling him down to me so I could kiss him. "I think I can spare a minute."

Kerian moved us to the left, away from the stove, and hoisted me up onto the counter, all while never breaking our kiss. He wedged his way in between my legs as his hands grasped my ass, pulling me closer. This was the sort of kiss you see in the movies, and let me tell you, it was just as fucking magical as you think it would be. It felt like I was the only person in the world to him right now, and he was in no rush to let this kiss end or to leave this moment we shared. Yet with all wonderful things, they must come to an end, but even though he leaned back from the kiss, he didn't pull away.

"Do you like dancing?" Kerian asked, catching me off guard with how out of the blue the question was.

"Aah..." was about all I could manage to get out as my brain tried to find that answer.

Kerian chuckled and kissed my nose. "Let me try that again. Lainey, I would love to take you out tomorrow night and go dancing. Would you be at all interested in doing that with me?"

"Did you have a type of dancing in mind?" I inquired.

"Well, I've been taking dance lessons for the past few years, and so far I've learned the waltz, tango, salsa, foxtrot, two-step, swing, and I'm currently learning the cha-cha," he answered.

My mouth popped open. "Holy shit, when in the hell did you find time to learn all that?"

"What can I say? I'm a man who likes to stay active." He shrugged. "My job has me sitting so much that I try my best to make sure I counteract that with biking, running, dancing, anything that gets me moving and my heart pumping."

"Here I was thinking you wanted to go to a club and do some bump-n-grind kind of dancing," I said with a laugh. "Now that I know what you *really* meant, I'm decent at swing, pretty good at two-step, but the tango is my jam."

"Sooo..." Kerian asked, dragging out the word as he jostled me from side to side playfully. "Does that mean you'll come tango with me?"

"Yes, I'll come tango with you," I agreed, pushing him back. "Now text the others so the food doesn't get cold."

The giant grin on his face shouldn't have made me so happy, but it did. He pulled out his phone, sent the message, gave me another quick kiss, and pulled me off the counter. "This is going to be a blast. Thursday night at this funky speakeasy I like to go to is tango night, so that works out perfectly."

"Guess it was meant to be then," I teased.

His face turned slightly more serious as he cupped my cheek. "I don't think you know how true that is about all this, Lainey. Call it a fluke of biology all you want, but I choose to believe that being scent-paired with someone is more than just pheromones and reproduction. You have seamlessly found your way into our lives to the point I don't know how we couldn't see we were missing something."

"You can't really believe that." I scoffed before I could think better of it.

"Sorry, my sweet, sultry vixen, but I absolutely do. Call me a fool or a romantic, but I truly believe there is that one person out there who completes the life you've been looking for. I already had Halstead and Quintin, both people I love with my whole heart, but once you entered the picture, I knew you would be the glue to hold us together for life," Kerian reasoned.

"I just don't know that I believe that exists in the world," I admitted. "Everything has taught me that you are the only person you can rely on not to fail you or turn their back on you."

"Well, I don't believe I heard Kerian say he wasn't going to do those things," Halstead interjected, drawing my attention to where he was leaning against the doorjamb, arms crossed as he watched us. Clearly, he'd been listening for a while to have such a certain tone of what Kerian did or didn't say. "He told you that he was falling for you, saw how perfectly you fit into our lives, and that he knew there was no other person in the world who could replace what you bring to this pack. Nowhere did he say that we wouldn't fuck up or let you down. That's part of being alive and dealing with any sentient being that has thought and will of its own."

He pushed away from the door and walked over to reach out a hand to me. I took it, and he pulled me away from the stove so I was now standing with Kerian at my back and Halstead's large body before me.

"Doll, if you decide to give us a chance, I will never promise you that we won't piss you off. I will guarantee you that there will be fights, disagreements, and butting of heads since you are such a strong-willed woman. The three of us are, for the most part, the typical Alpha who can't help but be opinionated assholes who believe they know what's right for everyone. It's in our DNA to protect, but I know for myself when I try to do that, it can end up feeling like you're being smothered," Halstead acknowledged, which I felt was rather self-aware of the man. "What I *will* promise you is that you will have our respect, affection, which I sense will soon be love, and above all else, the willingness to fight for you. Do you think living in a house with three stubborn men doesn't come with its battle of wills?"

I shook my head as I bit my lip, trying to quell the tears that were starting to pool in my eyes. *Damn these men and their fucking healthy communication skills.*

"No, you're absolutely right. In the early days, there were a few moments when I thought it might come to actual fistfights between Kerian and me. However, one thing I would never allow was for him to walk away from me. I'm not saying we needed to hash it out right then and there because sometimes tempers are too hot. If he needed to go in the other room to cool off before we could attempt to mend the argument, I had zero issue with that." Halstead took both my hands in his and held them tightly as he pinned me with his intense blue gaze. "The one thing I will not tolerate or allow to happen is for any of my pack members to leave this house in anger. No one can walk out unless they are prepared to never walk back in this door again. Here in this house and this pack, we fight for each other, and if you aren't willing to do that in return, then you were never planning on being part of this family."

My heart rate sped up at his words, mostly in terror that if I left, I would never get the chance to come back if I ever got the courage. Even still, there was a small flicker of hope that had been growing with each gentle touch, sweet word, and promise that I knew in my soul they would do whatever it took to keep me. This left me in an impossible position. How the fuck was I ever going to get out of this mess I never planned to be in?

That question had me thinking back on the message that the Syndicate sent me. *Would their opinion change if I had a child? If I left and then showed back up on their doorstep with their offspring, would they still reject me?* Hell, I would if it were me. In fact, I think if someone came back to me just because they decided they wanted to be a family after lying and running, I wouldn't trust them as far as I could throw them, and I doubt I could even pick Halstead up. All this turmoil had my mind racing to the point I thought it was going to start spewing steam like the cartoons. Then it all came to a screeching halt as lips pressed to mine, and I was wrapped up in a tight hug with both men trapping me between their bodies.

"Easy, doll," Halstead murmured. "That was unfair of me to drop that all in your lap when this is so new. In all those words, I only want you to hear one thing. We. Will. Fight. For. You. We all have messy pasts, and you've shared a bit about yours with us, but I just wanted you to know that it won't scare us off. We're Alphas... we like a challenge, and we most certainly like you."

Another soft kiss was placed on my lips, but I yanked my hands out of his and clung to him like a koala. He was saying all the things I've wanted to hear my whole life and never once received. You can't tell someone to want you, fight for you, and treasure and value the person you are. They do or they don't.

"Thank you," I managed to whisper, even though my throat was so tight with emotion.

Halstead nuzzled his nose against mine in an Eskimo kiss before unwinding me from his body. "You are more than welcome, Lainey. Anytime you need me to tell you that again, just say the word, even if it's ten times a day."

"What are we telling her ten times a day?" Quintin asked as he entered the kitchen with a handful of vegetables.

"That we like her and want her to stay," Kerian answered as he grabbed a large wash basin from under the sink and put it on the counter.

Quintin deposited the vegetables in the basin before washing his hands. "I think ten times a day might be a little unnecessary, but if that's what she told you she needed, then who am I to judge? By the way, breakfast smells amazing, Lainey."

"Thanks. I hope it tastes as good as it smells," I said, slipping out from between the men as Quintin grabbed plates.

"Silverware is in that drawer if you want to grab that while Keri and I bring over the food," Halstead suggested, pointing out the drawer.

Soon, we were all seated at the table with fresh coffee for us and tea for Quintin. A comfortable silence fell as we all dove into the food, the guys making happy grunting noises and going back for seconds before they even finished their first serving. Hiding my smile behind my coffee cup, I watched them as they worked out how to dish up the last slice of quiche.

"What if we cut it into three pieces?" Kerian suggested.

"That won't work unless two people don't want the crust," Quintin pointed out.

Kerian shrugged. "I don't need the crust. I want the good shit in the middle."

"Okay, what if we cut it in half lengthwise and then cut the top half down the middle so there are two pieces with crust," Halstead offered.

There was no way I could hold back my laughter at watching them figure out how to divide up this last slice as if it were some quantum mechanics equation to find the missing formula for the meaning of life.

Instantly, they fell silent, looking at me intently. "What?" I asked once I got my giggles under control.

"Did you get enough to eat?" Quintin asked. "Here we are talking about thirds when you've only had one serving. If anyone should be eating this, it should be you."

"Oh no, I'm stuffed," I answered, waving off his concern. "Really, I don't normally eat as much as I did since I would have made one or the other, not both dishes. You three have worked way too hard to figure out how to make this work. I wouldn't want to ruin the whole endeavor."

Quintin's face scrunched up in disapproval. "I'm sure this will sound rude, and I don't mean it to, but please know there is no reason for you to diet on our account. While you are a physically stunning woman, to expect anyone to maintain that their whole life isn't realistic. We work out and eat healthy to ensure our health is in a good place but not for any sort of vanity like the majority of people."

Kerian groaned and dropped his head into his hands, his locks creating a curtain around his face as if he couldn't bear to look at Quintin. "Quin, you don't ever tell a woman what to do about their physical appearance." Lifting his head, he looked at his partner with a slightly pained expression. "If she's healthy, happy, and likes how she looks, then that is all we need to concern ourselves with. Also, I'd like to point out that even though you didn't mean to, you just called her vain."

"I did not," Quintin snapped, then looked at me. "Did you think I called you vain?"

Taking a moment to compose myself so I didn't end up on the floor from laughing so hard, I answered, "Some might have taken what you said as calling them vain. I, however, did not because I know you well enough to understand where you were coming from. As for what Kerian said, he is right in some ways. It's best to keep your opinion to yourself when it comes to a person's view of themselves. Then again, if they are doing something that will cause them harm, then you absolutely should speak up."

"That makes sense, yet I don't see how it would be wrong of me to tell you that I like more than just your body. No matter what we do, bodies will change, but your personality and intelligence won't, and that I find even more attractive about you," Quintin clarified.

"Good Lord, you three are good for a woman's ego." I chuckled. "Thank you, Quintin. I appreciate you saying that and meaning it... not everyone does. For me, it's more of a checks and balances. I *love* sugary foods and munching on snacks if they are left out. Since I know this about myself, I try to keep a little more control over how much I eat during meals, knowing I will inevitably indulge in something else during the day. It's as you say, to keep myself healthy and be more aware of what I'm eating." This explanation seemed to appease the man as he relaxed into his seat, sipping the last of his tea.

"Lainey, could I steal you for a bit once we're done here?" Halstead asked.

"Sure, it shouldn't take too long for the four of us to clean up the kitchen, then I'm all yours," I answered.

"Oh, you're not cleaning up," Kerian cut in. "You cooked, we clean... that's the house rules. We even do it for Ruth since her work hours end for the night once dinner is done and ready to be served."

Blinking at them for a moment, I relented as Quintin grabbed my plate and stacked it with his. "Wouldn't want to break house rules."

"That a girl," Halstead said with a wink. "Now you get to come with me."

"Wait, why aren't you helping to clean up?" I questioned.

He looked at the other two then back to me. "They hate the way I do things, and no matter how many times they've tried to teach me, I never seem to match their standards. So I do the kitchen clean up once they are all done, like taking out the trash, sweeping the floor, things like that."

"You must be really terrible then," I reasoned as everyone nodded their heads.

Halstead got up and pulled out my chair, offering me a hand. "Shall we?"

"I don't know... are you two sure you're okay with this?" I asked, needing to be certain.

"Yes, go, we got this handled," Kerian assured me, waving us out of the kitchen.

Twenty-Three

Lainey

Halstead escorted me through the giant maze of a house, pointing out various things or rooms that I'm not sure I'd be able to find again without some trial and error. He then led us outside via a side entrance that placed us on the driveway. It was like a cul-de-sac of garages or what I assumed were garages that almost looked more like stone cottages. The driveway was made out of brick which only added to the aesthetic.

"Where are we going?" I inquired as Halstead tugged me along after him.

"I thought while you're here with us, it would be nice for you and me to get to know each other on a more personal level. We have the added challenge of being boss and employee, so I feel like I need to make damn sure you know who I am outside of that building. When we are at work, we work. However, the moment we clock out and get in our cars, we are Halstead and Lainey, a scent-paired couple," Halstead explained as he typed the twelve-digit number into the keypad on the door to one of the buildings.

The lock beeped, then he turned the handle and started to push open the door. "This is my most prized collection, and not many people know about it. As I'm sure you've more than gathered, I like to keep my private life to just my family and close friends. The reason

I'm telling you that is because if you were only a coworker or employee, you'd never know this existed."

He pushed open the door, stepped to the side, and flicked on the lights. It took them a moment to warm up and blink to life, but when they did, I gasped. The whole building was full of stunning, mint-condition vintage cars. Blown away at the sight, I slowly walked the main center path taking in each vehicle's beauty. There were some brands of cars I didn't recognize, making me curious to know if they were imports or just that rare. I spotted one in a bright cherry red color that was a two-seater with the soft top folded back, revealing the cream-colored leather interior.

This little beauty looked sporty with its curves and bright coloring, drawing me to it. "This is gorgeous," I whispered in awe.

"That is an Alpha Lonist 33," Halstead shared. "It was a race car back in the day boasting speeds of sixty miles an hour in six seconds, the fastest in its day and age, I'll have you know."

"So its looks match the goods under the hood," I teased.

"You know cars?" Halstead asked.

"If you mean how to drive one and where to put the gas and oil, then yes, I know cars," I answered with a completely deadpan serious face.

Halstead gave me an exasperated look. "You're lucky you're cute," he muttered. "Want to take her for a ride, see if she's as fast as they say?"

"She?" I asked, bemused. "Are all your cars women? Do I need to be concerned?"

"No, there are only a few that I've determined earned the title of 'she.' Most of the others are male, for damn sure, but there are some cars like this one that you need to prove just how skilled you are to be able to drive. It's not... can you drive a car or even a stick shift? No, no, it's can you speak the right language to unlock the car's true potential and see the hidden gem inside," Halstead enlightened as he lifted the door latch, and I gasped as the doors opened backward instead of out toward you.

"That is just too fucking cool," I blurted, rushing over to see how it did that.

He just chuckled, but the delight in his eyes shone brightly. "They call them suicide doors."

"I've never seen anything like it," I muttered, unable to get over the whole thing.

"Neither have I," Halstead said in a low voice full of double meaning.

Looking up at him, I found he wasn't even looking at the car but staring at me. "Okay, Mr. Smooth Talker, I think I've had about all I can handle in that department for now. You said something about taking a drive?"

"Hop in," he motioned.

Wasting no time, I ducked under the door and settled into the seat. It was low, making me feel like my ass was going to drag on the ground, but magically it didn't. Halstead walked over to a lockbox hanging on the wall, grabbed a set of keys, and opened the massive garage door. Once he was settled, he flipped a switch, checked the gear shift, and grinned at me.

"Ready? Warning... this baby is vocal," he cautioned.

I gave him a thumbs up as I clicked my seat belt securely into the buckle. He hadn't been lying when he said the car was loud. Then again, we were still in the building, so the sound echoed off the walls, making it even louder. Once we were outside, it toned down quite a bit, but I didn't think we would be having any heart-to-heart conversations unless we wanted to yell at each other.

We journeyed down the winding driveway I didn't remember from when we arrived. The sprawling green grass on either side with a smattering of trees made me feel like I was in some period romance novel. As we approached the gate, Halstead lifted a clicker remote, and the gates started to open slowly. I really should have been prepared for what would happen once we passed the gate, but I'd been too relaxed taking in the scenery to be bothered. There was a slight pause as we reached the main road then pulled onto it but came to a stop.

I glanced at Halstead, but he was just smiling like a fool seconds before the rear tires started to squeal and then—*bam*. We were shooting off like a rocket down the road, engine roaring, wind tugging at my hair, and laughter bursting out of us. The speedometer was maxed out, but Halstead didn't ease up. Instead, he kept that pedal to the floor as we twisted and twined through the once-upon-a-time farmlands. Then the fields dropped away in favor of the tall, wispy coastal grasses that danced in the breeze we created passing them.

Even though I'd spent eighteen years of my life in this city, I'd only been to the coast three times. It wasn't something you normally did with foster kids, and Trent sure as shit didn't think we deserved an experience as nice as all that. The first two times were with school trips, having won some contest or met some goal the teacher had set giving us a few hours in the sun and sand as a reward. The last time I went was after I found out Trent got put in jail, and I gathered anything that would trace me back to him and burned it like any melodramatic teen would.

Halstead turned on the radio, and it was set to an oldies rock station which he jammed out to, tapping out the rhythm on the steering wheel and enjoying the moment. I could see why he liked vintage cars—they were simple. There were none of the bells and whistles to detract from the simple joys of going for a drive. Taking a page out of his book to enjoy the moment, I tipped my head back and closed my eyes, letting the sun warm my face and breath in the fresh ocean air.

I was startled as a hand grasped mine, but when my eyes snapped open, I found it was Halstead. He took my hand and placed it on the gear shift with our fingers intertwined. This way, he could hold my hand and change gears when needed, something I found highly adorable. I gave him a soft smile before I went back to my relaxed position and allowed my brain to go blank as we drove.

Time seemed to stop while we were in this car. There was no syndicate, fear of being pregnant, worry about the future, or what would happen once I destroyed the code. All there was, was being in the moment. That was until we stopped. Cracking open an eye, I found we were in a parking lot facing the water with a beach in front of us and a tiki hut off to the right with people milling around it.

"You stay here. I'll be right back," Halstead instructed.

My brows rose as I watched him run toward the hut. He joined the line of people, and it took him a bit to get whatever it was they were selling. When he came back, he held a coconut in one hand and a massive bowl of shaved ice covered in fruit with something white drizzled over it.

"Do you mind opening up the trunk? There should be a blanket inside. I always make sure my cars have one since I love to come here on the spur of the moment," he shared.

Climbing out of the car, I followed his instructions on getting the trunk unlatched, which was far more complicated than I could have imagined. There were, in fact, two blankets, so I grabbed both and followed him out onto the beach, where we were close enough to the water but not too close. I took the items from him as he sat down then took them back so I could join him. When he saw that I was sitting next to him, he muttered something I couldn't hear under his breath, set down the bowl of ice, and tugged my arm until I was sitting between his legs.

"Here, now you hold this," he ordered, plopping the shaved ice in my lap. "It's a healthy dessert, so eat all you want. There is fruit, sweetened condensed milk, and shaved ice. What could possibly be bad about that? Then for a beverage, I have fresh coconut milk with watermelon puree mixed in for flavor."

"Did you plan this?" I questioned as I unearthed one of the spoons from the tropical fruit. "This seems far too perfect for it to be a coincidence."

"No, I didn't plan it, but as I said, this is a place I often go to on the spur of the moment. Once I saw how relaxed you were with the drive, I figured why not make the trek out here?" he reasoned.

My mouth exploded with the fruits' flavor and the ice's crispness, making me moan. "That is fucking incredible."

Halstead nuzzled into the crook of my neck and pressed a kiss there. "Good, I'm glad you're enjoying it. I wanted to spoil you but didn't want you feeling bad about gorging on something sweet."

"How did you even find this palace?" I asked, looking around to see if there was a town or any sign of a populated area.

"When I was first developing Enigma, I actually had a friend who I thought was going to be a business partner with me. He was brilliant at the average user viewpoint and integration, while I was the coder and mastermind of keeping it all secure. My mom had her identity stolen, and it was hell on her for years. She'd wanted to buy a new car for herself when I was still in high school. My mother worked and saved to put down a down payment on her first brand-new vehicle but couldn't since someone trashed her credit and took out all these loans under her name. Even now that she's passed, I still get calls about shit that this other person did under her identification number. You could say that's what pushed me to make security such a big priority for me.

"Anyway, this friend and I worked together on a project for college which, in essence, created the foundation for Enigma. Although it wasn't called that back then, but that's not really important to the story. We were so close to getting things off the ground when he told me that he'd trademarked the name we were going to use, found another business partner that would better fit where he envisioned the company going, and cut me out of all of it. I was devastated that everything I'd slaved over was gone in the blink of an eye, just like that," he said, snapping his fingers.

"Holy fuck, I would have murdered the bastard," I yelled, jerking upright from the lounged position I'd been in against this chest. "How the hell did he manage to get away with all that? If you both worked on things having an equal share in the concept, he never should've been able to pull that off."

"Oh, trust me, I was furious, and one of the only ways I knew to calm my temper was to take a drive. If I hadn't done that, I might have actually beaten the man to death, but that would have done nothing to solve the problem since he'd put everything in his name as well as his new partner's. Come to find out, it was a group of three other men who'd become his pack, and they were all wealthy sons of influential people, which is also how he managed to slip past all the rules that should have prevented it from happening," Halstead explained.

"So you just drove for who knows how long and ended up here?" I pressed.

He made the hand motion for 'kind of' as he made an undecided noise. "I guess you could say that, but the reason I stopped is because I'd driven for two hours and needed to piss and get a fucking drink. The drive hadn't been planned, so I had nothing with me. The

Tiki-Tiki Room was the first thing I found since I left the city, so I stopped. That place has all kinds of weird random things to eat and drink, always changing and evolving, except for these two things. Well, the flavor of the coconut water changes as does the fruit to what's in season, but you get my point.

"So here I was pissed off, tired, thirsty, my bladder about to explode, and I found this random tiki hut. Like anyone else, I stopped and took care of things, got a drink, and dropped onto the sand, trying to figure out what the hell to do with my life. It was then I realized this backstabbing asshole never had access to my security software or anything linked to it since it was my area to run. Eventually, we would have combined them, but at that point in the business, it was two halves of a whole... his intellectual property and mine. That was the only thing that saved me from complete and utter failure. Thanks to this place and allowing myself to simply take a moment to breathe and let my mind settle, I am where I am today."

"What about the other guy? Was he successful too, or did he crash and burn?" I inquired, then started to shovel the dessert into my mouth since it was melting.

Halstead rested his head against mine and let out a heavy sigh. "The other guy was Reuben Watts, founder and CEO of Cyclone Software."

The shock of that information made me speechless, unable to even finish swallowing the bite of fruit in my mouth.

"From what I can tell, he's doing just fine," he commented. "Well, except when he runs into a problem and has to come to my company and another person he's fucked over to fix it."

Gulping down the bite, I grabbed the coconut water before I started to choke on what I'd just swallowed before speaking, "Wow, does that guy have some balls daring to come to you after doing bullshit like that?"

"Yes, bullshit, indeed, but you see, in his eyes, I'm doing just fine and shouldn't need to hold a grudge about anything since it worked out in the end. He got his company, and I still managed to make mine happen without him. Now we are both at the top of the food chain for what we do as individuals," Halstead reasoned.

After that realization, we both fell silent and enjoyed each other's company as we finished the dessert. Once it was gone, we collected everything and started to head back to the car. Noticing that the sun was beginning to set, it was clear to me I had no sense of how long since we'd left the house.

"What time is it?" I asked once we were both seated in the vehicle.

Halstead glanced at his watch. "Half past four. We should be home before it gets dark and in time for dinner."

"What? We're two hours away from the house?" I exclaimed, gawking at him.

"Yeah... did you not realize how long we were driving?" he asked with a smirk. "I knew you were zenned out, but I didn't think it was that bad."

"Clearly, I needed this more than I thought," I mumbled, rubbing my forehead with my hand, trying to rationalize how I lost two hours that easily. "Wait, do the others know where we are?"

"No, I kidnapped you and left them to wonder what might have happened to us," Halstead said dryly as he started the car. "Don't worry. I texted them that we were making an impromptu trip to the tiki place."

The relief I felt knowing they didn't think we'd disappeared or run off was immense, and I didn't know how to feel about that. This whole thing was quickly spiraling out of control, and I had no idea how to slow things down.

When we arrived at the house and rejoined the guys, they were relaxing in the second-floor living room watching a movie. Neither of them seemed bothered at the fact Halstead and I had spent most of the day together. In fact, they were super curious about the tiki place as they called it.

"H won't ever take us there. He says it's his spot to deal with shit, and he can't do that if we're there," Kerian informed me.

I glanced at the grumpy bear who'd made me promise not to tell them too much about the place. This was a much bigger deal than I realized for him to have taken me out there and shared the experience.

"Look, Quin has his solarium we don't go to unless invited, you have your dance classes, and I have the tiki place. Everyone needs their thing or place to themselves... it's what keeps our relationship so healthy. No one wants to be needed *all* the time or the sole source of their happiness day in and day out," Halstead said in his defense.

"Are you two hungry? Ruth messaged me about five minutes ago to let us know dinner was ready, but there was no rush since she left it warming in the oven," Quintin shared.

"I have an idea," Kerian announced. "Why don't we do dinner up here so we can eat and watch a movie or two?"

"Yes," I cheered. "That sounds like an amazing idea. We had a snack, but I'm ready for some real food."

Decision made, we all traipsed downstairs, gathered what we needed for dinner, and brought it back up to the living room. I let the guys pick the movie since I was willing to watch just about anything, and they all seemed rather opinionated on the matter. Each of them picked out their choice, and then I was left to decide what one to start with. I closed my eyes and had them mix up the choices, then pointed to the CD.

"Looks like I'm the winner," Kerian said as he popped up off the couch to put it in the disk. "I hope you're ready for some epic action and impressive car stunts, my friends."

Action movies were one of my favorites, and I hadn't seen this one before, so I was thrilled. We dished up the pasta Ruth had made and snuggled into the deep-cushioned couch for the rest of the night.

Twenty-Four

Lainey

Fingers traced down the bare skin of my back, making me moan and arch into the touch, pressing my ass against whichever of my three guys was spooning me. Another hand circled my nipple before giving it a gentle flick, forcing a gasp to tumble out of my mouth. I half-opened my eyes to find Halstead in front of me, heat burning in his eyes as he met my gaze.

"Morning, doll," he murmured in a rough, sexy morning voice with a lazy smirk on his face.

"Hi," I answered, my brain still not really sure it was awake.

The man behind me slid his hand between my legs and stroked my pussy from bottom to top, using the slick already pooling to swirl his finger around my clit. "Good morning, beautiful," Quintin whispered in my ear before nibbling it.

"Oh, I think it's about to be a good morning if your hand is any indication of what's to come," I commented. "Is Kerian still asleep?"

"No, he's up and out of the house. Decided he wanted to take advantage of the time off and went to one of his favorite biking trails. He'll probably be gone most of the morning," Quintin answered.

"So it's just the three of us here in this big comfy bed. What could we possibly think of to do while he's away?" I mused aloud.

Halstead dipped his head, caught one of my nipples between his lips, and gave it a tug as he rolled his eyes up to watch my reaction. My head fell back against Quintin as I let him slide my left leg over his, exposing my pussy and allowing him more freedom to play. Halstead sucked my nipple into his mouth as he used his tongue to drive me fucking wild, thrusting against Quintin's hand.

Finally, Quintin plunged two fingers into my pussy, pumping them slowly in and out of me. He didn't remain there long but instead scooped out what he needed and started to massage my asshole. This gave me a pretty good idea of what these two had in mind, and I was in full support of starting my morning being doubled dicked and knotted. I could also tell from their energy that they wanted this moment to be tender lovemaking and nothing rushed or frenzied. I'm sure they'd gotten enough of that while I was in heat.

Halstead kept his mouth working my nipples, making sure each one received equal amounts of love as he lazily fingered my pussy. With his thick fingers, he only needed to use one for me to know it was there, but as I relaxed and my slick was now pouring out of me, he slipped in a second, making me cry out.

"God, I love the sound of your voice when we make you feel good." Halstead groaned, fisting his cock with his free hand. "Everything about you is so responsive to our touch it drives me out of my fucking mind. I keep telling myself to take my time and enjoy getting you all riled up, but I just want to thrust my cock so deep in your pussy you scream long and loud, letting the world know whose cock is making you writhe with pleasure."

Holy shit, the mouths on these men. They were about to create a new trigger for me that the moment any of them said something that dirty, I would come instantly. That's how much of a goddamn turn-on it was becoming.

"Fuuck!" I groaned out as Quintin slowly worked a finger into my ass.

He worked methodically to warm me up, using my slick as a lube and ensuring I was going to be comfortable when he filled me with his cock. I realized he was used to male partners who needed this consideration when it came to prepping for sex. Omegas, however, were made a little differently so when we were turned on, we became incredibly stretchy and malleable in an effort to accommodate an Alpha's knot.

It didn't take him long to catch on, though, as he slipped two fingers in the next time, and I stretched easily for him. "Are you that eager for me to fuck your ass, beautiful? You open up for me like a perfect flower blooming for all the world to see."

My whole body shivered at his words and the feel of his fingers stroking and thrusting into me. "Yes." I panted. "I want you both to fill me with your cocks and fuck me. To be pressed between you both as you fuck me together."

"What a good girl telling her Alphas what she needs," Halstead praised as I felt the warm, blunt head of his cock butt up against my pussy. "What our Omega needs, her Alpha is happy to give."

I half expected him to thrust up into me, but he didn't. Instead, the tip of his cock entered, but he didn't try to thrust but merely let my body slowly accept him in a moment of pure torture. The feel of him slowly working his way deeper had me wriggling, trying to press down on him but I couldn't as Quintin held me in place.

"Not this time, Lainey," Quintin scolded. "We are running the show, and the two of us want to savor every single moment of this. Nothing will be rushed because all good things come to those who are patient."

A whimper escaped me as I all but pouted at his words. His answer was to grip my chin and turn my face to him and kiss me. As he promised, it was languid, full of feeling, and had me melting into him just as he knew it would. Once I was fully relaxed, he took that opportunity to slide his cock into my ass, making me cry out, but he swallowed the sound with his kiss. When they both were finally balls deep in me, they didn't move but simply hugged me tight as they kissed each other.

Never did I think being with other people who loved each other would add such a difference to a moment. Right now, I felt so cherished and doted upon, even as they were the ones making out above me. There was just something about seeing the love they had for one another and how deep it ran, yet they managed to find a small piece of that emotion to share with me. My eyes burned with the threat of tears, but I wasn't going to fucking cry every time we had sex. I wasn't going to be that woman.

Pulling back from their kiss, they looked down at me with such tenderness, I was certain I would never recover. How could one person handle such an intense emotion from not one but two different people? They showered my face, neck, and shoulders with kisses and little nips that actually had me giggling.

"Now that is the sound I wish to bottle and listen to whenever I'm struggling with the darkness in my mind," Quintin shared, kissing my temple. "That is the sound of joy and happiness I hope to be able to hear for the rest of my life."

My brain skipped on that comment like a record with a scratch in it. "The rest of your life..." I repeated, just wanting to be sure that's what he'd said.

"That is my hope," he answered, nuzzling into my neck. "One day, I would love to see my mark on your elegant neck declaring to the world that you chose us. That we were found worthy of your love, allowing us to express that in a bond so deep and pure it can never be broken.

That is the wish I have and the dream I spent living in last night as I held you in my arms. It's a lot, I know, but I refuse to keep silent when I'm connected to you like this, and you hold part of my heart in your hands."

Those words had my heart bursting with hope and joy and simultaneously feeling like it was being ripped in half, knowing I'd been lying to them. A soft sob slipped out, but it was covered by the sound of both Alphas starting to purr as they held me. Once the purring reached peak intensity, they started to rock into me, turning me into a panting mess in mere seconds.

The vibrations echoed through their whole body, and I mean their *whole* body. Companies might try to make toys for women to use that replicate this exact feeling, but they weren't even fucking close. Their movements became bigger as they pulled out farther, but their pace stayed the same, building the orgasm until it spilled over, flooding me with endorphins.

I mewled my pleasure as my fingers dug into Halstead's back, and my teeth bit into his shoulder as I tried to keep from losing my mind at the intensity. Why I thought you couldn't get as intense of an orgasm from sweet sex, I don't know. Clearly, I hadn't had the right partner with the skills to pull it off because Quintin and Halstead just proved me the fuck wrong.

"That's it, doll... let us make you feel good. Don't hide that beautiful voice of yours. Let it out," Halstead encouraged as he and Quintin fucked me through the orgasm.

When they switched up the rhythm, alternating thrusts instead of doing them in time with each other, the next orgasm had me screaming. This time they came with me, both latching onto my neck opposite each other, but they didn't bite, just held me like that as if to promise one day they would follow through and claim me as their pack's official Omega. This sent me plummeting off the cliff and into another climax as their knots locked me in place between them. Two tears rolled down my cheeks at the realization they didn't go through with it and hadn't claimed me. It would have taken all my fears away had they just decided to make it happen, but instead, they were honorable men who wanted this to be something I offered to them in full submission and consent to live a life together.

"Lainey?" Halstead's voice was full of concern as he used his thumb to wipe away the tears. "What's wrong?"

"Nothing," I croaked. "Fuck, I said I wasn't going to cry during sex. I never cry... what the hell is wrong with me?"

"I'm fairly certain that's our fault," Quintin interjected. "We shouldn't have bitten you at all while we knotted you. That was unfair of us, and I'm sure your Omega instincts are in turmoil over it, making you second-guess everything we were just telling you."

He was half right, but I would let him believe it was the second half of that and not the wish for them to save me from having to hurt them.

"It's stupid, is what it is," I grumbled. "I know exactly why you didn't mark me, and I appreciate that you didn't. We aren't ready for that yet, but these goddamn Omega hormones can't understand that."

Quintin kissed the spot that still burned slightly from where he'd bitten down. "One day, this will be real, and you'll never have to feel like this again. For now, though, I think it might be best if we don't tempt fate. It was much harder to hold back than I anticipated."

"Same," Halstead agreed. "Once the need to bite reared up, it was all I could do to keep from finishing what I'd so carelessly started."

"I agree that might not be something you three should do, or myself for that matter, seeing how that went over with Kerian," I commented.

Halstead let out a loud yawn and snuggled against me. "I say we take a quick nap."

"We just woke up," Quintin pointed out.

Halstead lifted his head to look at his partner. "Did you have something else you wanted to do at the moment? If you didn't notice, we're a little tied up here."

I snorted, trying to cover up my laughter, but the expression on Quintin's face as he processed the fact that it wasn't just me he was knotted to, but Halstead was also part of the deal. "A nap sounds perfect. Then we need to make sure Lainey gets something to eat."

"Contrary to what you all believe, I have been taking care of myself for the past thirty-two years," I interjected.

Quintin kissed me quickly before making himself comfortable, tossing his leg over my hip. "I don't remember anyone questioning that, do you, H?" he questioned.

"Nope," Halstead answered.

"I think you're confusing the fact that we want to take care of you with the belief you don't think we trust you to take care of yourself, which, by the way, is entirely untrue," Quintin explained. "Now close your eyes and count our heartbeats until you fall asleep, beautiful."

"So bossy," I muttered but let out a heavy sigh as Halstead grabbed the comforter and pulled it over us. "God, this could get addicting."

"Good, that was our plan. Now hush," Halstead ordered and started to purr once more, lulling me back to sleep.

When we woke from our nap, we all scattered to get ready for the day and met in the kitchen. A breakfast spread awaited us with various pastries, fruit, bacon, and cheesy scrambled eggs. It would seem Ruth was back in action and more than ready to start feeding us all.

"Normally, this isn't how breakfast is for us during the week, but on the weekends, Ruth likes to spoil us with a *real breakfast*, as she calls it," Halstead shared. "Usually, I'm a man who needs a good cup of coffee and a piece of toast with peanut butter to sustain me until lunch. Kerian makes a smoothie, and I'm pretty sure Quintin survives off tea."

"No, it's that I'm the first one awake, so I make my breakfast and eat it before you arrive for your coffee. I make a bowl of oatmeal for myself with a side of eggs. You need food that will stick to your bones and keep you going on a busy day," Quintin corrected. "You just seem to catch me when I'm done and reading the morning paper."

Halstead gave Quintin a dubious look but shrugged and filled his plate with food. Everything was amazing, and it was nice to relax and chat with them after a leisurely morning. When we finished, we cleaned up, then Quintin decided to finish the tour that Halstead didn't before we ended up driving off into the sunset.

"As you saw yesterday, the main floor isn't used much, but if we ever had guests or a party, it would provide ample space. The second floor is where we spend most of our time since it's where our offices and bedrooms are. Offices are down the left hall, and bedrooms are to the right. I advised it wouldn't be smart to have them too close, or none of us could walk away from work," Quintin informed me. "Halstead's room is the double doors at the end of the hall, then my room, and Kerian is here at the start. There are two other rooms unused at the moment since I suppose we left the option for kids on the table but haven't really done anything on that front."

I opened one of the doors and pushed it open to reveal a simple room with a view of the driveway and front lawn. It had a built-in window seat, but that was about it for any kind of furnishings or personal touches. Even the walls were white and void of any personality—a blank slate.

"Wow, when you said you didn't do anything with it, you weren't kidding," I commented, looking back at the two who stood just outside the door. Chewing on my lip, I decided to take the chance since one of them brought up the subject. "So... does that mean you want kids?"

"We all love kids, and if the opportunity were to present itself to bring one into our family, I think we'd all jump at the chance. I think one reason we haven't is because we work so much and would have to have a nanny to raise the kid, which, to me, isn't really being a parent or giving the child the love and care they need. I'm sure if we started to talk about it seriously, our schedules would change, but it still wouldn't be ideal," Halstead answered as I stepped out of the room.

Quintin reached out and took my hand, twining our fingers together. "How do you feel about kids?"

"To be honest, I don't think I ever really thought about it," I admitted. "There was no one I would want to have a kid with, so it seemed logical to avoid that from happening. Like you guys, I've been focused on my career, and I move around fairly often because I like to see the world and have that freedom. It's not something I've spent much time thinking about, so I don't have a good answer for you."

"I think that was a perfectly acceptable answer," Quintin determined and squeezed my hand. "There are some answers in life you don't know until you're put in the time and place you need to think about it."

While I appreciated he wasn't going to demand an answer from me, I didn't think he realized just how little time I had to determine how

I felt. At the end of this week, regardless of what the Syndicate wants me to do or not, I need to know if I'm pregnant. It was clear that drug did something to me while I was in heat. It was different enough that it was apparent to the guys it hadn't been normal. Now I was left to wonder what the hell I would do with my life if that test came back positive.

"Hey," Quintin murmured as he pressed a kiss to my temple. "I hate to do this, but I need to get some work done. It shouldn't take me long, but since this wasn't a planned break, I couldn't put everything off I wanted to."

"Same for me," Halstead added. "I told the general in charge of the DOD I'd meet with him, and today was the only time he had in the next two weeks. I doubt it will take me long to listen to him apologize and tell me how it should never have happened for about ten minutes before he changes his tune and gets pissed I turned down the work and kicked out his employee."

I grimaced at his description of their conversation. "Oof, that sounds like so much fun," I said sarcastically. "Go do what you need to do. I could use a break from all the testosterone flying around this place. I think I'll go up and check out your library if that's okay with you?"

"You are welcome to whatever's in this house, Lainey. What is ours we will happily share," Halstead answered then kissed my lips before heading toward his office with Quintin.

I smiled as I watched Halstead wrap an arm around Quintin's waist and kiss him on the neck lovingly. It was a side that I was beginning to love seeing but knew it would never happen at work unless Halstead changed his mind about keeping their relationship quiet. Turning, I headed upstairs, but instead of going to the library, I walked toward the nest room, which I refused to call my own. Some sort of distance had to be maintained as I failed miserably in all other areas. It was like ordering a Diet Coke as you ate ten pounds of pasta. One didn't outweigh the other, but it certainly made you feel better.

Grabbing my phone off the nightstand, I went to the last message the Syndicate sent me. Now was the perfect time for me to sneak into Kerian's room and figure out if he had any devices there he might have the code on. What I needed was information on what to look for, a name of the code, part of a numeric sequence, anything I could search to tell me I was looking at the right thing on a programmer's computer.

I typed out my request and sent it along with an inquiry if they had anything in mind for destroying the code once I found it. There hadn't been a drive with a crash code or even a virus that would remove it from the hard drive. I was savvy around computers, but I was no programmer, that's for damn sure.

Ms. Caddel,

Thank you for reaching out with your request. Please wait one moment while we find the answer for you.

I cringed at the way the message had the overly perfect office response email like a robot had written it. Hell, maybe one did write it, and I've been letting some artificial intelligence rule my life the past week.

Thank you for waiting. Your instructions are as follows:

The code's name is UNVEIL, and we can confirm it is not the whole code, only part of it. At this time, we request that you destroy all copies of this section of code from Mr. Lewis' devices. Your phone is equipped with a virus already, so all you need to do is place the phone on top of the device, and it will automatically start to download the virus. In order for the virus to work, the code must be placed in a secure folder so that the virus does not spread to other parts of the computer. If you have any troubles or require further instruction, don't hesitate to reach out.

Thank you once again for helping the UOS create a world where we can place Omegas in power.

"Yeah, sure, no problem... happy to help, you fucking psycho organization," I muttered as I slipped my phone into my jeans pocket and headed back downstairs.

Twenty-Five

Lainey

Acting like I was going down to the main floor, I paused at the point no one could see me on the stairs to the ground floor, then stopped. Straining my ears, I tried to listen intently to every little sound in the house. I needed to be sure everyone was where they said they'd be. I also wanted to ensure that Ruth wasn't working on her cleaning chores and would then be making her way up to the second level. Nothing gave me the impression I was in danger or at risk of being caught, so now the only choice I had to make was—go for the office or the bedroom?

I landed in the office as it was the most logical choice, and being discovered in the bedroom would be far easier to explain. It was simple to figure out which two of the four doors *not* to open since I could hear Halstead talking and Quintin typing. I tried the one next to Halstead's office, but it was locked, so I moved across the hall, and that one opened. Peeking in, I found an incredibly modern-style office that could only be Kerian's. The other two like their traditional vintage vibes too much.

Slipping in, I closed the door behind me and took in the space, noting the wrought iron desk with the glass top as the focal point of the room. It was placed so the person sitting at the desk would have their back to the window allowing the sunlight to brighten the room and their desk. There was a closed laptop on the desk but also a massive triple-screen setup connected to a computer tower on the floor. As I rounded the desk, I noticed a tablet off to the side with one of those special pens allowing you to draw or write. I certainly had my work cut out for me going through all of this, but it was to be expected from a group of men who lived and thrived in the technology world.

Starting with the desktop, I felt like it would be the most logical place he'd be working. The screens lit up, and of course, the prompt for a password appeared. Taking a wild guess, I decided to try one before seeing if the Syndicate had something else to offer.

Tater-Tot!1

There was no way this basic-ass password would ever work, but I figured what could it hurt if it ended up working. Of course, it gave me an error telling me that wasn't right, so I placed the phone on the tower, and it buzzed with a message appearing.

Please select application:

- *Password cracker*

- *Decryption*

- *Code UVEIL destroyer*

"Holy shit, they were prepared for everything," I mumbled as I selected the password cracker.

The phone vibrated once more, and an alert telling me not to touch the phone appeared on the screen as a spinning wheel whirled in the background.

Please type in: **Bx$5goQ9*eq3**

I entered the complex combination of symbols and hit enter, praying to whoever was listening to me that it would work. If this didn't, I had no idea how I'd manage to get a group of men whose job it was to keep people like me out of shit to let me in. The screen went black then reappeared with the normal desktop main screen. I couldn't help but smile at the silly picture of Tater with his body wedged in the corner of the couch on his back, legs up in the air, sleeping with his jowls covering his eyes.

Shaking my head, I needed to return to the task at hand and pulled up the search function. I typed in the code's name, but nothing was found, so I tried Cyclone instead. Still nothing. Chewing on my lip, I tried to think what I knew of Kerian and what would be something logical he'd name this file. Taking a shot in the dark, I tried Reuben—nothing.

"Okay, think, Lainey... take a breath. We have time to get this done. Once I know what he calls it, finding it on all the other devices will be easier," I coached myself. "Now he would need to get it from work, so it's probably on some sort of cloud service not saved on the computer itself. So let's search for what program that would be."

I found talking myself through issues helped me to figure things out faster. I'm sure some therapist out there would tell me it had to do with my trauma and not having anyone else around, so I needed to hear the sound of my voice or some bullshit. Whatever the cause, it worked, and when I got stuck like this on a job, I couldn't afford to freeze up. Pulling up the list of applications on the computer, I scanned the names until I came upon one named 'Secure-IT.'

"Wow, could they make it more obvious?" I muttered then clicked on the icon.

The prompt for another password appeared, so I tried the one I'd already gotten, and it didn't work.

You have one more attempt before this account is flagged and frozen.

"*Fuck*," I swore.

Tapping my phone's screen to wake it up, I saw a new password had already been created with the application's name above. *Yeah, that's not creepy at all.*

Once in, I tried my search again for the code, and it popped up immediately. I clicked on the file and went through the settings to see if I could determine how many devices had accessed this data and when. There was a list of five devices—a phone, two computers, a laptop, and a tablet. A note was left saying it had been sent to another user, but it didn't say who or when so there was no way to tell where it went.

"Maybe he sent it to Halstead since he's a good programmer as well," I reasoned. "It's best if I check all their computers anyway to be damn sure I don't miss something and get fucked over. Now, for the next step, I needed to find a way to put this in a secure folder and delete it."

While I could manage my way around a computer, I was by no means an expert. Could I simply download this and destroy it, or did I have to destroy it here while it was on the cloud? If I could destroy it here, then all I'd need to do is see if it was saved physically on the other devices. *Goddammit, why did this have to be so complicated?*

Looking again at the settings, I found an option to lock this folder, but I didn't know if that meant I could access it again. Flipping to the internet, I searched the company and started scanning the webpage for the features they offered. Doing a quick read of the lock function, I found it was exactly what I wanted—a way to isolate the file so it couldn't be accessed by any device but the one I was currently on or opened with a password. Returning to the program, I followed the steps then when it was secure, I shifted my attention to the phone.

Flicking my finger across the screen, the list of options appeared, and I clicked on the one to destroy the code. It asked for the file location, the website name, and the password I'd created. Once all that was input, I got another reminder not to touch the phone or mess with whatever was happening on the screen. Running my hands through my hair, I leaned back in Kerian's chair and let out a heavy sigh.

The computer started to whirr and make funny noises like it was working hard or struggling to read something. Then the screen went black before yellow code appeared, scrolling across the blackness like I was suddenly in the *Matrix* or something.

"There's been a breach," a voice yelled outside the door before it was thrust open and slammed against the wall, nearly smacking Kerian as he rushed inside. "Shut down the rout—"

When he saw me sitting in his chair, he stopped. "Lainey? What are you doing in here?"

My gaze flicked to the screen, but there was no telling how long this would take, and it was quite clear what I was doing if he came over here.

"Oh... I just wanted to get online and check a few things since I've been a little MIA from life," I answered lamely. "Unfortunately for me, you have a password on your computer, which makes perfect sense for a man in cyber security."

Pushing up from the chair, I walked over to him, noticing how hard he was breathing like he'd been running. He also happened to be wearing skin-tight spandex bike shorts and shirt, which was an incredibly good look for him. "You were yelling something when you came in. Is something wrong?"

"No, well, yes, maybe?" Kerian answered just as Halstead and Quintin hurried into the office.

"I cut the router, so the Wi-Fi is off," Halstead blurted, then realized Kerian wasn't alone. "Lainey?"

I gave a little wave and smiled. "I think I might be the problem."

"What do you mean?" Quintin asked, frowning.

"You see, I was trying to borrow Kerian's computer to check my email and various other things, but it was locked. I tried to guess the password but only once to see if I could take a stab at seeing if I knew enough about Kerian to pull it off kind of thing. When it didn't work, I just planned to wait and ask one of you if I could borrow a computer," I explained, trying to keep my story simple and plausible.

"You should have just come to ask me. I wasn't on a call like Halstead, and I could have given you my tablet or laptop to use," Quintin scolded. "I realize we said you were welcome to anything and you could be in any room, but I suppose we meant personal things. These offices we use to deal with our business at the company. We have personal computers that we use for everyday use and then those we have connected to secure information within Enigma."

"Which is why we have elaborate software that tells us every keystroke, button clicked, and information accessed," Kerian informed me, his expression hardening as he spoke. "I know exactly what you did, Lainey."

Fear bloomed in my chest, and my pulse began to race. As if to seal my fate, the sound of the computer being tampered with as the hard drive and fan sped up, making it loud enough for them to hear.

"Kerian, what are you saying?" Halstead demanded.

"I'm saying that Lainey hacked her way into my computer and started to search for the code I'd been working on for Reuben. You're too late, by the way. I already finished it yesterday and sent it to him. I'd been close for days, but I wanted to finish it, so I could spend more time with *you*," he said, practically spitting that last word. "That damn thing had been looming over my head, and I wanted it over with so it didn't distract me from spending time with a woman I thought was going to be part of my life. A woman I could see easily falling in love with, but now I'm not sure if any of it was fucking real."

It was done.

Kerian had already given it to Reuben and unknowingly sealed my fate.

I. Was. Fucked.

My legs gave out from under me, and I crumpled to the floor, staring at their feet but not really seeing anything. I'd failed. The Syndicate would find out, and everything would be revealed. My life was over, and I'd probably end up in jail, where they could easily take my baby if I were pregnant. *Can't raise a child in prison, now can you?*

"Is this true?" Halstead roared. "You better tell me right the fuck now, Elaine Collins. Are you a spy? Did you lie your way into this family to steal from us?"

Hearing how angry he was, I knew there would be no point in defending myself and denying the truth. They had all the evidence they needed to know what I'd done, and if they looked at that phone, they would find even more proof.

"Yes," I whispered.

Licking my lips as my mouth had suddenly gone so dry, I forced myself to meet his gaze. "I was sent to destroy that code to ensure it never got finished or made it into Reuben Watts' hands. My job was to get close enough to you so I could gain access to Kerian's computers or any other device he might have worked on the code and obliterate it."

The pain and anger that washed over their expressions were like a nail in the coffin. This was all over, and there was no hope for me. I'd destroyed the one thing I've wanted my entire life—the chance for a family.

"Why?" Quintin asked, his voice raw with emotion. "Why do this to us?"

At this moment, I decided it might be better if these men hated me. Better to think of the woman who blew into their lives for a week was nothing but a coldhearted criminal who'd been caught. Stealing myself, I closed my eyes and pulled on the armor of being Elaine Collins, the woman they believed I was. She was the person ripping their hearts out, not Lainey.

Grabbing the arm of the chair I'd crumpled next to, I hoisted myself up. "That's because it's what I do. Really, the three of you should be honored that you caught me. As one of the best con artists, it's not a feat many can accomplish. Now the question is do you want to be brought in on the job and take part in the earnings?" I asked.

"Why the fuck would we do that?" Kerian snapped. "Who in their right mind would trust a word that comes out of your mouth after telling them you're a con artist? Not to mention none of us would take down our own company, no matter the price."

My brows shot up. "That's just the thing, your company isn't the one I'm after... it's the code. Someone has made me an offer I can't refuse to make sure it vanishes from existence. I found it was easiest to be planted in your company since you held the vital part of the code. My plan was to destroy it, then work on how to get rid of the rest. It's clear you have no love for Reuben, so why not help a girl out?"

Kerian was about to say something, but Halstead charged forward, grabbed me by the throat, and marched me backward until I was pinned against a wall. "What game are you playing right now?"

"I don't know what you mean." I gasped loudly. He was allowing me to breathe, but it was extremely limited. "You asked me why I did this, and I'm telling you why."

"No, you're still lying," Halstead countered. "Look me dead in the eye and tell me everything between us is a lie."

Realization hit me—Halstead was fighting for me. Even now, after all that I'd said and been caught doing red-handed, this man wanted to believe there was something worth fighting for.

"Don't!" I bit out. "Don't do this to yourself. I'm not worth it. Everything about me is a lie, it's all I know how to do and what I'm really fucking good at. I'm not some innocent woman who needs to be rescued. There have been a hundred of you. The stupid men I've lured into falling for me so they grant me access to what I need to complete my job. Once the job is done, then *poof*, I'm gone, vanished off the face of the earth. There is nothing real about me, Halstead. It's just easier if you accept that."

He tightened his grip on my neck, and I merely closed my eyes so I didn't have to look at him as he took out his pain on me. I deserved it and would take it because there was nothing he could do to me that would hurt more than the feeling of my heart ripping to pieces.

"*Look. At. Me!*" Halstead demanded, using the full power of an Alpha bark on me.

I had no choice but to do as he demanded, my eyes flicking open to meet his gaze. It was as if he was trying to look into my soul, and whatever he saw in my eyes had him shifting his hand from my throat to cupping my face. His lips slammed to mine in a punishing kiss as he forced me to open and surrender to him. This stubborn grizzly bear of a man was refusing to let me be the martyr and even now was fighting to give this vision of a family a chance. It was painful, yet at the same time, a balm to my soul that he *saw* me. Right now, he was cutting through the bullshit to gain access to my true emotions, which were anything but cold and callous.

"I need you to remember what I said the other day, Lainey. No matter what, we need to fight for each other. In order to do that, both sides must be willing to battle it out," he whispered urgently. "I won't let you leave this house until I know everything you're *not* telling us, which I have a feeling is a lot. I'm going to fight for you, even if you can't fight for us right now. Do you hear me, doll? I *know* deep in my soul you're ours. Don't give up on us, *please*."

The 'please' is what broke me, and out came the sob I'd been holding back since he pinned me against this wall. Never in my life had anyone fought for me, and when I found people who would, I betrayed them, lied, and used the trust they gave me to manipulate the situation. I didn't deserve them, not in this life or the next for all the bullshit I'd done.

Yet there was one thing I did know...

I wanted to fight.

"I'll tell you everything, but we can't do it here. We need to go somewhere that won't be overheard by any kind of technology," I whispered, my voice so soft I wasn't sure he could hear me. "Ignore everything about what I'm going to say because I mean the opposite of all of it."

Halstead frowned at me, confused but nodded.

"There's nothing to give up on since there was nothing there to begin with. I feel nothing for the three of you. Anything you think might have been real was all an act. Truly, it's why I'm the best because I know how to play with men's emotions and get them to believe anything I want them to. Do yourself a favor, either call the police and have me arrested, or let me go, and I'll be on my way. Calling the police will drag things out, and if you've already given the code to Reuben, then I have zero need to stick around here," I pointed out. "So what will it be? Draw attention to yourself by calling the police and revealing the relationships you've kept so hidden from the world, or simply let me walk out of your lives with no additional turmoil?"

"I'm not going to give you an answer right away. You don't deserve it after all you've done. Instead, I'm going to put you somewhere you won't be able to cause any trouble while we decide what your fate will be," Halstead answered, playing along. "Come on, let's go."

While it sounded like he was going to drag me out of there, he actually scooped me up and held me like I was a small child. Wrapping my arms and legs around him, I hid my face in his neck as he headed out of the room.

"Kerian, shut the door behind you. Quintin, I need you to unlock the secure room, please," Halstead directed, his voice low and gentle.

"What the fuck is going on?" Kerian asked in a harsh whisper.

I felt Halstead shake his head, then we moved forward, and I was set down on something soft. Bracing myself for the anger and hurt from these men, I took a shaky breath and opened my eyes to see where I was.

Twenty-Six

Lainey

The room was simple, but there was no window, the only light coming from the overhead fixture. A wall of screens that showed the property from various angles told me this was their security room. The hum of servers along the base of one wall informed me that I'd grossly underestimated their home setup. Soundproof paneling lined the walls making it clear why Halstead chose this room to talk.

He was squatting in front of me, eyes full of concern as he searched my face, waiting for me to speak. Kerian wasn't willing to be that kind, and he paced the room, arms crossed, muttering to himself before stopping to glare at me. "What the fuck is going on, and this time you better not lie to us, or I swear to God, I will hand you over to the cops myself, no matter what these two think."

"Keri," Quintin snapped. "Clearly, there is more going on than any of us realize. Let's not say things we'll regret later."

"How can you say that? She's been lying to us the whole fucking time," Kerian yelled, pointing an accusatory finger at me. "Tell me *how the hell* are we supposed to trust what comes out of her mouth now?"

"I suppose we give her a chance to speak, tell her story, then decide if we wish to believe it or not," Quintin reasoned as he turned to me.

"Unless you have proof to back up what you tell us, we would gladly appreciate it."

Nodding, I scrubbed my face with my hands, trying to figure out where to even start with this story. Then I decided on the basics, something they could look up recorded by police, lawyers, and an official criminal court. It would be the hardest part of my story, but it was the best I could do to prove I wasn't lying.

"The name I was given at birth was Elaine Caddel, but I always went by Lainey. I was entered into the social care system the day I was born, thanks to my deadbeat mother being a drug addict," I started. "I lived in a group home until I was ten years old, and a man named Trent came to adopt me. He was a con artist and would regularly take kids like me who had no family for him to worry about coming after him. Our purpose was to help him pull off some job or be used to further the plot of a con he was trying to pull. He used us for various fake ad campaigns for schools, hospitals, starving children in a foreign, war-torn country, and many other ploys."

Kerian headed for the simple desk he set up and started to type away. I assumed he was looking me up and knew he'd find it. For some reason, I never got up the nerve to wipe my past completely off the map, but you had to know exactly what to look for.

"Make sure you use Woville as the town to look me up. That's where the group home was and where he adopted me. He also changed my name legally to Lainey instead of Elaine at the time of my adoption to make it harder to find my information. Hard to have a daughter who pops up as an orphan if you google her name," I offered in hopes of proving I was being as honest as I could be.

Silence stretched as the sound of the keys clacking filled the room. "Found it," Kerian announced. "It's exactly as she says and has a photo of her at age ten when she was adopted."

He turned the screen so the others could see my smiling face with Trent standing next to me as I held the adoption paperwork. Tears flooded my eyes as I looked at that version of myself, so young, innocent, and happy, thinking I'd found a man who wanted to be my family.

"I was with Trent until I turned eighteen. The moment I knew I couldn't be put in the system again, I called the cops and ratted him out. I told them he was a con artist as well as the owner-operator of a hidden sex club that he filled with the kids he adopted and didn't need anymore," I shared, pausing as the memory of those times he would bring me to the club and threaten me with that fate if I didn't play my part. "As fucked up as it is to say, I was his favorite. It kept me out of that place, but it forced me to be by his side and trained to become exactly like him. The moment he signed those papers, I was his puppet to dress up and play pretend with, creating a new story for me at the drop of a hat. Daughter, niece, ward, princess of a foreign country, politician's illegitimate child... you name it, I've played it. As Trent said, I was a natural with an ability to make people believe whatever I wanted them to. I suppose it's why I ended up becoming just like him in the end."

The room fell silent, which only made the sound of my rapid heartbeat thunder in my ears. *Would they believe me? Is bearing my soul enough for them to see I'm telling the truth? Did I have to tell them everything?* Fuck, there were things I wouldn't even admit to myself, let alone anyone else.

"Lainey," Quintin said, finally breaking the silence. "Why did you come to our company? Are we your target?"

I shook my head. "No, you're not my target. I wasn't lying when I said my purpose was to destroy the code before it could be finished. However, it seems I've failed, and now none of it matters because

I'm ruined, and the Syndicate will do as they've threatened to expose everything about me. Oh, and let's not forget they plan to tell Trent I'm the one who sold him out, so even if I could run from the Syndicate, I'll never be able to outrun the man who taught me everything I know. So call the police, lock me up, and throw away the key. It will be the only way to keep you three out of my mess. I won't let the Syndicate use this as a reason to harm any of you."

"Hold on," Halstead cut in, raising a hand. "Backup a moment. I think you skipped over some important information here. Who or what the fuck is the Syndicate, and why the hell would they be threatening you or planning to hurt us?"

In my word vomit to try and get Quintin to understand, I'd shared more than I meant to. I'd planned to make sure they believed me before bringing in the Syndicate because it was hard for me to even make sense of it. Who grabs random Omegas off the street and forces them to do their bidding? Seriously, it sounded like something out of a thriller movie rather than something that could really happen.

"There is a group called the Underground Omega Syndicate, and they are the ones who put me up for this job," I explained, talking slowly to buy myself time.

Kerian frowned and raised his hands to search for their name, but I was up on my feet, diving across the room to slam his hands on the desk. "*No.*" I snapped. "Don't, please. I'm begging you. *Do. Not.* Search their name, or you might as well put a gun to my head right now."

He cocked his head as he looked at me with a frown on his face. "You're terrified of them."

"Yes," I whispered, a tear running down my cheek. "You have no idea what they've already done to me without provocation. I can't even fathom the fury that will come down on me if they know I've told you about them. There is nothing they care more about than keeping themselves a secret. It's why they drugged me, kidnapped me, dragged me from Marlios in the middle of the night, and brought me here."

My hands started to shake as I removed them from Kerian, and I tried to take a step back to give him some space, but my legs gave out. Instantly, Kerian caught and settled me on his lap, keeping his hands on my hips.

"Lainey, I think you need to tell us the whole story. Not about your childhood but from the point they took you and how you ended up here," Kerian instructed.

I wiped away the tears that wouldn't seem to stop and nodded. "Okay, I can do that."

Quintin appeared before me with a tissue in his hand and a box of more in his other. I took the offered tissue and tried to clean myself up before trying to stand, but Kerian didn't let go of his grip.

"You don't have to do this. I know you hate me right now, and you don't like to be touched when you're upset," I said, trying to give him the out so the others wouldn't judge him. "I'm used to managing on my own."

Kerian practically growled at that last statement. "Well, you're not on your own anymore," he stated. "Also, for the record, anger is the last thing I feel toward you right now, Lainey. I'm confused, hurt, and desperately want you to be the woman I believe you to be. The woman who I'm falling for so fast that it scares the shit out of me. It's like there is a war between my heart and brain about what to do and how to handle this. Let's just say I'm not managing them well."

"I understand that more than you know," I murmured, ducking my head. "That's been a war I've been losing since the moment I knew you were all my scent-pairs."

Halstead swore under his breath, drawing my attention. "That's why you lied to us and didn't admit you were an Omega. Did the Syndicate make you hide what you are?"

A harsh bark of laughter burst out of me. "Oh, fuck no, quite the opposite, in fact. You want to know why my heat was so bad and my scent was overpowering? Well, the Syndicate didn't like that I was posing as a Beta and suppressing my heat, so they took it upon themselves to force me to take a mysterious medication. Believe me when I say I tried to avoid taking it, but my driver, who was also being blackmailed by the Syndicate, made it clear that I took the medication, or he'd do it himself."

"That day I saw you get out of the car..." Quintin commented as full realization came to him. "You were furious, and now I can absolutely see why."

"Yeah, you caught me right after it happened," I confirmed. "When you sent me back to my place to get clothes, Halstead, I had the driver stop at the pharmacy after I learned that the medication would strip me of my suppressant. There, I was able to get another one, but it didn't work. Maybe it held it off, but I don't really know... the doctor I talked to wasn't forthcoming about the details of the drug. I pretty much got told that I needed to accept I was an Omega and proudly display my designation instead of hiding it."

Kerian leaned down and kissed my head before resting his cheek against it. "Are you okay now? Is there anything else we need to worry about? Should we get a doctor to come look at you?"

His question had my stomach clenching at what they'd told me yesterday. If I told them this, then there was no way I'd be able to walk away, no matter what danger I might bring to them.

"I don't think I'll need a doctor as of yet... but we will need to get something from the store," I admitted.

"Another suppressant?" Quintin inquired.

"No, a pregnancy test," I whispered as I rubbed my fist along my sternum with how tight it felt, to the point I wasn't sure I could keep breathing.

Cool hands cupped my face and urged me to lift it so I stared into Quintin's dark green eyes behind his glasses. "Are you saying you might be pregnant?"

"Yes." I sobbed. "They told me yesterday the drug made me ten times more fertile than normal, and there was an extremely high chance I would be pregnant. Quin..." I cried, grabbing his arms. "They told me I had to have this baby, and if I didn't want it, they would take it from me. I can't go to jail... they will take my child, I just know it. Please don't let that happen. They don't deserve the life I had... no child does," I pleaded, tears streaming down my face as I let him pull me from Kerian and hold me against his chest.

Soon, two more bodies wrapped around us, smothering me in their comforting scents and shielding me from everything I feared. I might not have planned to have a child, but I'd be damned if I didn't do right by them. Even if I might not be the mother of the year, I knew these men had more love in their little fingers than some fucked-up organization like the Syndicate. Every child brought into the world deserved the best we could give them. They didn't choose to be born. That was a choice we made, and if we also made the choice to complete the pregnancy, then we had the duty to ensure they had a good life.

"Lainey, I know you're scared, and you've been dealing with this all on your own, but I want you to know that we believe you," Halstead told me as he brushed tears off my face and tucked hair behind my ear. "We will protect you with all we have at our disposal, even if I have to sell my soul to make it happen. If we learn you are indeed pregnant, then I pray to God no one tries to harm a hair on your head. Not only would they be endangering *our* Omega, but our child as well, a sin I will *never* forgive."

"You believe me?" I asked, the desperation in my voice making me hate myself just a little with how pathetic I sounded. Gone was the woman who could look down at the world and give it the middle finger. These men had found all the cracks in my wall and wriggled their way into my heart with each and every touch and sweet word.

"I do," Halstead affirmed.

Twisting, I looked at Kerian. "Do you?" He'd been the one who'd been outwardly hurt by my lies, as he should be, but I needed to know if he had doubts. "Ask me whatever you like, and I'll answer it. If you want proof, I've got all the documents they sent me back at the apartment, and I can let you look at the phone they gave me with all the communications I've had since this started."

"There is only one question I want to know the honest truth about," Kerian said, taking my hand in both of his. "Do you want a life with us?"

"More than anything I've ever wanted in my life," I confessed. "All my life, I've only wanted one thing, and that's a family, but no one ever wanted me. So I decided it was easier to stop hoping it would ever happen and told myself the only person I could trust and rely on was myself. Then the three of you showed up, and the next thing I knew, you wanted me to be part of your family. I didn't know how to handle that, so I got scared and tried to hide behind the job, but that didn't work either. You kept fighting for me even when I wouldn't fight for myself."

Kerian pressed a kiss to my trembling lips, nose, and each eye before a final kiss on my forehead. "Thank fuck because I want nothing more than to fall in love with you, start a family, and spend the rest of our lives as the four, possibly five, of us together. So what do we need to do to make that happen?"

"Honestly, I don't know. My whole purpose was to destroy the code while you were still working on it. Apparently, its true purpose is to scour the dark web to find the syndicate so that Reuben can destroy it," I explained. "I have no idea why he knows about them or what they've done to make him hold a strong-enough grudge that he's willing to go to such lengths."

"I only gave it to him yesterday afternoon, so he hasn't had much time to do anything with it. If we go to the office, I should be able to create a virus through the link that was created to share information between our companies. The files were too important and far too large to transport any other way, so I created a secure connection I can use against him," Kerian revealed.

"Are you saying there's a chance we can pull this off?" I pressed.

"Yes, my sweet little vixen, that's exactly what I'm saying," he murmured, pressing a quick kiss to my lips. "Now I feel like we need to go back to my office and see what they're up to. Maybe even have a chat with your syndicate friends."

I didn't really love the sound of that, but I agreed all the same. Kerian stood and offered me a hand which I took instantly. Pulling me to my feet, he wrapped me up in a tight hug, burying his face in my neck. "I'm sorry I said those things to you. My fear of losing you made me lash out, even when I didn't mean a word of it."

"Let's call it an even draw on that," I suggested. "I'm not without blame in this, and I said hurtful things as well in a feeble attempt to get you to hate me. The thought of you three taking the blame for my actions wasn't something I could live with. Better for you to have a common enemy than to go after each other."

Kerian pulled back to look me in the face. "We do have a common enemy. Two, in fact, because if we can take down Reuben as well as the Syndicate, I can't say that's an all-bad situation."

"Couldn't agree with you more, especially after Halstead told me about their past," I said, looking over at Halstead. "I have a feeling I'm going to be like you when it comes to protecting people I care about. Once I've claimed you, no one else can fuck with you."

Halstead gave me a smirk as he ran a hand over his beard. "That really shouldn't be such a turn-on, but it sure as hell is. Let's go deal with these fuckers so we can put this all behind us and start our life together."

"I love the sound of that," I agreed.

Twenty-Seven

Kerian

Entering my office, it was quiet as if nothing had happened here thirty minutes ago. *Is that all it took for my life to have imploded and been rebuilt again?* One second, I thought my heart was going to shatter as Lainey ripped it out of my chest, only to have her replace it with her own. She felt the same way about us as we did her—it was clear in the way she looked when she thought it would all disappear. Then there was the shock of her telling us she most likely was pregnant.

Never did I think I'd have to try so hard to keep a grin off my face, but every time I thought about being a dad, I couldn't help it. I'd always loved kids and hoped it might happen for us one day, but the right time never seemed to happen. Now it was clear why—Lainey wasn't with us. She was the missing cog in the complex system we built for our lives. With her finally in her rightful place with us, things seemed to work effortlessly.

"The phone is sitting on top of your computer tower," Lainey said, pointing to the device.

Anger sizzled under my skin as I reached for the phone and handed it to her. She'd explained only her fingerprint would open it to the right screen. To anyone else, it would appear to be a normal phone.

"Here," she murmured, handing it to me. "I don't know what you want to do, but that's the screen they use to talk to me."

The screen was black with simple monospaced lettering. I read over what they'd instructed her to do in order to delete the code off my computer and was impressed. They had some incredibly skilled programmers and hackers at their disposal. Taking a shot in the dark, I typed out a message and assumed they would see it and respond.

I WANT TO NEGOTIATE A DEAL WITH THE SYNDICATE — KERIAN LEWIS

There was nothing but a blinking text cursor for a few moments as I held my breath. Then words started to appear on the screen, and they were not happy ones, that's for damn sure. I didn't even bother reading all the threats. Instead, I just hit the phone symbol, assuming it would call them. If it didn't call whoever was rage-typing, then it might give me someone more reasonable.

"*The UOS doesn't deal with Alphas,*" a voice clearly altered by some kind of technology answered. "*We of the UOS seek to put Omegas in positions of power to keep Alphas like you in their place.*"

"That's all fine and dandy with me. However, I would like to negotiate a deal with you on Lainey's behalf," I explained, hoping that would make a difference.

"*She failed her mission, and the enemy has the code. Ms. Caddel knew the consequence of failure, and now she's made things worse for herself by telling you about us,*" they responded.

Rolling my eyes at the dramatics, I forged ahead. "I know what her mission is, and I'm telling you I can make sure that code is destroyed so not even a zero is left behind. Reuben might have that code right now, but if you guarantee me that Lainey will be absolved of her connection with you, then I will complete the job for her. In fact, I'll even allow you to set the terms to hold me accountable so that I never try to recreate what I've worked on. Not having seen all of it, I can't say I'd be able to replicate it, but if I felt the need, I'm sure I could make my own version to hunt you down," I warned.

There was a pause, and I closed my eyes, praying that I'd made the right move by reminding them that I was as much a threat as an ally.

"If you succeed in obliterating the code and ensuring it will never again be recreated, then we agree to see this as full completion of Ms. Caddel's assignment. As far as terms to ensure you don't ever act on this knowledge, you will leave a backdoor in your systems to us using the password UVEIL so that we might check in on your data. Fail to do this or cut us off, and we will disclose all we have on Lainey Caddel and inform Trent Stone of her involvement in his permanent incarceration. Do we have an agreement?"

Lainey grabbed my arm and shook her head. It was clear she had no idea how far any of us would go to make sure she was safe. "You have a deal. As of now, Lainey will cease to contact you since I will be destroying this phone. The man you had as her driver is not to come anywhere near Lainey, and if I so much as feel the itch that someone is watching when our child is born, we will destroy everything you've built. I don't give a *fuck* how good you think your people are, we are better, and no one will be able to run from us when the right motivation is presented. Have I made myself clear?"

"*Yes.*"

"Excellent," I said, then hung up the phone.

Marching out of the room, down the stairs, and into the kitchen, I yanked open the microwave and chucked in the phone. "Let's see you fuckers work around this."

I slammed the door shut, hit the one-minute express button, then stepped back to watch the sparks fly. The satisfaction I felt watching that phone char inside our microwave shouldn't have been as fulfilling as it was.

"You know you're gonna need to replace that, right?" Ruth drawled. I jumped, not realizing she was there and found her sitting at the counter peeling potatoes for dinner.

"Worth it," I answered. "Besides, I think it was time for an upgrade. This time we could get one of those cool five-in-one with the air fryer built in."

"Why does it smell like something's burning?" Lainey asked as she and the others caught up to me. I just pointed at the microwave with a triumphant smile.

"Oh my God, you nuked the phone?" She gasped, then a grin tugged at her lips until she gave in and smiled. "That seems like a fitting end for them, I suppose. Too bad we couldn't put them all in the microwave. I'd like to give them a shot or two for the bullshit they've put me through."

Halstead wrapped an arm around her waist and pulled her against him. "Let's not look for more trouble just yet. We have a few loose ends to tie up, and if they don't do as promised, we will find a way to make it clear messing with us isn't going to work in their favor."

She hummed her agreement and leaned her head against his shoulder. A weight I hadn't known was weighing on her had clearly lifted, and in its place, she honestly looked tired. That was the fire I needed under my ass to get this resolved once and for all.

"I don't know about you three, but I'd like to get this over with sooner than later. The longer Reuben has the code, the more chance he has of causing trouble. We all know that man has no issue riding the line on what is or isn't legal. So I'm going to shower, change, and then

I think we should head to the office. I need roughly about two hours, maybe less, to create this virus if you're helping me, H," I shared.

"Fuck yeah, I'll help you. The faster we get this over with, the better. I don't like the idea of anyone having a target on my family, and right now, there's a giant one painted on the back of Lainey's head," Halstead grumbled.

With that decided, I clapped my hands with a decisive nod and hurried out of the kitchen. Taking the stairs two at a time, I made it up to my room, where I found Tater sprawled out on my bed, jerking awake at my abrupt entrance with a *woof*.

"Easy, killer, it's just me." I chuckled as I ruffled his wrinkles. "Guess what, T-man, Lainey's going to stay, so you won't have to lose your new friend."

He cocked his head at me as he listened, tongue lolling out one side of his mouth.

"Don't play innocent with me. Ruth told me how you stuck by her side the other day, totally ignoring her. You know how hard she worked to win you over with all those bits of chicken she supposedly dropped while cooking," I pointed out as I stripped out of my clothes. "Can't say I blame you for being partial to her because I am too."

He gave a big sneeze that seemed to have started at his tail and worked all the way to his nose. With a lick to his nose, he settled back down on the bed with a yawn.

"Good talk, bro," I tossed over my shoulder as I padded naked into the bathroom.

Turning on the shower, I piled my locks on my head, securing them so they stayed out of the way and didn't get wet. Hunting for one of my large hair ties, I didn't notice someone else entering the bathroom until I felt her hands smooth down my sides as she pressed her naked body to mine.

"Mind if I join you?" Lainey asked, pressing a kiss to the back of my shoulder.

I looked at her in the mirror, stunning hazel eyes staring back at me. "You never have to ask that question. Naked or clothed, you're always welcome to join me in whatever I'm doing."

The smile that lit up her face at my words and my cock hardened even more than it had, just with her touch and spicy cinnamon and clove scent. "Be careful you don't regret telling me that."

Sensing there was more to her visit than simply wanting to be with me, I turned as I snapped the hair tie in place. It was harder than I'd like to admit to keep my eyes on her face while she stood there like the goddess Venus in all her naked glory. "Why would I regret having you around? Isn't that how it works with someone you love?"

"I wouldn't know. I've never loved someone before," she admitted. "On that front, the three of you are light years ahead of me in the whole relationship thing."

"Are you worried you're gonna fuck this up?" I questioned, feeling like I might be getting close to her.

She shook her head. "No, pretty sure I've already done that, so I can check that one off the list. It's just all this is moving so fast. I get the whole scent-pair thing, but Kerian... what if I really am pregnant? We aren't even bonded and only met, what... roughly a week ago? All of this is crazy, isn't it?"

"Nah, it's not crazy," I assured her. "What you're feeling is the fear of allowing yourself to open your heart to trust others. Your mind is coming up with all the reasons this is a mistake and why you should run for the hills as fast as you can. Trouble is... none of us are going to let you go. You told us flat out that you wanted to create a family with us. Baby or no baby, it doesn't matter, you've been accepted into the pack."

Reaching out, I cupped her cheek, and she nuzzled into the touch, more starved for affection than she realized. It was easy to see how she gravitated to us now that we'd survived through her heat as if her body subconsciously realized what we knew the moment we caught her scent and fed off the comfort we provided. Lainey Caddel was meant to be part of our lives, and Halstead had been right to fight for her even when I succumbed to the doubt.

"Come on, a shower will help," I suggested. "They have magical powers to wash away all our worries so we can step out refreshed."

"Did Quintin tell you that?" she asked suspiciously.

I shrugged. "Just something I've come to believe and find true for myself, at least."

She seemed to accept that and took my hand, leading me into the large glass-walled shower. I'd never noticed before, but I was starting to wonder how much effort it would take to put in a bench of some kind. It would certainly open up a lot more scenarios for us to try out in the shower, but then again, being creative is just as much fun.

As if Lainey understood where my thoughts had been, she turned to face me with a sultry look in her eyes. Slowly, she backed into the shower, tugging me along until she stepped under the water's spray. Tilting her head back, she let the water soak her beautiful hair, making it even darker and a contrast to her golden skin. Water streamed down her neck, making me want to lick it off her before placing my mark for all to see.

No, you can't do that to her. The others had already told me how that went over like a lead balloon this morning.

Freeing my hand from hers, I grabbed the body wash and my handy shower mitt. No one likes ashy skin, and I found good exfoliation along with moisturizing is the best combination for good skin. Now I planned to buff all of my sexy vixen's body before taking the opportunity to help her massage that lotion in like the good-caring Alpha I was and maybe even throw in a few orgasms along the way. I read somewhere that endorphins keep you healthy and live longer, both of which seemed like a solid enough reason to give them to her often.

She moaned as I swirled the mitt-covered hand over her nipple, making sure I kept the pressure light. "Did you like that, my sweet vixen?" I asked, making the same motion again, this time getting her to arch into the touch.

"Yes," she answered, her voice so low I almost didn't hear it over the water.

"Do you want me to do it again?" I inquired.

"Yes, please."

I grinned and stepped closer so my cock brushed her stomach. "Please, what? I want to give you everything you need, Lainey, but you have to tell me what that is."

She grasped my cock in one hand as her other came to rest on the back of my neck. The woman looked me dead in the eyes as she spoke, "I want you to lather me up from head to toe so our bodies glide together. Then I want you to press me up against the glass and fuck me from behind until I'm screaming your name so loud the others come to check on us."

Fuck.

"Oh, you naughty vixen." I chuckled. "You want them to come in and see your breasts smashed against the glass as I rut so deep inside you that I will make damn sure you're pregnant if you're not already."

She shivered at my words, making me want to say more. It took the three of us all of two seconds to realize the effect of dirty talk on this woman. The more we said it, the tighter she got, the harder she rode us, and how fucking intense those orgasms were compared to others. Not only did our little Omega like the thrill of almost getting caught, but she wanted you to describe what it would be like if she did get caught.

Unable to hold back, I dropped my head to capture her lips with mine as I grabbed her ass, hoisting her up. Fuck the soap. Fuck the mitt. I needed my cock in this woman, and I needed it to happen now.

"Tell me, Lainey, if I called you into my office at work and fucked you over my desk... how loud would you scream?" I asked as I pressed her back against the glass, pinning her tight with my body and rolling my hips so my cock rubbed along her pussy.

"Hell yes, I would scream, especially if you didn't waste time with foreplay. I can just imagine the feel of your thick cock filling my tight and needy pussy," she shared, painting a picture of her fantasy.

Shifting her, I felt the head of my cock find her entrance. "You mean like this?"

Shoving into her with a single hard thrust, I got about half my cock in before I had to pull out and try again. Lainey shrieked as her nails dug into my skin, sending sparks of pain through my body, but the tightness of her pussy wrapping around my cock outweighed the discomfort.

"Fuck yes, Keri." She panted, using the nickname I only let the guys use, but it sounded right coming from her. "Fill my pussy with that fucking cock of yours and make it so no one but the three of you will ever be enough for me."

"Is that the game we're playing right now?" I challenged. "You want me to erase all memory of the shitty dicks from your past until only ours matter?"

"Yes," she screamed as I made it balls deep on the third try. "Yes, that's exactly what I want."

"Then hold on tight, you're about to get your wish," I warned, taking a beat before pulling back until I was *almost* about to fall out and thrust it back in.

I fucked her hard as I whispered in her ear, "If one of us hasn't already filled you with a child, then I promise you here and now, I will the next time. There won't be any more skipping heats for you, my vixen. We will turn those moments into memories you'll never forget as we rut into you, claiming you until our combined efforts create new life."

Lainey's heart hammered in her chest as she clung to me, moaning at the impact of my thrusts forced out of her with each stroke. When I felt like I was getting too close to finishing, I pulled Lainey off me, and spun her around so the story she'd painted for me first became a reality.

"This is what you wanted, right? To be on display for anyone who walked in to see me pounding into you from behind," I taunted as I teased the entrance of her pussy with my cock. A whine tumbled out of Lainey as she tried to back up onto my dick, but I held her in place. "What did I tell you? If you want something, you need to use your words."

"Please, Keri, fuck me. Shove your cock into me and fill me with your cum as you knot me," Lainey begged, desperation clear in her voice. "I want my body and mind to know what my heart does... that I belong here with you."

"Damn right, you do," I agreed, fisting her hair to arch her backward so I could kiss her as I filled her once more. Drinking down her cries of pleasure as I fucked her was a euphoric feeling I never wanted to end.

Breaking the kiss, I dropped my head to her shoulder as I fucked her with all the feelings I didn't know how to say or express. There was so much that had happened in the past week, not to mention the past hour. Feelings rioted in me, ranging from terrified we'd lose her to the fucking Syndicate, joy at the thought of her possibly carrying our child, and the warmth of love that was growing with every minute I spent with Lainey. I wrapped my arms around her, pulling her from the glass to hold her close as I felt my climax nearing.

It took everything in me not to mark her, to claim what I knew was mine to hold for the rest of my life. Yet it had to be her choice. She had to want it as much as I did, and I wasn't sure we were there. I knew in time Lainey would accept all we had to offer her, but a woman who'd been running from herself all her life wasn't going to adjust to settling down simply because we asked her to. Instead, I kissed her neck and latched my mouth on it working to leave a hickey where I eagerly wished to leave the real thing.

"Lainey," I whispered. "Can I mark you?" The words were out of me before I could stop them.

She gripped my arms, digging in her nails as I felt her tightening around me so close to coming herself. "Soon, but not yet. I want to know we're safe first."

Of course, she was right. It made no sense to do this when the danger wasn't gone from our lives. That gave me the awareness I couldn't knot her right now. We needed to shower and get this part of the deal over with. Pulling back just enough that my knot was outside her, I came with a shout.

"Fuck, you feel so good, Lainey." I groaned, feeling my cock pulsing in her core as it milked me within an inch of my life. "I wish I could fucking knot you tight, hold you in my arms, and spoil you the way I want to right now. However, as you said, we aren't safe yet, and I don't trust the Syndicate or Reuben not to find a way to fuck us over."

Sagging in my hold, she nodded absently. "You're right, it's too early for us to think we're off the hook."

"Man, it would be fucking nice to have a bench in here so I could let you rest as I cleaned you up," I muttered.

Lainey chuckled. "Funny, I was just thinking how odd it was you didn't have one. Normally, it wouldn't be a problem, but you see this Alpha who's kind of into me just fucked me until my whole body feels like Jell-O."

"At least the man fucked you, right?" I pointed out with a smirk.

"That he did," she agreed, her voice full of satisfaction and far more relaxed than when she joined me.

We made it work, and after about ten minutes, Lainey was able to manage on her own. Not that I let her get that far, feeling the overprotective urge to keep my hands on her hips. The thought of her slipping and falling because of something I'd done was my worst nightmare. When Lainey finished showering, I grabbed the towel I'd draped over the door handle and wrapped her up before setting her on the bathroom counter.

"Stay right there. I'll be quick," I instructed, pointing a warning finger at her.

"Yes, sir," Lainey answered, giving me a mock salute.

Three minutes later, I had a towel wrapped around my hips and combed through Lainey's hair as she sat on my bed. "I don't have a blow dryer in my room, but I'm pretty sure Quin does," I commented.

"There's one up in my bathroom," she pointed out. "I have to go back up there to get my clothes as it is."

That got me thinking. "The apartment here was provided by the Syndicate, right?"

"Yeah, along with everything in it. I'll have to hire someone to pack up all my shit and ship it here along with getting a new phone, bank cards, ID... basically replacing everything that the Syndicate took from me. Well, and transferring things to make it legit, but I'm not sure what to do about my birth certificate," she mused aloud as she processed what it meant to put down roots. "I might have burned that when I left here fourteen years ago."

"That's easy. I can get whatever you need with the right information," I told her. "Now head up and get dressed. We're going to stop by a pharmacy along the way."

The speed at which her head snapped around to look at me made me flinch. "What?"

"We're going to get you a pregnancy test, maybe a whole box of them so you can keep checking over the next few days. None of us are gonna be able to relax until we get a straight answer to this, and I'd rather not have you go to the hospital if we don't need to." I raised a hand to stop her argument. "It has nothing to do with not wanting people to know about us, I just don't want to hand the Syndicate information they don't need to know about you right now. Until I truly believe they will leave you alone, we're not going to put you at any unnecessary risk."

She snapped her mouth closed and nodded. "Okay, that makes sense."

I cupped her face and kissed her tenderly. "Now go so I can think straight. Having you in just a towel on my bed makes it incredibly hard not to fuck you again, which we don't have time for."

A wide grin spread across her face as she slid off the bed, dropping the towel on the floor. "Well, if the towel's the problem here, why didn't you say so?"

"Oh-ho-ho, you deliciously naughty vixen," I muttered, dropping my head into my hands so I didn't watch that perfect round ass walk out of my room.

"Keri—" I heard Quintin start to say before his words were cut off. "Never mind, I no longer need to ask my question. I'll see you downstairs when you're ready."

Not bothering to answer, knowing he wasn't there anymore, I walked into my closet and got dressed. My dick was hard once more, eager to please Lainey in any way she wanted.

"Sorry, buddy, we actually have something more important to take care of right now," I apologized to my cock as I zipped it away in my jeans, the only thing that wouldn't show my hard-on. At least, I hoped it wouldn't. "This woman is going to be the best kind of trouble, isn't she?"

Twenty-Eight

Lainey

Who would have guessed how hard it would be to keep three Alpha males in the car while you ran in to get a pregnancy test? None of them wanted to let me out of their sight, and I got it, I really did. However, they also needed to understand that even if I were going to be part of this family, I wouldn't give up my independence. Sure, at the moment, things were dicey with the Syndicate and Reuben having the code, but I could handle going into a store.

"You really should have three of these," the woman at the register commented. "Two for the first time you check, then save the third one for a few days later. Unless you're just checking before you go to a clinic to have your blood tested."

I hesitated, then darted back to the shelf and grabbed a third to be safe.

"First time?" she inquired, giving me a sympathetic look. "Trust me, I've seen that look on many a woman's face. Believe me when I tell you that you'll feel better once you know for sure. The worst part of it all is the guessing because it lets your mind spiral out of control. You're doing the right thing, knowledge is power, and once you have all the facts, you can make the best choice for your life. Oh, and if the man or men are still in the picture, don't you fucking dare let them pressure you one way or the other. They're not the ones who have to grow the damn thing and suffer with the results for the rest of your life."

Unsure how to even respond to all that, I simply smiled. "Thank you, that's all logical advice to keep in mind."

"I've got two kids of my own, and I wish someone would have been that honest with me for the first one. Don't get me wrong, I love the hell out of that girl, and I'm glad I kept her, but her father, the man who convinced me to keep the baby, split after three months of no sleep. Jackass couldn't handle it. Well, I say good riddance. As it turns out, he made room for the right man to come into my life who loved me and my daughter," the cashier shared. "All that to say things around you can change, but you'll forever be that child's mother. If you don't want that job, then accept it and deal with things before it's gone too far."

Taking the bag, I gave her a shaky smile and walked numbly out of the store. For the moment, I thought I knew what I wanted to do, but now after hearing her talk, I was left second-guessing myself. Kerian pulled the car up the moment I stepped out, and I climbed into the passenger seat, shaking off the turmoil the woman left me in. *Knowledge is power*. Once I have an answer, I'll know what I'm dealing with and can make a choice one way or another.

"You okay?" Kerian asked, looking at me with a slight wrinkle between his brows.

I nodded. "Yeah, just getting a little anxious. I'm sure I'll feel better once I have an answer."

Halstead reached an arm forward through the front seats asking for my hand. I gave it to him and smiled as he kissed the back of it. "No matter what those tests say, nothing changes for us. We want you to stay and be part of our family. Period."

"Good because I'm working really hard to accept the truth in that statement. My heart gets it, but my brain is taking a little longer to believe it," I admitted. "It seems like this is all too good to be true, and I'm living in a fairy tale."

"Didn't you know? All fiction is based on a bit of truth, so why can't this be *our* truth?" Quintin reasoned.

"It can," Kerian announced as he pulled onto the street. "Now all we need to do is defeat the evil trying to keep us apart, and we can start our happily ever after."

That got me laughing, and the fear that had been sitting in my chest evaporated. These men wouldn't leave me because of not getting enough sleep. Fuck, if I can tell them I'm a con artist who's ruined so many people's lives, and they still want me to be part of their family, I'm not sure much will scare them away.

"Mr. Norlund, I thought you weren't coming in until next week?" Sam said when he spotted us exiting the elevator.

"I should be saying the same thing about you?" Halstead challenged. "You were supposed to only be working until noon, and it's one o'clock now."

Sam blinked a few times before his brow crinkled. "I'm sorry, I didn't think you were serious about that."

"Son, what the hell is there for you to do when I haven't been here?" he questioned.

"Actually, I was getting ahead on a few things since I didn't have as much on my plate right now. I was able to catch up on—"

"Stop," Halstead said, holding up a hand. "Gather your things and go home. There is nothing vital for you to work on, and you're getting paid time off for this, so I don't want to hear anything about needing the hours. If you don't listen to me, I'll call Fernando and tell him to take you home."

Sam shot to his feet. "No, please, Mr. Norlund. After the incident with the gentleman from the DOD, he's been far more overprotective, and that's saying something."

"I can't say I blame him. If I found someone threatening one of my partners, I would have done more than just punch the man," Halstead grumbled. "I'll give you ten minutes, but if I come back out here to find you still here, then you sealed your fate."

"Yes, sir," Sam answered, nodding his head like a Bobblehead doll.

Quintin took my hand and gave it a little tug, drawing me to follow as we headed for Kerian's office. I hadn't spent much time here other than to know where it was. It matched the simple modern feel that his office back at the house had—all metal, glass, and white with pops of cobalt blue, yellow, and orange to liven it up.

Kerian dropped into his office chair and booted things up, flipped on screens, and made sure a few things were plugged in. "All right, so the plan is I will develop a virus that will seek out the one I helped to build. I'm pretty sure I reversed-engineered enough of it that I can give the hound a scent to track down and destroy. First, though, I'm going to make sure I still have access to the server through my link. If not, then I'll need a little time to get in the back door I created when I built it."

"Wait, you put in a back door even though you agreed to work with him?" I questioned.

Kerian paused and looked at me. "When the man has already fucked your partner over and put you in position to take the fall for something involving national security on a project you had nothing to do with... yeah, you put in a back door from the word go."

I couldn't argue that. I knew all about Halstead's drama, and I'd heard enough about Kerian's to know something bad happened, but national security, that was career-ending.

"That's what Halstead meant when he said, thankfully, you came to them so he could protect you," I blurted.

"Indeed," Quintin confirmed. "Interestingly enough, I think it might have had to do with this Omega syndicate. Reuben was caught looking into files he had no business having access to. They were data on a few prominent political figures who'd just been exposed for backroom deals on a drug to alter Betas into Omegas, but it was killing them instead of altering their designations. There was a whole sex-trafficking ring involved as well."

"The bastard used my computer to do the hacking so when they traced back the IP address, it had my name written all over it. Thankfully, we could show Reuben was piggybacking off my information, but the incriminating evidence was on his computer, not mine," Kerian informed me as his hand flew over the keyboard. "How he got off going to jail, I'll never know, but I bet every penny I own it was one of his packmates. Those fuckers picked their members based on giving each other the best advantage in life, not because they like each other. Honestly, I feel bad for their Omega. She's sweet, but they one hundred percent picked a woman they could easily manipulate and control."

Picturing what that must be like made me shiver. To think a woman could be trapped with that group of men and kept in the dark about all they've done, it made me even more thankful how important transparency and communication were to these three men.

"You don't have to wait here with us," Halstead commented, rolling a chair over to sit next to Kerian. "I'm going to jump in and help him get things rolling, so it shouldn't take more than an hour or an hour and a half at the most."

"Does that mean it will help if things are quiet, and you won't be distracted by me being in here?" I asked, cocking a brow.

They looked stuck as if they didn't know how to answer that.

"Guys, take a breath... it's fine. I'm a big girl and can handle being told you need space to work," I said with a chuckle, letting them off the hook. "Kerian reminded me that I need to get on top of settling my personal life to be relocated here. I'm assuming I can use one of the computers without setting off any alarms?"

Kerian rolled his eyes but went back to work as Halstead half rose out of his chair before Quintin waved him off. "Sit down. I'll set her up in your office since Sam is gone, and no one would dare step foot in there without your say-so."

"Good, her search history will also be protected so no one will be able to use that against her," Halstead pointed out as he sat back down. "Lainey, I don't know what your financial situation is like or if you have access to it, but part of being a pack means you get shares in the company. Until that can be arranged, you just tell us what you need to pay for, and we'll make sure it's covered until you have access to funds."

My jaw dropped. I was by no means in need of money—my nest egg would give me whatever life I wanted anywhere in the world. However, getting shares in Enigma would be a vomit-inducing amount of money.

"You don't have to do that," I argued. "I have more than enough money from my jobs until now to stop working and live a comfortable life."

"It's not about the money. To me, having you as an equal partner in this means we're equal in all areas of our life. No one can argue about money or power within the company because it's all distributed evenly," Halstead countered. "Now go do what you need so we can get you officially moved into our home."

Having dismissed me in a commanding and oddly adorable way, I sighed. "Come on, Quintin, let's leave the sexy nerds to their work as they save the world one number at a time."

Quintin snorted but placed a hand on my lower back as we headed for Halstead's office. Sam had gone home as he promised, so it was just the four of us up here, meaning I didn't need to hide our relationship from anyone. Stopping just outside Halstead's office doors, I grabbed Quintin's suit jacket and pulled him to me as I tilted my head up and kissed him. He didn't hesitate to wrap his arms around me as he returned my advances.

"What was that for?" Quintin asked, letting his forehead rest against mine.

I shrugged. "Because I wanted to."

"Good enough for me," he said, kissing me this time as he pulled open the office door, walking backward and drawing me in. "How much time did they say we had?"

A puff of laughter escaped me as I leaned into Quintin's hold. "As much as I love that idea, and trust me, I would be all for it, I think the first time in Halstead's office, he should be here with us."

"Yes, you're right," Quintin agreed dejectedly, pressing a quick kiss to my head before letting me go. "Let me get you to a secure profile on H's computer where you can access all you need, but there's no fear of anything happening to company files or information."

Moments later, I was in Halstead's giant leather office throne that was pretending to be a chair. I had to sit toward the front of the seat, or

I'd be too far away to type anything. "Any rules I should know about being in here?"

"Only one," Quintin said, holding up a finger. "No one but the four of us are allowed to be in here. There are security cameras everywhere on this floor that are kept on a private server so nothing that is ever said or done on this floor can be accessed by anyone but the three of us. That also means we have alerts set up if someone is trying to hack in or mess with any of our technology. The Syndicate can't get to you here. You are safe, I promise."

Hearing him tell me that was the reassurance I needed but didn't even realize it. "I trust you," I told him as I looked him dead in the eyes. "I trust all three of you to keep me safe."

"Thank you for trusting us. I realize what that means coming from you," Quintin murmured, his fingers brushing along my cheek. "I'm going to make some tea, would you like a cup?"

"That sounds lovely," I answered, giving him a soft smile.

He returned it with one of his own and headed out, leaving me alone here in this vast office thirty floors in the air overlooking the city. I glanced at the bag that held the tests and decided now was as good a time as any. Snatching it up, I headed for the attached private bathroom. Halstead offered it to me the other night when I was getting ready for dinner, but I wasn't ready to be that vulnerable in his personal space. Now, I didn't think there was such a thing as personal space for us, making me laugh as I shimmied my jeans down.

There I sat on the toilet reading the instructions for the test, feeling like an idiot. It couldn't be that hard to figure out, right?

"I have to pee for seven to ten seconds on the damn thing? Or I could piss in a cup and let it soak," I muttered as I read over the sheet for the second time. "Okay, if I'm going to do both, I'll have to do it at the same time. I don't know if I have enough pee for a second round, and I'm not going in search of a cup."

I took them out of the wrappers, removed the plastic cap, then took a few minutes to find the best way to make this work.

"Jesus, how the hell am I supposed to know where the stream is going to go. I'm not a fucking dude. Okay, seriously, girl, take a deep breath and let it out. So what if you have to adjust shit."

It was at this point my bladder decided it was going to be shy. I closed my eyes and thought of waterfalls, running rivers, ocean waves... *oh, thank fuck. It worked.* Having no clue if seven to ten seconds was achieved, I managed to aim well enough so I didn't make a mess and got the damn thing wet enough.

"This has to be one of the most ridiculous things I've ever done," I grumbled as I put the caps back on the tests and set them aside.

Pulling myself together, I ignored them as they sat there taunting me while they held my future fate. I hummed the happy birthday song three times as I washed my hands with my eyes closed hoping it would make the three minutes fly by faster. Now dry, I paced the bathroom, arms crossed, tapping my fingers along my skin as I focused on my breathing, keeping it calm and even. No matter what these things said, nothing would change for the guys and me. I would still go back to that desk and find a moving company to pack up my house and bring it here. These are the men I wanted to build a family with, so if I didn't get pregnant this heat, there was always the next and the one after that.

My feet came to a halt as I realized what I'd just told myself. "I want to be a mom..."

The revelation shocked me but, at the same time, made me smile. Unable to hold back any longer, I hurried over to the sink and looked down at the two white cartridges praying for two little pink lines to tell me that I would be a mom. I gazed at it, my eyes flicking back and forth between the two tests as my eyes watered. Covering my mouth, I tried to calm the wave of emotions hitting me and unsure how to process them. Then I heard the sound of the office door opening, so I grabbed the tests, wiped away my tears, and headed out to talk with Quintin.

"Hello, Emmalina," a voice not belonging to any of my guys said. "Fancy meeting you here since you're supposed to be back home dealing with a family emergency. Then again, who can ever trust what a con artist says?"

Twenty-Nine

Lainey

There standing in Halstead's office was Reuben Watts, his hands casually tucked into the pockets of his slacks as he leaned on Halstead's desk.

"What the fuck are you doing here?" I demanded, panic clawing at my chest.

"Oh, you can thank Kerian for that," he answered, pushing off the desk. "He finished the code... you know, the one you were supposed to destroy? I don't need to tell you what it does now, do I? No, I'm fairly certain the Underground Omega Syndicate told you all about its abilities and why they're so afraid of it. Unfortunately for you being so close in proximity, the alert for UOS activity went off, and I was able to trace who they were communicating with and work backward to find out all the dirt they had on you. Imagine my surprise when I found out the dear sweet Emmalina my friend Zarin fell for was none other than the bitch who destroyed his company. The doctored information you put in that report almost landed him in jail," Reuben roared as he advanced on me. "He lost everything and ended up in the hospital after he tried to take his own life. Are you proud of yourself, hmm? Is this what you hoped for... string the poor man along, make him fall for you, then burn his whole house to the fucking ground?"

I backed away, keeping the space we had between us as he hurled his rage at me. Once I was done with a job, I never looked back. Who would want to see the destruction they caused to a person's life? Not me. What I found more interesting is that Reuben was so personally appalled by this when he'd done equally awful things to those around him. What made Zarin different?

"If you're looking for an apology or any sign of remorse, you won't find it here," I stated, knowing he wouldn't believe any other answer. "I did my job, and unfortunately, in my line of work, there are people who get hurt. Truthfully, I liked Zarin. He's a good man but a lousy judge of character if he has you in his life as such a champion. If you want to see a person who fucks with people's lives, then take a look in the damn mirror. Really, I should be taking lessons from you because that behind-the-back takeover you did on Halstead was impressive. He didn't even see it coming until it was too late."

"I didn't have a choice," Reuben snapped. "You should know when the UOS wants something, they don't give a shit who they fuck over in the process. That's why I've spent every chance I get to hunt them down and wipe them off the face of the earth."

"What?" I said, trying to follow what this man was even saying.

"It doesn't matter. It's in the past... besides they got what they wanted out of me and my pack. What you need to be worried about is the fact I know *everything* about you, Lainey Caddel. With one phone call, I can end your life just as easily as they can. The UOS might say they will leave you alone after this mission, but they won't. Anytime they think you can help them, they'll drag out the same skeletons from your closet and threaten you with them," Reuben taunted, advancing on me once again until my back hit the wall of windows.

He stepped up until he was looming over me and grabbed my wrists holding the tests. I tried to fight against him using a move I'd been taught to twice get out of his hold. Reuben put an end to that as he used his forearm to press against my throat, keeping me from moving. I gasped for air as he put more weight on his arm, cutting off my air. With only one hand, I clawed at him digging my nails into his hand, trying to get him to release me.

"Fucking bitch," Reuben snarled, grabbing my throat and tossing me toward the other wall.

Disoriented from the lack of air and my eyes filled with stars, I tripped over my own feet so I couldn't catch myself. My shoulder slammed into the drywall hard enough, I felt it give under the impact before I slid down into a heap on the floor.

"Would you look at that, the con artist decided to make sure her newest targets couldn't get away from her. Was that the plan once you saw how good you could have it, get yourself knocked up then they'll have to keep you, right?" Reuben goaded as he shoved one of the tests into my face. "Two pink lines, that means pregnant, yeah?"

What?

No, it had only been one line when I looked in the bathroom.

Grabbing the test out of his hand, I looked, and sure enough, there were two clearly-defined pink lines. I must not have waited long enough the first time I looked. Joy flooded my body even as this man loomed over me, and my shoulder hurt like a bitch.

"I'm going to be a mom," I whispered.

Reuben scoffed. "Can't be a mom if you're in prison."

My gaze snapped to his. "What do you want?"

"I want you to help me destroy the UOS once and for all," he answered. "Just think, if they're gone, then there's nothing to fear from them, and you can live your happy life with your Alphas and baby."

"And if I don't?" I questioned even though I knew the answer, but I needed him to say it.

What I hadn't counted on was him grabbing me by the throat once more and slamming me against the wall. "Then the UOS is the least of your worries, Lainey. I'll make sure your dear daddy, Trent, knows all about you selling him out and even tell him where you are, who you're with, and that you're expecting a child. What do you think he's going to do then?"

"End up in a hole six feet under like you are, Reuben," Halstead answered.

I couldn't see him with Reuben's body blocking my view of the office, but even hearing his voice, I knew I would be okay.

"Now I suggest you unhand what is *mine* before I forget to give a shit about going to jail," Halstead instructed.

"Oh, I think we can get you off with a good lawyer and a self-defense claim," Quintin added.

Reuben looked over his shoulder at them with a sneer. "Do you even know who you're defending? This bit—"

"Finish that word, and I will make sure your mouth never opens again," Halstead barked. "I won't ask again. *Let. Her. Fucking. Go.*"

"So you really don't care that she used you three to get pregnant so she can bleed you dry and drop you for another man?" Reuben challenged.

Kerian let out a harsh laugh. "That's your story, man, not ours. I'm not gonna let your personal trauma fuck up our future together. Oh yeah, for the record, we know all about who she is, what she's done, and none of us give a flying fuck because she's *ours*. So, do as Halstead instructed and get *your* fucking hands off *our* woman."

Reuben did just that, letting me crash to the floor once again. Only this time, Halstead grabbed the man and hurled Reuben across the room into one of the armchairs in front of his desk. Kerian and Quintin rushed over to me, dropping to their knees before me. Quintin reached out first, and I threw myself at him, wrapped my arms around his neck, and began to sob. Kerian's body draped over my back as he hugged Quintin and me tightly while my body shook with adrenaline and tears.

"Shh... I got you, beautiful," Quintin whispered against the side of my head. "You're safe now. We won't let him touch you again."

There was silence for a moment before a knock sounded on Halstead's office door. I buried my face even deeper against Quintin's neck.

"It's just Fernando with the police," Kerian assured me. "We called them as soon as we saw what was going on. Lainey, I'm so sorry we didn't see it sooner. This should never have happened. We told you you'd be safe with us, and we failed you. I'm so, so sorry."

I tuned out what was going on outside of this cocoon of Alphas I was wrapped up in. Lost in the feeling of safety and comfort, I let out a whimper when Kerian sat back. Another pair of arms scooped me up and lifted me off Quintin's lap, only to be cradled like a child against Halstead's broad chest.

"We got you, my sweet girl, and we're going home," Halstead murmured, kissing my forehead. "The police took Reuben away along with a copy of his attack on you without the audio, of course. He's not going to get out of this one, I'll make damn sure of it, and if he does wriggle his way out of jail... let's just say no one will find the body when I'm done with him."

Licking my dry lips, I managed to find my voice. "Did you finish the code?"

"Fuck yeah, we did," Kerian answered instead. "The moment we hit enter, sending that virus to attack, is when the security alert popped up on my computer. It's my fault we didn't see the alert sooner. I have it set so when I'm in that code program, only certain level alerts make it past the Do-Not-Disturb setting. *Fuck*, I can't fucking believe that bastard managed to get into our building, up the elevator, and into the office. It doesn't make sense."

There was silence as we stepped into the elevator, and I scanned the panel, knowing you needed a keycard with the right permissions to get to the top floor. Only a limited few people had that access besides the four of us, Sam, and Fernando. Then it dawned on me.

"Fire the security officer. He was clearly paid off and has zero loyalty to you or this company," I stated, just as the doors opened, and there was the man.

"Heading—"

"You're fired effective right the fuck this second." Halstead growled. "Give Kerian your radio so he can contact Fernando to remove all sensitive Enigma access before escorting you from the building."

The man's stunned expression was genuine, but it was more the fact that he didn't think he'd ever get caught. "Sir, what is the meaning of this?"

Quintin stepped into the guard's personal space, not at all concerned that the guard had a hundred pounds and three inches on him. "I hope whatever he bribed you with was worth it because I'll see to it that you never work in security again. You fucked up, and I mean you fucked up bad. That man you let up who was then removed in handcuffs by the police, you know what he did?"

The guard shook his head furiously.

"He assaulted that woman who happens to be *our* Omega, who is also pregnant," Quintin spat. "Trust me when I say you won't even be able to guard a cemetery by the time I'm finished with you. Oh... you also want to be sure that Fernando never finds out that you were also the one who allowed that asshole up who attacked Sam."

"I'm sorry, Mr. Price... what did you just say about Sam?" Fernando asked through gritted teeth, eyes flashing in rage as he stared at the man. "This fucknugget is the one who let up the man who assaulted my partner as well as yours?"

"Oops," Quintin commented before stepping back from the guard, who now looked like he might throw up or pass out or possibly both. "I let you handle things from here, Fernando."

"Trust me, it will be dealt with to the letter of the law," Fernando assured.

When we exited the building, instead of Kerian's SUV pulling up, a sleek white car was in its place. The driver got out and opened the door, but rather than opening the normal way toward the front of the car, it did the opposite. Inside was plush and comfortable, with seats like a limousine facing each other. Yet the most amazing part was the whole middle was full of pillows and blankets like a nest.

"I thought it would be better like this so we didn't have to be separated," Halstead commented as he settled me in the pile of pillows. "If you hate it, then we can switch cars. I know you're not always comfortable giving into your Omega side."

Twining our fingers together, I kissed the back of his large hand. "It's perfect, thank you."

"Far from perfect, but I'm glad you like it," he grumbled, settling in beside me and tucking me under his arm.

"You know what could make this even more perfect?" I asked. All three of them looked at me with curious expressions.

Halstead pressed a kiss to my temple. "Tell us whatever you and the little growing life inside you need, and I'll make it fucking happen, baby doll."

"Tell the whole fucking world that we're a family, and if they fuck with us, then we'll destroy them," I answered.

Kerian and Quintin chuckled as they arranged themselves around me, awaiting Halstead's answer since he was the one who made the rule in the first place. The grumpy bear looked down at me then tentatively placed his hand on my stomach, letting his thumb stroke over my shirt.

"I thought I was doing the right thing keeping everyone out of the limelight, allowing them to have their own lives and not be hounded by people trying to garner a favor. Times change as do people, and I think I've let my fear keep me from telling the whole world I'm blessed with three people I love more than anything else in this world," Halstead admitted. "You're right, Lainey, not only should it have happened ages ago, but I won't raise a child thinking they need to be kept a secret. I'll make it happen... it's what all of us deserve."

Pulling him down to me, I kissed him, putting all the feelings I didn't know how to put into words behind it. "Thank you, and just for a little added motivation, none of you can mark me until it's been announced."

"You drive a hard bargain, woman," Halstead grumbled.

"Don't even try that on me, you grumpy bear." I laughed and gave him a quick kiss. "You love that I challenge you. It's part of my charm."

"Vixen, there isn't any part of you that we don't love," Kerian pointed out, twining our fingers together. "Let's just hope this kid of ours doesn't get H's personality... one of them is enough for this family."

That had us all laughing until our cheeks hurt, and Halstead got a stitch in his side, which he complained about even after we got home and everyone curled up in my nest, in my home, where I planned to spend the rest of my life with these three men... and the little one who would join us before long.

Thirty

Epilogue

Lainey

Two weeks later...

The past few weeks had been a whirlwind as my Alphas helped me gather all the pieces of my life scattered all over Breona. I had various stash houses and crash pads for one reason or another. Thankfully, I was a rather detailed person keeping track of where my things ended up. Now it was all finally under one roof, and Lainey Caddel had been reborn with official paperwork and identification. Kerian had kept his promise and found all the documentation I'd destroyed.

I stepped in front of the full-length mirror in my room and smoothed my hands over the satin dress the guys had left on my bed this morning. It was black, but with the satin, it had a slight shimmer to it. The classic sweetheart cut of the bust and the off-the-shoulder wrap gave it such a stunning simple elegance. It fell to midthigh, giving it that modern twist without being overdone. Truly, I don't think they could have picked a more perfect dress to fit my style, and that thought is what put a smile on my face.

There was a soft knock on my door before Quintin entered, looking dashing in his dark green suit. "I was just coming to check on you since guests will be arriving soon."

Halstead held to his commitment that he would announce us as a pack, which he did yesterday in a news interview. Tonight is a party with their friends at the house, where we plan to tell them I'm pregnant. We agreed that going on national television and saying we were a family was one thing, but to also share we were expecting seemed the wrong tone. None of us wanted people to think we were telling the world about us just because I'd gotten pregnant. Halstead handled the questions beautifully as to why he kept it a secret for so long. Many found it romantic that he would be so concerned for us, and their stocks went through the roof.

The lawyers were pulling together paperwork for shares to be taken from the three of them and given to me, creating an equal piece of the company. They were also waiting for the official documents stating that I was, in fact, their bonded Omega which we couldn't do until we were... well... bonded.

"I have to be honest, I'm really surprised Halstead offered to host the dinner here at the house," I commented as I slipped on my heels, holding onto Quintin for support. "He's always seemed so adamant about no one being here."

"Well, I suppose the fact the world now knows the truth, keeping us cloistered away doesn't serve a purpose," Quintin reasoned. "That, and I think he wants you to feel included in all aspects of our lives. These are friends we've had for years, and while we didn't admit we were together, we didn't hide it from them either. More like there was an unspoken rule to keep your opinions to yourself."

Doing a little twirl, I posed for Quintin. "How do I look?"

"Absolutely stunning. H was right when he picked out that dress for you. He said it would be perfect," he answered, pulling me to him and pressing a light kiss to my lips. "Don't want to ruin the makeup before everyone gets here."

"It's fine, I have more," I teased, kissing him back but still keeping it tame. "Shall we head down?"

Quintin tucked my arm through his, and we made our way to the first floor. Halstead and Kerian were talking about something in the foyer but stopped the moment they spotted us.

"Holy shit," Kerian blurted. "You look amazing."

"Why thank you, Keri," Quintin quipped.

He gave the man a patronizing look. "Quin, I already told you how good you looked the first time you put that suit on today."

Quintin cleared his throat and adjusted his sleeves, a slight pink blooming on his cheeks. "Pre-party quickie, I like it." I chuckled, giving Quintin a playful slap on the arm. "Hope you two aren't too tired to play with me after this party's over."

All the men started to purr with excitement at the mention of sex. There was an interesting phenomenon now that I was pregnant. It was almost as if my scent changed along with my hormones, even this early in the grand scheme of things to make me super fucking horny. Not to mention the ability to make all my guys hard in an instant as if they were in a perpetual rut. The whole thing made no sense, I was already pregnant. What did getting them all randy do? Well, it certainly kept me in a good mood, that's for damn sure.

"Are we sure we need to have this party?" Halstead questioned. "I'm more than happy to tell them that we changed our minds, so I can bend you over the dining room table just to show you how *not* tired I am."

Laughter burst out of me, knowing he'd have zero problem doing it too. "No, we need to be social... besides, I hear a car pulling up now."

Halstead muttered something under his breath just as Ruth walked into the room with a tray of drinks. "I figured you might need something to settle the ogre down," she commented, handing him a glass of whiskey. "Be warned... you only get four of them tonight per your fellow pack members' rules. Don't shoot the messenger, but when it's three against one, they win."

"Four?" Halstead demanded, looking at us. "Why only four?"

"Really?" I asked, hand on my hip. "What are the chances of you keeping up tonight if you drink more than four?"

That shut him up as he took a conservative sip from his glass just as someone knocked. Adem, one of Ruth's husbands, was manning the door tonight and pulled it open. Tabitha entered with two other men and a woman, who I assumed was her pack. When Tabitha spotted me, she smiled and reached her hands out to me.

"Lainey, you sneaky woman keeping secrets," Tabitha said as she greeted me with a light kiss to each cheek. "Why on earth didn't you say anything when we last spoke? It was only four days ago."

"Sorry, Halstead was adamant about making sure everyone found out at the same time, but also because he knew you'd be invited to this," I divulged.

"Well, it certainly explains things," she commented. "Oh, let me introduce you to Amelia."

Tabitha turned and held out a hand to the other woman, a petite thing with silky black hair and emerald eyes. The moment I caught her scent, I knew she was an Omega, but the marks on her neck and collarbone would have given it away too.

"Amelia, this is Lainey," Tabitha introduced. "Amelia is our pack's Omega and my wife of twenty years. We were together before meeting our other lovers, David and Edwin, who joined our family fifteen years ago."

"Oh, how fascinating, so I'm not the only one who was late to join her pack," I said, clasping my hands together, trying to contain my questions.

Amelia smiled and reached out to touch my arm. "Don't be shy, Lainey. Having your first child is a big learning curve, so feel free to ask me anything you like."

My jaw dropped as I looked from Amelia to my guys.

Kerian threw up his hands in defense. "I didn't say anything."

Amelia giggled a sweet tinkling laugh. "Oh goodness, no one had to tell me anything. I could simply tell from your scent. Having had three children, I know what that extra spice in an Omega's scent means."

Tabitha let out a cry of excitement before wrapping me up in a hug. "Oh, what happy news for you. God, it's about time these men had a proper family and such a perfect woman to fit in their lives. This is all just so exciting."

Now that the cat was out of the bag, I got hugs from all Tabitha's packmates along with introductions. Ten more guests arrived, and my head was spinning with all the congratulations, hugs, and introductions tossed at me. When we finally sat down for dinner, it was a welcome buffer for me to collect myself. Normally, I was never one to be overwhelmed by people or situations, but then again, I'd never been the center of attention either.

Ruth outdid herself, making a blend of all our favorite foods in a masterful four-course meal. Conversations flowed easily, and I found it was easy to pick up on the topics enough to share my thoughts. Tabitha just gave me a wink as I stumped one of the gentlemen who ran a telecommunications company. He'd been having trouble with his retention in a certain department, and so I offered an out-of-the-box suggestion.

"You know that might actually work," Carson muttered as he mulled over my idea.

"I'm telling you, this woman needs to start her own consulting firm so we can come to her with our problems and have her fix them," Tabitha interjected. "She sees the world in a whole different light, and that's what we need... innovation, my friends. Clearly, what we've been doing hasn't worked, so time to change it up."

To Tabitha's point, I hadn't really thought about what I wanted to do in the long run. Things had been so busy getting settled, and I hadn't looked much further than that. I'd still been working at Enigma as Halstead's executive assistant until we announced our relationship, but now I had the freedom to do what I wanted.

"Who knows, I might take your idea and run with it. That's certainly something I could do from home as I adjust to being a mom but feel like I'm doing something for me too," I reasoned.

"You just say the word, and we'll do whatever you need to make that happen," Halstead assured me. "Enigma will always have a place for you if you want it, but I know I can speak for the others when I say we want you to be happy with your choice."

I leaned in and kissed him on the cheek. "You're spoiling me, you know."

"Yes, and I plan to keep doing that for the rest of our lives," he pointed out.

The table let out an audible *aww,* making us chuckle before returning to another topic.

"Did you hear about Reuben?" Edwin asked.

I frowned as I looked over at my Alphas. "No..."

"Seems he died two days ago, got shanked during a prison fight. Never had a chance. Whoever went after him wanted that man dead," Edwin shared.

My brows shot up at the news. I shouldn't be surprised the Syndicate wasn't one to take chances, but I was surprised that it took them this long to take care of him. Either way, now I didn't ever have to fear that man spilling my secrets or anyone else's if Halstead's threats on trial day hadn't been enough.

As the plates were cleared away and dessert was brought out, a hand slowly started to work its way under my skirt. I surreptitiously glanced out of the corner of my eye at Kerian, who was happily talking to one of the guests I didn't know. The table hid his actions, but what I hadn't counted on was Halstead swooping in and tugging aside my panties, then stroking a finger over my pussy.

I let out a cough to cover up the gasp that I'd almost uttered. Taking a sip of my water, I set it back down, trying to minimize the slight shake as Halstead slipped his finger into me. Adjusting my seat, I spread my legs wider giving him more room, and he took advantage of it as he added a second finger. Kerian, determined not to be left out, got his finger wet from the slick pouring out of me and gave special attention to my clit.

My hands wrapped around the silverware, trying to keep seated and not let on that I was being finger-fucked by two of my lovers. A whimper slipped out as Halstead found my happy button and rubbed his thick fingers back and forth over it in an alternating pattern. Kerian must have some telepathic ability to know what Halstead was doing since he sped up his efforts, and before I knew it, I was soaring. The climax that hit me had me gasping and falling forward, knocking over my water and Kerian's wine which landed in my lap.

"Oh shit," someone at the table swore. "Are you okay?"

I nodded absentmindedly as I tried to clean up the mess I'd made. "Yes, I-I'm fine," I stammered, trying to function while still in a state of haze from my orgasm.

Not to mention Halstead's fingers were still inside me milking every last drop of this moment. Gripping the table's edge, I closed my eyes and tried to pull it together but knew it wouldn't happen.

"Dammit, it got all over your dress," Kerian muttered. "Come on, let's get you cleaned up. I suppose we should be thankful the dress is black."

"Let me get the club soda. It should help keep it from doing more damage," Quintin offered.

Halstead slipped his fingers from my pussy and immediately scooped me up in a bridal hold. "Can't let you walk and drip red wine all over the place, then Ruth will be cursing us all for the next week."

The others at the table merely watched us with curiosity and confusion. Wasting no time, Halstead strode out of the room with Kerian hot on our heels.

"Why do I get the feeling they're not coming back?" Amelia asked, her voice trailing after us.

Tabitha chuckled. "Because they're not. We'll finish our dessert and head out to leave the lovebirds be. It was foolish for them to think they could pull this off while she's pregnant."

I didn't know if I should be mortified at the fact they knew what was going on or appreciate that they didn't think I was an absolute disaster. Either way, I was about to be in the throes of passion, not giving a fuck about what anyone else thought of me.

Once in my room, Halstead set me on my feet, gripped the back of the dress where the zipper ran down, and he yanked. I jerked with the force of his efforts, but the cool air hitting my skin told me he'd been successful.

The dress ended up in a heap around my feet that I stepped out of. I was about to kick off my shoes when Halstead gripped my hips. "Leave them."

I glanced at him over my shoulder, and the heat in his eyes was enough for me to be more than willing to do as he asked. He urged me forward until I stood at the base of the bed where a padded bench was placed. "Bend over and rest your hands on the bench," Halstead instructed.

A shiver raced up my spine as I did as he asked, spreading my legs and wiggling my ass at him. He gave it a playful smack before dropping to his knees and feasting on my weeping pussy. No longer worried about whether people would find out what we were doing, I let out a moan as I leaned into the feel of his tongue lapping at my sensitive flesh. Kerian, naked as the day he was born, climbed on the bed and positioned himself in front of me, his cock bobbing eagerly. I couldn't use my hands, but I opened my mouth wide and trusted Kerian to take care of the rest.

"I have the..." Quintin started to say as he entered the room. "You did it on fucking purpose."

Kerian grinned as he fisted my hair, guiding me as I swallowed his cock. "In a way, but the spilling of the wine was all her."

Not at all pleased for being blamed, I made a grunting noise and let my teeth scrape along the tender flesh of his cock.

"Hey now," Kerian scolded, pulling out of my mouth. "I didn't mean it like that... simply that it gave us the perfect opportunity to get out of there without being ridiculously obvious."

I was about to share my thoughts on that when Halstead started to prod at my asshole, making my breath catch. "Oh fuck." I panted.

"That's the general idea," Halstead confirmed. "I plan for all of us to stuff you with our cocks and fill you with our cum as we mark your perfect ass as ours and ours alone."

The thought of that almost had me coming as Halstead slipped his finger into my ass. "Yes, please," I whined, adding to the urgency of my need.

He removed his finger and gave my ass another slap. "Get up on the bed and tell us who you want where, doll."

Needing no further instruction, I kicked off my heels and shoved Kerian onto his back. "Mind if I take you for a ride?"

He laughed as he guided me onto his cock. "Not at all, my sexy vixen. You help yourself."

I tossed my head back as I moaned at the feeling of him filling me. It was something I hoped I'd never take for granted. Once I was settled, I looked over at Halstead. "Will you fuck my ass, papa bear?"

"With pleasure, baby girl," he answered with a deep rumble in his voice.

Quintin crawled across the bed, wearing only his glasses, which I loved to have him keep on when having sex. "Does that mean I get that pretty mouth of yours, beautiful?"

"If you want it, it's yours," I answered as he cupped my cheek and kissed me.

"There isn't a doubt in my mind what I want," he whispered against my lips. "I want you, Lainey, because I'm madly in love with you, and I can't bear the thought of you not being in my life, sharing every day together with the three of us."

My heart melted with the earnestness of his words. "I love you too, Quintin Price, and I'm not going anywhere."

He slammed his lips to mine and feasted on my mouth as Halstead slid into my ass with a grunt. After a moment of letting me adjust to them both pushing me to my limit, they began to move in an alternating motion. Quintin broke our kiss with a shout, and I realized that Kerian had shifted the man so he could give Quintin's asshole some special attention. I knew how good it must feel as I watched pre-cum leak out of the tip.

Pushing Quintin back, I ducked my head and licked the bead of liquid off the tip, making him shout, "Oh fuck."

I chuckled as I rested a hand on his thigh and one at the base of his cock to hold it steady. Taking him in as deep as I could, I hummed my pleasure, making Quintin's hips buck and thrust into my mouth.

"Shit, Lainey, if you keep doing shit like that, then I'm going to come way too fast," Quintin warned.

"Don't worry, you'll only be down for a few minutes with how turned on she is right now. Pregnant pheromones are no joke," Halstead reassured him.

Not caring how long Quintin lasted, I lost myself in the feeling of all my men taking pleasure in my body. I was their Omega, and I would do everything in my power to make them know how treasured and valued they made me feel. Being honest with my words was a skill I was working on, but I'd always been honest in my physical reactions.

Kerian and Halstead picked up the pace, rutting into me deeper and faster now that I was properly warmed up. Omegas might be able to take pretty much anything you throw at them dick-wise, but as with anyone, you need to work up to a solid deep pounding, or you'll bruise something. Right now, my Alphas could fuck me however they wanted, and it would make my eyes roll back in my head with pleasure.

"Oh God, I'm close," Quintin warned as his hips thrust more erratically. "Shit, shit, shit."

He pulled out of my mouth as Kerian gripped his knot tightly, sending ropes of hot cum to land on my chest. Quintin grabbed my face and twisted it to the side so he could access the spot just below my ear. My body exploded with a euphoric feeling as our bond blazed to life as I orgasmed. Quintin finally released his hold on my neck, and he fell back on the bed, his chest heaving.

Moments later, Halstead's hips started to snap against my skin in short thrusts as he grunted, making sure his knot was as deep as he could get it before he shot off. His knot swelled, locking him in place, and with a roar, Halstead bit the lower side of my neck, throwing me off yet another cliff into a climax that had me seeing stars. My pussy clamped down on Kerian, who shot up, wrapping his arm around my waist and leaving his mark on the opposite side of my neck as he came. Unable to even process what I was experiencing, I just clung to my men, knowing they would take care of me. Body trembling with the overload of sensations both physically and mentally as our pack bonds fell into place, the three of us collapsed on the bed.

"Holy shit!" I gasped. "That was incredible."

Halstead chuckled, making his whole body vibrate, and his knot shifted inside me, setting off aftershocks, making me clench and all of them groan.

"Ha, payback's a bitch," I sassed.

"Oh, I wouldn't get too full of yourself. All I have to do is start purring, and your brain's going to melt," Kerian warned.

That had me shutting up. I fucking loved it when they did that, but right now, every nerve felt like it was a little frayed.

"God, that expression on your face." Keratin snickered. "I fucking love you, my sexy and naughty vixen. Don't ever change being who you are."

"Damn right," Halstead agreed. "We found ourselves the most amazing woman, didn't we?"

"Yeah, we sure as hell did," Quintin said as he draped himself over Kerian's body.

"Well, I'm pretty sure you guys have covered your bases," I said. When they gave me confused looks, I explained, "Guys, you've fucked me, marked me, got me pregnant, and rescued me from a secret underground organization. What more could a person do to make it really fucking clear that they love a woman?"

"She's got a point," Halstead mused aloud. "Then it should come as no surprise when we tell her how much we love her every day from now on since we've made it so clear and all."

"Is that your roundabout way of telling me you love me, Halstead?" I asked, peering over my shoulder at him.

His brows shot up. "The dinner party didn't make that clear?"

I grinned and pulled him down to kiss me. "I love you too, you old grumpy bear."

"What about me?" Kerian asked, giving me a dramatic pout.

"Oh... well, you see... I'm going to have to ask Tater-Tot's permission first," I teased.

Kerian then started to tickle me, and being trapped by two knots, there wasn't anywhere for me to go, so I had to admit defeat. "Uncle, I call uncle."

He stopped his tickle attack and switched it to peppering my face with kisses. "I love you, Lainey, and I'm so thankful you walked into our office that day. Syndicate be damned, but I will admit they gave us the greatest treasure we could ever have."

"I love you too, Kerian," I whispered, resting my forehead against his. "Thank you for fighting for me when I didn't know how to fight for myself."

"We'll fight for you always and forever, Lainey."

The End

About Author

Elizabeth is an International Best Seller, originally from Illinois but now living in sunny Phoenix, AZ. Elizabeth has been writing for nine years and started out in YA Fiction but recently found herself loving the Reverse Harem genre. Like her favorite books, Elizabeth loves to write about strong women of all varieties. Not all strength is flashy or apparent at first glance—some lies just under the surface.

Don't Miss Out!

Be the first to know what is coming next by following Elizabeth's social media! You never know when or what will be coming next!
Website: ElizabethKnightBooks.com
Facebook: Elizabeth Knight's Unicorn Queens
Instagram: elizabethknightauthor
TikTok: elizabethknightauthor
Newsletter: sign up here

Also By

Knot All Omegaverse
Knot All Is Lost: Part 1 & Part 2 (Complete)
Knot All Is Lost: The Complete Duet Omnibus
Knot All Is Ruined: Part 1 & Part 2 (Complete)
Knot All Is Ruined: The Complete Duet Omnibus

Caprioni Queen
Book 1 – Glitter & Guns
Book 2 – Blood & Heartache
Book 3 – Revenge & Truth (Summer 2023)

Standalone Books
Nicolette: Ladies of the MC
Lying Lainey: Underground Omega Syndicate

Hidden Empire Series – Complete series
Book 1 - Two Tricks
Book 2 - Three Tricks
Book 3 - Four Tricks
Book 4 - More Tricks
Book 5 - Our Tricks

Hidden Empire Novel
Harper's Renegades

Omega Assassin - Complete series
Book 1 - Dual Nature
Book 2 - Hidden Nature
Book 3 - Perfect Nature

Printed by Amazon Italia Logistica S.r.l.
Torrazza Piemonte (TO), Italy